Praise for

SWIMMING
WITH
BRIDGEF
GIRL

"Tambakis's outstanding debut is entertaining and sometimes sad, a superb portrait of a troubled but wisecracking gambler. Think Carl Hiaasen meets Fyodor Dostoevsky's *The Gambler*."

—*Library Journal* (starred review)

"Ray Parisi is making a spectacular mess of his life. . . . Tambakis keeps the humor from getting too broad and Ray from getting too sympathetic, though the reader usually roots for him anyway. His final confrontation with [his ex-wife] feels messy but true, just like a good Springsteen song. If this were a Springsteen album, it would be *Devils & Dust*: partly set in Las Vegas, it evinces hope and humor but is dark and gritty at its core."

—*Kirkus Reviews*

"Tambakis's first novel tackles some of life's toughest moments with humor, wit, and Ray's endless charm."

—*Booklist*

"*Swimming with Bridgeport Girls* is a sad, smart, funny-as-hell novel with a broken heart that beats powerfully between the lines on every sad, smart, funny-as-hell page."

—Jonathan Tropper, author of
This Is Where I Leave You

"Ray Parisi is an unforgettable character. His story demonstrates the terrible compatibility between the faith and idealism required for gambling and the faith and idealism required for love. Anthony Tambakis's *Swimming with Bridgeport Girls* brings its reader along on an incredible journey from casino to casino, making the romantic impulses of a gambler feel like one's own."

—Natalie Portman, Academy Award–winning actress

"This is the funniest book I've read in a long time—a bighearted story about one man's quest to save his ruined marriage. Ray Parisi makes one terrible decision after another, but I never stopped cheering for him."

—Jason Rekulak, author of
The Impossible Fortress

SWIMMING

WITH

BRIDGEPORT

GIRLS

A NOVEL

ANTHONY TAMBAKIS

SIMON & SCHUSTER PAPERBACKS

NEW YORK   LONDON   TORONTO   SYDNEY   NEW DELHI

Simon & Schuster Paperbacks
An Imprint of Simon & Schuster, Inc.
1230 Avenue of the Americas
New York, NY 10020

Copyright © 2017 by Anthony Tambakis

First Simon & Schuster trade paperback edition July 2018

SIMON & SCHUSTER PAPERBACKS and colophon are registered trademarks of Simon & Schuster, Inc.

For information about special discounts for bulk purchases, please contact Simon & Schuster Special Sales at 1-866-506-1949 or business@simonandschuster.com.

The Simon & Schuster Speakers Bureau can bring authors to your live event. For more information or to book an event, contact the Simon & Schuster Speakers Bureau at 1-866-248-3049 or visit our website at www.simonspeakers.com.

Interior design by Carly Loman

Manufactured in the United States of America

10 9 8 7 6 5 4 3 2 1

Library of Congress Cataloging-in-Publication Data is available.

ISBN 978-1-4516-8491-9
ISBN 978-1-5011-5833-9 (pbk)
ISBN 978-1-4516-8492-6 (ebook)

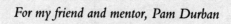

For my friend and mentor, Pam Durban

She wasn't doing a thing that I could see, except standing there leaning on the balcony railing, holding the universe together.

—J. D. SALINGER
("A Girl I Knew")

SWIMMING
WITH
BRIDGEPORT
GIRLS

I AM THE MILLION-DOLLAR STRANGER

April 6

. . . it's unfathomable to me that I would have to get a restraining order against R, but somehow that's what it's come to. I know he's been in the house, going through things and doing God knows what else, but he won't admit it, and he won't stop. I don't even know who this person is anymore. He's turned into a character in a Warren Zevon song . . .

OK. ALLOW ME TO SAY AT least this much in my own defense: I did not kidnap the dog. People said I did, and then it got repeated a bunch of times by the media, *Ray Parisi kidnapped a dog, Ray Parisi kidnapped a dog,* but it didn't happen. You can't kidnap your own dog. What you can do is a have a disastrous afternoon at Belmont Park, maybe commit what some would classify as a felony out there, and then it could be that you borrow the dog from your old yard and fall asleep before you can return him. And then L could get home from work in the city and find him missing. *That* could happen. If it does, then the Cobra CXT 1000 walkie-talkie in your motel room will go *kssshhh* for the first time in well over a year. If you'd given L the mate to it and instructed her to use it only when she'd decided to get back together with you, then you probably would've answered it whether a missing canine was conked out at your feet or not. If you'd given it any thought, you probably

1

would've realized you were being set up. But if you were half asleep and wholly lovesick, you might pick that squawking sucker up.

You shouldn't. You should take a second and think it through. But what's about to become very clear to anyone who hasn't already heard this story (or at least the story of the Million-Dollar Stranger, which I guess this sort of is) is that thinking things through has never been anything resembling a strength of mine, and when given a choice between doing something I should do and something I shouldn't, I'm a remarkably strong candidate to do the latter. Which is why I routinely found myself in situations like this:

Kssshhh. "Raymond?" *Kssshhh.* "This is so ridiculous." *Kssshhh.* "Raymond!"

"Ray here. Over."

Kssshhh. "Are you *sleeping?* It's five-thirty in the afternoon." *Kssshhh.* "Hello?"

"You didn't say *over*," I said. "Over."

Kssshhh. "What?"

"You have to say *over*. Over."

Kssshhh. "I said, *are you sleeping?* Or maybe you're just high for a change."

"You're not saying *over*," I said again, before surveying the motel room, where the dog, Bruce, was asleep at my feet. The room's nautical theme was supposed to suggest the feeling of mild ocean breezes and the boundless optimism of an encroaching horizon, but it only served to make me feel like I was on a sinking ship. In that regard, it was a shitty but honest room, and had been for well over a year, when things had taken a bad turn and paused.

Kssshhh. "Call me on a real phone. This is absurd."

"Copy that."

After L had banished me from the house and forced me to sign a shockingly quick no-contest divorce, I'd gotten a room at the Parkway Motor Lodge, which was just down the hill from where we used to live on Archer Street. The first thing I did was buy a pair of Cobra CXT 1000s from the Sarge, the ex-marine who runs the package store next to the motel. Since L wouldn't see me at the time for reasons we'll be getting into, I left her handset on the front porch of the house with a note telling her to tune it to Channel 3 and contact me when she was ready to reconcile. As the CXT 1000 has a radius of thirty-seven miles, I knew I was never more than thirty minutes away from having my old life back, and this was a comfort whether it sounds like one or not. Whenever I'd get depressed over the fact that L hadn't radioed yet, I'd reassure myself by speculating that her batteries had gone dead, or that perhaps she had forgotten the required channel number (this was folly, of course, as she was a lawyer and forgot precisely nothing, which was why I was living at a motel in the first place). Oftentimes, when I wasn't at the casino making matters worse, I'd drive up to the house and loiter around the neighborhood until she got home, at which point I'd tell her I was worried that her batteries might be dead, and she'd threaten to get a restraining order if I didn't leave the property immediately. This might have happened more than once. I should admit that. I should also admit that there might have been a couple of times where I checked on the state of the batteries myself, and needed to go inside the house to do that. I was not snooping around, however. Or at least I never intended to. It certainly wasn't my decision to store her handset in the same drawer she put her journal in. She did that on her own, and I'm not equipped with whatever set of characteristics make up the kind of person who would ignore that kind of thing once he stumbled on it. I'm sure there are guys like that out there, people who would just close the drawer without rooting around, but those are the guys who volunteered to join the military after 9/11, or became smoke jumpers, or members of Doctors Without Borders. Personally, I've never met a single one of those cats. There really can't be very many of them.

On the day I finally heard the *kssshhh* I'd been waiting for, the dog and I were both asleep, like I said, and any euphoria I felt when I first heard the sound of the Cobra was immediately extinguished by L's annoyed tone and refusal to use proper radio language. See, when we'd moved to Atlanta and L had started undergrad at Emory, we'd lived in a little apartment in a place called Cabbagetown and communicated with our neighbors via walkie-talkie. It started out as a cheeky birthday present we grabbed at Radio Shack for Kiki and Lew, the hippie couple who lived over the stained glass and pottery shop next door, and then it spread throughout the neighborhood in the way a gimmick like that can among young, carefree people to whom nothing has really happened yet. Within weeks, everyone in a three-block radius had handsets and a handle. If there was a dinner party being planned, or someone needed to borrow a shovel, or a pet had gone missing, you'd get a call on the walkie-talkie instead of getting, say, a text like you would in a normal neighborhood scenario. Why does this matter? It matters because L knew the proper radio lingo. She knew to say *over*. And she wasn't saying *over*. Which meant she wasn't calling to get back together. Which meant she had used the walkie-talkie to trick me. Which meant she was looking for the dog.

Confronted with a clear dilemma, I did what came most naturally: sat there and did nothing and hoped for the situation to resolve itself on its own. This tactic worked about as well as it normally did.

Kssshhh. "You have five seconds to call me or I'm getting the restraining order. You copy *that*?"

"Ten-four," I finally answered.

There was no getting around it, so I picked up the room phone, since my cell was dead and I had left my charger at Dawn's. But first I looked at Bruce. Locked eyes with him and sent him a message in the way you can with a dog you've had for a long time. "Hey. You. Listen to me," I transmitted. "You are *not here*, OK? Be good. *Be. Good.* I'm fucking serious."

He rolled over on his back, waved a paw in the air, and kept waving it until I grabbed it with my good hand (a cast was on the other) and sniffed it. It was his only trick, and it wasn't much of a trick at all. Now, other golden retrievers actually engaged in worthwhile domestic endeavors, like fetching the morning paper, or even noble societal ones, like leading the blind. Those dogs made some kind of significant effort to be more than animals. Rise above their station in life. Not Bruce. His thing was having his paws sniffed. Why? Because L had been doing it ever since we picked him out in Ed and Kay Kinder's barn near Athens years before, and he had gotten used to it, that's why. She lifted him out of a litter of eleven and carried him over to me, announcing, "This one's feet smell like Fritos." Every chance she got, she would grab his paws, sniff, and say, "Still Fritos," and somewhere along the line he developed a habit of rolling on his back and frantically waving his paws in the air until you sniffed them. It depressed me to no end, not because it was ridiculous, which it obviously was, but because I wasn't around to watch L do it anymore, and doing it myself only served to accentuate my loneliness.

I dialed my old number on the room phone. I was not looking forward to it. There was nothing to do but the thing the guilty have done since the dawn of man: deny everything and hope for the best.

"Hey," I said.

"Hey nothing, Ray. Where is he?"

"Where's who?"

"You know perfectly well *who*. And what's wrong with your cell phone? I texted you fifty times."

"Can't find my charger," I said, giving Bruce another stern look to remind him to keep his shit together. "Anything the matter?"

"I don't hear any slot machines. You must be calling from the Motor Lodge."

"Correct."

"How much longer are you going to stay at that place?"

"You tell me," I said, fishing.

"You getting on with your life has nothing to do with me."

This comment stung, but I had heard far worse from her without getting discouraged, believe me.

"I'll be coming into some money soon," I said. "I won't be here that much longer."

I knew that wasn't the right thing to say, but I was trying to put on the air of a man on the upswing, someone displaying growth and prospects, and not a person who had been living at a motel for over a year, circling the American drain.

"Ah. That's right," she said. "The father who miraculously rose from the dead only to die again. Good old Lazarus Parisi."

"I told—"

"I don't want to talk about that. I have no interest whatsoever in talking about that."

"Fine. What do you want to talk about, then?"

"Are you fucking kidding me?"

"Why would I be kid— Why are you swearing at me?"

"I want that dog back this instant, Raymond."

"What?" I said, scratching behind Bruce's velvety ear.

I looked to the nightstand, where there was about a third of a joint left, just enough to take the edge off, but I didn't spark it for fear L would hear.

"I'm only going to say this one time: If you don't get the dog back here in ten minutes, I'm going to get that restraining order. And I am *not* kidding. This is not the day for this."

"I'm sorry, but I have no idea what you're talking about."

"You're saying you don't have him?"

"Have *who*?"

"*Bruce.*"

"Bruce? Why would I have Bruce?" I said, scratching his other ear and looking at the joint. What was the best thing to do here? The cast and the old-school telephone made this a very tough situation. I figured, what, tuck the phone between my ear and shoulder, put the

6

joint in my mouth, and light it with my good hand? Would that be audible?

"He's not in the yard."

"Maybe he's in the house," I said, experimenting with the joint-lighting strategy. The phone between the shoulder and ear was a shaky proposition.

"*I'm* in the house."

"Well, how the hell do I know what's going on over there?"

"Because you're in here as much as I am," she said. "There's a ring from a soda can on my journal, by the way. I don't suppose that's something you know anything about, either."

I did know something about that. I was drinking a cream soda a few weeks earlier when I went to check on her Cobra batteries and stumbled on her journal, which I took to Kinko's and then returned to the drawer. That might sound wrong, photocopying someone's diary, but she was my wife, after all, or had been for ten years, and she wasn't talking to me, so how else was I supposed to get a feel for her state of mind? I mean, in times of war and crisis, hasn't espionage always had its rightful place?

Before I could deny knowledge of the soda ring, my bronchitis or whatever the hell I had kicked in, and I went on a major coughing jag. When it subsided, I gave up on the joint idea and took a swig of the minuscule amount of NyQuil that was left on the nightstand.

"You sound like shit," L said.

"I'm good," I managed. "I'm OK."

I cleared my throat and looked up at the oil painting hanging over the TV: an aging sea captain shaking his fist at the heavens as a wild storm breaks all around him. I thought of my early days as a fledgling sportswriter, when L came with me on a tour-of-minor-league-ballparks article I did for the *Journal-Constitution*. We stayed in places like the Parkway Motor Lodge in a variety of Southern towns, faux-wood-paneled shit boxes that all had low-grade oil paintings of angry mariners and morose clowns and winged horses on the walls. We used to love to lie in bed and make up titles for them. I used to get high at the Motor Lodge and imagine her curled up next to me. She'd look at the painting in my room and say, "*Misfortune Knows No Shores.*" I'd laugh and offer, "*Curse of the Scalawag.*" And then *she'd* laugh and say, "*The Old Man and the Plea.*" And then *I'd* laugh and say—

"Raymond!"

"What's that?"

"Are you listening to me?"

"Copy that," I said. "I mean, yeah."

"Where could he be? I'm at a total loss."

Just then I heard a commotion out in the parking lot. Bruce jumped off the bed and ran to the window to investigate, his sudden leap shaking the recently replaced nightstand lamp, a wooden ship with a lightbulb in the crow's nest. Bruce shoved his snout between the drapes and broke out a low growl. This normally would have amused me, seeing as how he was a coward through and through, only this time it wasn't funny because I didn't need him making a racket and tipping L off to his whereabouts. While I was stalling her, it occurred to me that I could use his curious disappearance as an excuse to head over to the old house and search for him with her. It wasn't what I had intended when I took him, but it was certainly an improvisational opportunity with a lot of promise. I mean, she and I could team up, get the old camaraderie going, and then after a while I could suggest splitting up to cover more ground, wherein I'd take the opportunity to race back to the motel, scoop Bruce up, and arrive back at the house in triumph, claiming to have found him roaming the eighteenth fairway over at the municipal golf course. I'd throw in a funny anecdote about some shenanigans with him and some humorless duffers on eighteen, she'd invite me in, we'd fire up some mai tais, crank some Springsteen (anything but *Tunnel of Love*, which was his divorce record and something I just couldn't listen to), and soon all would be forgotten. It was an idea very much worth exploring.

"What's that noise?"

"It's nothing," I said. "Hey—could you hold on a sec?"

I shoved the phone under the pillow and dashed over to the window, then walked out the door and into the late-day sunlight. I leaned over the balcony and stared into the parking lot with as much authority as a grown man living in a motel could muster. Two preteen boys, one fat, one skinny, sat on the curb with a pack of bottle rockets. They looked like every comedy duo there ever was.

I raised my finger to my lips and furrowed my brow. I felt like it was a very adult "Shut up or else" gesture. Confident that I had gotten my position across, I closed the door with a little extra oomph and went back inside, dragging Bruce away from the drapes and onto the bed. It took a while to get him up there. He didn't move as well as he used to.

"Sorry about that," I said, climbing next to the hound.

"I'm worried about Bruce," she said. "Where could he have gone?"

"Beats me. Maybe it's those landscapers. Wouldn't be the first time they haven't, you know, latched the gate or whatever."

"It's not the landscapers."

"I'm just saying."

"Boyd's out looking for him now. He's checking the golf course."

Just like that, my new plan was shot. I had to shake my head. Was this losing streak ever going to end? *Jesus.*

"Old Man River still in the picture, is he?" I said.

"You know perfectly well what the situation is, Raymond."

The situation was that while I was attempting to get L to engage in even the most preliminary of reconciliation talks (an effort roughly as uplifting as working in a prison laundry), a fifty-five-year-old silver-haired snake in the grass named Boyd Bollinger had somehow slithered in and ensconced himself in her life despite: 1) being old enough to be her father; 2) having not one but *two* bumper stickers on his champagne Lexus (I'D RATHER BE GOLFING and THE MERCHANT OF TENNIS); 3) owning a champagne Lexus in the first place; and 4) having been the guy who invented those plastic contraptions people use to throw tennis balls to their dogs instead of just winding up and tossing the ball like a normal person. Which of these four facts was the most appalling is subject for debate, though any one of them should have precluded L from ever giving him the time of day, since he was exactly the kind of person we used to make fun of. But she hadn't been herself since Lucille had passed, and she was furious with me for a variety of things, not least of which were lying about my past, developing a gambling addiction while she was taking care of her dying mother in South Carolina, and having an innocent yet seemingly inappropriate friendship with a woman who lived up by Mohegan Sun with her five-year-old daughter. So this Boyd character had slipped in at a weak moment.

I had seen his car in our driveway one night when I happened to be driving around my old neighborhood after another regrettable evening at the casino, and then it started appearing there more and more often. After I noticed it parked there *in the morning* one time, I wrote down his plate number and fired up Web Sleuth, one of those online investigative services that tells you everything you need to know about a person for $49.99. I printed out some pertinent data and took the information up to L's door later that night.

"I'd like to have a word with your Memphis-bred fifty-five-year-old sleepover friend, Boyd, if I may," I said. "It's adorable that you two have the same birthday, by the way. That'll be fun for the eight or nine that he has left."

L looked stunned for a moment, but she gathered herself, and that's when she started throwing around the phrase *restraining order* with conviction and regularity. I also began to realize that forgiveness might not be my only obstacle to getting L back. I also had to contend with Father Time in golf cleats.

While I was contemplating the evil curiosity that was Boyd Bollinger, I heard a high whistle and a pop out in the parking lot. Bruce lumbered over and gave a low *woof* at the drapes. I immediately grabbed a half-full can of Pringles that I had been munching on before falling asleep and chucked them across the room. He turned away from the window, stuck his nose in the can, and started hoovering them up but good.

"What was that?"

"What was what?" I said.

"I heard barking."

"That's nothing. That's the TV. *Scooby-Doo* reruns."

"Scooby-Doo talks."

"Not always. Sometimes he, you know, barks and whatnot."

"That's the second time you've said *you know*."

"I have no idea what you're talking about."

"That's the second time you've said that, too. Those are the two things you always say when you're lying."

"I honestly don't know where you come up with some of this stuff," I said.

It was at this point that things took a distinctly negative turn. The unsupervised, troublemaking little hot dog and hamburger out in the parking lot decided to spark the entire pack of bottle rockets at once. They whooshed and whistled and rat-a-tat-tatted for a good ten seconds. Let's just say that Bruce failed to keep his shit together. It sounded like feeding time at the city pound.

"You son of a bitch!"

"No!" I said, though I have no idea why. What on earth was there to say *no* to? I had the dog. She knew I had the dog. Everything pointed to *yes*, not *no*.

"If he's not back here in ten minutes, you're going to get a visit from the police. And I have never been more serious in my life."

"Listen—"

"Ten minutes."

I got off the bed and looked at the dog. He had quit barking and returned his attention to the chips. I transmitted, "Hey, man's best friend. Terrific work. Really." He looked up, the Pringles can stuck to his nose, blameless as can be. But he had a glimmer in his eye. I knew it and he knew it. And that glimmer said, "Remember when you left me at the Prince and Pawper Kennel Club for six straight weeks last year while you were bingeing on blackjack eighteen hours a day and sleeping on Dawn's couch? Remember that? I do." And I looked right at him and thought, "Yes, I remember leaving you at the Prince and Pawper for six weeks. But I sprang you, didn't I? You had a pretty good time staying at Dawn and Penny's after that, if I remember correctly. And I made it up to you by taking you to Myrtle Beach with me. A trip you totally spoiled, I might add."

He looked at me. Gave me nothing.

"Anyway, this was no time to make a point. Now drop the fucking chips and let's go."

I hauled him down the stairs and tiptoed past Maurice the day manager's office. All four hundred pounds of him were at his desk, gnawing on a Hot Pocket and listening to WFAN on the radio. He looked right at me as I went past, which meant I'd be answering a series of questions later regarding the no-pets policy.

I tossed Bruce into the F-150 as the two perpetrators of my demise looked on smugly. This was simply another case of bad luck for me. In a day and age when parents put webcams in the bathroom in case Junior wants a juice box while he's taking a crap, I had found the last two unsupervised children in America. Kids who were allowed to play with fireworks, no less. I gave them the finger with my good hand, pulled out of the motel lot, drove up past the golf course, and rumbled through my old neighborhood, where the sight of my truck had gone from being one that inspired waves galore to one people averted their eyes from. It had gotten so uncomfortable that I often parked down by the driving range and walked through the woods to my old backyard on days when I was worried that L's Cobra batteries had died. I had done that earlier in the day, which is why reasonable doubt was still on the table before the hound blew it. I knew the first thing L had done was canvass the neighbors and ask if they had seen my truck in the driveway. She would have come up empty there. If a couple of things had broken my way, the search party/mai tai idea could very well have been successful. But you don't get the breaks you need when you're on a downslide. You get shit, and then you get more shit, and when you think you've maxed out, you get a little more shit on top of it all.

As I took the corner onto Archer, I could see the dreaded champagne Lexus parked where my old basketball hoop used to be, moronic bumper stickers on display. And there in the front yard, looking for all the world like he owned the place, was the Old Rooster himself, Boyd Bollinger. He was chipping plastic golf balls toward where my hammock used to hang. Now that was gone, too. I parked on the street. Walked past a good deal of high-end luggage sitting at the end of the driveway. He broke out a Silver Fox smile as I strode past him. He fancied himself a regular George Clooney, this motherfucker.

"Ray."

I looked at him. The Kentucky Derby mug I'd gotten on a trip to Churchill Downs was at his feet, steaming with tea. Who the hell drank hot tea in the goddamn summertime?

"Boyd."

When the dog who blew my cover and I got up to the door, L tossed the screen open and Bruce raced in. Her hair was shorter than I had ever seen it. It made the delicious blue speck on her bottom lip even more pronounced, and her eyes looked like a pair of little moons. Though I had known her for sixteen years, the girl got more breathtaking every time I saw her. It was unsettling.

"First-rate cut. Very stylish," I said, smiling and nodding at the luggage in the driveway. "You going somewhere?"

She shoved her Cobra CXT 1000 into my chest and slammed the screen door; it was still rattling as I trudged back across the grass.

"Have a good one, Ray," Boyd chirped.

The geriatric was relishing the situation. I would have clobbered him except for the cast on my right hand, which was one thing, and the fact that the cops were probably already in the process of figuring out who I was after the incident at the racetrack earlier in the day, which was another. Plus, he was six hundred years old. He'd keel over on his own soon enough.

I took a couple more steps toward the truck as a limousine pulled into the driveway. I turned around and looked at Boyd Bollinger. He was smugly holding a pitching wedge, wearing a lavender V-neck from the Republican Casual line. I walked over to him and gave him a menacing look (I had a solid six inches on him, not to mention being twenty years younger), then picked up the Kentucky Derby mug, dumped the tea out, and tossed it, left-handed, across the driveway. Because I'm a righty, it was a lame, ineffectual toss, and the mug bounced off the pavement and into the bushes without even breaking.

As the limo driver began piling luggage into the car and Old Man River tried to tether down the slightest of smiles, L watched from the window and shook her head in disgust. The neighbors across the street did the same. Jesus. Hadn't anyone ever been on a losing streak before?

THE GAMBLER'S GUIDE TO HAPPINESS

March 11

. . . and where I came from, therapy was a tremendously suspect thing. Airing your problems and grievances to a total stranger? Ridiculous. Mom thought analysis was just another industry invented to pamper rich people. If you needed to talk, that's what your mother was for. When I think about it, in all the years with R, I never really spoke to him about anything substantial. I always called my mother. I remember when I told her I was pregnant. We joked that I already had one rambunctious child, so what was another?

AT THE BOTTOM OF MY OLD street, past the municipal golf course entrance, the road splits and affords a person in my position two clear and equally depressing options: 1) turn left and go back down Rabbit Hill Road to the motel of exile; or 2) turn right and head up the Merritt Parkway to the casino that led to the exile in the first place (and from which I'd recently been banished by security). While I'd strung together so many lousy days in a row that I'd forgotten what a good one looked like, this one had been aggressively shitty even by my standards. The trouble I had gotten in out at the racetrack earlier in the day was likely just beginning (my escape from the confusion being nothing more than an illusion of freedom and barely dodged consequences), the dog incident had further damaged my reconciliation campaign with L, and the limo and bags outside my old house suggested that the Boyd Bollinger issue was getting more problematic. All of this was on top of the fact that I had lost my job at ESPN, owed my bookie $52,000, and had maxed out my final credit card two weeks earlier on a cash advance that had led to a disaster at the blackjack table, one which resulted in a brawl that had led to both a broken right wrist and my banishment from Mohegan Sun. I might have been a glass-is-half-full guy, but there was no getting around the fact that the glass was now shattered all over the floor, and I spent the better part of each day doing a nice little merengue on the shards.

I sat in my truck at the bottom of the hill and paused. Going left meant an awkward conversation with Maurice, where I'd have to lie about having a dog in my room, then face another night sitting in that nautically inspired shit box, watching lousy network TV under that outraged image of the hopeless sea captain and taking personality and life expectancy tests online. While I had discovered through multiple tests that I had a dynamic personality, I had also learned that I was projected to live to ninety-one years old, a fact that I would have been thrilled about if it didn't mean I might be spending another fifty-six years in a fucking motel.

Going right meant a trip to Mohegan Sun, which I wasn't allowed back into and would likely be removed from the second I walked in the door. Even if I wasn't shunted off the property, I had no money to gamble with, and Dawn Dondero, the only person on the premises who might be inclined to cough up a small loan so I could play a little, was also a person who wasn't speaking to me at the moment. Given a choice between being alone and facing my situation, or being surrounded by people and possibly making it worse, I made the obvious decision and turned right.

It was a lousy time of day to be heading toward the casino. The two-lane parkway was clogged, and the last light was fading from the summer sky. All around me, cars and SUVs were filled with people living either the kind of life I used to live or the kind of life I *would* have been living if I hadn't started gambling.

It had started, benignly enough, in New Orleans. I was on a four-man panel show on ESPN, and the producers sent us in for a Saints playoff game, setting up a makeshift studio in the concrete dungeon that is the Superdome, and informing us in the preshow meeting that it would be appreciated if we didn't mention the place had basically served as a third-world refugee camp during Hurricane Katrina, a national disgrace even if you were someone like me who had no interest in politics and didn't even watch the news. This set me in contrast to L, who at some point went from being blissfully in the current-events dark to keeping MSNBC on around the clock and listening to something called TED Talks, which basically seemed to be smart people going on about how the world would be a better place if everyone were as smart as they were. L was living in what seemed to be perpetual outrage about the state of the planet, which didn't strike me as being any worse than it had ever been. I mean, I'm no scholar, but isn't history just an unbroken line of catastrophes and misdeeds? Haven't the same fucked-up things been happening since the start? What's the point of paying attention to things you can't possibly change?

Once our show in the Dome wrapped, a couple of local crew members invited me out for a drink. We ended up at a joint in the French Quarter called Lafitte's Blacksmith Shop, which apparently was the oldest bar in the country and named after a pirate who used to plot his marauding there. One of those features is plenty enough to recommend it as a spot to do some day drinking, and two makes it pretty much a no-brainer, so I joined the locals and we proceeded to line 'em up. We drank and dominated the jukebox until Rowdy Ronnie the piano player came in, then we pulled up some stools around him and spent all night reveling in the fact that every time a tourist requested Billy Joel's "Piano Man," Rowdy would instead play Warren Zevon's "The French Inhaler," which he said was the only song that truly captured the desperate, lonely essence of a bar, a handful of Tom Waits songs notwithstanding (unlike L, I didn't find anything wrong with resembling a character in a Warren Zevon song—they were always very colorful). Ronnie considered "Piano Man" an abomination, utterly phony and representative of everything that was wrong not only with music but with life itself, and he refused to play it even when a cluster of Wall Streeters offered him a hundred bucks for just a verse. Everything about Rowdy Ronnie suggested he could use the cash, but New Orleans has a curious integrity despite its general poverty, and he wouldn't play "Piano Man" no matter how much they tried to muscle him with their money. I remember being very impressed by this, as I usually was with any genuine display of principle.

At around midnight, it was suggested that a moonlit stroll along the Mississippi and a trip to Harrah's casino were the logical next steps. My phone had one bar of battery left, so I called L on the chilly walk along the river, left her a message, and then rolled into the casino with about half a dozen of my new Louisiana compadres, most of whom were shocked and appalled that I had never gambled before, despite having both Foxwoods and Mohegan Sun in my backyard.

A couple of the crew gave me a quick lesson in the fundamentals of blackjack, how to play what they called "basic strategy," and then we sat down at a five-dollar-limit table to give it a whirl, each of them taking pride in advising their "celebrity" guest on how to play his hand and adjust his wagers. I cashed in for a hundred dollars, and the feeling I got when I placed that first chip down on the felt was—Jesus, what *was* that? It was as if someone had taken an extension cord, plugged one end into the French Quarter's electrical grid, and shoved the other end right between the back pockets of my Levi's. Everything—nerve endings, lights, sound—was heightened, acute and new, yet at the same time I felt outside of myself. Plugged in yet floating. Time somehow accelerated and stood still at the same time. It was strange and magnificent. The dealer kept busting, everyone at the table was cleaning up and raising hell, the drinks were free—where in Christ's name had this been all my life?

After nearly sixteen hours had somehow evaporated, I went back to my room at the Royal Sonesta and plugged my phone in. Aside from a slew of voicemails, I had no fewer than twenty "Where are you?" texts from L, which was alarming because she never texted when she was at work and was most definitely not one of those girls who needed you to check in all the time. If she said "I'll see you at the house tonight" when she was going out the door in the morning, then that was exactly that— she'd see you later at the house. She didn't feel any need to correspond throughout the day. She'd never send you a picture of the salmon salad she was eating for lunch or forward you some allegedly hilarious video a colleague had sent her of a cat hanging on to a ceiling fan. The more the world threw the seeming simplicity and ever-presence of technology at her, the more she ignored it. L used no social media, something she'd managed to quite freely and happily live without before the world conspired to make everyone feel like they were missing out if they didn't participate and do so aggressively. She wouldn't even use the GPS in her car. She was a girl who thought maps were beautiful. In fact, now that I think about it, her office was filled with framed maps. I had always assumed the firm decorated all the offices, but that might have not been true. I'm not really sure. We didn't talk about things like how to decorate an office (or anything meaningful, according to her, though I don't consider office decoration important, and I believe we discussed the issues of the day quite routinely no matter how L remembers it).

I called her back, and before I could brag about my blackjack prowess, how I had won $365 on my very first attempt at the game, she blurted out that she'd had a miscarriage.

"What?"

"I had a miscarriage."

"But you just found out you were pregnant," I said.

"What does that have to do with anything?"

"I'm not sure."

And I wasn't. I wasn't entirely sure what a miscarriage was. I mean, I knew *roughly* what it was. But how it actually played out I had no idea. My knowledge of that topic was basically limited to wealthy mustache-twirlers tossing heartbroken girls down the stairs in old movies, usually in mansions, or any dwelling with a deep and dramatic staircase.

"You're probably relieved," she said.

"Are you OK?" I asked.

"I'm fine."

"Then of course I'm relieved."

"That's not what I meant."

I knew what she meant. My initial reaction to the pregnancy news, which I'd received less than a week earlier, was apparently unsatisfactory. L had always been adamant about not even considering kids until she was thirty-five, and I guess I was under the impression that the Pill was one of the many things I didn't know much about from a technical standpoint but which was nonetheless fail-safe, like Treasury bonds or the weather in Southern California (or what happens when a man with a family name to protect pushes a pregnant girl down an antebellum staircase).

After wrapping my head around the fact that you could take the Pill and still get pregnant, I started to worry about the things I'm sure most people obsess about when they find out they're going to have a kid (deformities, swimming pool tragedies, things of that nature), but that doesn't mean I wasn't excited, or wouldn't have *gotten* excited, once the deformity and swimming pool images subsided. I'd barely had time to digest the news before that morning in New Orleans. To be honest, the whole thing was pretty much over before it ever got started.

I hopped on the first flight back to New York, but by the time I got back to Connecticut, L was gone. Not an hour after we had spoken, she had gotten a call from her mother, who was living down in Myrtle Beach. Breast cancer. I arrived home to a note on the table. L had gone to South Carolina. I was to get Bruce from the Prince and Pawper and await further instruction.

And that's life, isn't it? You're just going along, going along, going along, and then *boom*, words like *miscarriage* and *cancer* bully their way into your everyday vocabulary, and suddenly you find yourself in an empty house in the middle of winter. You get the dog and await instruction, but no instruction comes. So maybe you end up with a lot of time to kill. Too much time, since the person you're used to spending it all with isn't around anymore. This could prove disconcerting, and to combat the loneliness, you might hop in your truck and go to Barnes & Noble to buy some books you should have already read. It could be that you recently got skunked in a video trivia match in a Sheraton lounge by some roofing supply salesmen and vowed to fill in some of the considerable gaps in your arts-and-letters knowledge. For example: While you may know that the clock in Tony's car reads 10:22 in the opening-credit sequence of *The Sopranos* and Penny Lane's real name in *Almost Famous* is Lady Goodman, you've never read *The Great Gatsby* (this would later prove to be even more problematic than you thought). Maybe the roofing supply salesmen thought it was absolutely hilarious that you didn't know your own country was named after Amerigo Vespucci, which they claimed was something any child would know. If you didn't have that information, they wondered, what the hell else were you in the dark about? Maybe they made you realize that the handful of credits you got at Rutgers wasn't enough.

So it could be that you decide to rectify this situation, head to Barnes & Noble with the best of intentions, but come to find that the place is a fucking maze. Maybe it's like the hedges outside the Overlook Hotel in there. You could wind up in Games instead of Fiction as a result of the poor layout. A mistake made at the blueprint stage and not corrected, or maybe just the misguided floor plan of a confused low-level manager. Who can say? But this being the case, you might end up in Games, and perhaps the New Orleans outing has piqued your interest in a world you never considered. Maybe you wind up buying yourself some books on blackjack and craps instead of investigating the work of the dead Russians and Brits you CliffsNoted your way through in prep school. The piece of paper in your pocket might read:

War and Peace
Anna Karinia (sp?)
Tale of 2 Cities
Oliver Twist
Weathering Heights (sp?)
The Great Gatsby

While the books in your bag end up being:

Breaking the House in 5 Easy Steps
How to Play Winning Blackjack
The Gambler's Guide to Happiness
Lil' Joe from Kokomo: A Guide to Craps
The Gambler
The Great Gatsby

Now, you might get home and empty the bag and feel a little ashamed of yourself when you look at the contents relative to what's on the piece of paper. It might even seem like the dog is disgusted with you. You're probably glad someone accidentally put Dostoevsky's *The Gambler* in Games and not Fiction, where it belonged, and you crack that open first to try and realize your initial impulse toward self-improvement (*Gatsby* was right by the cash register, fortunately, but you figure you can deal with him later, and put that one on the nightstand, where it will stay until it becomes one of the items L packs up and sends to you down at the Motor Lodge in the duffel bag you kept your softball gear in, tucking it amid a variety of small items you purposefully left behind after your banishment).

So the reading of Dostoevsky commences, but all that book makes you want to do is gamble. Yeah, there's a lot of people running around a suite at a German hotel who are either royalty or claiming to be royalty, and they all have agendas and grudges and the stuff of stories, but in the end it seems that the book is basically about playing roulette, and how a guy named Alexei gets completely consumed by it, as does a rich old woman who has come to the town for its healing waters but instead gets sucked into the action at the casino and blows pretty much her entire fortune. This is sickening but also kind of satisfying, since everyone back in the suite is waiting for her to kick so they can claim their inheritance, which you really don't want them to get their hands on, since they're a pack of vultures.

Now, no matter what the roofing supply salesmen think about you and Amerigo Vespucci, you're not a complete idiot. You're sure there are themes of class as well as male-female dynamics in *The Gambler* that some professor could gasbag about for a good while, but all you really get out of the book is an intense desire to go to a casino despite the fact that everyone who gambles in the story ends up in the shits and pretty much an addict. No normal person could read that book and think gambling was anything but a dead end, but you're not a normal person. This is another case of bad luck. If Dostoevsky hadn't made gambling so enticing right after New Orleans did, you might have been able to treat it as something you tried once and moved on from (like lox or Swedish movies), but that's not the way it went, because that Russian can fucking write, and was a degenerate gambler himself, which was another push toward the tables, since anything that was appealing to a genius like Dostoevsky couldn't be bad for a regular Joe like you. Gambling was obviously an intellectual pursuit of some kind, which is what led you to the bookstore in the first place, wasn't it? A lot of factors seemed to be pointing toward giving this thing a try.

One more factor: It could turn out to be unseasonably warm that winter, and as a result there might be dead squirrels all over your yard and driveway. And it could very well be that sitting alone with the dog, the both of you eating French-bread pizzas every meal of the day, is a little depressing. Maybe looking at those dead squirrels piling up is a downer, too. You could easily start thinking the folks in New Orleans were right. Maybe it *is* kind of a waste to be a little over an hour away from Foxwoods and Mohegan Sun and not play. After all, why not support the Indians? Don't they deserve it after all they've been through? Maybe the roofing supply salesmen were right. What kind of American are you, anyway?

So, let's say that you read all the books, play thousands of mock blackjack hands, and keep track of your progress on your wife's legal pads. Let's say that those pads show winning session after winning session after winning session. Maybe you never lose, and are seemingly born to play the game, even winning every time you practice online. Perhaps your wife wants to be alone with her mother and doesn't want you to come to South Carolina. Maybe she surprises you by being pretty adamant about this being a time they need to spend together without you. As she's telling you this on the phone, you can hear the *thunk* of a dead squirrel falling off the roof onto the patio. Maybe the poor, confused thing dies in a puddle of warm rain on the other side of the sliding glass door. It's very possible that the dog won't shut up about it. He might start scraping his nails on the glass and generally going insane for no good reason. At that point, your wife might say goodbye without an *I love you* for the first time (though you won't think about this until much later and don't even notice it at the time). You could say fuck it, grab your keys, take a hundred, hundred and a half, from the petty cash jar under the kitchen sink, and head toward the front door. Maybe you tuck a laminated "Ten Keys to Being a Winner" card that came with *The Gambler's Guide to Happiness* in your wallet (where you'll always keep it and never refer to it), yell "Knock yourself out in there, I'm going to check out the casino" to the howling dog, hop in your truck, and roll down Archer. When you come to the fork in the road, you might go right for the first of many, many times, and find yourself taking your initial steps into a great and disastrous unknown. A gambling addiction is under eighty miles away, after all. And it's a straight shot there.

LOVE AND
EVERYTHING ELSE

March 11

. . . it became something of a constant refrain afterward. What did you know? When did you know? Why didn't you know? All the girls bring it up constantly. Hope. Beth. Fiona. It's one of those things that's very easy for people to say after the fact, but they didn't see it any more than I did, I don't think. They all held us up as the perfect couple until everything came to light. But even if they hadn't, I wouldn't have done anything differently. I wouldn't have seen or known more. I was so in love then. My God. I was so in love, I was sick with it.

I PULLED THE F-150 BENEATH THE enormous wooden teepee out in front of Mohegan Sun and tossed the keys to Chip, one of the valets who would leave a loose joint in your ashtray from time to time if you'd had a bad night and looked like you might need it. He smiled and shadowboxed when I got out of the car. "Sugar Ray. How's the paw?"

"Be back in the ring in no time," I said, holding up my cast.

He smiled and hesitated before getting in the truck. He knew I was banned from the casino but didn't want to be the one to enforce it. It was just a summer job, after all, and he was still young enough to think that any edict issued by higher-ups was, by definition, complete bullshit.

"Whatcha doing here, dude?"

"Research," I said. "I'm thinking of buying out the Indians."

He grinned and shook his head. What was it to him whether I got hauled out by security or not?

"Dawn's over by the Triple Sevens in case you're looking for her," he said, hopping in the truck. "Or in case you're not."

Chip peeled out. He was twenty years old and going to UConn. His girlfriend was cocktailing inside. They had just spent three weeks in Amsterdam. He had the world by the fucking collar.

I walked into the casino. It was after eight o'clock and there was a lot of action, a lot of other things the pit bosses needed to be paying attention to besides me. The stakes at the low-limit blackjack tables were being raised, the better-looking cocktail waitresses were starting their shifts, and the drivers of the senior buses had already herded up the old-timers and hit the highway, leaving a younger crowd in their wake. I took a look around. Mohegan Sun, despite being a house of horrors for me, was a fine-looking casino and, unlike nearby Foxwoods, made at least a passing attempt at a Native American motif, which seemed only right, since they were ostensibly sitting on Massapequa Indian reservations (though the closest thing to a real Indian I ever laid eyes on up there was a croupier named Lawrence Littlejohn, who claimed to be one-eighth Massapequa but was practically albino). Mohegan Sun had the teepee out front, and the interior featured a lot of blond wood, with carpeting that vaguely suggested the American Southwest. In the wintertime, the valets wore hooded fur parkas that had a somewhat authentic hunter-gatherer look to them, and some of the $25 chips featured a howling timber wolf on one side. Add the nightly Trail of Tears from the tables to the parking lot, and you could make a case that the natives were finally exacting a sliver of revenge on the ancestors of those who had done the unthinkable to them and gotten away with it. The casinos weren't much, but down 50–0 to the Cowboys, the Redskins had managed a field goal to get on the board.

Still cognizant of keeping a low profile, I walked past some craps tables, ignored an "*Hola*, Ray!" from a couple of drunk Mexican landscapers who were regulars, and strolled into the slot salon to see Dawn Dondero, whom I had met when I first decided to try casino life and who was at least partially responsible for my banishment to the Parkway Motor Lodge.

Dawn was a petite, pretty dishwater blonde who, at the time we met, had a crappy job at a strip mall hair salon, lousy luck with the slots, and a deadbeat ex-husband who was habitually showing up at her apartment when she was at work and helping himself to whatever loose cash he could ferret out of her dresser drawers. All these things remained permanent fixtures in her life, with the exception of the ex-husband's unannounced visits, as he had recently become a guest of the state of Rhode Island after making some surprise appearances at the homes of people he hadn't been previously married to. All Dawn had in the black was a sincere "Today's the first day of the rest of your life" attitude and a charming five-year-old daughter named Penny. Like a lot of people, Dawn could never quite figure out why it was that she couldn't get what she wanted out of life despite lowering her asking price year by year. But she never dwelled on that fact for long and was, quite honestly, about as upbeat a person as you could ever hope to know.

We met through her sister, KC, who was a cocktail waitress up at Foxwoods before they canned her for salting away a dozen White Russians every shift. To protest what was an undeniably just dismissal, we moved our play over to Mohegan Sun and started hanging out pretty much every day. I'd ask her how Penny was coming along in school, and she'd ask me how L's mom was doing, and oftentimes she'd sit with me when I'd play blackjack, or I'd kill time with her at the slots. We became friends. One night there was a pretty treacherous ice storm, and she invited me to crash on her couch, since she lived close to the casino, and not that far from Bristol, where the ESPN campus is. Once I started gambling every day, I wound up staying over there more often as a matter of convenience, and for a while I found I could play cards in the morning, make it to the taping of my panel show, and then get back to the tables before dark. I didn't share any of this with L, naturally. I figured I was just killing time until her mom got better and she came home from Myrtle Beach. Only that didn't happen as quickly as I expected it to.

I found Dawn perched in her usual spot, working the lever of an American Glory Triple 7s slot machine whose legendary refusal to pay off was matched only by her mulish insistence on feeding the sucker until it did.

"You ever consider the fact that this one may be a dud?" I said.

"They're going to give you the bum's rush if they see you," she said, continuing to pull the lever without looking at me.

"You're not going to rat me out, are you?"

She ignored me. She was trying to send a message. But Dawn was a talker, and silence was anathema to her. She held out for almost ten seconds. It must have felt like a week and a half to the poor girl.

"I thought we weren't going to see each other anymore," she said without conviction.

I looked at her. When she had been playing for a while, she'd get a thousand-yard stare going like Walken at the end of *The Deer Hunter*, and a quick look at her ashtray suggested she'd been at it for about four or five hours. This meant Penny was with the convict's parents in Mystic on a sleepover.

"And if you're looking for money, forget it," she added. "I'm not sharing with you anymore."

Dawn had long harbored hopes that our friendship might turn into something more substantial, particularly after I got divorced, and she was always telling me she didn't want to see me until I got over L. She would invariably change her mind a day or two later, so I ignored her comment and assessed her outfit. She was wearing a suede caramel-fringe vest, dark jeans tucked into red cowboy boots, and a Harley-Davidson tank top, none of which I'd seen her wear before.

"You on your way to a Bon Jovi concert?" I asked.

"*Very* funny. This is the only thing in my closet I've never worn here. Everything else is unlucky."

"If clothes are to blame for what's happened to us in this place, then we might as well start coming here in our goddamn underwear," I said.

Dawn continued to hammer away at the Triple 7s as I kicked the tray of a Wheel of Fortune slot to her left. An elderly woman who must have missed the last senior bus limped by, pulling an oxygen tank on a metal roller. I sighed. When I first started frequenting the casino, my eyes were always drawn to hopeful sights, like people nailing big jackpots and high-fiving each other at craps tables, but after a while the grind set in and all I ever seemed to notice were Civil War widows pulling oxygen tanks, their final hours ticking away under artificial light. Life will do that to you, but casino life will do it quicker.

"I thought you were going to start going to the track instead," Dawn said.

I thought about telling her that I *had* been going to the track. That I'd come one horse away from winning the Pick Six at Belmont that very day, but a certain jockey named de la Maria had eased up at the wire and cost me what could have been close to $90,000 and an end to my financial problems. If I told her that, then I would also have to mention that I went a little berserk, jumped the rail, and pulled de la Maria off his horse after the race, and if not for the security staff being completely inept, I might not have been able to make it out of there before the real police arrived (not that the situation was even close to being over, since the jockey had been knocked unconscious, and everything gets recorded by somebody nowadays, so if you fuck up in public, you will most definitely not get away with it).

"I never said I was going to the track," I said. "Plus, didn't you say you were quitting this place, too? I thought the dream was over."

"The dream *is* over. I'm not going to be able to send Penny to some fancy college by hitting a jackpot. All I'm trying to do is get something back," she said, yanking down the arm again. "I just want to break even."

I watched her stare at the spinning 7s, blankly accept another loss, and pull on the lever again. The room hummed. There was nary an empty seat at any of the slots or the tables. It was a world that non-gamblers could never understand. For most people, the thought of risking their hard-earned money on games of chance that were designed to favor the house was incomprehensible. I used to feel sorry for them when I thought of all the action they were missing out on, but after enough time in there, it wasn't that difficult to see where they were coming from.

"You ever notice we don't even talk about winning anymore?" I said. "All we talk about is breaking even."

"What's wrong with breaking even?" she said, hitting a row of single BARs that paid ten measly credits, then shouting, "Good for you, Camilla!" to an old black woman who had just hit a small jackpot a few rows down.

"Breaking even's just getting back what was yours in the first place," I said. "Doesn't that make it all seem like a big waste of time?"

"Not to me. To me, breaking even means getting back to where you used to be and being happy to be there. Breaking even means appreciating what you had before you started gambling."

She was right, of course. She had a way of saying things like that, things that were very simple, and true, and completely useless to me. I started coughing and couldn't stop. It had been going on for two weeks.

"I think you've got bronchitis," she said, turning to look at me for the first time. "I'm sorry for throwing you out of the car. I feel terrible about that."

This was typical of Dawn, who'd had every right to throw me out of the car. Without getting into details, suffice to say that I'd been behaving *precisely* like someone who deserved to get thrown out of a car. She had been good enough to take me to the hospital to get a cast put on my wrist after my meltdown at the blackjack table, and then I had said some things that I knew would get me pitched out of the car whether it was pouring rain or not. She hoped for things out of me that it was obvious she'd never get. She knew I adored somebody else. She knew, even, that I hung out with her because I hated being alone. Yet despite the fact that all I ever did was disappoint her, she was still good to me. And instead of being grateful, I punished her for not being L. I know I'm not the first guy to do this kind of thing, but it doesn't make me feel any better about it.

"I don't know why you even mess with these stupid things," I said, kicking the tray again. "I mean, you see that guy over there with the tool belt? He *opens* these suckers. The casino *pays* him to work on them. Why would you trust a game that the house literally has the keys to?"

"And the house doesn't have it over you at the blackjack table?" she said. "I don't see you getting rich playing Twenty-one." She reached down into her purse and handed me my phone charger. One of her "I'm clearing your stuff out of my place" gestures that I was used to.

"Nobody calls it Twenty-one anymore," I said bitterly. "They stopped calling it Twenty-one about the time people stopped naming their first sons Jasper."

"You used to like that I called it Twenty-one," she said quietly.

This was true. I used to think it was charming that she said things like that, but those days were long gone. Everything I ever found endearing about L (that she had a blue speck on her lip, that she liked to sit on the floor of the shower and talk until the hot water ran out, that her Southern accent came out when she drank, that she sniffed the dog's feet, that she drank mini-creamers but not coffee, that she'd named our dog after Springsteen, that she'd run naked to the ice machine in hotels, that she liked the drive-in, that she knew how to change oil, that her freckles bunched up when she got a lot of sun, that she wore an anklet, that she cried when she saw dogs with gray hair on their chin, that she was smarter than me, that she wrote "You 'n me, babe—how 'bout it?" in lipstick on the dash during our first road trip, that she loved the batting cages and fireworks and trains and maps and walkie-talkies and every last thing about life and how you could wait for her to get ready for an eternity and never be disappointed when she walked out), those things never went away. They only got more delicious over time, while Dawn's habits just grated on me as the repetitions accumulated. And that, you'd have to say, is the undeniable difference between love and everything else.

I didn't have much time to mull this fact over, however, as I looked up to see two stone-faced security guards and a bemused pit boss heading my way. I was given two choices: They could call the state police, or I could end my relationship with Mohegan Sun and kindly leave the property forever. As with taking a right or a left at the bottom of Archer, this was an easy decision, so I said so long to Dawn and was walked out of the casino by security. Dealers, regulars, staff: Everyone was watching me, thinking God knows what, but I was far past the point where I worried about that kind of thing. Some of them probably considered me something of a folk hero (I mean, what gambler hasn't wanted to take a swing at a dealer who rolls himself a 3, 10, 2, then lets a hint of a grin form when he slaps down a 6 for 21?), but most of them probably just felt sorry for me, because I used to be a somebody and was on my way to being a nobody, maybe worse off than all of them. Whatever they were thinking, they couldn't know any more than I did that I just might not be through, and that maybe, just *maybe*, the kid might be primed for a comeback. Stranger things had happened, after all. And I was the kind of person they happened to.

SCHNAUPH & ASSOCIATES

September 19

. . . it's a question of knowing who you are. Having some fundamental understanding of the person you are, or at minimum the person you want to be. Prince wrote a song called "Funk Machine" when he was seven years old. He knew who he was. R never did, and so of course I didn't, either. How could I? How could I have known any of it? I used to think that he had the greatest attitude a person can have. Easygoing. Nonjudgmental. It took a long time to realize that the reason he never judged is because he didn't want to be judged himself. He never went in search of anything because he didn't want to be searched for himself. He accepted everything and challenged nothing by design. It's just that simple. "I had a lover's quarrel with the world" is written on Robert Frost's grave. R? He has a nonaggression pact with the world . . .

ONE OF THE WAYS GAMBLING IS like life is that things can go from bad to worse in an instant, yet right when it seems like all hope is lost, there's often a turn of events that might just herald a change of fortune if you can seize the shift in momentum and eliminate all the mistakes that created your current predicament. The morning after I was escorted out of the casino is an excellent example.

I woke to a thunderous banging. Now, there were a lot of candidates in regard to whom I might have pissed off enough to start hammering away at my door at eight-thirty in the morning (which was why I always parked the F-150 in the secret spot behind the motel), but the first place my mind went was the police and the Belmont Park incident. My instinct was to go for the bathroom window and make a run for the truck, but there were two problems with this: 1) I had no idea whether the window was big enough for me to climb out of; and 2) I was on the second floor. The drop couldn't have been that bad, provided I hung from the ledge. I'm six-three, and if I could extend, I might be able to drop down into the parking lot with minimal damage. Problem was, I couldn't extend, since my wrist was broken, so fleeing was out of the question. Hiding wasn't going to work, either. So I crept to the door as stealthily as I could and looked out the peephole, where my bookie, Bing Buli, stood. He banged on the door again and started yelling. "Parisi! Parisi son bitch! You hide Bing Buli! You pay! You pay!"

Bing was an immigrant from the Philippines who'd sold doughnuts and loose cigarettes on the streets of Manila as a child, then fought his way off the island as a flyweight boxer. He'd eventually established himself as a bookmaker in Connecticut, of all places, brought his parents over, and lived with them in a tiny South Norwalk apartment. I had met him through people at Mohegan Sun (getting hooked up with a bookie at a casino is roughly as difficult as finding a cigarette butt in an ashtray) and quickly tumbled into the hole betting on sports. Bing had allowed me to work off my original, much smaller debt to him by recruiting new clients. He was entirely enamored with the fact that I was a television personality; considered me his only friend; and agreed to give me a percentage of the business I brought him. Sensing an opportunity to manipulate lines in my favor and gain an insider's advantage, I proceeded to invent new customers who were really me under assumed names. This went about as well as most of my other schemes, and I eventually racked up the aforementioned $52,000 debt before Bing figured out what I was doing. He was brokenhearted when he discovered my scheme, then had his hurt calcify into seething bitterness when he realized how thoroughly I had taken advantage of him. The fact that a furious Filipino boxer was the best-case scenario for me at the door that morning certainly highlights the dodgy state of affairs I found myself in.

As Bing kept shouting his threats in broken English, I could feel a coughing jag coming on. I covered my mouth and raced to the bed, burying my face deep in a cluster of pillows to avoid being heard. I reached for the NyQuil, but that was spent, so I kept my head buried until the fit passed and Bing gave up outside. As soon as he climbed into his ancient sea-foam Honda Accord and pulled away, rotting muffler roaring, the room phone started ringing. This was safe, as only Maurice ever used it. Lord knows it wasn't L again.

"What is it, Maurice?"

"Ray? Bing—"

"Buli's looking for me. I know."

"OK. But he's really PO'd, Ray."

"I know, Maurice."

"You also have a FedEx."

"A what?"

"A Federal Express package?"

I threw on a pair of cargo shorts, trotted downstairs in a light drizzle, and mentally prepared myself to face Maurice Boudreaux, about whom I can tell you this: Aside from being four hundred pounds, he had a face that most resembled an old catcher's mitt, a wispy, half-hearted mustache that curled into his mouth at both ends, and a toupee that sat on his scalp so precariously that it looked like it dropped out of a loose ceiling tile and landed on his head by sheer chance. Maurice was so obese that he had the driver and passenger seats removed from his Capri and drove from the back with the help of foam blocks that extended from the brake and gas pedals like shoe lifts. Watching him struggling to get in and out of that car was always a couple of blocks past heartbreaking, and it could drop me into a deep funk if I was having rough sledding in the head on that particular day, or if L had refused yet another of my overtures to reevaluate the state of our relationship, which, as you can already tell, was pretty much constantly the case.

Maurice had been letting me live relatively rent-free at the Motor Lodge, usually accepting autographed sports memorabilia in lieu of hard cash (I hate to admit that the items were all forged, but there you have it). On days when I didn't stay at Dawn's, I'd go out and get Maurice breakfast before I went up to the casino so I wouldn't have to watch him fighting his way into the Capri, and so the Sarge, the ex-marine who ran the package store next to the motel, wouldn't stand outside with his phone and videotape him when he did, uploading the results onto YouTube with regularity under a series titled *I Spy a Fatty*. Whether it's more depressing that a decorated Vietnam War veteran has a YouTube account or that there's a sizable audience for videos of an obese man struggling to get into a Capri is anyone's guess.

The Sarge tortured him on a daily basis, and Maurice never defended himself, opting instead to bunker in behind a stack of papers at his desk in the motel lobby, where he used a love seat as a chair and did nothing all day but scour the *New York Post* cover to cover, listen to WFAN sports radio, and suck on his inhaler. He was roughly the size of a utility shed, and among his three or four hundred pressing health concerns was that he was asthmatic, a condition mocked relentlessly by the Sarge, who carried a deep and unshakable belief that anyone who had not been subjected to the rigors of Parris Island was doomed to a life of weakness, failure, and shortness of breath.

As far as Maurice knew, I used the Motor Lodge for writing purposes and spent a good deal of time there because my house was being renovated and my wife was in South Carolina taking care of her sick mother (because this once was perfectly true, I found it had no expiration date as a domestic fallacy). Maurice asked very few questions of anyone as a general rule, and even fewer of me because I was a minor celebrity due to both my old ESPN sports adventure series and the fact that I had been a regular on a popular afternoon panel show. I had been canned from the panel for missing a couple of tapings due to getting hung up at the casino and failing to make it to studio headquarters in time, but I didn't share this detail with Maurice, choosing to tell him that I was on sabbatical from ESPN while I wrote a book. This, like my wife's absence and failure to have any access to cash whenever rent was due, was never questioned. I further secured my cost-free living situation by allowing him to handle all postings on my Twitter feed, a role he took on with the sobriety and care of a White House press secretary. He was so shy, and so grateful for our spotty friendship, that he allowed himself to be oblivious to the fact that the first thing I ever said to him ("Hey, my name's Ray, and I need a room") was probably the last thing I ever said to him that could be described as wholly accurate.

As I headed for the office, I saw the Sarge opening up the packy. I gave him a nod, and he did what he usually did when he saw me, which was shake his head as if I weren't one person but rather a van full of hippies. I opened the door to the lobby and walked in. Maurice was gnawing on a McMuffin and pawing at the *Post* while someone who lived in a Staten Island basement bitched about the latest failure by the Mets' front office on the radio.

He smiled when I walked in, then sifted through four empty Big Gulps, seven or eight spent inhalers, two dozen old copies of the *Post*, and thirty or forty bled ketchup packets before uncovering a FedEx package. How it had made its way to the bottom of that catastrophe, I'm not sure. It was a pretty good bet it hadn't arrived that morning.

"We picked up a bunch more followers last week," he said, taking a pull on a forty-four-ounce Cherry Coke to kick the day off. "People miss seeing you on TV, but they're excited about your book. I think it'll be a big success for sure."

"Great. You're doing a hell of a job, Maurice."

I had consistently lied to Maurice about following his social media efforts on my behalf, mostly because I wanted to keep him on my side and also because I knew he took pride in it and didn't have that many things in his life to take pride in. You have to give people that kind of thing when you can, even if you think all of that stuff is bullshit, which both L and I did. She said she couldn't think of anything less appealing than knowing what everyone was up to all the time, and I felt the same way (though I would come to discover that Facebook does have its benefits as a purely investigative tool). The Twitter thing had been a mandate from ESPN. Some intern had set it up and kept it current until I got canned and gave the honor to Maurice, and I suppose I was able to rack up a bunch of followers because of the shows I was on, and also because of an impromptu speech I gave on the field at the Little League World Series over a decade before. It was televised and became a very big deal, heralded for its inspirational qualities and message of tolerance (both of which were entirely accidental, as all I was really trying to do was get the kids to stop crying on national television).

"I was thinking maybe we could do an 'Ask Ray' thing for like an hour one day, if that's OK with you," Maurice said, taking another bite of his McMuffin. "The fans would really like it. Being interactive is a great way to grow our base."

"Do whatever you want," I said, grabbing the FedEx envelope and looking at the sender. *Schnauph & Associates.* It rang a bell.

"Awesome. When?"

"Whenever you want. That social media stuff is all you."

"OK. But it's 'Ask Ray,' so you'd have to answer the questions."

"Maurice, you pose as me every day. Answer the questions yourself. I can't get involved in that stuff. I need to stay focused on the book."

He nodded. The air for the "Ask Ray" idea went right out of his balloon. He was easier to discourage than a foster child.

"Um, Ray? Listen. You by any chance have a dog in your room yesterday?"

"What's that?"

"You by any chance have a dog in your room yesterday?"

"A dog?" I said.

"Yeah. Like, yeah. A dog."

"I have no idea what you're talking about."

"You didn't have a dog in your room?"

"I thought you guys had, you know, a no-pets policy here."

"We do," he said.

"There's your answer, then."

He looked at me, shrugged, and turned his attention back to the McMuffin. As I said, it didn't take much to persuade Maurice to give up. It was his first impulse in nearly every situation, and his having seen me hauling a ninety-five-pound golden retriever right past his window not fifteen hours before was not going to change that.

"Ray?"

"What's that?" I said, itching to get out the door.

"It's OK if you had a dog in your room. I had a dog once, too."

He had a forlorn look on his face and a bit of egg hung up in his mustache. I sighed. Any interaction with Maurice was, by its very definition, depressing, and I shuffled out of there with my FedEx before I started to feel too heavy.

Outside, the Sarge was hosing down the lot in front of the store despite the fact that it was starting to rain. He looked at my bare feet. "You and the fat boy need to pull it together," he said.

I looked at his hose. Up at the sky. He kept spraying.

"I don't count on Him," he barked. "I count on me. Think about that."

"I will," I said, trotting up the stairs and kicking myself for not confronting him about the deer situation, which the Sarge had also counted on himself to take care of, the results of which had been bothering me in a way things usually didn't.

I had spotted a beautiful doe in the back parking lot a few months earlier, when spring just refused to come and the roads were so bad that I couldn't make it up to the casino. After spending an entire day watching a *Rocky* and *Rambo* marathon, I went outside to get some fresh air and smoke the last of my weed. It must have been two or three in the morning. Out in the lot, sniffing around in the snow, was a doe, who must have crossed the parkway to get there. We looked at each other for a while, and then I figured, Hell, this thing has gotta be starving, so I went upstairs, filled a bowl with some Cinnamon Toast Crunch, and left it outside. Waking up to find the bowl empty, and feeling a bit of pride that something I'd attempted had actually produced the desired result for a change, I started leaving a bowl of cereal out every night. For a few weeks, the only decent part of my day was seeing that empty bowl in the lot as I walked to my truck. And then it stopped. One morning there was a full bowl of Cinnamon Toast Crunch out there, and it remained untouched for days, got soggy with rain, and that was when Maurice told me that Angel, the overnight manager, had seen the Sarge dragging a dead deer across the back lot, a rifle slung over his shoulder. He was a committed hunter, the Sarge, and had held court about his woodsy exploits numerous times. I occasionally indulged him, since I'd found you could crack a beer in his store, listen to one of his rugged stories, polish it off before he was finished, and get yourself a little two-for-one action when it came time to pay up.

Anyway, I don't even know why I'm still thinking about this. I didn't witness the shooting. There are no haunted tales of a rifle crack waking me from a dead sleep. I never even said a word to the Sarge about it. Part of me wanted to call him out for what he'd done. Give him a good lashing over it. I rarely got the opportunity to take a position on any kind of moral high ground, and it might have been nice to check out the view from up there. But another part of me knew that it was my fault. That feeding the deer cereal was just another case of me thinking something was a good idea, acting on it immediately, and failing to consider any kind of consequences until it was too late.

I tossed the FedEx on the bed and knelt on the floor, fishing in the pocket of my jeans for the weed Chip had slipped me after the Mohegan Sun boys sent me packing. I extracted the joint (three-quarter joint, really, since I had taken a few drags on the drive home) and pulled my phone out. I had more voice mails and texts than I had ever seen before. If I had hit the Powerball or assassinated a sitting president, I couldn't have expected greater volume. Like a FedEx from a law office, this couldn't have been good, and as with the FedEx from the law office, I ignored it and climbed on the bed, sparking the joint and turning on ESPN. The bronchitis made smoking a little difficult, but I powered through it, and within a couple of minutes a buzz started to kick in, right about the time shitty and distant cell-phone footage of me at Belmont Park appeared on the screen. The anchor was saying this over it:

"In what can only be described as news of the weird, New York State Police are searching for an unidentified man who stormed onto the track at Belmont Park Tuesday afternoon and attacked Colombian jockey Jorge de la Maria following the day's sixth race. De la Maria, who had ridden three-year-old Brother Rick to a place finish, was pulled from his saddle by the mystery assailant and struck his head on the turf after falling from the horse. The veteran jockey is listed in stable condition at this time, and the circumstances surrounding the attack are unknown. Police have received several tips regarding the potential identity of the perpetrator via social media, but no definitive announcement has been made."

Well, fuck. That wasn't good. The only positive thing I could glean from the situation was that the footage was crap, though the fact that my cast was visible made an eventual positive ID very likely. I was halfway decent friends with the anchor delivering the story, and I could tell by the look on his face that he knew it was me and was glad he didn't have to report it yet. Then the room phone started ringing. Maurice must have checked the Twitter feed and found people starting to ask questions. I ignored that, too, and sat back on the bed, staring at the sea captain on the wall. I was beginning to look at him with new appreciation. Kinship, even. We were brothers, he and I. Men carrying on nobly in the face of adversity. Sojourners tossed about on the unyielding waves of life, both seeking firm land after rough passage, a return to hearth and home. I sighed. Looked at the FedEx at the end of the bed. Relative to what I had just seen on television, there was nothing in that envelope that could possibly stoke my inferno of misfortune any higher, so I ripped it open. And this, my friends, is where that turn of events I was talking about comes in. That momentum swing that can change everything if you just seize it and make the behavioral adjustments you need to make.

In the FedEx were two separate envelopes along with a cover letter from Ira Schnauph, Esq. I wasn't two sentences in when I finally remembered where I'd heard that name before. It was the last conversation I'd had with L prior to the alleged dognapping. It was back in February, I think, or March. Sometime before the Sarge had decided he had nothing better to do but murder my deer for eating cereal. I'd been driving back from a rare winning day at the casino when I'd seen L's name pop up on my cell. I couldn't believe my eyes and nearly drove off the parkway in my haste to answer. "Hey there, pretty baby."

"Ray, a man named Ira Schnauph called for you."

"How are you?" I gushed. "I miss you."

"Never you mind how I am. Just expect a call from Mr. Schnauph."

"Is he a debt collector?" I said. "I'm working on getting all that stuff straightened out."

"He's not a debt collector."

"Who is he?"

"He's an attorney."

"You already divorced me once," I said cheerfully, since making light of the situation made it less real, and the Knicks game on the radio had just gone final and they had covered the spread on a meaningless shot at the buzzer.

"He's an estate attorney. Apparently you're inheriting some money from your father. Which is remarkable."

"I can explain," I said.

"Raymond, in lieu of telling it to a therapist, which you badly need, you can explain it to your friends at the casino. Or tell it to your hairdresser girlfriend. Or go swimming with Bridgeport girls and share it with them. You will not, however, be telling it to me."

Click.

I never spoke to Ira Schnauph, and outside of using its impending arrival as an excuse to hold off Bing Buli, I never thought about the inheritance at all. I figured the old man had left me fuck-you money. A check for a dollar or something like that. I had no desire to be reminded of my father for any reason, and the fact that his attorney had called my old house and told L about it felt like the bastard was sticking it to me from beyond the grave. I considered it a terrible break and a crushing blow to my reconciliation campaign. Considering L thought both of my parents had died in a car accident when I was one and I'd been raised by my grandparents, news of my father's actual death certainly did not further the cause of me getting her back; it merely cemented her growing impression that she didn't really know who I was and never had. She wouldn't let me explain that my mother had been dead for six years before we met, and my father and I had cut ourselves off from each other, so he was dead to me, too. I had invented an alternative past for myself out of spite, the mutual friends who introduced us in New Jersey had told L the invented story prior to our meeting, and there never seemed to be a reason to dredge it all up. I had moved on, we were insanely happy—who gave a shit about the past? What was everyone's fixation on things that had already happened?

I sat on the bed and looked at the two envelopes. One had my official address on it ("c/o Parkway Motor Lodge" looked ridiculous in print and was strange to see), and the other just had "RAY" written on the outside in my father's unmistakable handwriting, which I recalled from the specials board in the kitchen of his restaurant, and from the only letter he ever wrote me at prep school, advising that I stay out of a situation I'll be telling you about later that factors into all of this.

There was no part of me interested in opening the "RAY" envelope (I have no idea why he used quotations like it was an alias, since he'd named me after his father), but I held out a little hope for the other one, once it was actually in my hands, as I had under a hundred bucks in cash and anything that was in there would help, even if it was fuck-you money. I took a last pull on the joint, snubbed it out, and opened the envelope. Inside was a check for $612,500. I stared at it. Stared at it a little longer. Looked for loopholes.

From? Schnauph and Associates, Attorneys at Law.

Pay to the order of? Raymond J. Parisi.

In the amount of? $612,500.

Signed? Ira H. Schnauph.

I didn't know why it was happening, what the hell the old bastard had been thinking, or how he'd chosen a number like that, but the check was official despite it making zero sense. It had been almost exactly half my lifetime since we'd even spoken, and if there was an explanation, it was surely to be found in the "RAY" envelope, but I decided to stop thinking about how this mysterious gift tied into my past and instead focused on how it could shape my future. I looked at the check, glanced over at the bedside table, where my paperback copy of *Gatsby* sat untouched, and smiled. The Kinder House Plan could finally be put in motion.

The Plan had come to me a few months earlier, right around the time I had let myself into my old house on Archer via the garage and found all of the *Our Life* scrapbooks L had made rotting in a pool of antifreeze at the bottom of a plastic garbage pail. See, every year we were together, she would keep every last memento from our lives—torn movie tickets, photos, notes, concert stubs—and arrange them in handmade scrapbooks. If Boyd Bollinger's Lexus sitting in my old driveway wasn't enough to worry me, finding the scrapbooks ruined and discarded was, and from that moment on I understood that it was going to take something major to get her back, some gesture well beyond anything that had ever worked in the past. She was not the same person once her mother died. There was her obsession with the school shooting up in Sandy Hook. The religious books that had started popping up around the house before I got tossed. The exasperated tone she had adopted with me on the phone during her stay in Myrtle Beach and never relinquished. Now she had short hair and did yoga. There had been a major shift, and it was obvious that I needed to pull off something significant. Something jaw-dropping. Buying the Kinder house was it.

See, we used to drive up to Athens just about every Saturday in the fall when we lived in Atlanta. We'd roll up for UGA games, drive the red-clay Clark County roads where L had grown up, and visit with Ed and Kay Kinder, an older, childless couple who lived in a farmhouse just outside of Athens and bred golden retrievers out in a barn behind the main house. L had grown up in an apartment with her mother and been unable to have a dog. She had visited the Kinders' barn nearly every weekend as a child. We'd bought Bruce as a puppy from them, and the Kinder property always represented a kind of Shangri-la to a Southern girl who'd grown up poor, living in run-down apartment complexes on the wrong side of the university tracks and riding her bicycle for miles to gaze upon kudzu-draped railroad trestles and old sunlit barns in wide-open spaces. We always joked that we'd buy the place from them someday when we got a windfall. Take over the massive property, the breeding, everything. It would be the perfect life.

While never cracking the book I had gotten from Barnes & Noble, I had watched *The Great Gatsby* at Dawn's and come up with the plan, or rather just stolen the general idea from Leonardo DiCaprio, who bought a house directly across the bay from Carey Mulligan and waited for her to come to one of his splashy parties as part of his grand design to win her back. I fell asleep soon after their first rainy afternoon together, due to having stayed at the casino until six that morning, but I had seen enough and decided that I needed to do something Gatsbyesque to sway L, though my idea would be longer on sentiment and shorter on patience. The second I got the idea to buy the Kinder place, I knew it was the most brilliant plan ever conceived. It was nostalgic. It was epic. It could not possibly fail.

I had been pestering Marty Tepper, my old Realtor friend in Atlanta, about it despite the fact that I was badly in debt and living in a motel. That had changed, though. A miracle had taken place, and now I was mere days away from another one taking place. I picked up the phone and called Marty.

"Jesus. What now, Ray?"

"Marty. I need you to call the Kinders."

"Oh, for Chrissakes."

"I'm serious."

"How many times do I have to tell you? That property is worth two million dollars. You don't get a discount because you bought your dog from them or because they like you and L. They aren't going to give you the place because they never had kids and you used to visit them. It doesn't work that way. Hold on. *What? It's Ray Parisi. Oh, what do you know about it?* Sorry, Ray. Look, I've got to show some McMansions. I don't have time for this right now."

"I'm serious this time, Marty."

"Ray, not for nothing, but you said you were serious last time."

"When was that?" I said.

"When you called me at three in the morning from a fucking casino and asked if they'd take twenty thousand down and finance the rest."

"This is going to be a cash deal," I said.

"That's great. Put it in a knapsack and have a pig fly it down here. I'll take it up to Athens. Ed Kinder will be thrilled."

"Marty, it's— What's today?"

"July first."

"Call the Kinders. I will have every penny within a week."

"You're going to have two million dollars within a week? That's amazing. I heard money was falling from the sky in Connecticut, but CNN has been wrong a lot lately, so I disregarded the story."

"You ever hear of a little thing called an inheritance, my friend?"

"An inheritance? From who?" he said.

"Never mind that. Just set it up."

"Who could you possibly have an inheritance from? You're a fucking orphan. No offense."

"Marty, are you listening? Set it up."

"You're serious?"

"I've never been more serious in my life."

"You better not be dicking around, Ray. I'm not in the mood for one of your— *It's none of your business, is what we're talking about. Go work on your quilt or something. Fine. You do that. Tell him I said hello. Tell him it gets old quick.* Sorry. It's that time of the year, if you know what I'm saying."

"You'll call Ed Kinder, then?"

"If you're serious about this inheritance, I'll call Ed Kinder. But I wouldn't mind a little more information. Not to mention the six grand you owe me."

"It'll all be taken care of. Just make the call. Someday I'll tell you the whole story, brother. You and Sher come out to the house—"

"At this rate I'll be coming out solo."

"Fine, you come out to the house when this is wrapped up, and I'll tell you the greatest story you've ever heard."

"You're an optimistic son of a bitch, Ray. I'll give you that much. Call me after the Fourth. I'll be in Sanibel all weekend, looking for a place to bury the body."

"Awesome. Hey. Marty?"

"What?"

"Do you know who this country is named after?"

"Amerigo Vespucci. Why?"

"No reason."

I hung up with Marty Tepper and pulled out my wallet. I had one credit card that wasn't entirely maxed. It was useless for a cash advance, but it had a few hundred in credit on it. And while a few hundred wouldn't get you far, it'd most definitely get you to Vegas.

TODAY, I CONSIDER MYSELF

R didn't have any real friends. I was always encouraging him to take people more seriously. To actually befriend someone instead of just yukking it up all the time. On some level, I knew he was Don Quixote and needed a Sancho Panza. But he didn't see it that way. He had the guys from the show. The crew members. The neighbors. Everyone loved to see R. He could read any situation and give a person what they wanted. That was his genius. We never left a party without pretty much every single person telling me how much they loved my husband. But real life isn't just about giving people what they want, is it? It's about giving people what they need. And to know what a person needs, you have to be paying the kind of attention it wasn't in him to pay. To take the kind of care it wasn't in him to take. R was like one of those old songs about having a dollar in your pocket and a girl on your arm and everything being hunky-dory. And maybe life was really that way to him. Or maybe he was so committed to keeping things positive, to walking on the sunny side of the street, because he was afraid of his own history. Afraid of the other, shadowy side of the road. I've thought so much about this, and I can feel as I write that I don't have it in me to think about it anymore. It's like studying an equation you no longer desire the answer to.

I ARRIVED AT MCCARRAN INTERNATIONAL AIRPORT a little before three in the afternoon, toting the Kinder House Plan, a duffel bag, and a new head of hair. I got recognized a lot from being on TV, and with the

Belmont Park video circulating, I figured it'd behoove me to change my appearance; so I stopped at CVS on the way out to JFK and bought some Just For Men hair dye, figuring a switch from my usual blond to their H-45 Dark Brown would do the trick anonymity-wise, provided I parlayed it with a Red Sox cap and long sleeves to cover my cast.

Half an hour later, I found myself strolling across the cool, gleaming marble lobby of the MGM Grand with a casino host named Bob Mota. He was roughly five-nothing and half that wide, and walking across the white tiles with a cleanly shaved head and black suit, he most closely resembled an eight ball that had just rolled off a pool table and onto the floor. He led me to his office, told me to take a seat, studied the Schnauph check that I had handed him, and looked up at me. I was hopeful that my dyed hair and hat would keep him from recognizing me, but then it dawned on me that I hadn't done anything, nothing that he'd know about yet, anyway, and that calmed me down until it quickly occurred to me that my name was right there on the check, so of course he'd know who I was, unless he was one of those guys who didn't follow sports. Except he worked at a casino and looked exactly like a guy who spent the majority of his nonworking hours sitting on a black leather couch and binge-watching games on multiple flat-screens.

This was the problem with always having something to hide. You could never really relax. I'm sure honest people have their problems, too, but I have to imagine that they have less of them.

"So what do we have here, Ray?"

"It's my inheritance," I said, surprising myself by telling the truth when confronted with a direct query for the first time since my gambling life started.

"I see."

He looked at me. At the check. Back at me. If he knew who I was, he didn't let on.

"He had a heart attack," I offered. "In a kayak."

"What's that?"

"My father. He had a heart attack. In a kayak. In Michigan."

Mota looked at me again.

"Not a good place for that kind of thing," I said.

"Michigan?"

"A kayak."

"Oh. No. It isn't."

Let me be honest here: I've been embellishing, or just flat-out lying, since I was a kid. I have no idea why. I suppose it entertained me to make things up at first, and then it got to the point where I just wanted things to be different than they were and found that they could be if you just said it was so. Most of the time there would be a germ of truth to whatever it was I was lying about. My father did used to kayak, for example, but the chance that he had died in one was slim. I probably said it because I liked the image.

"He used to kayak around the Meadowlands," I said, which was true.

"The swamps?"

I nodded. "You're from back east, right, Bob? Accent gives you away a little."

"Queens."

"I was going to guess Queens," I said, though this wasn't true.

"Maybe he was looking for gold."

"What's that?"

"Your father," he said, continuing to eyeball the check. "Maybe that's why he was kayaking in the Meadowlands."

"I don't know what he was doing," I said, which was also not true, since my mother was an ecologist when they first met and they used to spend quite a bit of time kayaking through the Meadowlands doing research. I suppose he kept going after she died as a way of remembering her.

"Probably looking for gold," Mota said. "Pirates used to—whattya call it? Maraud. Pirates used to maraud in New York Harbor. They'd bury their gold in hollowed-out tree stumps in the Meadowlands. I read it in a book, believe it or not."

I wasn't sure whether Mota was referring to the buried treasure or having read a book as unbelievable, but it didn't seem to matter. I simply needed to show some interest and curry his favor. The dream was close all of a sudden. I needed to turn $612,500 into $2 million. Technically, I was two winning hands of blackjack away from having my life back. One winning play, you're looking at 1.2 million. Another, 2.4. That's the Kinder House with $400,000 left over. I'm not saying I was going to put it all out there like that (you'd have to have balls of molten steel and brains like grits to be that aggressive), but it goes to show how close to my fingertips all of it was. I just needed this bald motherfucker to give me a room and a credit line.

"For real?" I said.

"Yep."

"Pirates?" I said. It sounded like one of my stories.

"Pirates."

"In the Meadowlands?"

"In the Meadowlands."

"That's something," I said, before I started coughing for a good twenty seconds. The bronchitis, or pneumonia, or whatever it was I had come down with after walking four miles in the rain, was still hanging around. I'd get on coughing jags that I couldn't stop. It hurt the ribs more than anything else.

"You OK, Ray?"

"Summer cold," I finally spat out.

"What's up with that cast?"

"I attacked a blackjack dealer and broke my wrist on his head" didn't seem like the right call, so I went with "Damn dog went after a squirrel. Practically ripped my hand off."

"Fucking animals," he said in an unsettling tone. There was a whole story there that I didn't want to hear, likely involving Mota and missing-cat flyers stapled on utility poles throughout his neighborhood, so I changed the subject by nodding at the Lou Gehrig Cooperstown Collection bobblehead he had sitting on his desk.

"Now, that's outstanding."

"The Iron Horse," he said proudly.

"Great player."

"*Great* player. Reminds me to come to work every day. Make the best of things."

I cupped my hands over my mouth and approximated the public address echo of his famous speech at Yankee Stadium.

"'Today I consider myself, myself . . .'"

"'The luckiest man . . .'" Mota jumped in.

"'Man, man, man . . .'"

"'On the face of the earth . . .'"

"'Earth, earth, earth.'"

Mota smiled broadly. You could tell it was a rare occasion.

"Great speech," he said.

"Courageous."

"Fucking A, it's courageous. You seen *The Pride of the Yankees*, Ray? Gary Cooper played Gehrig. He was forty and looked ridiculous in the fraternity scenes, but you can't worry about shit like that. That's the small stuff. You have to look at the big picture. Cooper was right in the big picture."

"I agree. I'm all about the big picture."

"Good."

He stood up, said he had to take my check down to finance, and told me to fill out a credit application while I waited for him to come back. He handed me a clipboard. "Where you from originally, Ray?"

"Jersey."

"Jersey girls are all right by me," he said.

"Down the shore, everything's all right," I said, smiling.

He nodded and left the room. It was the third time I had told the truth in that office. I was practically a new man. And the lyrical reference I had hit him with got me thinking about the old days with L, which always felt good.

I'd met her at the Parker House in Sea Girt, New Jersey. She had escaped the Georgia heat and was visiting friends who had a place in Point Pleasant before heading back south to start school at Emory in the fall. We met while getting drinks at the bar, then partnered up at bumper pool against a pair of Waspy fraternity brothers who treated the finesse game like they were hazing pledges. It was awful.

"These guys are a fucking disgrace," L whispered to me. She altered her voice when she said it. Changed the cadence. I recognized it immediately from one of my favorite comedies.

"Did you just hit me with a line from *Slap Shot*?" I said.

"Did you just recognize that as a line from *Slap Shot*?"

"I certainly did."

"Paul Newman is the perfect man," she said. "Do you have Paul Newman qualities? Tell me you do. Say it with conviction."

"I have Paul Newman qualities."

"We shall see about that."

We held the table for nine straight matches, and then she said she wanted to go back to Point Pleasant and see a band at Martell's Tiki Bar. What could I say? She had smooth, fair skin, delicate freckles, silky blond hair, a tiny blue speck on her bow-tie lips, and the widest, clearest eyes I'd ever seen—if she had said that she wanted to hitchhike to Morgantown and put in a night shift at the coal mine, I would have grabbed a canary and a pickax in two seconds.

We ended up hopping in a Briggs van and heading over to Martell's, where the house band played Tom Waits's "Jersey Girl," which Bruce had made famous on the *Born in the U.S.A.* tour and was forever a big hit down the shore. L and I were thick as thieves by that point, and she grabbed my hand to dance when it came on. I can tell you that there are few things in life that compare with being nineteen years old, holding the tiny waist of the most beautiful girl you've ever seen, and slow-dancing on an outdoor deck while a summer breeze eases in off the Atlantic and pinwheel lights from a distant Ferris wheel bleed across the water. Can you even imagine that? Can you imagine everyone in the place singing "'Cause down the shore everything's all right, you and your baby on a Saturday night, nothing matters in this whole wide world, when you're in love with a Jersey girl" and, during the "Sha-la-la-la-la-la-la-las," closing your eyes and burying your face in her hair and hoping the band would never, ever stop playing? And then, right when you think there's no way the moment can be topped, she looks up at you with those eyes that are neither gray nor green nor blue but something unto themselves, some color you've never seen, and you stare at that mesmerizing blue speck and whisper, "I think you have something on your lip," and she stares straight into your eyes with those little moons of hers and says, "Maybe you could get it for me." And then your life begins.

And the thing is: That moment held, people. Trust me. It held for well over a decade of our lives, right up until her mom got sick. We had never been apart, and then suddenly we were, and I guess it turns out that I'm not the kind of person who excels when left to his own devices. On some level L intuited that, because once it became clear that she was going to take a sabbatical from work and stay in Myrtle Beach with Lucille, she continued to handle all of the household duties back on Archer, no doubt figuring that things like bills and whatever else went into running a home were likely to fall by the wayside on my watch. I was given one job: to collect all "pertinent" mail, put it in a bubble envelope, and send it to Myrtle Beach. To be honest, I don't think I had ever looked at the mail before. I ignored it like I would ignore, say, the plants (or birth control, for that matter). They were things that seemed to get taken care of without my worrying about them. But when L left and I started gathering the mail for the first time, I began to notice something interesting. There were a good deal of letters addressed to me from credit card companies. A *very* good deal of them. Apparently, thanks to the reliability of my partner, a lot of people were under the impression that Mr. Raymond J. Parisi himself was an excellent credit risk.

I avoided mailing in an application at first because I didn't really believe those offer letters could be true. Why the heck would someone give me free money? I could see L getting that kind of treatment since she was a lawyer and earned legitimate bank, but despite what people think, you don't make that much being on TV, or at least not on ESPN a handful of hours a week.

I ignored the credit card offers for a while, but then I started going to the casino every day before the show, and once I'd blown through the petty cash in the kitchen, I found that it wasn't easy for me to get my hands on more money, since my ATM card was tied to our joint account and it wouldn't take L long to notice that I was making cash withdrawals every day. I thought about asking ESPN to stop putting my checks into direct deposit, but she would have noticed that, too, so my options were limited. I certainly couldn't call her and say, "Hey, honey, I know your mom has cancer and all, but can you wire me a few grand for the casino, because it's winter, and I'm bored as hell, and there're dead squirrels everywhere, and they're depressing the crap out of me, and did I mention I play blackjack pretty much constantly now?"

So I sent in for a Chase credit card. And some good folks at Mohegan Sun were happy to show me how to get a cash advance off it. Then I got another one. It was mind-boggling. Do you know how easy it is to get free money if you have good credit? And do you know how long it takes word to get out that everyone was wrong about your perceived reliability? In time I got a third card (why not?) and a fourth (sure). When the mail came, I separated my credit card statements from the "pertinent" mail pile bound for South Carolina and hid them in my desk, and when I got paranoid, I moved them to the toolshed, where I stuffed the envelopes into a wading boot that the previous owner of the house had left behind.

Before you could say *trouble*, I was $25,000 in the hole. Thirty. Thirty-five. Forty. Every day, instead of hoping today would be the day L came home, I prayed for today *not* to be the day L came home. I was consumed with how I was going to gamble my way out of the ditch I had gambled myself into. It was all I thought about. I stayed at Dawn's, which was twelve miles from the casino, and kept Bruce at the kennel before finally springing him in a fit of guilt one day, wherein he, too, became a fixture at Dawn's apartment, a fact that L got her hands on somehow and bludgeoned me with along with everything else, constantly accusing me of "setting up house with a hairdresser" when all Bruce and I were doing was sleeping on the sofa and helping out with Penny. I went from buying in for $100 and playing red nickel chips at the small tables at Foxwoods in January to playing in the VIP salons at Mohegan Sun with nothing but black $100s by April. When it became obvious that I wasn't going to win it all back playing blackjack, and after a misguided "can't miss" craps strategy that cost me $3,000 on a Thursday afternoon and $5,000 more on a new card Friday morning, I met Bing Buli through people at the casino. Bookies require no cash up front, just your good name or someone's say-so on your good name, which I guess is really no different from the whole credit card thing, with the notable exception of a definite philosophical difference in the area of collection methodology. Bing was more than happy to sign me up as a customer. To him, I was famous, and having a client like me was a feather in his cap. He liked to joke that he was playing with fire by having someone who talked sports for a living wager on games with him, but anyone could look at my betting patterns and see that they resembled those of a garden-variety schizophrenic more than a professional prognosticator (my mother was a schizophrenic, so that probably wasn't the best word choice, but let's just carry on and get to that later).

I proceeded to handle sports gambling about as well as I handled casino gambling. Something Bing and all the credit card companies would agree on, and I certainly wouldn't argue with, is that there are certain kinds of people who cannot be trusted with a credit line, and I would be the prototype. Given the opportunity, I bet on everything. I played mostly blackjack. Some craps. A little roulette (thanks for nothing, Dostoevsky). I also tried my hand at baccarat, mini-baccarat, three-card poker, Pai Gow poker, and Caribbean stud. Outside the casino, I played the Lotto. Bought scratch-offs. Wagered on horses, dogs, boxing, baseball, college football, the NFL, NCAA hoops, the NBA, the NHL, and even golf. I bet on everything from the World Series to the opening round of the NIT. I wagered on both the Super Bowl coin flip and the outcome of the Academy Awards. Straight bets, parlays, teasers, halftimes, props, wheels, sides, totals. I tried them all.

When I met Bing Buli, I was convinced that I could dig myself out of the hole in no time, since I could be betting on games while I was playing at the tables, thus doubling my opportunities to get on a roll, pay off all the cards, and quit immediately (never mind the fact that this indeed happened on at least two occasions, and I pressed my luck each time, figuring I might as well get a little ahead for all my trouble). I would go up to Mohegan Sun in the morning, sit in the coffee shop, and study the day's matchups, or sit next to Dawn in the slot salon and *try* to study the day's matchups while she talked about the cast of one reality show or another. Then I would hit the tables until one-thirty, cash in, dash outside, grab my truck from Chip, and race over to Bristol to give my opinion on the sports topics of the moment, which I wasn't even following anymore, a fact that I covered up by choosing a different member of the panel to agree with every day and parroting whatever his position was.

After taping in the walk-in cooler that doubled as our set at ESPN, I'd pass up any offers to go over to the cafeteria on campus to grab a snack and catch up with whoever was doing the asking, claiming I had to get home to the dog due to my wife's absence (you use the word *cancer* in any context, and the excuse is immediately accepted). I'd race back to Mohegan Sun for some more cards, breaking around six-thirty to hit the coffee shop and study the evening lines. No matter the season, the nighttime action always cranked up around seven and continued through the ten-thirty West Coast games. I'd grab a quick slice from the food court, play more blackjack, and get up from the table between the shoes to check my phone for game updates, as if compulsively looking every ten minutes would somehow alter the course of, say, a Duke-Clemson game being played a thousand miles away by a bunch of teenagers in baggy shorts. By one in the morning, I'd be completely burned out and would run numbers in my head on the ride back to Dawn's, tabulating the day's gains or losses, figuring the overall debt, and frantically trying to concoct a plan that would get me square before L found out what I had been up to.

I benefited from the fact that she had too much on her mind to keep tabs on me. Addicts are first-rate liars, generally speaking, and I managed to hide things pretty well with the help of the liar's greatest aide: the cell phone. It wasn't beyond me to text L from the casino bathroom, for example, and say Bruce and I had just crawled into bed and were watching *Boardwalk Empire*, or step out onto Dawn's stoop and leave a message about how cold it was in Kansas City, where I had allegedly been sent on an assignment. After I got fired, I told her the network was considering a new show for me, since I knew her mother loved to watch me in the afternoons, and I needed to come up with a reason I was no longer on the panel. But I had no illusions about really getting away with anything. I knew I was leaving a paper trail. And I knew time was running out. I was worried sick. I never ate. I never slept. I owed everybody. How did I let it happen? I really don't know. You always hear a lot of talk about people self-destructing, but I don't think that's true. People don't self-destruct. They *unravel*.

As I was contemplating the events that led to my downfall, Bob Mota came barreling back in the room, check in hand.

"You know we can't verify anything today, right?"

"OK."

"This is just a piece of paper to me right now. But I like you, outside of the Red Sox hat, and I like the numbers on the paper. I think we can do business. Can I tell you something, Ray?"

"Sure, Bob."

"It's been nothing but pigeons and screamers in here lately," he said. "Plungers all over the floor. I swear it's been like a goddamn sawdust joint this summer. Fucking economy. They keep saying it's recovering, but that's blue-state propaganda."

"I hear you, Bob."

"You have no idea, Ray."

I nodded. He'd probably never been more right about anything in his life, since he'd lost me at "pigeons and screamers."

"I'll tell you how we're gonna play this," he said.

I tapped Lou Gehrig on the head, sending a subliminal message to Mota to say something positive. I needed money. I needed a room. I needed to put the plan to buy the Kinder place in motion as soon as possible.

"I'm gonna put you up on good faith. Not in the mansion, but we'll give you a nice suite upstairs. Everything checks out, we'll get you set up on the floor ASAP. Folding money till then, though. You need anything in the meantime, meal, massage, whatever, you call me, OK?"

Lou Gehrig and I nodded. I might not have been the luckiest man on the face of the earth, but I had been before, knew what it felt like, and was primed and ready for my second act.

ONE, TWO, THREE . . .
BREAK

November 23

. . . hell, I loved the guy on TV as much as everyone else did. Why wouldn't I? He was beautiful and amazing. I couldn't get close enough to him. I wanted to crawl inside him and live there forever. I wanted us to be like Herbert and Zelmyra Fisher. To break their record. But that's such a young way to think. Who knows what the Fishers' life was really like? Who knows what anyone's life is really like? It takes forever just to begin to understand your own . . .

I GOT AN EXPANSIVE SUITE WITH a marble whirlpool tub, loaded bar, wide-screen TV, wraparound sectional couch, and thirty-foot stretch of glass overlooking what Hunter S. Thompson called the "main nerve of the American Dream," the Vegas Strip (I got the quote from a chamber of commerce–sponsored magazine in the back of the taxi to the MGM, if you want to know). Out the window was the vast expanse of the Mojave Desert. It looked like the end of the earth, a place where things came to die. But, as Bob Mota had said, to focus on that would be to worry about the small stuff. The big picture was clear and looking good. I had gone from the miserable confines of Room 23 at the Parkway Motor Lodge to a suite at the MGM Grand. From being flat broke and thigh-deep in the sludge of debt and despair to more than half a million dollars in the black, assuming I paid off everyone I knew, though, that was not holding the top slot on my list of priorities. I was focused on one thing and one thing only: turning the $612,500 into a couple million, buying the Kinder house, presenting it to L in a dramatic moment of heartfelt grandiosity, moving the hell out of Connecticut and back south, and resuming a life that had been interrupted by a series of unfortunate circumstances and misguided decisions. It was just that simple.

I stood in front of the window in the suite and wondered how soon the check would clear. Outside, directly across the boulevard, a crew of workers was rocking empty cars back and forth along the Manhattan Express roller coaster outside New York, New York, a mini-Gotham-themed casino that featured an enormous replica of the Statue of Liberty that was absurd even by the impossibly campy standards of Las Vegas. I thought for a moment of the story my father used to tell about my late grandfather. How he'd come to Ellis Island with nothing, not even shoes on his feet. It never interested me. I continued looking out at the sprawl of Vegas. To the north, I could see the medieval-themed Excalibur, the turrets and spires above the bell towers looking like they might melt at any second. The radio in the cab on the way to the MGM had reported the temperature at 112 degrees and rising, and the desert out beyond the Rio and the Gold Coast was baking and cracking under the relentless sun.

I took out the unopened letter from my father and put it on the coffee table, along with the paperback copy of *Gatsby* I had finally started reading on the plane (again losing interest when it was obvious he had gotten Daisy back), $86 in loose bills, and the envelope Maurice had given me to place a futures bet on the Giants winning the Super Bowl. I knew that telling Maurice I was Vegas-bound was a bad idea as far as secrecy was concerned, but he'd been going on about how he had a vision of the Giants winning the Super Bowl for months, and I knew I'd need some spending money beyond the crazy check I was carrying, so I told him they were going off at 40–1, I was heading to Sin City, and you couldn't take visions lightly in this world. If he was ever going to make a big move, I said, this was it.

Maurice pulled himself off the love seat, ambled into a back room, and returned with an envelope full of cash that he handed over with great ceremony. It was like he was bequeathing me a samurai sword.

"Be careful, Ray," he said as he forked over the envelope. "There's some crazy people out there."

I stared out at the desert and pulled out a pack of Marlboros, extracting what was left of Chip's joint, which was camouflaged between the cigarettes. This was how I'd always get my stash through airports during the days when I had a job. I once was a recreational dope smoker (just a little here and there to take the edge off things), but the stress of my breakup with L and my nonstop gambling had caused a condition where my heart became permanently stuck in a state that can best be compared to an engine being revved in neutral, and I couldn't make it stop without sparking a joint. A little weed would calm me, slow the world down to a reasonable pace, and let me breathe and think things through. You could say I smoked every day if you wanted to.

I sat down in front of the window and put the joint in my mouth. Across the street, a security guard pulled a couple of kids from the fountains in front of the Bellagio, and as I watched the killjoy ply his trade, I fired up the joint and put my cell phone on the floor. I had 136 text messages, 58 missed calls, and 37 voice mails. It didn't take peerless intelligence to assume that word had gotten out about exactly who had yanked Jorge de la Maria off his horse at Belmont Park. The texts were a litany of "Wuz that u?," "WTF?," and "Ur fukked." I knew the voice mails weren't going to be much better, but since things were looking up in every other way, I figured I could endure the avalanche.

Hello. You have thirty-seven new messages.

First message, received at 11:02 A.M. . . .
Hey, man. What the fuck?

Second message, received at 11:21 A.M. . . .
You son of a bitch!

Third message, received at 11:38 A.M. . . .
What's your problem? You walk out of the casino without saying good-bye, and then you don't even call to explain or answer your stupid phone or anything. I'm so sick of this crap. It's just . . . You're just ridiculous, Ray. You can't keep doing this all the time. And did you tell Penny you'd take her to Central Park this weekend? She's Central Parking me to death over here. Call us. We love you.

Fourth message, received at 11:31 A.M. . . .
Is it me, or was that you on TV doing some really fucked-up shit? It's Keith.

Fifth message, received at 11:49 A.M. . . .
I go motel. You trouble Bing Buli.

Sixth message, received at 12:15 P.M. . . .
Raymond Parisi, please call 1-800-984-2100, extension 100, regarding your past due account; 1-800-984-2100, extension 100.

Seventh message, received at 12:41 P.M. . . .
Ray? It's Maurice. Bing is back. He's not happy, Ray. I need you to call me right away, OK? Call me right away.

Eighth message, received at 1:02 P.M. . . .
Hey, man. Miss you around these parts. If that's you we're seeing, we're gonna have to report it, brother. Call me and tell me you don't have a cast on your arm.

Ninth message, received at 1:18 P.M. . . .
Ray, it's Maurice again. I had to let Bing in your room. I'm sorry. He

insi— Ray? This Bing Buli. You trouble no friend. I find. He tell. You tell fat!

Tenth message, received at 1:33 P.M. . . .
Yo, fuckstick, it's Angelo. Don't be a douchebag your whole life and straighten that thing out you said you was gonna straighten out. Come by Bobby V's tonight. And what's this shit I'm hearing about you and a horse?

Eleventh message, received at 1:51 P.M. . . .
This is Robert Barnes. Again. We talked about this dog thing, Mr. Parisi. Please. L does not want to get the restraining order, but you're leaving us no choice. You understand that, right? It's simple. You're leaving us no recourse. None whatsoever. Please be reasonable and stay off the property. And leave the dog be already.

Twelfth message, received at 1:55 P.M. . . .
Estivation is like hibernation except in hot weather. And sometimes an animal can be in a deep sleep and doesn't hear anything going on around him. But he's not hibernating or estivating. Just really, really sleeping. This is called a torpor. Can't wait to go to the park with you, Uncle Ray!

Thirteenth message, received at 2:03 P.M. . . .
The Las Vegas? Take Bing money the Las Vegas? Oh, Ray, you . . . oh you . . . oh. I find! Bing find! No Thanksgiving no more. No more friend. You lie Bing Buli!

Fourteenth message, received at 2:07 P.M. . . .
Ray, it's Marty Tepper. You sound retarded on your message. Do something about that. I put in the call to Ed Kinder— Hold on. Put it in the car, not on the car. There you go. That's terrific. Now it's got a much better chance to make it there. Anyway, his wife's not well, so this may

be a good time after all. He's talking Florida again. Don't fuck me on this.
Have a good Fourth of July.

I decided to skip the rest of the messages and focus on the great news from Marty Tepper (there was no sense worrying about the other stuff). It was too bad that Ed Kinder's wife wasn't doing well, but they were old and would be better off in a condo down in Fort Lauderdale than worrying about chasing after dogs and all the stuff that was better left to me and L to do. All I had to do was roll the inheritance money over and the place was ours. The plan seemed ingenious, which set it in stark contrast to the rest of the ideas I ever had about getting L back. As I'd figured, telling Maurice I was going to Vegas had been a terrible idea, since he couldn't keep a secret and was scared to death of Bing Buli (though he was in his early fifties and checked in at no more than five-four, 130 pounds, Bing looked like he had once done terrible things to American soldiers in faraway huts). Maurice Boudreaux would have made the world's worst prisoner of war, and while I traded the quick cash for the risk that he'd spill the beans about my whereabouts, I knew Bing would never find me in Vegas even if he was inclined to look for me. Which I doubted he would, since his parents made him look fluent in English by comparison and were for the most part bedridden. There was no way he'd leave them alone. I had spent the grimmest Thanksgiving of my life at the Buli apartment the year before, but again, what kind of thing was that to concern myself with? This Thanksgiving, L and I would invite everyone we knew in Atlanta up to our new place. Hounds would be running around the barn. The leaves in Georgia would be golden on the ground. The Dawgs would be getting ready to kick off against the Jackets. You could practically smell the turkey already.

I poured myself a vodka from the bar, splashed in some pineapple juice from a mini-can, and contemplated opening my father's letter before deciding to turn on the big screen instead. I flipped over to ESPN.

Lo and behold, there I was again, though this time it was not footage from Belmont Park but rather my speech at the Little League World Series, which accidentally started the career I had gone on to squander.

The anchor, also a former friend of mine to whom I owed a few grand, was noting that the qualifying games for the LLWS were going on all over the country, and since it was about to be the tenth anniversary of my moment in Williamsport, they thought they'd run the clip again. I was just a low-level scrub at ESPN in those days, gathering stats and monitoring games for highlights, and with L in her last year of law school, I had a lot of time on my hands, so I helped a guy I worked with named Stu Lock coach his son Ben's Little League team, or rather the regional All-Star team Ben had been selected for and that Stu offered to coach. These kids were phenomenal, and the Connecticut team wound up going on a run, making it to Williamsport as winners of the New England region and ultimately representing the United States in the championship game against a precise Chinese squad that hadn't made an error the entire tournament.

The game was a nail-biter. Ben was pitching, and Stu never went to the mound when his son was on the hill on account of the kid not forgiving him for divorcing his mother two years earlier. In the fifth inning of a scoreless game, the wheels came off. Our shortstop booted a routine roller, our right fielder lost one in the sun, Ben started pouting, and then the floodgates opened figuratively as well as literally, as the Chinese jumped all over us and half our team started breaking down and crying on the field. Stu asked me to go out and say something, anything, to stop the bleeding, so I called time and trotted to the mound, waving the entire team in to join me. Since it was the finals, ABC asked us to wear microphones, and all of it was captured live.

I sat and stared at the TV. Watched myself walking out on the field. The kids, tears streaming down their faces, gathered around as the Chinese players stood stoically on each base and their manager stared from the dugout with an inscrutable look on his face. This is what I said:

"I can't believe what I'm seeing. Not the errors. Who cares about the errors? Unless you're trying to miss the ball on purpose—unless you're the mini Black Sox running some crazy conspiracy to throw the Little League World Series—then you gotta ease up on yourselves. People make mistakes. It's nothing to cry about. I don't want to see any more crying, OK? Not because it's unmanly—there's no such thing as that—but because it's ridiculous. It's summertime. You're playing ball with your friends. What the hell is there to cry about? Look: I don't know a lot about China, but if you look at how serious those kids are, you can see that they have a lot of pressure on them. In a couple hours, they have to go back and deal with a bunch of Communists while we all go down the shore to ride the Tilt-A-Whirl and eat Carvel. Some of you guys are going to be meeting girls down there, and trust me when I tell you that meeting the right girl is a lot more important than anything that happens on this field. You meet one half as good as mine and it'll save your life, believe me."

At this point, the umpire began to walk to the mound to break up the meeting. As I sat there and watched it all these years later, he seemed to take his time, though I don't know why. Maybe it was the crying. Or the fact that I'd had the entire team sitting on the ground like we were around a campfire and not a pitcher's mound. It was an odd scene any way you looked at it.

"I should say that if you're leaning the non-girl way, that's fine also. Meeting the right guy is more important than this, too. A lot of people are going to give you crap about it, but to hell with them. That's their hang-up. Don't apologize for who you are."

The ump got within five or ten feet, said, "Wrap it up, coach," and walked back toward the plate. I motioned for everyone to stand up. Cameras were everywhere. There were thousands of people crammed into the grandstand. The hill behind the outfield fence was filled.

"I know you feel pressure," I said. "There're adults all over the place, which is never good, and there're a lot of cameras, and those are never good, either, but screw everything and have some fun. It's just baseball. We're on a field in Williamsport, Pennsylvania, not Gettysburg. No one's shooting at you. There's nothing to cry about. If those Chinese kids beat you, then you shake their hands 'cause they were better, and you move on with your lives. They get a bigger trophy but have to live in China. You get a smaller trophy and get to live in the greatest country on earth. Who's really winning?"

I had them all put their hands in the middle like we always did before we took the field.

"This isn't the high point of your lives, OK? You're just getting started. These aren't your glory days. This is just something cool you did when you were young. Let's start having a good time out here. Break on three. One-two-three . . . *break*."

That was it. And when I walked back to the dugout, I didn't think anything of it. Ben pitched out of the jam, but the damage was done, and the Chinese took the title. Later, it all exploded. The speech was shown everywhere, and I not only became the golden boy in Bristol but was also embraced by a variety of pro-American groups as well as gay rights organizations. Much to L's chagrin, most of the Republican candidates that year quoted the speech and hailed its American values (aside from the gay stuff), and Sunday-morning shows broke down the content of what I'd said and claimed it not only put sports in perspective but redefined masculinity in post-9/11 America. Hell, a women's magazine put a picture of me on the cover under the headline IS RAY PARISI THE PERFECT MAN? due to what I'd said about L ("You meet one half as good as mine and it'll save your life, believe me"), which was heralded as one of the most romantic things a lot of women had ever heard. L had the magazine cover framed and hung it in the living room until she got back from Myrtle Beach and it "accidentally" fell off the wall one day and broke, putting an end to an item that had given us a lot of laughs and one I still think was the victim of something other than an accident.

But that moment had made my career, like I said. It immediately led to a book deal and a lot of offers to deliver commencement speeches, which is pretty ironic, since someone who's never finished anything probably shouldn't give life advice to a bunch of people who just did. I guess it doesn't matter, since I never took any of the speech offers and ended up returning the advance from the publishing house because I never got around to writing anything. L and I did go out to LA for a summer when a producer set me up with a screenwriter to work on a script about my life story, but we never really got past the one scene we had with the LLWS speech in it (and an opening sequence based on a debacle with a skywriting pilot when I first proposed). I ended up spending most of my time in Cali drinking beers and learning how to surf with the writer's brother, Cyrus. I really loved it out there, but L hated Southern California and wouldn't even consider a conversation about staying and practicing law there. She said New York had suffering, which she could deal with, but LA had despair, which she couldn't. She also noted that while New York serial killers were usually pasty white loners like Mark David Chapman and David Berkowitz, only California could produce the Manson family.

When we got back east, ESPN seized on my sudden popularity and gave me a kind of adventure show, which, if you never saw it, was a cross between your average sports fan's wish-fulfillment fantasy and *Jackass*. Among other things, I ran with the bulls in Pamplona; spent an entire day drinking with Manchester United fans on the eve of the Premier League championship; competed and threw up at the Coney Island hot-dog-eating contest; and tore my rotator cuff in the hammer throw as a guest and competitor of honor at the Scottish Highland Games. I was reminded of some of these things as I watched the TV, since clips from my show followed the footage of my LLWS speech. And then the Belmont Park footage followed that, because apparently it was the fucking Ray Parisi Hour in my old studio. I mean, I know it was the dog days of summer in sports, with football not yet begun, the NBA and NHL playoffs over, no Olympics, and baseball lumbering through its season, but it still seemed excessive. I mean, I hadn't pulled an OJ, for Christ's sake. I went on tilt a little at a racetrack. Big deal. Show some goddamn Wimbledon highlights, why don't you.

"Parisi, who is no longer employed by the network, has been identified as the perpetrator in the bizarre incident out at Belmont Park yesterday," said my former coworker. "Details remain murky, but we here at ESPN join authorities in encouraging our former colleague to turn himself in to the New York State Police. When we come back, can Joey Chestnut win his sixth consecutive title at this weekend's Nathan's Famous hot-dog-eating contest in Coney Island?"

I sipped my drink. Mulled things over. This media outing of me as a fugitive from justice was a bummer, certainly, but not an unforeseeable event by any stretch. I mean, I had Just For Men H-45 on my head. I knew this was a possibility. I put my shades on, walked into a bathroom the size of a studio apartment, and checked myself out from a variety of angles. Brown hair. Sox cap. Sunglasses. Long-sleeve shirt to cover the cast. Shit, I barely recognized myself. I had no reason to worry. I was as incognito as a person could be. Then again, if recent history had taught me anything, it was that whenever I thought I had things under control, I really didn't. Was I safe, or did I just think I was? If I was going to emerge from this mess as a new and improved Ray Parisi, I needed to start examining things a little more deeply than I normally did. Just an extra step was all it took. If you thought, Hey, no worries, I'm safe, you needed to add a Wait, are you *really*? beat, then think about whatever that answer might be. It was just a minor adjustment. Really, that's often all it took to fix things.

After another brutal coughing jag, and with my wrist starting to throb, I went back into the suite and poured myself another vodka pineapple. ESPN had moved on from their All Things Ray segment, thank God, and with nothing but time to kill before the check cleared, I figured I'd head downtown and see about getting some supplies. I was out of weed, out of painkillers for my wrist, and once I analyzed the question of my safety a little deeper, I realized that I could probably use a fake ID of some kind, just to be safe. While I had mastered the art of meeting locals wherever I went, and quickly gaining their trust (and their weed connection), this list of supplies was a bit of a taller task. But then I exercised my new strategy and thought one step further. Was it really such a tall task? This was Vegas, after all, and of all the things a person might be looking for in Sin City, pills and documentation were nothing extraordinary. Getting a passport and some painkillers in Vegas was basically the equivalent to scoring a loose joint in Salt Lake City. Problem was, I only had $86. Once again I thought further and remembered Maurice's Super Bowl bet. Jackpot. I smiled, grabbed the envelope, and headed toward the door, marveling at what could happen, what could open up for a person, with a minor adjustment in act and attitude. One modification and you could go from being broken down to up and running in a flash. It was a beautiful thing, right? It was a beautiful thing.

NOT EVEN AVA GARDNER

March 29

. . . Katherine likes to check in on the stages of grief. It's become something of an inside joke for us. A way to lighten up the sessions. I think she's starting to see the entirety of the picture in a way I can't or am only starting to. She's really helped me stop beating myself up over not seeing what was happening sooner. I was focused on Mom. As I should have been. It wasn't my fault. God, I'm so fortunate Grace recommended her. She's been a blessing. She's so bright, but her sense of humor really sets her apart from a lot of academics. Today she said that if Elisabeth Kübler-Ross had ever met R, she would have written an entirely different book . . .

Two A.M. THAT FIRST NIGHT IN Vegas found me sitting on a bench on Fremont Street downtown. I was camped out under a sign for fried Oreos, talking to an eightysomething-year-old guy everyone called "The Professor" who had just hooked me up with a whole new identity (because it's Vegas, your friendly neighborhood counterfeiter is closing in on ninety, and there's nothing strange about it). I had made the connections I was looking for at the Girls of Glitter Gulch strip club earlier in the afternoon, the day eventually leading me to a couple of different apartments on the outskirts of Vegas, where I was able to use Maurice's Super Bowl money (the Giants didn't have the defense to win it all, in my opinion) to procure half a dozen prerolled joints, two bottles of painkillers that were of indeterminate origin but living on the same side of the street as Oxycontin, and the complete identity of one Raoul McFarland, of Omaha, Nebraska. I imagine you'd be hard-pressed to find a family tree anywhere in the world with a branch crooked enough to have someone by that name hanging from it (and if there were a place a Raoul McFarland could call home, it'd be a stretch to imagine Nebraska being it), but there was no getting around the fact that it was a grade-A piece of work by the old man sitting next to me. I had a Raoul McFarland Nebraska driver's license, assorted cards from local grocery chains and pharmacies, and a faculty ID from the University of Nebraska, as apparently Raoul McFarland was an English teacher, much like The Professor himself had been. With this new tool kit at my disposal, I could very likely weasel my way out of a modest questioning by authorities, provided they didn't have me dead to rights or ask me about the plot of *Anna Karenina*.

The strip-club posse I had ingratiated myself with was long gone, bolting with their cash once they dropped me off at The Professor's place out on Boulder Highway, where I watched a Civil War documentary while he worked on the McFarland portfolio. He had finished up his work well after midnight (and just after Stonewall Jackson had been accidentally shot by one of his own men at Chancellorsville) and come downtown to participate in his weekly poker game at the Four Queens, one that was played by old-timers for small stakes, and one no casino would accommodate unless they played in the early hours of the morning, which The Professor said was fine with his crew, who rarely slept anyway. He wore a blue-and-white seersucker suit and thick-lensed blue-framed eyeglasses that suggested he was either legally blind or had been at a tag sale at Elton John's house in the early seventies. His neck was so thin that his head seemed to rest on it like a wedge of cheese on a toothpick. Though he didn't say five words to me at his apartment, I liked him and was happy to accompany him back downtown before his game started.

We drank a cup of coffee at the Golden Nugget before walking out onto Fremont Street and sitting down. The avenue was nearly empty. With all the lights blazing away, it looked surreal and sad somehow, like an elaborate party that no one had shown up for. Next to our bench, a Mexican maintenance worker scaled a ladder, replacing some burned-out bulbs on Vegas Vic, the iconic smoking cowboy cheerily perched above the Pioneer.

Downtown is the old Vegas that you always see on TV and in commercials, with all those colored lights splashing and zipping every which way. There's an enormous white canopy about a hundred feet high that stretches over four blocks of Fremont and plays host to laser light shows on the hour, but the reality is that only small-timers and those on the margins go down there, while most everyone else stays at one of the newer joints on the Strip. The city keeps trying to lure people back downtown, but its heyday is not likely to return. It's more depressing than anything else down there. A quick glance around showed: a bunch of *Breaking Bad* extras drinking sixty-four-ounce rum drinks out of plastic flamingos; a one-armed man riding a zip line; and two Vietnamese men spraying a chow with gold paint without bothering to cover the dog's eyes. This was not the kind of place that made a comeback.

I had taken a couple of painkillers with my coffee at the Golden Nugget, but they hadn't quite kicked in yet, and I had never felt so shitty in my life. My eyes were puffy and bloodshot, my wrist was throbbing, and my throat was so swollen that it felt like I was trying to gulp down a dozen sets of car keys every time I swallowed. The hacking fits had returned, and my chest felt like it was being whacked with a croquet mallet whenever I coughed. I was in the middle of an extended jag on the bench when The Professor patted me on the back and handed me an embroidered handkerchief.

"You need rest and medicine," he said. "And not the kind of medicine you just washed down with your coffee." He smiled. Looked up at the awning over the street. "I simply cannot get used to that monstrosity. But of course so much has changed. Downtown and all over, really.

76

The old Overland Hotel, that used to be right over there," he said, waving a bony finger. "The Sal Sagev there. On the other side of the Horseshoe, where they added on, that was the Mint. That was all long ago, though. You know something, Ray? If you head that way through the desert for a good while, you'll come across the old nuclear test site at Nellis. When I was in the air force back in the fifties, the Atomic Energy Commission packed all of us soldiers into the area to expose us to the effects. They were called Doom Towns, where we lived."

"Really?"

"That's where I met my wife. Can you imagine it? From Dachau to a Doom Town to falling in love in ten short years."

When he said "Dachau," I remembered a couple of things the strip club posse had told me on the drive out to his place. One was that he had gone out for breakfast one morning in 1980 and lost his wife in a fire at the old MGM. The other was that he'd been in a concentration camp when he was young.

"She was Miss Atomic Blast," he continued with a kind of heart-breaking reverence I understood all too well. "That's what they called the bathing suit contest. Of course, everything then was Atomic this and Atomic that. Atomic burgers. You name it. Peg was Miss Atomic Blast. She won because of her legs, but I tell you, Ray, the special thing was her face. She had a face like nobody's you've ever seen. Not even Ava Gardner could hold a candle to her. She was even more beautiful in 1980 than she was when I met her in 1954. That's how it is with the great faces."

I thought about how L had looked a few days earlier when I'd brought Bruce back to the house after the alleged kidnapping incident. Jesus Christ. Was this my future?

"My wife has a face like that," I said.

"I didn't realize you were married."

"Oh yeah. She's down in Myrtle Beach right now, taking care of her mother. Breast cancer."

"I'm sorry to hear that."

"Yeah. It's OK. I just saw her. She's gonna be, you know, fine. She'll be fine."

"That's good to hear," he said sadly.

"Everything will be fine."

He looked at me and patted me on the leg. We didn't say anything for a while. Just looked at all the sorry lights. Somehow he knew I was lying, but I didn't care. Maybe this sounds odd, just sitting on some bench on the other side of the country with a ninety-year-old stranger, but it was par for the course for me. I met people easily. They opened up to me all the time. It was very normal as far as I was concerned. It was simply a matter of personality.

I had taken the Myers-Briggs personality test online one lonely night at the Motor Lodge. The roads to the casino were closed due to a major snowstorm (the Sarge had failed to open the package store, which was unheard of), and I was trapped inside with nothing to do but play online poker for worthless credits and take personality tests for both me and L, trying to determine if there was something in our essential makeups that I hadn't accounted for and that might have something to do with the problems we were having.

On the Myers-Briggs test, I was categorized as an ESFP, and when I took the test for L, she was categorized as an INTJ, which was the precise opposite. All my answers indicated that I was an extrovert and based nearly all of my actions on feelings and instinct rather than on reason and clear thinking. Suggested careers for an ESFP were acting, advertising, and sales, and my closest celebrity comp was Steve Irwin, the gregarious Aussie "Crocodile Hunter" who basically fucked around with extremely dangerous creatures for a living until a stingray decided enough was enough. L's career suggestions were all much more substantial, and her celebrity comps included no fewer than six US presidents and a variety of other historical heavyweights. After the

Crocodile Hunter, I had Arsenio Hall and Kathie Lee Gifford on my team. I chose not to focus on that and instead took solace in the fact that the oldest adage in the world was "opposites attract." An ESFP was a perfect fit for an INTJ, even if you did answer sixty specific questions in the very way she didn't.

I turned to The Professor. "You mind if I ask you something?"

"Not at all."

"Something personal?"

"All the better."

"What's it been like since losing your wife?"

He took off his glasses, wiped the lenses with a small orange cloth, and placed them back on his face. He sighed. Rested his hand on my leg again. For some reason I covered it with my bad hand, and he gripped my fingers absently. I didn't mind. It was nice to touch somebody.

"Thirty-six years this November," he said. "Almost exactly as long as I knew her. That seems impossible. But all the things you think can't happen, do. That's the story of life."

"I'm really sorry."

He nodded and said nothing.

"Is that when you stopped teaching?"

"And writing," he said. "I don't think I ever wrote anything that wasn't about her in some form or fashion. Colleagues used to tease me about it. After, I couldn't bring myself to write about her. I couldn't bear to look at her name. I think I thought if I wrote her name in the past tense, then I would be saying goodbye to her, and I didn't want to do that. I tried using just her initials once, but that felt ridiculous."

"It doesn't sound ridiculous to me," I said.

The pills started to work their magic. The lights seemed to get more intense.

"Do you know what I've been doing for the past thirty-six years, Ray?"

"What's that, Professor?"

"My name is Victor Bellow. You can call me that. She was Margaret Bellow. Peg was."

Tears started to well up in his eyes, and then tears started to well up in *my* eyes, because how many people have you ever seen crying over someone who's been gone for thirty-six years? Most people will forget you after thirty-six minutes in this life. Thirty-six days if they liked you some. Thirty-six months if they were crazy about you. I pictured myself in thirty-six years if I didn't get L back. There was no way I would make it. Who was I without her? I tried to put a positive spin on things (in thirty-six years, Boyd Bollinger would be either dead or a vegetable, provided he didn't live as long as The Professor), but it didn't work. When you're away from the person you love, everything is depressing. The best you can do is not think about it and keep working to fix it.

"Mr. Bellow it is."

"Victor," he said kindly.

"Victor."

"What I've been doing for thirty-six years, Ray, is waiting. I eat when I'm hungry. Sleep when I'm tired. Play cards on Wednesdays. Help some folks with identification from time to time. But mostly what I do is wait."

"What are you waiting for?"

"For it to be over, of course."

"So you can see her again, right?"

He grinned sadly. "And where might that happen?"

I didn't say anything. It occurred to me that someone who had been in a concentration camp and lost the love of his life in an inferno might not believe in heaven. He looked off down the avenue. I thought I had lost him to memory, but he sprang back.

"One thing I remember about the camps is how different people were," he said. "How differently they acted. Some of them would do anything to survive. Anything at all. Those were the ones who thought of nothing but seeing loved ones again, or finishing something important they had started before the war. Whatever it was, they had hope, and that's all there is to have in life. There's nothing else. Hope is greater even than happiness, you know. It's more powerful. More useful. In the camp, the ones without hope fell into two groups. One group ran into the wire. That was the most popular form of suicide there. Running into the electric wire along the fences. The other group just sat and waited for the end. They didn't yearn to survive, and they didn't run into the wire. They lived in that empty space in between. That's how I've become, it seems. That's how I've spent these years. I don't take pride in that. But you have to call a thing a thing in life. You can always do that much."

Suddenly there was a popping sound, like a gunshot, and we both looked up. The repairman had dropped a bulb from Vegas Vic on the sidewalk. He looked at us apologetically at first, then less so when he noticed us holding hands. Even at three in the morning in the strangest city on earth, the sight of a nearly ninety-year-old man in a seersucker suit holding hands with a guy less than half his age had to qualify as an odd sight. The Professor smiled and released my fingers. He took off his glasses and rubbed his eyes. "I'm so sorry, Ray. I must be a terrific bore to you."

"Not at all," I said. "What you said about the wire—that's something else."

"Yes. It was. But a person can get to that point easier than you might imagine. I thought about it a great deal after Peg died, but I couldn't do that. And I couldn't do the other thing, either. There were opportunities. There are always opportunities, no matter what you think. Friends in California urged me to come manage their land for them. Orange groves, you know. There was a woman there I could have shared something with, I believe. Mutual acquaintances suggested as much. But I never went."

He took off his glasses and wiped them with the cloth again. "And I never did that other thing, obviously," he said. "Neither of those options seemed to suit my nature. I regret this. A person should find something that suits his nature and make some kind of decision in life. Carry on from there and forget everything else. You should remember that."

"I will," I said.

He put his hand on my shoulder and helped himself up. "Tell me, Ray: What the devil do you need false identification for?"

"I don't know. Why do you make it?"

"A tenant in my building left the machine a while back. I learned how to use it. But to answer your question, I have a lot of problems with the government and how it operates. It's getting worse by the day. People think they're living in a free country, but they have no idea how wrong they are. At any rate, I like to help people out when I can. I'll spare you all my thoughts on Big Brother."

I smiled at him. The pills were kicking in, and it was time to get back to the MGM. "Good luck tonight."

"*Luck*," he mused.

"Yeah. I don't suppose you're a big luck guy. Philosophically speaking."

"Not particularly, no," he said. "I studied the idea for some time. I could have stayed in bed that morning, for example. Or woken Peg when I left for breakfast. But she didn't feel well and wanted to sleep. She never slept in. I played it a million different ways. But the fact is that someone left a pie display on in the restaurant downstairs, and there were faulty wires, and there was a fire, and some people were in a position to get out and some weren't. You could call it luck, but it was just what happened. That's half of life, I'd say. Just what happens, and whether you're in the way of it or not. The other half is what you decide to do yourself, and what the consequences of those choices are. If you think there's something more to it, there isn't. You take good care of yourself, son."

And just like that, he hobbled off toward the Four Queens. I was sorry to see him go, and for a second I almost called after him, because he was someone I might have been able to tell the truth to. Someone who could have given me some fatherly advice, maybe. But I didn't say anything. Instead, I sat there and considered what he'd said about luck, and I thought of the series of events that had landed me on that bench in the middle of the night, and how everything might have been all right if just one thing had gone one way instead of another. As the pills kicked in harder, I closed my eyes and replayed the series of events that had led me here. The countdown to my top 10 hits played out like this:

#10

As I was playing blackjack one afternoon at Mohegan Sun, Dawn came running up to my table. She had just hit an $800 jackpot. I gave her a high five, and she said she was going to the gift shop to buy me a present, which I told her not to do. I distinctly said, "Get something for Penny," but she said, "*Everybody's* getting something, buddy boy," and went running off, returning fifteen minutes later with a turquoise and silver western shirt. It looked like someone had put a dolphin in a blender. When I said, "Jesus, I can't wear that," she got pouty.

"All right," I said. "I'll wear it *one* time, but then we take it out back and shoot it."

"Fine," she said. "But I choose when."

"Suit yourself," I said.

#9

One night a couple of weeks later, after another spirit-crushing string of beat hands and misguided impulse bets, Dawn once again came trotting over to my table. She said the casino was offering free country line-dancing lessons in the Wolf's Den lounge.

"Take a break and learn how to Texas Two-Step with me," she said.

"What the hell," I said. "It might be the only time we get something for nothing in this joint."

#8

We were sitting around Dawn's apartment on her twenty-ninth birthday. No one had gotten her anything except for this papier-mâché raccoon Penny had made in school, and her ex-husband had just phoned from prison and called her a bitch. I felt bad for her.

"Go get dressed," I said. "I'll take you wherever you want to go for your birthday."

She ran into her bedroom to change, emerging a few minutes later with a bright smile and a brighter shirt. She tossed it to me and said, "Button her up and let's dance."

"I've been afraid this might happen," I said.

#7

We drove to a place called the Littleton Saloon, which was just about halfway between my house and her apartment. While in the middle of performing something called "The Montana Kick," a bartender started taking Polaroids on the dance floor.

"Say cheese, y'all!" he said.

"Cheese, y'all!"

#6

Sometime after that evening, the owner of the Littleton Saloon (a person I do not know but clearly someone who cannot leave well enough alone) made a pair of decisions: 1) to open early and start serving lunch; and 2) to make the decor more customer-friendly. He removed most of the steer horns and cowhides from the walls and replaced them with framed candid photos of customers he'd been having his staff take for months.

#5

Less than a week after returning home from her mother's funeral, L got a call from Sandy Flynn, her freshman-year roommate at Emory who had lost her own mother to breast cancer. How she knew about Lucille I have no idea, since she hadn't spoken to L since they'd graduated. How did this happen? Was there some cancer newsletter that went out every time a doctor dropped that shitty hammer on someone? Where did this Flynn woman come from?

#4

One morning the following week, Sandy Flynn invited L to lunch. I was in the study, making believe I was doing research for a potential new show, when I heard L say, "No, no, you're due soon. I'll come up your way."

Five minutes later, she poked her head in the office and said, "Hey, Ray, where's Littleton if I take the parkway?"

"Where?"

"Littleton."

"No idea," I said.

#3

My wife drove to Sandy Flynn's house (again, where did this woman even *come from?*), which was being sprayed for termites or flying squirrels or caribou or what the fuck ever, and so they were forced to go out to eat. The Flynn woman was pregnant and craving chili, so she took L to a "cute place that just started serving lunch."

The Littleton Saloon.

#2

A hostess led the two of them to a booth, where they started nibbling on corn bread. A waiter approached the table, and as this

Sandy Flynn person ordered a bowl of Uncle Mickey's Firehouse Chili, the love of my life looked at the wall. Hanging thirty-six inches from her nose was an eight-by-ten photo of a familiar face in an unfamiliar shirt.

#1

L returned home from lunch and poked her head in the office, where I was studying baseball lines.

"Whatcha doin'?" she said.

"Working. How was lunch with Sandy What's-her-face?"

"Sandy *Flynn*. And it was fine. We went to a place called the Littleton Saloon. You ever hear of it?"

I stuck my head farther into the paper and said, "Nope, how was it?"

"Interesting," she said. "I'd say it was very interesting."

And welcome to Fucked City. Population: Ray.

As I contemplated this brutally unfortunate sequence of events, I felt a slight kick and opened my eyes to see a girl wearing white capris, a yellow halter, and a silver and turquoise belly ring that was about eye level for me. Her stomach was flat and brown and magazine-perfect, and when I glanced up and saw her straight blond hair and bangs, I recognized her as the cashier at the Girls of Glitter Gulch.

"Aren't you, like, a little young to be sleeping on benches?"

"I was just resting."

I launched into an extended coughing jag. She backed away and reached into her denim shoulder bag. "You sound like ass. Here, have some gelcaps."

"Much obliged," I said. "You work at the club, right?"

"I work *at* the club, not *in* the club. Like, I don't dance."

"I didn't say you did."

"Well, I *don't*," she said, putting her hands on her hips.

"OK."

"Sorry. I just don't like people thinking I'm sketchy," she said. "I'm Renée."

"Raoul," I said, trying out my new moniker and extending my good hand.

"You don't look Mexican."

"I'm not. It's a random name."

"I'll say. But it's cool," she said, casually blowing a bubble. "That old man you were with—he your pop?"

"No. Just a friend of mine."

She pulled a pair of earbuds and an iPhone out of her bag. When she asked what I was doing snoozing on the bench, I attempted to explain that I had a VIP suite up at the MGM, only it took me twenty seconds to get it out on account of another coughing fit. She gave me a professional eye roll.

"*Riiiiight.* Every time I have a fat place to stay, I like to sleep on benches downtown, too. See ya around, high roller."

And with that, she flashed me a peace sign, put in her earbuds, and sauntered away. I could hear her singing the words to some song I'd never heard before as she made her way down the avenue and hopped into a cab on Third Street. As she did, the maintenance worker climbed down from the ladder, mopped his brow, and gazed at his work. He turned and looked at me. *"Es bueno?"* he said.

I looked up at Vegas Vic, his cigarette dangling and red neon boots shining. He was smiling and waving. Not a care in the world. If the cowboy could have spoken, he would have said, "Ray, pardner, everything's gonna be A-OK. That old plan 'a yers is gonna work out juuuust fine. You 'n the little lady's gonna live happily ever after. Ride right off into that sunset. You have faith now, ya hear? And don't you be sweatin' an old sack 'a feed like Boyd Bollinger. That old bastard's got one foot in the grave 'n one foot on a banana peel, ya hear me? He ain't nothin' t' nobody. Tell him t' piss up a rope 'n run him out on a rail."

I gave the maintenance worker a thumbs-up. *"Sí,"* I said to him, grinning like a man with some kind of future. "It's really *bueno.*"

THE WONDER OF IT ALL

Where I ever got the impression that R was Paul Newman, I have no idea.
It is quite literally the stupidest idea I ever allowed myself to indulge. If Paul
Newman had pulled one tenth of the crap that R did, Joanne Woodward
would've driven him down to the Westport train station and shipped him back
to Hollywood no matter how blue his eyes were.

I WOKE UP THE NEXT DAY around five in the afternoon. Sick. Jet-lagged.
Delirious. I looked out the window at the Statue of Liberty for a solid
half minute without knowing where the hell I was. After a while I
snapped to, poured myself a drink, popped a couple of painkillers, and
saw that a note had been slipped under the door.

RAY—YOU'RE GOOD TO GO. SIGN FOR ANYTHING
YOU LIKE. CALL ME WHEN YOU GET THIS.
BEST,
BOB MOTA

I slipped on a cushy MGM robe and matching slippers and sat on
the couch, flipping the tube on and checking my messages. It was a
bloodbath. The texts were in the hundreds, so I figured I'd try my voice
mail, since that was where the most urgent stuff generally landed.

Hello. You have fifty-nine new messages.

First message, received at 11:58 A.M. . . .
Pick. Up. The. Fucking. Phone.

Second message, received at 12:16 P.M. . . .
Damm it, Ray, where are you? Why do you have to pull this crap? You can just be the sweetest thing, and then you always turn around and flake out. KC always says you're unreliable and hung up on your ex-wife and I should never talk to you again, and maybe she's right. Maybe you're a hopeless case, like she says. I hope you show up to take Penny to Central Park Saturday. She's so excited to see the fireworks. I really hate this shit, you know? I hate it.

Third message, received at 12:34 P.M. . . .
Oh. Son gun. I come the Vegas.

Fourth message, received at 12:48 P.M. . . .
If you cut the arms off a starfish, guess what happens? They grow back. It is the only thing that re— Hey, what's this word? Not that one, this one. Whisper it—regenerates. It is the only thing that regenerates. That's awesome! And the Tooth Fairy came last night. Her wings were blue this time.

Fifth message, received at 1:37 P.M. . . .
Ray, it's Maurice. Sorry about the whole thing with Bing. He just—he scares me, Ray. You should probably call him, OK? Call Bing.

Sixth message, received at 3:11 P.M. . . .
KC just called and said you were on TV. What's going on? Are you in trouble? Call me back. I'll help. I hit for four hundred dollars today. I love you.

Seventh message, received at 3:45 P.M. . . .

Uh, Ray? It's Maurice again. Sorry to bother you, but, um, did you know that you were on TV? You're right there on the TV and . . . yeah. What happened? The police are looking for you and everything. Call me and let me know how things are. I mean, you're right there on the TV. Right on SportsCenter. Oh, I think we better take the Twitter down. Should we take it down? Maybe we should take it down. All right, then.

Eighth message, received at 3:54 P.M. . . .

Ray, man, it's Dinger and Lou at Bobby V's. What the fuck, brother? You're on the big screen!

Ninth message, received at 4:12 P.M.

Sugar Ray. It's Chip. Dude. Everyone at Mohegan is talking about you, bro. You're a lunatic! That video is awesome! That jockey was, like, what the fuck? Craziest thing ever! You're a legend! Janie says what's up.

Tenth message, received at 4:29 P.M.

Hey. It's Ronnie and April in the ATL. Is that you?

Eleventh message, received at 5:02 P.M.

Raymond, you have done it this time. What on earth have you gotten yourself into? The police called. Boyd may have given them your number. You better straighten whatever this is out. You're unbelievable.

Twelfth message, received at 5:07 P.M.

Ray, Boyd Bollinger. A Detective Jack Keller is going to be contacting you regarding an incident in New York. I'm sure you know what it's in reference to.

Thirteenth message, received at 5:16 P.M.

Maurice again. The cops called. I told them I didn't know where you are.

And again, I'm sorry about the Bing thing. I should have kept my mouth shut. Don't worry about my Super Bowl bet. It doesn't matter. Hold on, the Sarge wants to say something . . . Ray, you and this boy here are a couple of weak, sorry sons of bitches. That is all, soldier.

Fourteenth message, received at 5:22 P.M.
Ray Parisi, this is Detective Jack Keller. We'd like a few words with you. Obviously. Call me back at 212-422-6899. We don't want to chase you around on this. That won't be in your best interest.

Fifteenth message, received at 5:39 P.M. . . .
You know what? Screw you. I'm going out to dinner with Ken from the aquarium.

Sixteenth message, received at 6:12 P.M. . . .
I Vegas.

Seventeenth message, received at 6:22 P.M. . . .
Ray, I think you should come on the show. I know they let you go, but you're still one of us here, and we should have the exclusive. You can do the interview with me.

Eighteenth message, received at 6:38 P.M. . . .
Oh, Ray, no make Bing look. You call . . . 7 . . . 0 . . . 2 . . . you call Circus Circus. You ask Bing Buli.

Nineteenth message, received at 6:41 P.M. . . .
What in the hell?

There was no way I was going to sift through another twenty minutes of that landfill, so I clicked my phone off and thought for a second. The continued fallout from Belmont wasn't anything I hadn't been expecting, or would have been expecting if I were giving a second thought to anything other than the Kinder House Plan. If anything, the acceleration of the story just meant that I needed to get started on the plan ASAP, and the unexpected note from Bob Mota meant that I could. I hadn't known the check would get cleared so quickly, so I was actually *ahead* of where I expected to be, not behind. The cops on the other side of the country weren't something I was going to worry about, and Bing Buli was in needle-in-a-haystack territory, so I wasn't sweating him, either. I was annoyed that Bollinger had called (leave it to the decrepit son of a bitch to give my number to the cops), but again, his days were numbered, and I was used to people out there talking about me over one thing or another, so why let that faze me? Once you got used to being regarded as a disappointment and a fuckup, your threshold for shame went up considerably. You could deal with things that would cripple your average person. It was one of the few advantages to having almost nothing left to lose.

Penny's Tooth Fairy message made me think about L for a change. About how we were at a party up at Lake Lanier once, at the home of one of the partners in a firm she was interning at. There was a kid there, a little girl about Penny's age, and she lost a tooth and had a complete meltdown. The parents couldn't settle the little monster, so L told her this elaborate story about fairies and how they love to swim when they come for your teeth, and if you put a glass of water on the nightstand, they'll take a dip in it, and you can tell what color their wings were in the morning by looking at the color of the water. The kid calmed down, L helped put her to bed, and then she put some food coloring in a glass of water to make it light blue. Why do I mention this, other than the fact that I swiped the idea and did it for Penny? Because L was always coming up with stuff like that, things that were decent and surprising and that you'd never heard of before. Things that made your heart warm when you were with her and your chest go cold thinking about when you weren't.

I poured another vodka pineapple and popped on the tube. I saw myself again, this time on CNN, and turned it off immediately. I started to get riled up, thinking about Boyd Bollinger sticking his nose into all this, finking to the cops and taking my girl out of town, but I realized that wasn't productive and headed toward the bathroom to clean myself up for the big night. What the hell was he besides a blip on the radar screen of our lives, anyway? When it was said and done, would the Old Rooster merit a footnote? Would we even remember the time we were divorced at all, or would we delight in joking about it, a wink to a silly and misguided patch of history long since put in perspective and tossed away as a relic from another time?

I showered and headed down to the floor. When you have cash on account like I did, you sign a marker for whatever amount you'd like to play with, the chips are brought to you in plastic racks, and you get a table all to yourself if you want one. The house prefers that you play alone for a couple of reasons: 1) it looks good for the casino to be hosting the kind of people who play with stacks of colors the nickel-and-quarter crowd like to gawk over (lavender $500s and canary yellow $1,000s and chocolate $5,000s and even pumpkin $25,000s); and 2) if a heavy player is sitting by himself, he will not only play faster, but the likelihood that he'll start playing multiple hands increases, along with the probability that he'll blow his stake much quicker than if he were seated at a table with six other people. With the slight edge the house has, it's all a matter of dealing as many hands in the shortest time possible, which is why, of all the great gambling-related inventions, the automatic shuffle machines that eliminate the time wasted by dealers shuffling in between shoes is the most ingenious. Increasing the speed of the game is the surest way of shuttling a player to the inevitable ahead of schedule, because nothing is truer than this: A small crack, given time and pressure, will always break open. Casinos were founded on this principle. Which is why they never close. You don't hang a BACK AT 6 sign on a sure thing.

Now, let's get something straight: Most things in life reward commitment, obsessive attention to detail, and a go-get-'em attitude, but gambling is not one of them. To gamble successfully, you need a plan. A clearly defined goal. You need, in war terms, an exit strategy. The problem with most gamblers is that they don't have any of those things. They play for the sensation, the action, and even when they're winning, they can't walk away from the game because the action means more to them than the money. They have no plan. They have no purpose. That was my glaring weakness as a player. I had gambled for a variety of vague and wasteful reasons up until then, and eased down into the shithole inch by lousy inch because of them. But walking across the floor of the MGM, with my dreams of L and the Kinder House firmly in my grasp, I realized the error of my former ways. I understood that a person without a goal had no business gambling. No business living, really. For the first time, I knew exactly what I was doing and why I was there. And because I had a purpose, the casino became a hall of light, sound, and promise once more. You can't go home again? The fuck you can't.

I strolled merrily past the craps tables and roulette wheels. Was cheered by the sound of jackpot bells tolling among the slots. Delighted by every last thing I saw, from the recently arrived and hopeful, tentatively walking across the floor and trying to decide what machines looked ready to pop, to the newlyweds trotting gaily past the Race and Sports Book, all lace and cocktails and big plans. It felt great to be in a casino again. The direness of the routine in Connecticut was a thing of the past. Never again would I see busloads of retirees filing grimly through the parking lot, their aluminum walkers placed gingerly on the snowy pavement, or construction workers hastily signing over their paychecks on Friday afternoons, eager to join the parade of local grinders nickel-and-diming their way down the slow road to bankruptcy. That blue-collar misery was behind me. This was different. This was *Vegas*.

I ran into Bob Mota and told him I would like to be referred to as Raoul McFarland from here on out. He nodded casually (for six hun-

dred grand, he'd be happy to call me Louise) and then introduced me
to Manny C., a quietly surly, pockmarked Chilean pit boss who led me
to a table. It was cordoned off with a velvet rope and metal stanchions.
I requested $100,000 in chips, and while I was waiting, I popped a cou-
ple more painkillers, ordered a vodka pineapple, and chitchatted with a
friendly dealer named Patrice who lived in Henderson and had five kids
she loved and one ex-husband she didn't. Not drinking at the table is
pretty much gambling rule number one, but I didn't care, and I didn't
care because I knew I was going to win. There was nothing that could
keep me from it. For over a year I had sat at that motel and tried to figure out how to get back home. How to backtrack to the point where I
had gone off course, and reclaim the rightful arc of my life. A journey
that had been interrupted by unforeseen forces and events, all of which
had tumbled into each other like dominoes and none of which I'd
been able to quite see coming or keep from happening. But why talk
about it? The time for talk was over. The Kinder House Plan was all
about action. There was no use for talk. Did Gatsby show up at Daisy's
house one day and say, "So, listen, I'm thinking of reinventing myself,
becoming ridiculously wealthy, and then, as a grand gesture, I may just
buy a place across the water and throw a bunch of parties in hope that
you might show up one day and be blown away by the grandeur of my
love?" Of course not. What the Old Sport did was get the plan in his
head and then put it into action. It was a matter of vision and execution.
Vision and execution—that was all it took.

I started out playing conservatively. A thousand or two thousand a
hand. This went on for about fifteen minutes before a voice in my head
said, "What the fuck are you doing, Ray? Air it out already. Time's
a-wastin'." I was short-arming it big-time. Playing tight. The problem
was, I was still in the Mohegan Sun mind-set. It was a question of colors. I had never played with anything beyond black ($100 chips). Had
never seen monster stacks of anything that wasn't red or green. But the
plan didn't have anything to do with red, green, or black. The plan was

going to be realized only with the colors I mentioned earlier, the yellows and chocolates and pumpkins, and I needed to adjust my thinking, because $2,000 a hand when you've got $600,000 to play with is like taking $6,000 down to Fremont Street and playing the minimum at the $2 tables. You could conceivably spend the rest of your life sitting in front of the same bankroll without anything ever happening besides developing hemorrhoids, getting old, and dropping dead. I had $100,000 in front of me, another half million in the cage, and Boyd Bollinger drinking chamomile tea out of my Kentucky Derby mug. What was I dicking around for?

I put out a stack of ten yellows and breathed deeply. Patrice smiled and put an 8 in front me, then a jack. She showed 7, turned a queen. She paid out the $10,000 and I left it out on the table, stacking it about as high as a card turned on end. She dealt again. Out came a 7, then a 4. She rolled a 5. I breathed deeply again, reached into the rack, leveled a stack of yellow next to my first one, and doubled. Patrice tapped the table with her knuckles, turned a 9 for 20. She flipped a 7 to go with her 5, then a 4, then a king, and see you later. Winner. I had just made $50,000 in under a half minute.

And that was the beginning of it. Soon the lavender and yellow went in, never to be bothered with again, and the chocolate and pumpkin came out. Bob Mota might as well have stood over me with an umbrella, because it was raining face cards at that table. Just *pouring* face cards. And Patrice and I were having a party. She'd put out a face card and I'd say, "Put a bullet in that monkey," and then, voilà, there was the ace.

"It's like a shoot-out at the zoo," she'd say, "nothing but bullets and monkeys," and I'd say, "You got that right. It's a regular bloodbath on the grounds. Someone should call PETA." And then, moments later, I'd double up on a 6–5 and say, "You know what this house needs, Patrice?" and she'd smile and say, "Looks like you need some paint, Ray," and then, of course, the "paint," the 10 or face, would come.

It was magic. I'd put out a play, $20,000, say, and then I'd hit a natural, which paid $30,000 at 3 to 2. And then I'd hit another. And another. Queen-ace. Ace-ten. Jack-ace. Whatever combo you wanted, there it was. And when the house finally replaced Patrice with a dour Swede named Ingmar, it made absolutely no difference. I buried him, too. I won so many hands in a row, my chip stacks grew so quickly, that people started lining up behind the rope to watch. I should have worried about this. Should have been afraid that someone would recognize me. But I felt bulletproof. My hair was brown. I had a hat on. Was sporting blue-lensed Ray-Bans. It was free and easy down on that floor, and I was playing it fast and loose, like Eddie Felson. I mean, why worry? These people had come to Vegas, after all. They were seeing magic shows at the Monte Carlo. Riding in gondolas at the Venetian. Taking pictures of the Eiffel Tower at Paris. They had better things to do than sit around their rooms watching ESPN or CNN. There was a good chance that none of them knew what I'd done out at Belmont Park. Plus, word had spread that my name was Raoul, and every time a shout of support went up, it was for Raoul McFarland, not Ray Parisi. I was rolling in plain sight.

After an hour or so the spectators were four or five deep, all of them cheering like they were at an English soccer match every time I hit a 16 and a 5 came tumbling out of the shoe. I tipped the cocktailers $100 every time I ordered another vodka pineapple, tossed the dealers $1,000 chips every time I hit another big hand. I could not lose. The pit bosses just sat back and shook their heads. Every time I had a questionable call, say, a 12 on a 2 or 3, I'd ask the opinion of the crowd, and they'd shout out advice like I was a contestant on *The Price Is Right* who was trying to get the audience's read on how much to bid on a dinette set. It was raucous down on that floor. It was a good time. They loved Raoul.

Now, normally, shoes run hot and cold. You crush one, the next one buries you. At best you might get a couple of sweet ones in a row before things start evening out. Runs rarely last. But that night, everything was different. None of the usual rules applied. Even when I got dealt garbage up, I knew I'd get bailed out. If I sat 13, I knew without a doubt that a 7 or 8 was on its way. If I called for it, or the crowd called for it, it would come. If I sat 15 and the dealer showed 5 or 6, it was just a matter of waiting until he turned his hole card, which was always a face, and then turned another one, to bust and pay out. Everything played out as it should according to the basic strategy of the game. I knew *exactly* what was going to happen two seconds ahead of time—it was like living inside a dream you've had before, a glorious kind of déjà vu that wasn't unlike the zone some athletes talk about, when they know a shot is going to go in before it leaves their hands, or can clock the rotation on a ball before it hits the bat.

I knew what was coming before it came, and I knew it was happening because I was finally gambling for a reason. Before, I was just like the others, doing it for the adrenaline rush. But once I found a legitimate cause, there was no stopping me. As I sat there drinking vodka pineapples and listening to the crowd cheering and watching the stacks of chips grow higher and higher, it was obvious to me that the only reason I had ever gotten into all this trouble in the first place was because I was being punished for not having a clear purpose in the casino. Having suffered bitter losses and myriad humiliations, I had finally learned the golden lesson and seen the light that is Purpose, and so the gambling gods had pardoned me then and there for all past transgressions. It was no longer a game of chance—anyone could see that. Fate and Just Cause were arranging my passage back to the place I belonged and the person I belonged there with, and as I chased another painkiller down with another cocktail, I had no doubt that right at that moment, in the glow of the emerald lights of the mighty MGM Grand, winged angels were working furiously to lift Vegas Boulevard into the clouds and stretch it all the way to my new house. They were preparing a gilded road for me to travel on, the west wind at my back the entire glorious way.

Through it all, Bob Mota did his best to appear happy for me. He raced about offering suite upgrades; show tickets, meals at Emeril's and Pearl, massages, helicopter tours of the Hoover Dam, anything and everything my heart desired. Manny C., on the other hand, wanted nothing more than to put a permanent dent in my forehead with his pinkie ring. He wanted to turn a fire hose on the crowd. Wanted to tell them that this was the MGM Grand, not an Alabama-Auburn tailgate, and to shut the fuck up already. But he didn't. He just grinned as the crowd swelled and rumors began circulating about me. "Where's he from?" "What's he do?" "Who is he?" "He's somebody famous, but who?" "Wasn't he in that movie with what's-his-face?" "Wait, isn't *he* what's-his-face?" And you know, in that moment, I *am* famous. I *am* what's-his-face. Hell, I'm *everybody* who was *ever* famous. I'm American-made, baby. I'm Paul Newman in the pool hall. Willie Mays in center field. I'm Billy the Kid on the draw and Rocky running the stairs and Brando in a T-shirt. I'm Mickey Rourke in the eighties. Hell, I'm Bruce *and* Clarence on the cover of *Born to Run*. I'm the chorus of "Thunder Road," too. The window *is* rolled down. The wind *is* blowing back my hair. I *am* pulling out of here to win.

I have waitresses bring out trays of shooters for everyone. Because I am Hope Springing Eternal, I make toasts to Possibilities. Raise a glass to the Wonder of It All. I change chocolate to black, and every ten minutes I toss those $100 chips into the crowd like I'm pitching pennies into the Fountain of Youth. Guys slap my back. Girls sign my cast. And in the middle of it all, one of them touches my hand and says, "Well, I guess the high roller wasn't lying after all."

Renée.

W LCOME TO T E HAP IEST P ACE ON EAR H

January 25

. . . and it's something that, while he never says anything, makes me feel like Boyd might think less of me for it. But that's just me projecting. He's wonderful. He's truly nonjudgmental. Not in R's democratic, "hang out with anybody at any time no matter who they are or what they've done" way, but in the way of an older man who sees the world in the way it's meant to be seen and engages it in the way it's meant to be engaged. With care and reverence. Not greed and gratification. R is a child to him, and he's either not threatened by his antics or simply man enough not to show that it bothers him. But I know he wonders how I lived my entire adult life the way I did. Why wouldn't he? I wonder about it myself all the time.

WHEN THE RUN FINALLY ENDED, I met Bob Mota over by the cage and watched my racks of chips counted off. Renée was with me, filling me in on pertinent details, such as her age ("greatteen"), where she was from ("Blowhio"), what her hometown was like ("crap"), what her ex-boyfriend was like ("total crap"), and what it was like working in the paper factory in town ("beyond crap"). As she was talking, Mota informed me that my account stood at $1,252,500. Less the check I had deposited, I had just won $640,000 in four hours. You know how people are always saying, "It takes money to make money"? Believe it.

I asked for $252,500 in cash for three reasons: 1) it brought my account to a clean million, which was exactly half of the way back home (and only one winning hand away, if I chose to play it that way); 2) I was curious to see what a quarter million dollars in cash looked like; and 3) Bob Mota kept telling me to leave it all on account, just take some "walking-around money," and it was entertaining to watch him squirm, because the last thing in the world he wanted to see happen was for me to sashay off with his cash. He would rather have slathered himself in barbecue sauce and walked nude through the tiger exhibit at the Bronx Zoo than have me take a quarter million dollars and saunter off with Renée for the night. As long as the money remained sequestered in the MGM vaults, he figured it had a relatively reasonable chance of staying there, but once cash went the wrong way out of the cage, it probably wasn't coming back, and he knew I wouldn't be donating the entire $612,500 check as expected. This had to come as a disappointment to Mota, who only had to take a cursory glance at me when I'd walked in the previous morning to be pretty certain that emotional stability, reasonable behavior, and I hadn't sat down for a chat in a very long time. I didn't look anything like a guy who could be trusted to hang on to a quarter of a million in cash, and Renée looked like a girl who might have an idea or two how to spend a buck, and Mota knew this, only there was nothing he could do about it. He had to keep me happy. If an out-of-state check for $612,500 gets you VIP treatment at the Grand, take a wild guess how another house would treat you if you walked in their front door with $1.25 million in cash. Vegas is the kind of town where, if you strolled into a hotel with a million dollars under one arm and a severed head under the other, not a single person working the front of the house would think to ask about the head.

The money came in bricks of $100,000: ten straps of $10,000 each wrapped in cellophane. I got two bricks, five unwrapped straps, and $2,500 in loose hundreds. It all fit in an MGM tote bag with room to spare. This surprised me. In the movies, someone can owe as little as, say, fifty grand, and they'll go through this whole rigmarole where a big suitcase is hauled out and the latches are popped and boom, there's this sea of cash, but that's not what that kind of money really looks like. It's a movie thing, like how they always show some insanely lucky couple who just hit a big score celebrating on a king-size bed. They scoop up huge gobs of cash, toss it in the air, and watch the bills fall from the ceiling in slow motion like autumn leaves. But that kind of money in real life is crisp and new and sticks together, and even if you took off the wrapping and the straps and flung a couple of packs in the air, it would just kind of plunk down on the bed no different than if you had tossed a couple of pounds of sliced ham toward the ceiling. The movies consistently ignore this kind of reality, which is precisely why I like them.

Renée and I waited for the elevator to go up to the suite, chatting away, and again, this was nothing new for me, as I was always making fast friends when I traveled. I would say that I enjoyed and excelled at meeting new people, and L would say I was terrified of being alone, and as usual, I was kind of right and she was exactly right. We got into the elevator with an elderly couple in matching Windbreakers, khakis, and fanny packs. They stared at Renée like they had just gotten a memo that the world was coming to an end and young women like her were directly responsible. She was wearing a black leather miniskirt, black high heels, and a white halter top with SAY WHAT? written in rhinestones across the chest. She was oblivious to how they were eyeballing her, but not to the way Mota and Manny C. had been looking at her downstairs.

"That Bob dude and that GD pit boss were looking at me like I'm a whatchamacallit," she fumed. "A working girl."

"You are a working girl."

"Oh, for Mike's sake. Not a working girl. A *working girl* working girl. *You know.*"

"Oh, I'm sure they didn't think *that*," I said, though I was certain they had.

She took a look at my cast. "What'd you do to your arm, fancy pants?"

"I fought off a mugger."

"On the real?"

"Yep."

"God. People are so fucked-up."

The Boca couple looked at her. They were clearly offended by her language, but Renée saw their interest in a different light and failed to notice that the husband kept hitting their floor button over and over in a pointless attempt to get there quicker.

"Hey, you guys have been around for a while," she said. "Have people always been this fucked-up, or is it worse now?"

The older couple looked down without answering. Renée got defensive. "I don't dance, if that's what you're thinking. And I'm not a whattyacallit, either. Tell them, Raoul."

"She's not a whattyacallit."

The couple kept staring at the ground. They wanted no part of us. Renée shrugged it off and looked at the signatures on my cast. "Who are all these bitches?"

"Random girls from downstairs. They were signing when I was playing."

"They're a bunch of skanks," she said. "You can tell by how they write."

"They seemed all right."

Her defensive look came right back. "Better than me?"

"Obviously not," I said.

I had taken a couple of pills down at the table, and they were starting to kick in, or had at least jump-started the pills that were on the fade. It was getting hard to concentrate.

"You don't think I'm a bad person, do you?"

"Not at all."

"I really don't want you to think I'm a bad person, OK, Raoul? I mean, I'm a good girl. Like, I haven't been with as many guys as you think I have. Do you think I've been with a lot of guys? You do, don't you?"

"I haven't really thought about it," I said.

"Well, I haven't. I had a boyfriend from the time I was thirteen to the time I got out of that stupid factory last year. He still works there. He wouldn't leave that disgusting town if you gave him a trillion dollars, 'cause everybody knows him. Like that's a big whoop or something. He was always like, 'Why go somewhere else?' and I was always like, 'Uh, *get a clue*, dude.' Even the *air* stinks like paper. Leslie liked how it smelled, if you can believe that. That's his name. Leslie."

"Your ex-boyfriend's name is *Leslie*?"

"I know. It's a girl's name, right? Every time I talk about him, people think I'm a lesbo. I Frenched a girl at a party once, but I don't see what the big deal is. It was on a dare. His parents named him after some old actor, I think. I don't know. I don't want to talk about his sorry butt, anyway. All he cares about is deer hunting."

"I can't believe people still shoot deer," I said, thinking of the Sarge and the cereal.

"Uh, *yeeea-uh*. Him and all his dipshit friends spray themselves with deer piss and go sit in trees all day. It's totally disgusting."

When we reached their floor, the Boca couple dashed off the elevator like they were grabbing the last chopper out of Saigon. Then Renée and I got to my floor and headed toward the suite. She linked her arm in mine as we made our way down the hallway.

"You're pretty young to be Joe Money Bags," she said. "You're not one of those Bernie Madoff people, are you? I saw a thing on him on TV. What a pecker. I mean, if you steal and you're way poor, it's like, OK, I get it, no worries, but rich people who steal are just total scuzbuckets."

"I agree," I said. "But I'm in plastics. That's where, you know, I made my fortune. Pretty much."

"Ohhhhh. Plastics. *Cool*," she said, though she had didn't have any more of an idea what I was talking about than I did. "I was just kidding about the Bernie Madoff thing," she said. "He's a bad person and you're a good person. I can tell."

When I opened the door to the suite, Renée raced over to the long stretch of window to take in the view while I found the room safe.

"*Cheese and rice!*" she yelled from across the suite. "This place is sick. It's like that movie with the Scientology dude and that retarded guy."

"*Rain Man?*"

"*Sí, señor!*"

I took a $10,000 strap out of the bag and locked the rest away, using L's and my anniversary, 1123, as a code. Then I poured a couple of vodka pineapples and fired up one of the joints I had scored. I took a pull and offered it to Renée.

"I will if you gimme a shotgun."

I took another drag, held the smoke, and then she put her mouth close to mine and I blew it in.

"This place kicks so much ass at night," she said, looking out at the Strip. "During the day it makes you want to kill yourself with a razor."

She was right. There is no place on earth that looks more different from day to night than Las Vegas, Nevada. It's like the difference between despair and hope.

"Gotta beat Ohio," I said.

"Hell yeah it does. That's why I call it *Blow*hio. Look! There's the Excalibur! My friend Teresa's retarded crush CJ works up there at the show with those guys with the horses and the big sticks."

"The jousts?"

"I don't know," she said. "Whatever you call those old-fashionedy people with the clanky metal suits. It was like a hundred years ago, so I don't really know. CJ's not one of those guys, anyway. He just, like, cleans horse shit, pretty much. Hey—you gonna ask me what I'm doin' here or what? It's kinda weird you haven't. I mean, you're acting like we're old friends. Which is awesome. But it's a little weird, right? You don't think it's random that we were talking last night and now I'm here?"

"I hadn't really thought about it," I said.

"Probably 'cause you were too busy winning a skillion dollars."

"Maybe."

"Well, I had an interview at Wet Republic. Which is gross. That lazy river is nothing but sweat and pee and Coors Light. Anyway, I'm not a stalker or anything. I had a reason to be here. Then I saw this whatchamacallit in the casino, this commotion, and I checked it out, and there you were. I was like, holy moly, it's the cute dude from the bench! I watched you for a while. You were really cool with everybody. They all liked you. I mean, they liked you besides for the fact that you were giving them money. Some people give people money, but they're dicks about it," she said, her face clouding. "Like all those gross guys who come into the club. They're, you know, a hundred percent disgusting, but they think since they have cash, they're God's gift. Deep down they hate the girls 'cause they have to pay to see good-looking ones, and the girls hate them 'cause they try and treat them like whores. Who makes someone pick up money off the ground? Even animals don't do that. Not that they have money, but if they did, I bet they'd just give it to each other and not be asswipes about it. Or at least not make each other feel like shit on purpose."

She walked around the suite, picking things up and putting them down like she was at a high-end yard sale.

"People are like that, you know. They'll try and make you feel like crap if they feel like crap. You'll be with a guy, and he'll be in a pissy mood or something and tell you your ass looks flabby even if it doesn't, 'cause, like, he wants you to *think* it's flabby so you don't get to where you feel too good about yourself. Guys think that if they make you feel crappy about how you look, then you won't leave them, 'cause you won't think you can do any better than you're already doing."

I thought of L. Of what an emotionally generous person she was. She used to call me her "beautiful boy." And I was constantly reminding her how perfect she was. We were not stingy with those things. Not ever. Some couples are—Renée was right—but we weren't. And that's important, you know? Because after a while, when you look in the mirror, you start to see what the person who loves you sees and not whatever it was you might have seen before, if that makes any sense. After L and I were together for a while, we came to see ourselves like the other saw us, and I think that's one of the most amazing things love can do. Maybe *the* most amazing thing, if you think about it.

Renée reached into her pocket and pulled out her iPhone. Her face lit up. "Oh my God. Raoul. We gotta go to the Rio! Ryan Gosling's at VooDoo!"

Renée had received word from one of her "posse" that the actor and an entourage were at VooDoo, the rooftop bar at the Rio. She was crazy with excitement and insisted she simply *had* to meet him before she died because he had changed her life, since it was after seeing *The Notebook* on cable that the true nature and possibility of love had been revealed to her. As Renée explained it, when she saw the love Ryan Gosling had for Rachel McAdams, she decided then and there that it was time to get out of Ohio and her emotionally unsatisfying relationship with Leslie Womack, whose displays of romanticism were limited to: 1) yearly Valentine's Day outings to the Paradise Motel (a by-the-hour eyesore still within a quarter tank of the factory); and 2) ceremoniously dragging a twelve-point buck up to her parents' front door as a gesture of apology after bypassing her sixteenth-birthday dinner in order to go deer hunting with his coworkers from the paper factory. Gosling's unyielding, incalculable love for McAdams was made even more resonant by the fact that Womack fell asleep next to Renée during the movie, thus sealing his fate and finally squandering the enormous emotional credit he had built up as a result of being the only guy she had ever slept with. I ignored the obvious parallels between me and L and focused instead on the fact that Gosling had built a beautiful house in the hope that McAdams would return, thus cementing the fact that I had indeed come up with the perfect plan, or at least one that had worked multiple times in American fiction of varying quality. Renée made it clear that she didn't "want to, like, hook up with Ryan or anything sketchy like that," but merely wanted to meet him and express her gratitude for his having helped her understand that there were men in the world who would lay their lives down for a woman. Anything short of that, she said, was no longer acceptable to her.

"Can we go, Raoul? Can we? Even if you don't care about Ryan, VooDoo has a kick-ass view. It's just like this one, only there's no glass in front of you, which makes a pretty big difference, I think."

"Sure," I said. "Let's do it."

"Awesome. You want me to call Carmelo for party favors?"

"What kind of party favors?" I said.

"You know. Rhymes with *joke-brain*."

"Ah. You like that stuff?"

"Never buy it, never sell it, never turn it down. I heard a girl at the club say that. Do you like it?"

"Not really," I said. "I just like the way it smells."

She looked at me. For a long time.

"That was a joke," I said.

"*Ohhhhhhhhhhhh*. Holy moly, that's, like, *genius*. I gotta use that! Can I use that?"

She called Carmelo to discuss the procuring of party favors while I poured another drink. Now, I know what you're probably thinking: You're on a roll, Ray, and so close to seeing the Plan through. Why not hit the sack, wake up fresh, and get after it in the morning? Take the suckers down and get out of Vegas before night falls again. Which makes sense. Complete sense, really. But I'm a social person, for one thing, and I hadn't felt this good in a very long time, for another. I wanted to celebrate a little. It wasn't that I had any interest in sleeping with Renée or anything like that (in my mind I had never gotten divorced, and no matter what L thinks about the Dawn situation, I hadn't looked twice at another girl since the day I'd laid eyes on L at the Parker House, and you'll never find anyone to say otherwise), and though time was an issue, it didn't seem like *that* much of an issue. L and the fossil were off God knows where on vacation. I had a little time. I mean, I'd been exiled for so long already. Didn't I deserve to enjoy myself a little?

Bob Mota arranged a limo for us, and we headed down Vegas Boulevard with a young Asian kid named Coco behind the wheel. Renée informed him that he had "the coolest name ever, besides for this girl Pooh Jeter who lives in my apartment complex." I poured a couple of drinks from the wet bar and lounged on the leather seats, enjoying the way the pills slowed everything down and made the lights outside the tinted windows shimmer. Renée stuck her head out the sunroof, and Coco did his best to keep his eyes on the road and not on the rearview as she leaned on the roof with her butt up in the air.

On Renée's direction, he pulled into a parking lot off Flamingo where a decrepit shack of a bar stood. Out front was a white plastic sign like you usually see outside used-car lots. It read W LCOME TO T E HAP IEST P ACE ON EAR H in black letters. Missing letters notwithstanding, it probably should have billed itself as "the place on earth that has the least interest in truth in advertising," since the dim-light, dead-end clientele and deathly glow from the video poker machines made your average Cambodian sweat shop look like a month of Sundays in comparison. I waited by the door as Renée made a quick exchange with the bartender (Carmelo, presumably), and then we headed back toward the limo, where she handed me some cash. "Here's your change, Raoul."

"Keep it for drinks."

"Nuh-uh. Lou Ann says never take money from a man."

"Who's Lou Ann?"

"This old lady I play bingo with at the Plaza. She made me a scarf. Now that my real family doesn't talk to me anymore, she's like my grandmother. I'll probably eat Thanksgiving with her. She brings it up every five seconds even though it's still a skillion degrees out and the last thing I want to think about is freaking gravy," she said. "Yo, Coco Loco! Head over to Harbor Island. I gotta pick up some of my peeps."

Standing outside in the parking lot of the Harbor Island apartment complex were seven friends of Renée's (most of them likely carrying fake IDs, though so was I), one of them toting a Chihuahua in a leather side bag. Within seconds they had all piled in the limo and started snorting lines off a local travel guide. Then Renée started talking a mile a minute to one of her friends. I watched her in drugged-out amazement.

"This driver's name is Coco how freaking cool is that Raoul's in plastics I don't know he doesn't look Mexican at all that girl in sixteen should move to Bitch City yeah tell me about it two-faced where's Pooh what do you mean she moved she didn't even say goodbye what a lame-o she can be such a basic bitch cheese and rice is it hot I'm sticking to these seats yo Coco Loco fire up the AC it's like being in jail working there Pooh Jeter moved that's crazy that guy is a big-time loser Rio I know totally Raoul is at the MGM holy moly you should see his room it's like *Rain Man* I don't know some movie the place kicks ass yeah the music is gay there for sure what do you mean you hate s'mores that's crazy I don't like bingo I just feel obligated I know he's cute look at him plastics I don't know you've never seen so many freaking chips a hundred dollars a drink no Wet Republic ya huh screw Hard Rock they suck don't be gross I have no idea he's not wearing a ring why don't you freaking announce it Camille you never should have got that stupid dog it pisses on everything where the heck are you gonna put it holy Einstein that's genius no not Britney S. Britney P. I would not I don't care what you say Leslie still thinks I'm gonna move back there and marry him fat chance deer piss Ryan Gosling totally Channing Tatum is not you can have him never in a million years I'd rather die little pecker no I haven't talked to her of course it's insane he is not now you're being disgusting don't buy it don't sell it don't turn it down I know uh-uh not really I just like how it smells thanks no that's Raoul's yeah totally woo to the hoo let's go Coco time to do this thanks Raoul you rule no this way party-time people!"

A handful of cash got everyone into VooDoo, including the Chihuahua, who was smuggled in the bag, and Coco, the driver, who abandoned all pretense of working and whipped his shirt off on the dance floor. At one point a member of Renée's posse, Kevin G. (aka Chickenhead), vomited during an *Off the Wall*–era Michael Jackson song, and the Chihuahua appeared in the strobe lights and started lapping it up, at which point the bouncers descended and requested that we vamoose, which was fine with me because the outrageous view was offset by the triple-digit heat. By then Renée had heard that Gosling and his posse had gone to Cheetahs strip club, and she informed the bouncers, "We're outy anyway 'cause we're going to party with Ryan at Cheetahs and this place is so over so suck on that why doncha?"

We climbed back in the limo, stopping off at T E HAP IEST P ACE ON EAR H for a re-up, at which juncture Coco climbed in the back and started doing lines off Renée's stomach, which was reasoned to be the flattest object in the limo. That left the wheel to Kevin G., who was feeling better after relieving his stomach of its contents at the Rio and was driving with great confidence after Renée announced that "No one rolls like the Chickenhead!" I called L's home phone twice from the limo (she had changed her cell number on me), getting the machine each time and not leaving a message. What I thought I might say if I got her on the phone I'm not entirely sure, since the fact that I was partying in Vegas with a bunch of teenagers wouldn't have been high on the list of things she was interested in hearing about. I realized that I wasn't aiding my cause, and making those kinds of calls was probably why staying in would have been a better idea. I knew I needed to get the money and get out of Dodge before I screwed everything up. I did not make good decisions when I was alone, obviously, and the more time I spent alone, the worse that trend got.

Gosling was not at Cheetahs, a fact we learned after I gave another doorman a fistful of cash and then spread out enough to get everyone in the VIP room, where four things of note happened: 1) Renée convinced Coco that he should quit the MGM and go to work for my plastics company; 2) Coco left a series of messages on L's machine informing her that, in his opinion, she was making a big mistake choosing an old sack of bones like Boyd Bollinger over a prince like me; 3) a fat Polynesian businessman mistook Renée for a dancer, offered her money for a lap dance, and got a White Russian tossed in his face for his trouble; and 4) we were thrown out of our second consecutive establishment, which is actually difficult to do in Vegas if you're spending a lot of money (see previous severed-head analogy).

Once we got pitched from the strip club, Coco gave the limo keys to a homeless guy outside the club as a kiss-off to the MGM. He and the rest of Renée's "peeps" dispersed one by one, and we ended up taking a cab to the In-N-Out Burger, where I gave Renée a handful of cash and told her to buy dinner for everyone in the place. She put on a paper In-N-Out cap and stood up on a table, yelling, "Yo! Las to the Vegas! Who wants a free Double-Double?" It damn near caused a stampede among the drunks (who else would be at In-N-Out at five A.M.?), and somewhere in the commotion Renée decided she wanted eggs, not a burger, so we wound up eating at Denny's on the Strip, where I watched Renée stuff as many mini-creamers in her purse as it could possibly hold. This brought tears to my eyes because I was reminded of the five million times L and I had gone to breakfast at the old Majestic Diner in Atlanta, and how she used to peel the lids back and drink the mini-creamers, happily turning them over and stacking them in a pyramid as I smiled at her and wondered how it could be that something so small could be so consistently thrilling to me.

"I can't believe Pooh Jeter just moved without telling anybody,"

Renée said, polishing off the last of a stack of silver-dollar pancakes. "It's the sketchiest thing ever. I'm totally going to get to the bottom of this."

She whipped out her phone and also pulled an iPad from her purse. Her fingers started flying, and she began scanning her devices and talking to herself.

"Oh my God, here's where she met him. Ew. He's a magician. Augh—she uses the worst filters. Holy moly—that was less than a week ago. They have time to spray-paint a car but not say goodbye? What's wrong with people? Pooh is crazy. But that can happen when your mom has a bunch of shady boyfriends that don't always go back to the right room in the middle of the night. 'Oh, is this not the bathroom?' As if."

She showed me a picture of Pooh Jeter and her magician.

"God, he's not even a good magician. Poor Pooh. She thinks that's all she deserves. That's what happens. You don't think you deserve anything. It's like that story about the guy who's, like, eating shit for so long. Someone goes, 'Hey, buddy, why are you eating shit?' and the guy goes, 'I'm not eating shit, I'm eating dinner,' 'cause that's what he's used to. That's a whattyacallit. Story that means something else. I think it is, anyway. It seems like it is. Oh well. So long, Pooh. Hope you like Utah."

It had taken her under ninety seconds to figure out precisely where this Pooh Jeter was, whom she was with, and what the circumstances of her leaving town were. It was remarkable.

"That's pretty amazing," I said, wondering for a second where that snake in the grass Boyd had taken L. They had a lot of luggage. A *ton* of luggage, now that I thought about it. L was a light packer. Why hadn't this occurred to me when I went over there? I should have focused on the volume of luggage, not the Kentucky Derby mug.

"It's easy. I can find anybody."

"What if they don't do any social media?"

"Doesn't matter. Their friends probably do. You can't hide anymore, Raoul. People will find you," she said, looking at me in what I felt was a meaningful way.

Renée got up to go to the bathroom. For a second I wondered if she knew I was a fugitive, then I decided I was being paranoid. I paid the check and walked outside onto Vegas Boulevard in the full brutal light of morning. I watched as an obese bearded man in a red visor and powder-blue tracksuit hauled a wheelchair out of a white van and set in on the sidewalk in front of the curved covered driveway leading to the Imperial Palace. The pain was returning, so I popped a couple more pills and watched him waddle over to the passenger side of the van, where he emerged carrying a cripple who appeared to be about my age and looked like Howie Rose, my old best friend who had been paralyzed after falling out of a tree while playing flashlight tag in the summer when we were nine. The cripple's arms, legs, neck, and hands were twisted in every direction, and the guy carrying him dumped him in the wheelchair with all the care of a gardener tossing a sack of fertilizer into a toolshed. He made his way back to the van and grabbed a plastic bucket, a name tag, and a new straw cowboy hat. He set the bucket in the cripple's lap, attached the name tag to the cripple's ratty pearl-buttoned western shirt, set the hat crookedly on the cripple's head, and hauled himself back into the van, where he squealed off into the Imperial Palace driveway.

Renée came walking out of Denny's, and we crossed the street to catch a cab at Caesars. I couldn't stop turning around to look at the cowboy cripple. I thought of Howie Rose. I thought of the beam from the flashlight that cut across the lawn after he fell out of the tree. And the way tears rolled down his cheeks that one time I went to visit him, though he couldn't move to wipe them and seemed to know I wasn't coming back after that first visit. The longer I looked at the cripple, the more I thought that it might actually *be* Howie Rose, so I raced back across the street to get a look at his name tag. It read Cowboy Bob. His eyes were vacant and moist, just like Howie's were. I said "Howie? Is that you?" He just looked at me with those eyes. He couldn't speak. I didn't know what to do but stick a $100 bill in his bucket. Renée started hollering, "Raoul! *Vamos!*" so I ran back across the street, where we hopped in a cab.

I looked back across Vegas Boulevard, where the fat guy in the tracksuit had reemerged and was reaching into the bucket with a heavy paw. He held the hundred up to the sun, inspecting it, then looked around suspiciously before stuffing it in his pocket and disappearing into O'Sheas. I had the urge to get out of the cab, to go back, but I didn't, partly because I didn't know what I would do, and partly because none other than Bing Buli was walking past the guy on the other side of the street, studying each foot of sidewalk like I might be hiding in a crack. He was either wearing shorts that were a foot too long or pants that were a foot too short. I ducked down in the cab before he could see me. I cursed Maurice in my mind for a second, and then I thought that I had clearly dodged a bullet, had just survived the impossibly long odds of ever running into Bing Buli in a town the size of Vegas, and proceeded to forget about him entirely. I surely didn't waste any bandwidth beating myself up over the fact that he was so out of sorts that he had flown across the country to scour a strange city on foot on the off chance that he could get his hands on his old friend.

Renée put her head in my lap and fell asleep. I absently brushed her hair, imagining that I was back in Cabbagetown and L had fallen asleep watching one of her favorites, *The Purple Rose of Cairo*. I held the thought for a long while, imagining Mia Farrow staring at the movie screen in the film and me staring at the freckles on L's face in the same wondrous way. I kept petting Renée's head as the sun bore down, and then I closed my eyes. It was time to call it a night.

MR. PARISI

I want to kill him with my bare hands. It's just that simple.

I WOKE UP LATE THE NEXT afternoon on the couch in the suite. I had never felt worse in my life. There was no way to determine how much of the agony was from my bronchitis and broken bones and how much was from the night before, when we'd drunk roughly half the agave extract of central Mexico and inhaled the entire gross national product of Bolivia. My wrist was throbbing away, my stomach was churning (think Denny's Grand Slam in a bingo tumbler), and my throat felt like it had survived a dull guillotine. It was abysmal and depressing. I had tears in my eyes. The sun was already setting through the windows. The dimming desert was endless. Was this any way for a millionaire to feel?

I made it into the bathroom, dry-heaved, then stuck my mouth under the faucet and managed to get down a couple of painkillers. Renée was passed out on a chaise longue, her stomach caked in so much drug residue that she looked like one of the natives on Kurtz's island at the end of *Apocalypse Now*. I crawled to the couch and went back to sleep, and the next thing I knew, I was being awakened by a horrible shrill clinking sound. I looked up to see Renée standing over me, banging a fork on a wineglass and looking none the worse for wear. Never had the difference between thirty-five and eighteen been clearer.

"Rise and shine, Buster Brown."

I squinted up at her. She was wearing a bubblegum-pink thong and bra, and her hair was wet. It was like waking up in a beer commercial.

"Who are you, and how'd you get in here?" I said.

"What?"

"How did you get in this room?"

"I, like, came with you! You don't remember me?"

"Are you Pooh Jeter?"

"Pooh Jeter? Pooh Jeter moved!"

I would have kept it up but was restrained by the fact that she was about to start crying and I was about to vomit. One of those things will pretty much put the kibosh on any protracted jocularity, and two of them, forget it.

"I'm joking, Renée. It's a joke."

"Well, sometimes your jokes are for the birds."

"It's true."

"Do you remember what you promised me today?"

She put her hands on her hips, reached behind her back, popped off her bra, and slid out of her underwear, all of which took about three seconds. Her skin was as taut as an extended rubber band. I mean, if you followed Renée around with an airbrush all day, you probably couldn't find anything on her body to touch up. I had no doubt that her ex-boyfriend spent many nights polishing his hunting rifle and thinking about that very fact.

"I'm gonna take a hot tub. Get up off the thingamabob and come in with me. I'll wash your hair. And you said you'd take me to the Forum Shops, by the way. Like, at Caesars."

"I know that," I lied.

"Come on, old man."

Renée reached out her hand and pulled me up. Her strength surprised me, not to mention her comfort level with thorough nudity, which was yet another trait that reminded me of L. You'd think, Oh, she's a lawyer, she must be uptight (and I realize that the version of L I'm describing here *is* uptight, at least where I'm concerned), but that was never the case. She was as game as they get.

I took my shirt off. Renée looked at me curiously. "Why is your chest hair blond and your hair hair isn't?"

"I don't know," I said. "It's always been that way."

"Huh. That's pretty random. But I kinda like it."

We got in the tub, and Renée had me sit in front of her while she poured water over my head and washed my hair, which felt good, as did the pills, which were starting to work their wonder. My chest and throat eased and softened, and my wrist went numb. The world was starting to right itself. My optimism was returning.

"Who did you keep calling last night?"

"I don't know," I said. "Did I call someone?"

"Only about eight skazillion times. It was fishy."

"If I could remember, I'd tell you."

What an idiot I was. L and the Silver Fox were no doubt commiserating right that very second about her train wreck of an ex-husband calling from the 702 area code. And the creaky bastard would look it up and say, "Honey, that's Las Vegas," and then he'd start in on how I was a gambling addict and bring up the credit card debt I had gotten into and probably mention Dawn and Penny just to turn the knife. I could hear it all now. What the hell was wrong with me? Why couldn't I just stay quiet until the plan was executed? And did I have *Coco* call her? Did that happen? That couldn't have happened. Not even I was *that* stupid.

"How come you remember telling me you'd take me shopping but you don't remember who you kept calling on the phone?"

"Maybe I only remember the important stuff," I said, and then I remembered seeing Bing Buli out on Vegas Boulevard. I decided then and there that I needed to keep it tight for the rest of the time I was in Vegas. No more fucking around.

"You're weird," she said, scrubbing my scalp. "But weird-in-a-good-way weird. A lot of guys are just *weird* weird. Everybody who comes in the club is just *weird* weird. Why are you not, like, married or anything?"

"Do you think it's weird?"

"Duh. You're a total catch."

I considered telling her about L. My plan. All of it. But that's not how it works. You don't all of a sudden turn into a truthful person just because you're sitting in a bathtub and have a million dollars.

"You don't think I'm a busybody, do you?" she said.

"Not at all."

"OK. Good," she said. " 'Cause, like, nobody likes a busybody, and I don't want you to think I am one. My mother's one, though. *Cheese and rice*, is she a busybody! Or at least she was. She doesn't talk to me anymore 'cause I left Buttholeville and don't wanna marry Leslie. Close your eyes and let me wash your sweet face. There you go. Leslie eats over there like twelve days a week and calls her Mama and then he calls me and says she won't let anybody mention my name at the table 'cause I'm like the devil for leaving and not finishing high school and working in that GD factory till I drop dead, like everybody else in that town. He's always like, 'Everybody here hates you and I'm never speaking to you again 'cause you're a bitch for leaving and thinking you're too good for this place,' and then he'll hang up and call back five minutes later and tell me about one of our old friends who got another one of our old friends pregnant or something like that. Like he didn't *just say* he was never speaking to me again two seconds before. Sometimes he gets drunk and plays songs we used to listen to over the phone to try and make me homesick. Like if they're having a camping party with girls or whatever. He'll hold the phone while they're all singing so I'll get FOMO and want to go back. One thing I learned so far in life is that people who stay places are totally against people who don't. Everybody always wants you to stay where you are so they don't feel bad about never doing anything themselves."

"It's not right," I said.

"Nope. 'Course, I don't care, 'cause I'm not going back. Not ever. I want to see things and, like, you know, *go somewhere*. My mom never went anywhere—that's why she won't talk to me. But, I mean, whoever heard of someone not talking to their kid anymore? That's fucked-up, right?"

Again I thought of saying something personal, something about my old man, but as always, I didn't, even though I knew she could have used some support in how she was feeling. She was only eighteen. She was putting on a brave face in a new place. She probably knew that Vegas wasn't going to work out for her and she'd end up back in Ohio. Her fear was transparent beneath her attitude. She wouldn't dance, and the money went to girls who would dance. And the money gave you freedom. Or at least more freedom than you had without it. I knew she'd either end up back in a dirty house with deer heads on the wall or on the stage herself. But I didn't mention any of this. I merely nodded and agreed. "Yes," I said. "It's very fucked-up."

She rinsed the remaining shampoo from my hair and stood up. "OK, you," she said. "Take me shopping or take me to bed."

When I asked Bob Mota for another limo, he grinned tightly and said, "See if you can't get this one back to us, hey, *Raoul*?" and then we were off down the Strip. I was feeling dreamy again because of the drugs, and I stared out the window at clusters of families inching their way down the sidewalks, sweating all over their fanny packs in the heat of the desert evening. You couldn't help but wonder who took their children to Las Vegas in the flaming heart of the summertime. Or any time, for that matter. The chamber of commerce goes out of its way to make the place seem kid-friendly, sure, but Vegas is Vegas. I mean, if a madam put a kiddie pool behind the bordello, would it really change what was happening in the house?

In the least surprising news of the day, Coco hadn't shown up for work, so we had a new driver named Lyle. He was all sideburns and self-confidence and chatted up Renée while I contemplated giving her some money, dropping her off, and hotfooting it back to the MGM to hit the tables. She was extremely excited for her shopping spree and firing on all cylinders, blasting through topics even faster than she usually did. Did I think it was strange that roses had the shame shape when they were dead as they did before they bloomed? Why was Arkansas pronounced Arkan-*saw* and not Ar-*Kansas*? Why are all girls named Sam nice and all girls named Alex bitches? Would *The Girl with the Dragon Tattoo* have been as sexy if she didn't have any tattoos? Should Renée herself get a tattoo? I tried to pay attention, but there was something gnawing at me, some vague recollection of something L had said on the answering machine when I'd heard it the night before. Something about how, if it was the police calling, she had no information about me, which seemed unnecessary to put on an outgoing message. She also said she'd be unreachable, which I didn't like the sound of now that it was coming back to me. Time *did* seem of the essence all of a sudden.

Renée socked me in the arm. "Lyle just asked you a question. Geez. You're like that old-timey song with that Major Tom guy who bit the radish."

"Man, I got high as *fuck* to that song a couple weeks ago," Lyle said.

That reminded me I had a loose joint in my pocket. I asked whether he minded if I fired up, and he said, "Hell no—that's the best thing I've seen all day," before adjusting the rearview, eyeballing Renée, and adding with a grin, "Well, second best." He was a good-looking kid and a very smooth character. I had no doubt he had limo stories to tell.

Renée took a drag and blew the smoke into my mouth, but my throat was too swollen to take it, and I started hacking.

"Dude, you sound like you've got pneumonia," Lyle said.

"He's very sick. I'm his nurse."

"Where's your uniform, then?"

"I'm not, like, a *real* nurse. I'm just taking care of him. And not in a pervy way, either," Renée snapped.

"Whatever it is, it's not a bad deal," said Lyle. "What's a guy gotta do to get his own personal nurse?"

I kept coughing. There was no end to it in sight.

"You know, I feel like I've definitely seen you somewhere before, dude," he continued.

"He's in plastics," Renée said. She sounded so proud that for a minute I kind of wished I *were* in plastics.

"You sure you're not an actor or something? You look like someone I saw on TV."

"He *could* be an actor. He's, like, good-looking enough."

"I swear I've seen your face before. I don't know. Let me hit that thing again."

Lyle took a professional toke and passed the joint back to Renée.

Renée took a toke. Looked at me seriously. "What do you call the guy who takes back your car if you don't make your payments?"

"A repo man?"

"*Reeeeeeepo* man," she said, cracking up for no apparent reason, though there didn't seem to be any logic to the question in the first place.

Before I could put together what was so funny about a repo man, we pulled into the driveway at Caesars, rolled past a twenty-foot statue of Julius Caesar himself, and cruised alongside the fifty-foot Italian cypresses that line the drive. I think the limo was still moving when Renée whipped her door open and starting dashing under the geodesic dome out in front and on into the casino, where girls dressed like Cleopatra and guys in gladiator getups meandered around the floor. It was all I could do to keep up with her. You have never seen anyone so excited in your life.

"Hey, Raoul, look! I'm kicking this gladiator's butt."

She had stopped her sprint toward the Forum Shops and was playfully punching a guy with arms as big as my thighs. He wore the put-upon expression of a classically trained actor forced to slum it until the world recognized his prodigious talent. He gave Renée a once-over and said, "I'm not a *gladiator*, baby, I'm a *centurion*."

She said, "Whatever," and pulled me through the casino by my good hand, though I had to stop her short at one point when I was overcome by another coughing jag. Renée pounded me on the back, yelling, "Shake it off! Shake it off!" like a football coach, before charging on past a couple of empty craps tables and into a gold and marble foyer where a replica statue of Michelangelo's *David* stood. A cluster of Canadian girls wearing backpacks and hiking boots were standing around the base of it, giggling and pointing. I heard one of them say, "Not much of a pecker, eh?"

Renée walked over to read the plaque at the base of the statue. All the Canadian girls stopped talking and looked at her critically. She was wearing white short shorts, a tiny black tank top, white sneaker-shoes with four-inch soles, and the kind of big black bubble shades Jackie Kennedy used to wear after things fell apart in Dallas. The Canadians rolled their eyes and walked off, one of them sticking her finger down her throat, one throwing her chest out, and the others laughing. It pissed me off. Canadians are usually better than that. Renée was oblivious to them. "Hey, sickly, guess how high this statue is?"

"Five feet," I said.

"Seriously."

"Five-six."

"Uh, *I'm* five-six. You're not even in the whatchamacallit. The ballpark. It's eighteen feet. Guess how much it weighs."

"Twelve pounds."

"Twelve pounds! It says it's, like, an exact replica made with the same Italian marble. Listen. 'David is an exact replica made with the same Italian marble.' See? So how can it be twelve pounds? It's *marble*. I mean, I'm a hundred and eight and a half!"

"Twenty pounds, then."

"You're impossible," she said. "It's *nine tons*. Eighteen feet, nine tons."

"How much is a ton?" I said, amusing myself, because every time you asked her a question, you were seconds away from solid entertainment.

"A ton? I don't know. But it's a lot, 'cause every time somebody says something's heavy, they say, 'This thing weighs a *ton*,' you know? So a ton must be, like, insane."

"So he's eighteen feet, nine tons," I said. "Some underdog."

"Whatever, goofy. Let's roll."

She dragged me past the Cartier window and Le Paradis, and then through another deserted stretch of casino before we ended up amid the piazzas, statues, and fountains of the Caesars Palace Forum Shops, the mother of upscale malls. Above me, a ceiling painted like an afternoon sky was moving around, swirling and swaying, and I thought for certain it was the painkillers playing tricks on me until Renée pointed up and said that the roof of the Forum Shops shifts from day to night over a stretch of three hours. Another flashy and pointless Vegas gimmick.

"The girl who cuts my hair for free 'cause she's a student and they make them told me that," she said proudly.

I pulled out two $10,000 straps I had brought along and handed them to her. Her hands started shaking as if I had just plopped a pair of grenades in them.

"No way," she said.

"Way. But I'm feeling a little weak. I'm just gonna sit over by the fountain for a little while. I'll be right over there. At Bertolini's. Knock yourself out."

"This is the coolest thing ever," she said, kissing me. "You're such a babe."

Then she marched across the mall. Outside of watching Bruce fetch a tennis ball, I'd never seen such a blend of joy and determination in my life. I walked past Spago and sat at a table outside Bertolini's, where I ordered hot tea for my throat and checked out the marble statues of Greek gods behind me while I waited. There were angry bearded men wielding tridents and winged horses in midflight and all manner of ancient madness. Renée waved at me from the Versace store, then proceeded to do the same thing from the windows of Bernini, Gucci, Escada, and Salvatore Ferragamo, where she held up a black leather shoulder bag and hollered, "Whatcha think, Raoul?" across the plaza. At some point during the twentieth century, possibly on the eve of the end of one great war or another, there may have been a human being who was *equally* happy, but it's inconceivable to imagine anyone more so.

I rested my head on the table, and a surly waiter, irritated that I had ordered only tea, tapped me on the shoulder and said, "Try and stay awake, guy." I reached into my pocket and produced a C-note, which I held up between my index and middle fingers without raising my head. The money exited my hand, the waiter put the tea on the table and said, "Rest is actually the best remedy for a cold," and if I failed to adequately describe exactly what kind of town Vegas is, there you have it.

Sometime later (minutes, hours, who really knows), Renée woke me. She was clutching a couple of armfuls of bags and beaming like Mother Sunshine. She showed me some of her purchases, then insisted I get something for myself, dragging me into Hugo Boss for a three-button black suit she said was "too hot for words." Next was Kenneth Cole for some shoes, and then to bebe, where she attracted the attention of every straight male in the place (and even some boys who might have been on the fence) by trying on a series of belly chains. She then ran into Bulgari to try on watches, and I stood outside, where a cluster of statues suddenly started moving. Then the ceiling went dark and lightning ripped across it. Trumpets started blaring and operatic voices rose from the fountains, and then a statue of an old sage in a toga came to life and a voice boomed out, "Atlantis! His kingdom was destroyed by foolish pride!"

It was too much for a hungover, drug-addled, bronchial catastrophe to deal with, so I wandered off alone, past the Gap, where chipper workers were busy putting out fall jackets and sweaters despite the ungodly heat outside. A Gap girl put a lemon-and-lime-striped sweater around my neck and said, "These colors totally work for you." I shrugged the sweater off and walked on toward FAO Schwarz, where I stopped to get my bearings in front of a giant replica Trojan horse. It was then I heard someone say, "Mr. Parisi?" behind me.

I don't know why I turned around. There was no possible benefit to it. But it was hard to keep track of, the Raoul McFarland thing, and your instincts tend to take over when you hear your name whether you're fucked-up on pills or not. There was also the fact that it was *Mr.* Parisi, which was generally something people used to call my father. No one called me Mr. Parisi. I was always Ray. Even the interns at ESPN called me Ray without my having to tell them to. I just wasn't the kind of guy anyone called Mr. I mean, I couldn't remember the last time anyone had ever used it. Until I turned around. And then it dawned on me exactly where the last time I heard it was. "Miles?"

It was Miles Smithson, the shortstop who'd booted the grounder that had started the fifth-inning unraveling of the Little League World Series championship game. Stu Lock was the son of an air force officer. He insisted on protocol. He made everyone call him Mr. Lock and me Mr. Parisi. It was a nonnegotiable thing before I came on as a coach.

Miles nodded without smiling. I tried to recall something about him, but all that came to mind was that he was a beady-eyed, humorless little bastard with a cannon for a right arm. That and the fact that he was a dead ringer for the runt who fell off the Verrazano-Narrows Bridge in *Saturday Night Fever*.

"How you doing, man? How's the old wing?" I said, touching his right shoulder. "You go on to play college ball?"

"I blew it out in high school," he said.

I shook my head sympathetically. "That sucks."

"You know what also sucks? Having everyone think you're a fag when you're twelve years old."

"What?"

"That shit you said about it being cool if we were gay? You looked right at me when you said it."

"No, I didn't."

"Yeah, you fucking did. Next thing you know, you're Johnny Television, and I'm in line for ten years' worth of queer jokes."

"That wasn't my intention," I said. "I was just trying to calm you guys down. Everyone started crying after—"

"I booted that gimme. Thanks for reminding me."

"That's not what I was gonna say."

A couple of guys in matching Yankees caps and Derek Jeter tank tops came strolling over. Friends of his. They looked as humorless as Miles was.

"Take a guess who this is," he said to them.

The Yankees looked me over. Shrugged in unison.

"Ray Parisi."

"Who?"

"Ray Parisi."

"From ESPN?"

They sized me up. Looked at the cast.

"You're in deep shit, man. Fucking everybody's looking for you."

"Yeah, they are," said Miles, smiling for the first time in his life. "I bet there's a pretty big reward, too."

I offered a weak smile before slowly turning on one heel, casually resting my hand on the Trojan horse, and then dashing off into the heart of the mall, dropping my bags as I ran. Lightning continued to rip across the ceiling, and thunder cracked as I raced through the crowd and Miles and the boys from the Bronx gave chase. The ridiculous Atlantis show worked to my benefit, since the shoppers were all clustered and staring straight up and the mall was dark.

I did a nice spin move around some jewelry carts and ended up in front of Kenneth Cole, where I stuffed a couple of hundreds in the hand of the salesman who'd sold me shoes. Without explanation, he led me to the employee bathroom and shut the door behind me. I sat on the toilet in the dark and caught my breath. After a minute or two, I decided to check my texts while I waited for the coast to be clear of shortstops from summers past.

It was the usual. People asking about Belmont Park. ESPN colleagues looking for an interview. Threats from Bing Buli, who was combing Vegas for me. Guilt trips from Dawn, ending with one that read, "I would have loved you if you let me. Goodbye, Ray." And then one from L saying, "We need to talk," which are four words that have never managed to appear next to each other and connote any kind of positive feeling whatsoever. I started erasing them all. As I was flushing the sewage of drama and disappointment from my phone, the door to the bathroom eased open and the salesman hit me with an "OK" sign. I handed him whatever loose bills I had left in my pocket and scurried back out through the mall, where the sky on the ceiling had returned to blue and announcements of lost kingdoms and foolish pride were momentarily past. I made it out of the Forum Shops, through the Caesars casino, and hopped back into the limo, where Lyle was waiting.

"Where's the nurse?"

"She went to do some volunteer work," I said.

"Volunteering to spend some of your money, maybe. Where to?"

"Base camp."

"Right on. You got any more weed on you?" he asked.

"Not on me. I'll hook you up later, though."

"Sweet. Hey, let me ask you: You the dude who was with that fag Coco last night?"

I looked out the window as we pulled onto Vegas Boulevard. Cowboy Bob was back on the sidewalk in front of the Imperial Palace, his broken body jerking this way and that amid the neon chaos. Tourists walked around his chair, ignoring him. I thought again of Howie Rose. What if it was him? I mean, if someone were putting him out there to collect money, they wouldn't use his real name. They'd stick a stupid hat on him and call him Cowboy Bob or something equally pathetic, wouldn't they?

"You hear me, dude?"

"What's that?"

"Coco. You the guy who was with Coco last night?"

"He was our driver, yeah," I said.

"Fuck happened to him? Pole smoker totally flaked. They just found his ride out near Barstow."

I closed my eyes and laid my head back as we inched up the boulevard in bumper-to-bumper traffic. "I don't know," I sighed, staring back at Howie Rose/Cowboy Bob. "I really don't know what could have happened."

CLOSURE

February 11

. . . then he left some crazy note about how he was starting to read the Bible because he wanted to take an interest in the things I was taking an interest in. He read a little bit of the New Testament and concluded that Peter was worse than Judas. Judas had sold Jesus out for thirty pieces of silver, he said, but he had felt bad about it and hanged himself, so that made it OK, whereas Peter kept denying Jesus, and then when the coast was clear, he was right back by his side as if nothing had happened. So that was his takeaway from the New Testament. That Peter was a jerk, and Judas got a bad rap.

WHEN I GOT BACK TO THE MGM, I signed for a quarter million and started playing $10,000 per hand, three hands at a time, right off the bat. The casino was relatively empty, nothing like the night before, and neither were the cards. I'd win two hands, lose two. When I caught a nice shoe, a shit shoe followed. I'd get up a little, give it back. Get down a little, win it back. Mota and a couple of the pit bosses stood nearby with their arms crossed, waiting impatiently for a collapse. In the back of my mind, I knew that if it came down to it, I could arrange to play one hand, win the Kinder House, or go bust, but I never really thought about doing it like that. I had won the first $650,000 so easily that it didn't seem like it would be long before another run came along and I'd get where I needed to be. If I went for it all and lost, it would all be over, and I couldn't bear to think about that.

An interesting thing happened after a while: Playing the chocolate $5,000 chips provided no substantial sense of excitement whatsoever. In gambling, as in all things, the longer you do something, the more you get accustomed to it, and the quicker it becomes a grind. Your first $5 bet is as nerve-racking as any you'll ever make, and over time you have to keep raising the stakes to try and replicate the feeling you once got with a single red chip sitting in front of you. And this is ironic, because the reason a lot of people wind up in casinos is because their lives are short on the spark, the jolt of adrenaline that gambling gives you, yet in the end the betting life loses its juice in the same way that all the other things that led you to the casino lost their juice. I could see this phenomenon occur with just about everyone I ever played blackjack with. There's no getting around it.

I know what the logical question is: Why do it in the first place? And if you start doing it, why not stop once you've figured out that it fades like everything else? Well, the first part I've talked about. You start because there's something lacking in your life, and it's pretty easy to get into it after that, because gambling is the type of thing that makes you forget all about whatever it was that got you into it in the first place. Any boredom, any loneliness, is forgotten pretty quickly once you start playing, because the world of gambling is designed to allow you to think about exactly nothing outside of it. There are always new books to read. New slang to learn. New strategies to try out. There is nothing that happens in the outer world that you don't begin to think about in gambling terms. Even the weather becomes not a series of meteorological patterns but specific events you can bend into opportunities if you can solve the riddle not of the causes behind them but of the results they will yield. When you watch the rain falling outside your motel window on a Saturday night, you don't think about the things normal people think about (how this will affect my garden, will Uncle Doyle's party have to be moved inside?), but rather what impact it will have on the total number of points scored in the Giants game up the road at the Meadowlands the next day. You lie in bed and listen to the rain fall and think it will make for a low-scoring game, since it will be too slippery to pass the ball and both teams will rely on the running game. Running plays keep the clock moving, you think, and that will shorten the game and keep the score down. You make a mental note to call Bing Buli in the morning and drop a bomb on the Under. A minute later, you roll over and consider the fact that the receivers know where they're going and the defensive backs don't, so the slippery turf will lead to a lot of broken coverages and big plays, thus actually making it *easier* to score, not harder. You pat yourself on the back for your cleverness and make a note to call Bing Buli in the morning and drop a bomb on the Over instead.

"Fine," you may say. "I can see how you could possibly get sucked into it. But why not get out when you can see the trouble it's causing? Or at least stop when it gets as dull as everything else?"

This is an understandable position. After all, a logical person with a modicum of perspective would begin to tabulate the financial losses, or at least the personal ones, and make some changes. But gamblers are not logical people. They have as much use for practicality and logic as a baboon does for silverware. And most of them don't think they have a problem, or at least not a problem that one good run couldn't fix. While it would be easy to write this off as typical addict denial at work, I have to point something out: Gambling is unlike any other thing you can get hooked on. Why is it unique? It's unique because gambling has a possible payoff built into the rush. With other addictions, the equation is simpler. Take cocaine, for example. With a habit like coke, the deal is pretty basic: You put your money down, you get the rush you paid for. You do it again, same thing. Buy, get high. Buy, get high. You can like how it feels, you can look forward to the sensation, but there is no larger history of anything positive coming out of the experience. The shortest book ever written is probably titled *Cocaine Success Stories*. Once you start down the road, the map is pretty clear. There is no upside outside of the moment itself.

And this is where gambling differs, because it's the only addiction that offers these twin attractions: heroes and takebacks. Amarillo Slim. Nick the Greek. Johnny Chan and everyone who's ever won the World Series of Poker. Arnold Rothstein fixing the 1919 World Series. Hell, even Newman and Redford, all smiles at the end of *The Sting*. All those guys were action junkies, sure, but they *won*. And that's why betting offers a complexity that drugs or booze or sex or food or whatever else it is a person gets hooked on doesn't. Gambling gives you the takeback. The opportunity to experience the rush *and* win money after you do. And for extra encouragement, it gives you a glamorous group of people who succeeded before you.

See, with gambling, you place a bet, and inherent in that act is buying yourself some juice. Some action. So you get your adrenaline rush, and then after you get the boost, there stands close to a 50/50 chance that you'll come out *ahead of the game*. Even when the dream of winning is gone, it's easily replaced by the dream of getting even, which can be almost stronger than the dream of winning. After all, winning involves imagining what you don't have, while getting even merely requires you to remember what you did.

In the end, of course, getting even is just as much of a mirage as winning was, because it's not only money the gambler loses but time itself. This is a beneath-the-surface fact, though, and can be easily ignored when you're deep in the betting life. It's relatively simple to lie in bed at night and plan your grand comeback in a way that other addicts can't. For this reason, there's not a drug user in the world who hops out of bed at seven A.M. and thinks about what an amazing day it's going to be, but I can promise you that seven A.M. will find scores of gamblers eagerly and optimistically scouring the morning lines, or cranking up the cars they've let the maintenance slip on and tooling up the highway to the casino. And all of these people, no matter how far in the shits they may be, are thinking the very same thing: Today is the day. Today I turn it all around. If you were to advertise for it, "Gambling: The Hopeful Addiction" would probably be as good a slogan as any.

I treaded water for about ninety minutes before Renée came marching through the casino, followed by one of the bellhops, a thin, acne-riddled kid who was about six-six and straining badly under the weight of about fourteen shopping bags he was carting for her.

She came up to the table and laid in to me. "I appreciate you letting me get all this stuff, but what gives, leaving me in the middle of the GD mall?"

She had her hands on her hips, and the way she was standing reminded me of the way Dawn looked whenever I'd go MIA for a few days and pop up next to whatever slot she was working at Mohegan Sun. It was a look of bitterness and exasperation, and behind it were confusion and hurt feelings more than true anger (if you pissed people off as often as I did, you learned the subtle differences pretty quickly).

"I mean, *cheese and rice*, Raoul, even Leslie never left me alone like that. Well, he did, but that's how he is. I don't know how *you* are, but you're not supposed to be like *that*. You're supposed to be a whatchama-callit. A gentleman."

"I'm really sorry," I said. "I was feeling sick as hell and couldn't find you in the crowd after that whole Atlantis thing. I needed to get back here and rest."

"You don't look like you're resting to me."

"I was just, you know, playing a quick hand."

"Well, you didn't have to take the thingy," she said. "The limo. It was, like, a real pain to get all these bags in a cab. And then I had to tip him extra for his help. He was a perv, too."

The bellhop looked at me and shook his head as if to make sure I knew she was talking about the cabdriver and not him.

"I mean, you could have taken a cab if it was so GD important to run off on me. Unless you were, like, ditching me. Do you want me to go away?"

"Who said anything about that?"

"I'll go away if you want me to."

"Nobody said anything about anybody going anywhere," I said.

"I was afraid I was getting on your nerves."

"Not at all."

"Leslie used to say I talk too much. Do I talk too much?"

"I don't think you talk too much," I said. "Plus, Leslie shoots deer. You can't listen to what anybody who shoots deer says. They're the *last* people to listen to."

"OK. But if I start talking too much, just tell me and I'll zip it."

I started to get up from the table and then was overcome with the urge to let it all ride. There was about $250,000 in front of me, and if I lost, I'd still have a million (including my cash), and if I won, I'd be at 1.5 and only $500,000 from the Kinder House. I could scoop that up in a night.

I looked at Renée and asked if she'd ever seen anyone bet a quarter of a million dollars on a hand of cards.

"As if," she said, while I waved my hand toward Mota and the pit bosses to indicate that I wanted to play it all.

Mota said, "Whatever you like, Raoul."

"Let's do it," I said to Mota. "Let's play the two-fifty."

Renée covered her face with her hands. "I'm, like, not even looking. Tell me when it's over."

In the movies, a hand like that takes forever. It's agonizing. Every turn of the card takes thirty seconds. The dealer breathes deeply before each turn. Time stands still. But in real life, time doesn't stand still at all. This is how fast a hand of blackjack happens in real life: about seven seconds.

.01: 7 my way.

.02: Dealer card down.

.03: Jack my way: 17.

.04: Dealer card 6.

.05: "Stay" hand wave.

.06: Dealer hole card king.

.07: Dealer draws an 8. Busts.

Done.

"You can open your eyes now," I said to Renée.

Mota plastered a pained smile on his face and croaked out a "Nice one, Raoul" as Renée jumped into my arms.

The bellhop who was saddled with the bags took a long look at me, then at the half million in chips being stacked up on the table, then at Renée. He sighed and lowered his head for a moment. There was no doubt that he was either: 1) contemplating the gross, immeasurable injustice of life; or 2) very seriously considering choking the life out of me with Renée's belly chain. Suffice to say he thought I had it all.

I added the chips to my account, and Renée and I went back up to the suite. She threw her bags down and glanced at the new watch she was sporting. "Augh. I'm outy. I gotta cover for Cecily tonight."

"At the club?"

"Duh."

"Call in sick."

"*She's* sick. That's why I'm covering."

"Quit, then."

"Are you Froot Loops?" she said, fixing her hair in front of the mirror. "I need that job. I mean, it's not like I have some sugar daddy taking care of me. This girl's on her own."

She took a quick glance at me in the mirror to gauge my reaction. I looked away. I could feel her face fall. But then she bounced right back. She was a rubber ball at heart.

"Oh, 'member the girl I was telling you about last night? The one I moved here with who thought she was hot shit 'cause she used to be in a Nielsen family a million years ago?"

"Yeah," I lied.

"She couldn't wait to get out of Blowhio 'cause it sucked so bad, but then she forgot how shitty it was and started saying things like 'Don't you miss back home?' And I'd be like, 'Are you *crazy*, Denise? What's to miss about a bunch of losers and some shitty factory? I mean, even the snow's dirty.' But she forgot what it was really like and ended up going back, and now she's knocked up. All she does is text all day and complain how much she hates being preggers and how Donnie the loser won't even admit the kid's his. She's one miserable bitch right now. Her and her swollen feet. I just got a text from her. That's why I'm whattya-calling. Talking about her."

"That's too bad."

"It is for her," she said, popping a piece of gum in her mouth, kissing me, and heading for the door.

"When are you coming back?" I said.

"I gotta work, and then I gotta do a girl thing, and then I gotta play bingo with Lou Ann, and then—wait, do you want me to?"

"What?"

"Come back?"

"Of course."

She looked at me skeptically. The ball had bounced back the other way. "I thought that maybe you were gonna Laika me."

"I do like you."

"Not *like*. *Laika*. Laika the Space Dog. I thought maybe you were gonna do me like the Russians did her."

"I'm gonna go ahead and say I have no idea what that means."

"I did this report at school once. It was about Laika the Space Dog. See, the Russians, they wanted to get to space faster than us. I don't know why. There's nothing out there. Anyway, they figured they'd put an animal in orbit. See how that went. So they got this stray dog named Laika. It was the cutest thing ever. They brought her to the astronaut place and trained her, and then the night before they were gonna do the launch, one of the scientists took her home. She got to go to a real house for the first time ever, and there were kids there. She was super happy and finally had a family, only it was BS, 'cause he took her back the next day and put her in a rocket and blasted her into outer space. The Russkies tried to tell everyone she was fine. They made a big hero out of her, and lots of people thought she was still out there alive, a dog in space, but that wasn't true. She didn't last but a few hours before burning up. It was all a lie. Every part of it was a lie, even though they put her on a stamp, I think. Anyway, I didn't want to get Laika'ed, you know?"

"I'd never Laika you," I said.

Renée smiled broadly. Ran over and kissed me again. She was such a sweet kid. "Well, I'll see you tomorrow, then! Like, maybe around dinnertime or something like that? I literally know this place that sets your dessert on fire, if you want to go there."

"That sounds awesome."

"Right?"

And out the door she went. Why I had invited her back when I had no intention of even being there the next night, I have no idea. Her instincts were right. I was treating her exactly like Laika the Space Dog. I mean, the way things were heading, Marty would have the Kinder House paperwork in motion before Renée finished her shift. I made a mental note to text her before I left so she wouldn't arrive back at the MGM and find me gone. A girl like that would be devastated to learn I had vamoosed after I had just promised not to. Once she had a few years in Vegas behind her, she'd come to expect it. Her trust would be shot. I thought about how it would be for her after a few years in that neon Dumpster. Eventually someone would talk her into doing something for money because they knew how desperate she was to avoid going back home in defeat. It wouldn't be anything too bad. A local automotive calendar, maybe. One of those garage, bikini, wrench shoots. Then they'd suggest a thing similar to it, just a little worse, and then something a pinch more compromising after that, and well, that's probably how it'd go until she wasn't a rubber ball anymore. I had met a lot of girls like Renée during the summer L and I lived in Los Angeles. Girls who worked on porn shoots in the Valley. Cyrus, the screenwriter's brother, knew a lot of them, and all of their stories seemed to start with a garage, a bikini, and a wrench. It was too grim to think about. I decided to text her right away and tell her there was an emergency with my plastics company and I had to split on the first flight out I could get.

I took out my phone. Again, there were just numbers everywhere. Six billion missed calls, twelve billion texts, a couple billion voice mails. Before I could start writing to Renée, I saw L's new number near the top of the scroll. This time, her text read, "We REALLY need to talk."

If the four words *we need to talk* are about as bad as it gets, adding an all-caps *REALLY* takes it to a level you just don't want to go to. On one hand, I was dying to hear her voice, and any contact was better than no contact, but on the other, there didn't seem to be much of a chance that she had anything positive to say to me. If she knew how well I was really doing, that'd be one thing, but she didn't. All she knew was that the police were after me and I was all over the television. I decided to hold off on calling her and turned on the tube to see exactly what information was out there now. I figured I'd find out what she knew, and then at least I'd be prepared to explain myself and assure her that it would be sorted out soon. I popped a couple of painkillers, poured myself a vodka pineapple in a silver tumbler, and turned to ESPN. It was my old show, and a roundtable of reporters was discussing my situation. They were all guys I used to be friends with. People whose destination weddings I attended. Men I'd shared a lot of laughs with. And they were killing me.

"I don't know what the man is thinking. Ray, my brother, you lost the plot, kid. You gotta stop runnin' and own this."

"From what we're hearing, he's obviously got a gambling problem."

"'Course he's got a gambling problem. Why do you think he's not here anymore? Let's get real."

"Neighbors are saying he kidnapped a dog."

"That's crazy right there."

"You got time to take your Twitter down, you got time to turn yourself in."

"From that new video going around, Ray's in Vegas. That's not a good place for him to be. Man's gotta get some help."

They cut to footage someone had taken on a cell at the Forum Shops: Miles and his pals chasing me through the mall. It was like watching someone else entirely. I turned it off. It wasn't what I needed to see before calling L back. I killed the tumbler of vodka in a big gulp. That got me going. Then I did a little shadowboxing in front of the window to pump myself up. Maybe I was looking at this the wrong way. She had reached out to me. Twice. I had no proof that it was going to be negative. Those four words (and then the all-caps fifth) were *usually* harbingers of doom, but not *always*. Life was unpredictable, after all. You never knew what was coming. A life of following sports had certainly shown me that underdogs like the '04 Sox pulled off upsets all the time. And who was a bigger underdog than me?

I refilled the tumbler, took a deep breath, and dialed. And I'll be damned if the Ancient Mariner himself didn't pick up L's phone.

"Let me talk to my wife," I said.

"Excuse me?"

"I said let me talk to my wife." I was agitated. Enough was enough with this motherfucker.

"*Your* wife? I've got a little news flash for you, Ray—"

"*Give me that.*" It was L. She had yanked the phone out of old Gray-beard's mitts. You had to love that. She still had the old spark in her. Yoga hadn't taken that away.

"I've been trying to reach you, Ray."

"I know. I've been kind of busy."

"Busy being a fugitive, maybe."

"I'm not a fugitive," I said, going on another coughing jag.

"Raymond, you may recall that I know a thing or two about the law. Trust me when I tell you you're a fugitive."

"I've got everything under control," I spat out.

"That's fantastic. You can tell that to all the policemen and reporters back at the house. You're in a lot of trouble, Ray."

"I'm telling you: I've got it covered. Everything's gonna work out a lot better than you think it is, trust me. I'm on the verge of—"

"You're on the verge of going to jail, is what you're on the verge of. If you don't die first. You sound horrible."

This was an excellent sign. She was showing concern.

"I'm not worried about it."

"Naturally."

"I was surprised Old Man River answered the phone," I said. "Isn't it past his bedtime?"

"Don't start, Raymond. I will hang up this phone."

"Where are you and the Old Rooster at, anyway?"

"Never you mind where we are. And you're not getting any younger yourself, mister. At the rate you're going, your next birthday cake is going to have a file in it."

"Good one, Boo."

I figured any form of humor, even at my expense, was a good sign, though I needed to shift the conversation away from my legal difficulties and from exposing too much about the plan. I was a rotten secret keeper, a giver of birthday and Christmas presents days too soon, and if I stayed on the phone too long, I could well blow the surprise. Then again, hearing her voice was so sweet, I didn't dare shorten the conversation. Plus, she hadn't told me why she wanted to talk to me yet. I walked toward the window. The roller coaster twisted and turned over at New York, New York. People threw their hands in the air. They were having a good time. Why not? You only went around once.

"Hey," I said. "If we got back together, do you think we can still beat the Fishers? Or does the divorce screw that up?"

Right before I got exiled, we saw a story on TV about this couple, Herbert and Zelymyra Fisher, who had gotten married in the 1920s and stayed together eighty-seven years, which was the record for the world's longest marriage. It was a dream of mine to top it. A long shot, I know, but still.

"I've got something to tell you," she said.

"I've got a lot to tell you, too."

"Listen. Boyd and I—"

There was a knock at the door.

"Hold on just a sec," I said.

I walked over and opened it. It was room service. They had the wrong suite. I shooed the guy away and strolled back to the window. "Sorry about that. It was room service."

"I'd ask what you were doing, but I really don't want to know," she said in that new tone of hers that wasn't all that new. "I got a series of strange messages from someone named Coco, by the way. I don't suppose you know anything about that."

"I have no idea what you're talking about."

"That's what I figured you'd say," she said.

"I'm in Vegas right now."

"Another stellar decision. Nice, Ray."

"It is nice. See, I finally got that money from the old man—"

"I am *not* talking about your father. I forgive you. I pray for you. But I cannot talk about that. Do you understand?"

"I wish you'd let me explain."

"I'm going to hang up this phone if you say another word about it," she said, and she meant it. I was already kicking myself for having brought it up.

"Fine. Fine."

"Do we understand each other?"

"Roger that."

"Good, then," she said.

"But can I tell you one thing? About the frogman coming out of the lake? I've been dreaming about him, and it may mean something important."

"I'm hanging up."

"OK. OK. Jesus." I took a swig from the tumbler. Changed course. "Want to talk about the Bible?"

"No, I do not want to talk about the Bible. Why on earth would I want to talk about the Bible?"

"Because you're into that kind of thing ever since you met Father Phil."

"His name is not Father Phil. Father Phil is a television character."

"You know what I mean."

There was silence on the other end. I shouldn't have mentioned Father Phil, either. I needed to shut up. Or stick with something I knew.

"I've been getting back into Warren Zevon," I said. "He has very unique characters in his songs, don't you think?"

More silence. Stolen-journal references weren't smart. C'mon, Ray.

"I told you I took personality tests for us, right? We're total opposites. And I took a life expectancy test. I'm going to live till ninety-one. I tried doing one for you, but I didn't have all of the answers healthwise. I texted you about it."

Nothing.

"You seen any good movies lately?"

"No," she finally offered.

"That's because you haven't been with me," I said cheerfully.

"I don't want to talk about the movies."

"You love talking about the movies."

"Not anymore."

"Does Boyd like them? Or does he miss the silent ones he grew up with?"

"I'm getting married, Ray."

I've been accused many, many times of hearing what I want to hear.

Usually by L, come to think of it. What I wanted to hear in this case was "I want to get married again, Ray," which meant "I want to get married to you again, Ray," which meant "We're still married, Ray." I swear I heard it that way.

"That's so great," I said.

"What?"

"I feel the same way."

"The same way as what? What are you talking about?"

"I feel like we're still married, too," I said.

There was silence for a second or two. It was nice. I basked in it.

"I'm getting married to *Boyd*."

"I'm sorry?"

"I'm marrying Boyd. That's why I wanted to talk to you. I felt like I owed you that much. I felt like I owed you this conversation. So we can finally have closure."

"Closure?" I mumbled.

"Yeah," she said very, very softly. Sweetly. Her old voice. "Closure."

I didn't say anything for I don't know how long. I just stared at all the brake lights blinking on and off and on and off up and down the boulevard. Where was everyone going? Where was there to go?

"Boo?"

"I'm here," I said.

"I'm sorry. But you need to accept this."

"It doesn't make any sense," I said.

And it didn't. It couldn't. I had a million and a half dollars. I had a plan. And she was my wife. Someone else can't marry your wife. It doesn't work that way.

"I'm sorry."

"You're supposed to come back," I mumbled.

"You don't want me back," she said. "Trust me."

"I don't— Where are you? I'm coming there right now."

"You're not coming anywhere," she snapped. "This is the end of all this craziness. Do you understand me? *The end of it.* I want you to let this go once and for all. I want you to let me live my life."

"I never touched Dawn!" I shouted. "Why won't you believe me?"

"I *do* believe you. This doesn't have anything to do with that. This is just—this is just what it is. This is where I need to be."

"And where exactly is that?"

"Ray," she said, and then I heard her say *five minutes* very softly to someone else.

"Put that old bag of bones on the phone!"

"No, I will *not* put him on the phone," she said. "This doesn't have anything to do with him."

"That decrepit old poacher steals my wife, and *it doesn't have anything to do with him?* Are you insane? Put him on the goddamn phone."

"Ray, you keep talking like that and I will hang up on you. I don't want this conversation to end like that."

"I don't understand this," I said. "This doesn't make any sense."

"You're not going anywhere. And if you don't turn yourself in, you'll be arrested at the airport anyway."

"Why?" And I meant that. A guy like me didn't belong in *jail.* That made no sense.

"Are you kidding me?"

"Where are you? L? Where are you? I want to know where you are."

She didn't say anything. I wish I could tell you what I was feeling then, outside of waves of panic and confusion, but I can't. Panic and confusion don't let you feel anything *but* panic and confusion. They *own* you.

"You were born to be with me," I said.

"That's not true."

"You're telling me you were born to be with Old Man River? Mr. Personality is going to take my place? Are you serious? He's gonna be your Clyde?"

"We're not Bonnie and Clyde, Ray."

"Sure we are. We said we were."

"We said that a million years ago. And even Bonnie and Clyde weren't Bonnie and Clyde. She was an uneducated woman in the Depression. Her family was poor. She had no job prospects outside of prostitution. She stayed because she had no options, OK, Ray? It wasn't a love story. It was pragmatism."

I had no idea whether she was right or not, but why spoil the story like that? Why was she being so hateful?

"You blame me for everything," I cried. "But I was on tilt."

"I was angry. Of course I was angry. But I prayed and prayed, and I'm not angry anymore. I just want to move forward with my life. Be a better person. No one's to blame. This is just what happened."

"How can you be a better person? You're the best person I know." Tears started streaming down my face. I didn't even bother to wipe them.

"I'm not, Ray. I'm not. I'm trying to do better. I'm trying to change some things."

"This doesn't make any sense. We didn't have to change anything. We were perfect."

"That was a lifetime ago. And we weren't perfect. We were children. Don't you see how selfish we were? We only did for each other."

"Who the hell else were we supposed to do stuff for?" I cried.

"I can't get into this with you, OK? I can't. I just wanted to tell you about me and Boyd. I just wanted to say goodbye to you with a good feeling in my heart. You were my whole life for so long. I'll never forget you. I'll carry you everywhere. But this ends for me right now. This part of my life is over."

That was too much. I started sobbing. I was wailing so hard I could barely breathe. L didn't say anything. She didn't comfort me. Maybe because she had never heard that kind of sound come out of me. I don't know.

"This can't be happening," I finally choked out.

"It's already happened," she said quietly. "It happened a long time ago."

I slumped down against the window. The room got fifty degrees colder. My God. It *had* already happened, hadn't it?

"But—"

"Goodbye, angel."

UP POPS THE DEVIL

October 30

. . . one time I even heard bells going off and asked him about it, and he said it was someone from the Salvation Army. I said, "But it's April," and he said, "I know. It's weird, right?" Another time he sounded terrible and wondered if he had seasonal affective disorder. That was in July, which I pointed out. His response? "Can you not get it in July?" How was I supposed to know he was gambling and doing God knows what else? Casinos are the saddest places in the world. It never occurred to me that he'd have any interest in that.

AFTER SOBBING TO THE POINT OF throwing up, popping one too many painkillers, and drinking two full tumblers of Absolut, I tossed on an MGM robe and slippers, put on my Ray-Bans, and shuffled to the elevators like a zombie. Bob Mota found me down on the floor within half a minute (the man was *everywhere*). He looked me over and said, "Hey, Raoul, how's your night?" like I was wearing a three-piece suit and not a fucking robe and slippers. Then he led me to a table, gave me a marker for a quarter million in chips, and handed my tumbler to a waitress to refill. There was obviously something very wrong with me, but Mota had a million and a half reasons not to ask questions, and so he didn't.

The chips had absolutely no value to me. I might as well have been sitting in front of a stack of peanut shells. The numbers on the cards meant nothing. Eights. Fours. Threes. I stared at them like I had never seen them before. I looked at the haughty little mustache the king of spades was sporting. Who did he think he was? Fuck him. The jack of diamonds gazed at me with weary eyes. What was *his* problem? He thought *he* had problems? Did he know what just happened to *me*? I sat there and looked at all the people playing cards nearby. Chewing their nails over some nickel bet. Praying for good things to happen. Celebrating minor detours on the road to the inevitable. What were they doing there? What did they think was going to happen? Didn't they understand what a rigged game looked like? Didn't they understand what a gross waste of time it all was? Didn't they know that you're supposed to take vacations to places of great beauty? Places touched by history and the imprint of true human endeavor? Places where you could learn something? Be astonished? Feel a sense of genuine possibility and community? What were they doing gathering in a rancid man-made shithole that appealed to the least original impulses in the human race? Didn't any of them know that the story always ended up the same way? Didn't anyone have any interest in saving themselves? Didn't they know that almost any endeavor in life was a better use of their time and resources than sitting at a stupid felt-covered table? And what the hell kind of material was *felt*, anyway?

I sat there and drank vodka like it was water and did whatever struck me at the time. Sometimes it was to play right, to hit and stick like I was supposed to, and other times it was to do the unthinkable, just to see how it felt. Which it didn't. Nothing did. You could have cattle-prodded me and I wouldn't have flinched. I stood on 7. Hit on 19. Doubled on 14. I played one hand at a time, $10,000 a hand. The dealers looked to the pit bosses whenever I asked for a card on an 18 or sat pat with an 8, and the pit bosses shrugged and acted like they didn't see what was going on. I never said a word to the dealers. When people who recognized me from my big run walked by and said, "Hey, Raoul!" I ignored them. Who were they? Did they know about L and Boyd? Were they trying to rub it in?

When my tumbler got empty, I'd silently hand it to the waitress, and she'd fill it. Every twenty minutes or so Bob Mota would ask if I wanted to take a break, if I was feeling all right, and I'd tell him I was fine. He didn't know what the hell had gotten into me, and he didn't care. If you live in Vegas long enough, chances are that you've seen everything there is to see many times over, and if some wack job in a robe wants to hit 19 on a $10,000 bet, then, well, so be it. Plus, what did he care about my motivations? What did he care if my life was over? He wanted the Grand's money back. He would have let me sit there stark naked, blowing a kazoo, if I was going to make it that easy.

When I got bored with blackjack, I wandered over to the baccarat salon and put $10,000 on one hand, even though I had forgotten how to play. A couple of Japanese guys in tuxedos looked at me like I was insane. After losing a quick ten Gs there, I put another ten on a hand of Caribbean stud poker, which I had forgotten how to play as well. I carried my plastic rack through the casino, stopping wherever it struck me. I put $10,000 on a counter in front of a giant wheel that looked like it belonged on the boardwalk. As I watched it spin 'round and 'round, I thought of the summers in Point Pleasant with L. The Bloody Marys on the deck of the Parker House. The nights dancing to the Springsteen cover band at Jenks by the Sea. The rainy afternoons drinking Rolling Rock and playing bumper pool at the Broadway on Randall Avenue. All the long, deep kisses in the glow of Ferris wheel lights. Tears were streaming down my face. The dealer looked at Bob Mota and Manny C., who had appeared and was following me like he was in the Secret Service. They shrugged as the wheel spun and clicked and spun and clicked. I leaned on the counter and wiped my face as the wheel finally stopped. I stared at it. "Did I win?"

"No, sir. I'm sorry."

"I understand," I said. "It's all right. No one's to blame."

I told Mota and Manny that I wanted to throw some dice and shuffled off to the nearest craps table in my robe and slippers, easing in among a small group at the south end of the oval. It was a $5-limit table, but Mota whispered to the box man and told me to go ahead and play whatever I liked. I signed another $250,000 marker. By that point, I could barely stand. I tried to focus, but I couldn't. I couldn't feel anything. The painkillers were overwhelming me, so I purposefully smashed my cast on a drink shelf on the underside of the table. *That* I could feel. *That* got the blood flowing. Then people started in on me. Commenting about my sunglasses. My robe. Calling me Howard Hughes. A group of frat boys at the end of the table kept asking to borrow money. I went from being on the verge of passing out to the edge of killing somebody. I felt aggressive all of a sudden. Unreasonably angry. I felt like everyone was on Boyd Bollinger's side somehow. That they had all been working against me. The frat boys especially. So I called Mota and Manny C. over. "Tell those Sigma Nu fuckers to beat it or I'm going to the Mirage."

Within fifteen seconds, the college boys were encouraged to go play elsewhere, and when the others at the table saw me flex my VIP muscle and ruin the run they had all been on, they grabbed their chips and left, too. The only person who stayed was an amiable office-supply salesman who wore a name tag reading HI, I'M EVERETT! He had hair the color of dead grass and was wearing an orange Illinois sweatshirt and matching hat. He was about Boyd Bollinger's age, and I figured it wasn't inconceivable that they knew each other. Bollinger looked like a guy who went to a Big Ten school that never won anything.

"Damn, Raoul. You really put their dicks in the dirt the other night," Everett from Illinois said. "I watched the whole thing. And thanks for that hundy you gave me. Or my wife thanks you. Women! They can smell it when you got a little extra scratch on you, can't they?"

I thought: Can you believe the nerve of this guy? Getting all chatty with me after going to school with Boyd Bollinger? *Rooming* with Boyd Bollinger, most likely. Writing fucking *papers* for the guy? I ignored him and looked at the table. It was filled with proposition bets. I knew those were for suckers, so I figured I'd play one of them. I wasn't sure what they paid, and there was no way I was going to ask Everett, who was a traitor and deserved to be shunned.

"Saw that little filly you were with the other night," he said. "She's a piece of work, isn't she? With all due respect."

I ignored him and grabbed a handful of chips. "Hard ten," I said.

The box man turned around and looked at Mota and Manny C., who nodded.

"Gentleman has a thirty-thousand-dollar hard ten."

"How much?" I said.

"Thirty thousand, sir."

"What does that pay?"

"Ten to one, sir."

"Stop calling me *sir*."

"Yes, sir," he said.

I glared at him, then grabbed another fistful of chips and tossed them on the table. "Same way."

Everett let loose a low whistle as the box man turned around and looked at Mota and Manny C. again. Manny said, "*Jesus Christ*, Vernon," and waved his hand as if to say, "How many fucking times are you going to ask the same question? Let the burnout do whatever he wants."

"Eighty-thousand-dollar hard ten," he said.

The stick man shoved five dice my way. I looked at them. Went completely blank for a few moments. Started seeing black lights.

"Any two you like, sir."

"Are you being lippy?" I demanded.

"No, sir."

"You call me *sir* again, I'm shoving that stick up your ass. It's just that simple."

"Easy, fellas," said Everett the Mediator, grabbing a couple of red chips. "Gimme a ten-dollar hard ten. Gotta go with my man Raoul. He's a lucky son of a gun."

I grabbed two dice, glared at the stick man, glared at Everett, and pitched them down the table.

"Gimme them puppy paws!" Everett shouted.

A pair of 4s finally settled down.

"Point is eight. Eight's your point."

Everett clapped his hands. "Eighter from Decatur. Got yourself a square pair, Raoul. Right in the old neighborhood. Now gimme that pair of roses."

I fired the dice angrily across the felt. They ricocheted around.

"Nine."

Everett slapped me on the shoulder. "What shot Jesse James? A forty-five. Almost, buddy. I know you got those sunflowers coming up next."

I took a swig from the tumbler. I could feel something boiling inside me. They weren't roommates at Illinois, they were *fraternity brothers*, Everett and Boyd. They knew secret handshakes and hazed farm boys who didn't know any better. Who just wanted to fit in. I whizzed the dice in disgust. A 7.

"*Seeeeeven out,*" said the boxman.

"Six one, we're all done," Everett said.

My chips were scooped off the table. I glared at Everett, then at the box man, the stick man, Mota, and Manny. I wanted to kill every one of them. I dumped the rest of my chips on the table like a child. "All of it. Hard ten again."

There was $170,000. Mota grimaced. He was thrilled when I was back at the blackjack table, inexplicably giving my money away, but now two random 5s on the dice would pay off $1.7 million. I grabbed the foam padding on the table and took a deep breath, not because I was nervous (my life had ended on the phone, what did I care about anything else?) but because I could barely stand up. Everything was blurry. I banged my cast on the shelf again.

"I like your style, Raoul," Everett the Two-Faced said. Then he made an elaborate display out of taking a $25 chip from his pocket and setting it on the table. Judging by the look on his face, you would have sworn we had the same bet out there.

"Heck with the dinner buffet," he said. "Gotta go with my partner in the fancy robe again."

In my former life, I would have liked the man. Would have valued his sense of camaraderie and pleasant nature. His sincere desire for fellowship and unassuming midwesternness. I'd met countless people like him on the road over the years, and normally I would have spoken to him as a friend. Asked about his kids. His take on parenting in the modern age. I would have asked for his and his wife's origin story. Perhaps encouraged some recollections regarding his collegiate affiliation. Memorable games. Favorite halfbacks. Opinion on concussions. I would have shown a great deal of interest in getting his take on the lay of the land from his corner of the world. We would have made fast friends in the Sheraton lounge. Maybe teamed up for group trivia. Bought each other drinks. Made vague plans to hook up next time I was passing through. Heck, Everett might have even wanted to get high for the first time since the late seventies, when everyone was experimenting. He might have kicked off his Thom McAns, taken a toke, and coughed his lungs out. Joked about being out of practice. All of these things could have happened once, but not now. Now I wanted Everett from Illinois in a wood chipper. I wanted to go *Fargo* on him.

"Make it happen, amigo," he said.

I whipped the dice so hard that one of them hopped off the table and plunked Mota in the shoulder. Everett said, "Whoa, Nellie!" and I was given two fresh ones. Threw a pair of 4s again.

"Mmmm, mmmm, mmmm. Ozzie and Harriet. Old Raoul likes the windows, boy."

My hands were shaking as the stick man sent the dice back my way. I flung them and came up with another 9. Everett started chirping immediately. "Nina from Pasadena . . ."

I whirled around on him. "Will you *shut the fuck up, Everett*? I mean, *Jesus Christ*."

His face sagged with shock and hurt. He put his hands up like I'd pulled a gun on him. He had no idea what had just happened. It was like kicking a friendly dog.

I grabbed the dice, tossed a 4, and looked at him. You could tell he wanted to say something, but he held it in. Same thing on the next throw, a 5. Then an 11. Another 11. A 6. Silence. Three. Five again. Eleven. Nothing from Everett. Another 6. Biting his lip. Still nothing. And then I tossed a 7.

"Up pops the devil," he muttered.

Before it was out of his mouth, I swung wildly and brained him with my cast. Pain shot through me like buzz saw to bone. We fell to the floor and rolled around a little before Manny C. and a couple of security guards separated us. Everett's Illinois hat sat on the carpet with his hair under it. He was balder than a bad tire. They led him away, red-faced and bewildered.

"You're a crazy person!" he shrieked. "A crazy person!"

Mota put his arm around my shoulder and walked me through the casino. Everyone was watching. You couldn't even hear slots being played. He told me to tie my robe, which was wide open. Members of a wedding party walked past and eyeballed me.

"What the hell are you looking at?" I hollered at the groom. "You think she's gonna stay with you? She's not gonna stay with you. She'll find somebody else. You hear me, you son of a bitch? She'll find someone else!"

When we got back to Mota's office, he told me to sit in the same chair I had a few days earlier. I felt like I was back in prep school, waiting to get expelled. The Lou Gehrig bobblehead seemed to move imperceptibly. Was he judging me, too? I slumped back in the chair. Rubbed the lapel of the robe on my cheek. It was a miracle I hadn't passed out. You have never seen someone so messed up in your life.

"Seems like you're a little under the weather tonight, Ray."

"I'm fucked-up, Bob."

"Well, how's about you call it a night and hit 'em again tomorrow? The tables, that is. Not the customers. I don't think you really want to be drawing that kind of attention to yourself. All things considered."

"All things considered."

"Right. Lot of these people probably watch the news, if you hear what I'm saying."

"I hear you," I said, and sighed.

"Good," he said, standing up. "Then we understand each other. You and the little lady need anything, you just call downstairs. Try and get some rest for yourself."

I suppose I should have been grateful for his kindness. He could have dropped a dime right there. But he wasn't motivated by goodwill. It was greed. I still had something he wanted, after all. Then again, what did it matter? Intent. Outcome. Goodwill. Greed. Luck. Fate. What did it really matter? Who gave a shit about the fine line that divided every last thing? Life was arbitrary. It was unfair. What you had today would be gone tomorrow. All was temporary. Anybody could be forgotten. The feeling love gave you—that you were heroic, that your life was epic—was a lie. You weren't heroic. You were nobody. Everything was nothing. In the end, your life was like a strand of Christmas lights wired in sequence. When one bulb went out, everything went dark. Everything stopped working. The light was gone. It would never come back.

"Fuck you, Bob."

"I'm sorry?"

"Fuck you. You're not my father. You don't tell me when to go to bed."

"Now hold—"

"Gimme the rest of my goddamn money. I'll go play at Caesars."

There is little to no question that he wanted to stomp the shit out of me right then and there. The New Yorker in him was telling him to climb over the desk and dish out some East Coast–style justice. But he wasn't on the East Coast anymore. And he had a job to do. And that job was making sure I left with nothing. Not even the robe.

"You want to keep playing, toughie?" he said, getting up. "Fine. G'head and play."

We marched across the lobby, where a boxing ring was being set up to promote a major fight. I had no idea who it was. That world was another I was once a part of but was now lost to me. Mota led me on into the casino. He was walking at a pace, no doubt wondering whether he'd done the right thing by not kicking my ass for telling him to fuck off. I weaved behind him, everything on the casino floor stretching and contorting like reflections in a fun-house mirror. I sat at my own table again and told Mota to get me a marker for $500,000. A young, handsome Korean dealer shuffled up. His name tag read HO. SEOUL.

"Hey, Ho," I said.

He remained expressionless.

"Little Ho Hum tonight?" Nothing.

Screw him, I thought, as another pair of newlyweds and their wedding party barged through the casino, making a big scene. The bride was falling-down drunk, and the groom had his arm around one of the bridesmaids. When Ho asked me if I was ready to make a bet, the groom reached down and grabbed a healthy handful of the bridesmaid's ass. I sighed, then put out a $100,000 play and adjusted my shades. Ho dealt me a 7, then a 4, against an 8. I doubled up, measuring another stack next to my first one, and drew a 9 for 20. He flipped a 6 next to his 8, snapped down a 7, and racked up my chips like he hadn't just handed me a brutal beat. It irritated me. A dealer's job is to say "Ouch" or "Tough one" or at least something that indicates he sympathizes with what just happened to you. Not Ho. Old Stoneface didn't make a sound. I contemplated my next bet as a waitress I vaguely recognized from the night before came over and put a vodka pineapple in front of me.

"What the hell is this?"

"It's what you were drinking last night."

"It's not last night anymore, is it?" I said.

I waved it away and ordered tequila. If she had brought me a tequila, I would have waved it away and ordered vodka pineapple. I wondered what Boyd Bollinger drank. Dewar's, probably. The fucker had Dewar's written all over him.

"Wait. What do old guys drink?" I said to her.

"I'm sorry?"

"Old dudes. Bring me whatever old dudes drink. Dewar's or something."

"What about the tequila?"

"Bring that, too."

I stacked up another $100,000. Ho fed me a 17. Turned an 18 without blinking and snatched my chips.

"You gonna ask me if I want a card next time, Hi Ho Silver?"

Ho sighed. Turned around to look at Bob Mota and Manny C., who had appeared. They were like peas and carrots, those two.

"Raoul's an unpredictable player," Bob said. "Don't deal without seeing what he wants to do."

"He had a seventeen."

"Don't deal without consulting the player. Understood?"

"Yes, sir."

"So I gotta eat that last one, Bob?"

"You tell me. Sharp guy like you gonna hit seventeen?"

"You never know," I said. "You never know what's going to happen in life."

My heart was still racing and my blood was sizzling. I kept seeing Boyd in bed with L. Revolting images caromed around inside my brain. I saw flashes of things that were horrible. Things you should never imagine. I shook my head and emptied the rest of my rack, stacking up $200,000.

"You ever heard of a guy named Boyd Bollinger, Ho?"

Mr. Personality shook his head. Dealt a 14 against a face. I hit. El busto.

"You gonna answer me or just fucking stand there?"

"Never heard of the gentleman, sir."

I told Mota to bring me another $500,000. In the meantime, my drinks arrived, and I slammed them both. I nearly threw up. But I told the waitress to bring me two more anyway. When my chips arrived, I dumped them on the table like a four-year-old playing with LEGOs. I must have looked like a maniac.

"Boyd Bollinger is the man who stole my wife," I continued.

"Sorry to hear that, sir."

"I don't believe you," I said. "I don't believe you care about that."

Ho turned around and looked at Mota and Manny C. again.

"Why do you keep looking at them? Bob, why does Ho Chi Minh keep looking at you?"

"Let's just relax a little bit, Raoul."

"I'm very relaxed. I'm cool as a fucking cucumber," I said. "Just tell your boy to deal the cards."

The waitress plunked down two more drinks, which I hammered back. I covered my mouth to keep from throwing up. More images of Boyd and L tumbled in my head. I couldn't shake them.

"I'm from Korea," Ho said evenly.

"I can read a name tag. Seoul. With an E."

"Ho Chi Minh is Vietnamese."

"Yeah? Well, Merry Christmas for him. You gonna deal cards or teach geography?"

I put out another $100,000 bet. Before I could even read my cards, Ho rolled an ace-queen. I could swear I saw a smile crease his lips.

"Like that, didn't you, Ho?"

"No, sir," he said.

"Bob, Manny, put this motherfucker on the next boat to Saigon. I want a new dealer."

Ho wiped his hands and gave me a curt bow that was soaked in disdain. There was no telling who wanted to kill the other more. Difference was that he was just a polite kid doing his job, and I was a chrome-plated asshole. There wasn't a lot of nuance to the situation. I stared into space until my old friend Patrice arrived at the table.

"How you doing, honey?"

"How'm I doing? How I'm doing is I lost my wife."

"That little blond girl? I'm so sorry."

"Not *her*," I said. "She's not my *wife*. She's nobody. She's from fucking *Ohio*."

I leaned back in my chair and turned around. A small crowd had formed, but not like before. Now they were keeping their distance a good ten feet behind me. Bob Mota went to disperse them after I hollered, "What the hell are you buzzards looking at?"

"Sorry about that, Raoul."

"It's not the fucking zoo, Bob," I said, ignoring the fact that I had turned his floor into a raging house party not a day earlier.

"You're a hundred percent right," he said.

"I mean, *it's not the fucking zoo*. Do I look like a panda to you? Patrice?"

"No, Raoul."

"Exactly."

"You sure you want to keep playing, sweetheart? You look worn out."

"Oh, for fuck's sake," I said without placing a bet. "Deal the cards."

I just sat there for a while, Boyd and L doing the most heinous things imaginable in my head, before Manny C. coughed and said, "What's

the play, guy?" I glared at him and shoved my entire rack out in front
of me: $400,000. No one in the history of legalized gambling deserved
to lose more than I did.

"This is the play."

"Raoul."

"What, Patrice?"

"Look at me," she said.

"Deal the cards."

"Maybe you want to go slow? Have some coffee?"

"Deal," I said. I couldn't even look at her. She was too sweet.

"I'm really sorry about your wife."

"Deal."

"Honestly I am."

"Deal the fucking cards, Patrice."

"Yeah, Patrice," Mota said.

"Shut up, Bob," I snarled.

"Hey."

"You, too, Manny."

Finally she started dealing. She had no choice. But I never looked
at her. I just stared straight down. A queen slid into my line of vision.
Then a 5. I looked at her up card. A 3.

"He's fifty-five years old," I muttered.

"Who is?" said Patrice.

"The guy who stole my wife. Can you imagine?"

"Handsome fella like you won't have a problem finding someone
new."

"I don't want someone new," I said. "I want L."

"The pretty blond girl seems to like you."

"I told you, she's nobody."

"Don't give up. You never know what's coming your way in life.
That's the best thing about it."

"Really? I think it's the *worst* thing about it," I said.

"Everything has a way of working out, even though you can't see it."

"I don't know," I said. "I don't know what to do."

"Fifteen on three. You know what to do."

"Hit me."

"That's not what to do," she said.

"It doesn't matter. He's fifty-five. He'll be dead soon. We'll all be dead soon. Hit me."

Patrice hesitated. I could feel her trying to make eye contact. I couldn't look at her. She was so earnest. I didn't deserve her kindness.

"You heard the player," Manny C. said. "Hit him."

She sighed and gingerly turned over a king. "I'm sorry, Raoul."

I sat there and didn't say anything. I had just gone through more money than some people will make in their entire lives. Bob Mota came around the table and reached into his coat pocket.

"Gimme another five," I said.

"There is no other five. You're done."

"I'm done?"

"This is what's left."

He handed me a thin envelope. I handed it right to Patrice.

"And we checked your credit. It's not so good."

"No?"

"Not particularly, no. And there's something else I didn't tell you, *Ray*. I'm a big racing fan. I was at Pimlico when de la Maria won the Preakness. So I'll give you, say, thirty minutes before I place a few calls. Have a nice evening, scumbag."

Just as he said it, a cold wave hit me in the face, like someone had dumped a vanilla shake on me. My shades were coated and I couldn't see a thing. When I took them off, there was the bride I had insulted earlier, holding an empty White Russian. Why did girls drink those things? Didn't they know how fattening they were?

"I'm never leaving my man. You hear me? *Never.* We're gonna be happy, you stupid faggot!"

She marched off toward the elevators. Bob Mota took out his handkerchief and handed it to me.

"Here you go, Ray. It's on the house."

YOU LIE BING BULI

June 4

Today he came trudging through the woods with a flashlight like a crazy person. If I were a gun nut, I probably would have shot him. He wanted to tell me about a friend of his who had fallen out of a tree when he was a kid. This after that insanity last week with the newspaper article. Do I have him arrested? Do I move into the city? What?

I GOT IN A CAB OUTSIDE the MGM and rolled off down Vegas Boulevard, a Grand duffel bag holding more than $200,000 on my lap, the remnants of what was left in the safe. I had thought about tossing it all on a hand of blackjack before I left, but Mota was serious about calling the police, and what did it matter, anyway? While I wasn't really thinking about anything other than the news about L and Boyd, I'd eventually need money to survive, because there was little to no chance that I'd turn myself in at any point. I mean, no matter what mental state I was in, I just wasn't the kind of person who would surrender to authorities and take his punishment. I certainly didn't think I belonged in jail, though there's no way that fate could have been worse than the one I'd just suffered.

The cabdriver was from somewhere in the Middle East. He wore a turban. Normally I would have asked him about that, since wearing a turban post-9/11 can't be comfortable, socially speaking, but what did I care about that? Why should I give a shit about his problems? Did he care about mine?

The TV screen in the back of the cab played an ad for some movie in which Liam Neeson played the father we all wished we had. I pawed at the screen until the sound finally muted.

"The movies—they all are the same now, my friend," the driver said. "Boom boom boom."

I gazed blankly out the window. Lights. Cars. People. Pointless bullshit piled onto pointless bullshit. Boom boom boom was right.

"He is a fine actor," he continued. "A learned man. I do not like this Charles Bronson nonsense he does now. It is insubstantial. The man played Oskar Schindler, for heaven's sake."

I thought of a story I'd heard about Neeson's wife, Natasha Richardson. She'd fallen while learning how to ski on a bunny slope in Canada. She'd thought it was nothing. A pedestrian thump on the noodle. A handful of hours later, she was dead. L had cried about it for days. She had met her in New York once.

"You must honor your talent," the taxi driver said. "Talent is a gift from God. What you do with it, that is your gift back to God."

I ignored him. Thought of the Professor. The pie case. The ruination of the world. The hopelessness of it all. All around us, horns blared. People stood three deep, watching the fountains dance in front of the Bellagio. Jesus Christ—they were watching fucking water. It was so depressing.

"Why should Liam Neeson give a shit about God?" I said.

The driver kept his hands steady on the wheel, but his eyes darted to the rearview. They said, *What the fuck kind of question is that?*

"Seriously. His wife died on a bunny slope. Normal day. Beginner's ski lesson. *Poof.* It's over. God can take away your wife on a fucking bunny slope, and you're supposed to give a shit what kind of movies you do after that? He lost everything. What does it matter what he does now? I mean, Liam Neeson is supposed to care what— What's your name?"

"Sameer."

"He's supposed to care what Sameer the cabbie thinks about his artistic choices? He lost his wife. Do you even know what that means? To lose someone like that?"

We stopped at a light. Drunk college kids ran across the clogged boulevard, holding plastic fish bowls filled with grain alcohol and a dab of food coloring to make the poison palatable, all of them racing toward some more pointless bullshit. That's the crummy cycle of life right there. Lovely colored water for fairy wings turns into grain alcohol in plastic fish bowls.

Sameer turned and looked at me through the plastic divider. "I have lost three children," he said evenly, holding up a trio of crooked fingers.

He turned back around. He no doubt saw me as someone who didn't get it (and you couldn't argue with his instincts), but at that moment, all I could think of was how *he* didn't get it. How *no one* got it. The only person who got it wasn't around to get it anymore. It occurred to me that the only thing worse than no one in the world getting what you got was one person getting what you got whom you couldn't see anymore. Whom you'd lost. It was worse that way. Lonelier.

I stole a glance at Sameer. He probably thought I didn't care that he had lost three children. Maybe he thought I was one of those Americans who didn't give a shit about the terrible things that happened to anyone who was brown and spoke in halting English. He might have thought I felt like he had brought it on himself, with his turban and his opinions on Hollywood. But that's not what I was thinking. What I was thinking was, what was so terrible about being dead? I mean, what did the dead have to worry about? Did the dead care if some silver-haired motherfucker was waking up on their side of the bed? Of course not. The dead didn't give a shit about that kind of thing. If you were dead, what would it matter whom your wife was talking to in the shower? What would it matter whom she was watching movies with? Or having sex with? If you were dead, you wouldn't care about any of those things. The dead didn't have those kinds of images searing their eyeballs out. The dead didn't have rusty hacksaws pulling down hunks of their hearts. Even if there were a heaven and hell and you ended up catching a bad beat on that decision, what could happen in a cauldron of eternal fire that could possibly be any worse than losing the greatest thing there ever was? What did I care about the devil? I already knew him. He drove a champagne Lexus with a MERCHANT OF TENNIS bumper sticker. He'd RATHER BE GOLFING. He invented a plastic contraption to throw tennis balls to dogs with. The devil didn't wear red, he wore khaki. And the devil didn't carry a pitchfork. He carried a sand wedge. No one needed to tell Ray Parisi to worry about the devil. It was too late for that.

I leaned my head against the window. To the left, the fountains in front of Caesars were awash in pink lights, and then farther down, the volcanoes in front of the Mirage rumbled and burst, the flames glowing orange over a rock pool of rippling water. Farther up the boulevard, a huge crowd leaned on thick rope railings and watched a pirate ship in front of Treasure Island. Cannons boomed, and swashbuckling thirtysomething actors swung from crow's nests and ripped sails, most of them having fruitlessly spent their twenties in Los Angeles and were now on the slow road back from where they came. Everyone ooohed and aaahed and took cell phone videos. It was all anyone ever seemed to do there. *Watch.* The place is the watching capital of the world.

"Those people should all have to walk the plank," I said, nodding at the group in front of Treasure Island.

Sameer ignored me. I glanced to my right. Another crowd of gawkers was surrounding a Plexiglas booth set up on the sidewalk just past O'Sheas. A young, toothy guy in a tuxedo wielded a bullhorn, announcing that a cash-giveaway promotion was about to begin, and I watched as an elderly woman was led inside the booth. There was a countdown, and then money started swirling around her. She grasped futilely for dollar bills, moving far too slowly to have any chance. When her time was up, she was empty-handed, and the crowd booed her. She had to be eighty years old. As the onlookers dispersed (with the promise of more humiliation to come in exactly half an hour), I spotted Cowboy Bob/Howie Rose out in front of the Imperial Palace. He was sitting in his miserable chair and jerking his head from side to side. The more I looked at him, the more I was convinced it was Howie. No one was fooling me as to his real identity, and whether it was the pills, the booze, or the heartbreak, I felt like I had to do something. Set one thing right before whatever became of me became of me.

"Let me out right here," I said, reaching for the door.

"Sir, you cannot—"

I handed Sameer a hundred through the opening in the divider. He sighed and switched lanes. I jumped out. The heat was ungodly. Brake lights blinked for miles in either direction. I started to walk away, then turned and knocked on the passenger window. He lowered it.

"I'm sorry about your children," I muttered.

He looked at me curiously. Didn't say anything.

"Sameer?" I said. "I'm sorry."

The light turned and he inched away. I crossed the boulevard, weaved my way through the crowd in front of O'Sheas and the Imperial Palace, and before you knew it, I was gripping the handles of the wheelchair. I had no plan whatsoever. I just started rolling the cripple down the street, pushing him along the crowded sidewalk stretching in front of Harrah's and Casino Royale. Right as I got near Denny's, out came the fat son of a bitch with the beard and the van, wiping his filthy face on his Margaritaville T-shirt. Suffice to say he was startled to see someone making off with his meal ticket. I whirled around and headed back the way I'd come, weaving in between clusters of tourists, with him hollering, "Hey! Stop! Hey! *What the fuck are you doing?*"

I got as far as the Imperial Palace when a guy handing out sex leaflets grabbed an armrest and sent Bob/Howie pitching forward onto the sidewalk. Just as he went tumbling from the chair, I heard someone shout, "Oh, OK. Oh! You son gun Parisi!" and looked up to see none other than Bing Buli standing on the other side of Vegas Boulevard, shirt buttoned to the neck despite the heat.

Clutching the bag of cash, I left Howie and bolted off through the Imperial Palace driveway, where the giant lightbulbs on the roof of the covered drive make you feel like you're inside a pinball machine, and then continued down an alley between the Imperial and O'Sheas. I looked back and saw Bing dodging traffic. He was still yelling, "Oh, Parisi! Oh, OK! Parisi!" I ran another hundred yards down the alley, ducked under a grove of trees, and emerged in a parking lot, where I could smell fresh tar from a steamroller. Across the street, two kids sat on top of a corrugated tin carport roof and tossed pebbles at me. Bing's voice was getting fainter, and by the time I zipped past an empty Ramada security booth and hopped a low stucco wall outside the Cascade Warren Apartments, I was safe. I crouched behind the wall to catch my breath, and for a good ten minutes I watched a woman do a graceful backstroke in the apartment pool. I thought of L. Of how we used to sneak into hotel pools in Myrtle Beach, and how she liked me to carry her around in the water. I could feel her slick legs. Her arms around my neck. The sun on our faces. Her eyes as she looked at me, full of love. I cried softly in the darkness, but the woman never heard me; she just glided across the surface, lost in her own world. I closed my eyes and pictured L's face. It floated at the end of a long string, and I pulled it toward me. I looked at her eyes. What color were they? I could not say for certain. But I could say that if you took two perfect gray stones, set them in a lush green field, let a blue rain fall down for ten thousand days until the rain seeped into the stone, and the grass seeped into the stone, then you could *begin* to get an idea of the color. But that wasn't quite right, and I tried to look closer, to describe it to myself another way, but I heard the splashing of water, the woman getting out of the pool, and L's face floated away. The string slipped from my hand. It was gone.

I opened my eyes. Though the pool was empty, I heard some chattering around the corner. The kids. And Bing Buli. No one else sounded quite like him. I could have stayed hidden. There was no chance he would see me. But I didn't. For some reason I stood up and started yelling his name. I'd love to tell you why, but I can't. Maybe I wanted to punish myself. Maybe I wanted to feel something other than what I was feeling. Maybe I wanted to see a familiar face. Who fucking knows?

"Bing! Bing Buli!"

Moments later, he entered the gate to the pool area. His shirt was buttoned up. It was 738 degrees out. He had been running. But he was not sweating.

"Hey, Bing."

He squinted, his small, rough face illuminated in the glow of the swimming pool lights. We looked at each other for what seemed like a long time. He was no doubt taking in my appearance. Cast. Dyed hair. Scratches on my face from my scrap with Everett from Wisconsin. Bloodshot eyes from pills, booze, crying, bronchitis, and crushing and eternal defeat at the hands of an elderly foe.

"You TV," he finally said.

"I know."

"Lot TV."

"Yeah," I said. "A lot of TV."

I looked closer at Bing's face. Hard times were etched all over it.

"Fat man say you here."

"Maurice. His name's Maurice Boudreaux."

"You lie everything," he said.

"I know."

"Mother say Ray good. No believe. You Thanksgiving no more."

"I'm sorry," I said.

"You have money?"

"No."

The money was in the bag at my feet. I have no idea why I said I didn't have it. I think I knew that if I gave it to him, that would be it.

He'd take it and move on. But that shouldn't have been it. I had screwed him over thoroughly, and then when he'd given me a second chance, I had screwed him over again, only worse. I didn't deserve to just hand over my father's money and walk away. I deserved something worse. I *wanted* something worse. I wanted what was really coming to me.

"No money?" he said wearily.

"No."

"Oh. Oh. Son gun. Son gun, Ray."

"I, you know, had it," I said. "But I blew it. I gambled it away."

Bing nodded. Put his hands behind his back like he was standing in front of a casket. "You gamble."

"Yeah."

"In the Las Vegas."

"In the Las Vegas."

I looked him in the eye. He didn't seem mad. Just sorry.

"You run Bing Buli," he said.

"I know."

"You lie Bing Buli."

"Yeah."

He sighed. "Oh. No choice. No choice."

"I know," I said. "I understand."

He shook his head grimly, and then he put me down with an open hand to the throat. He followed it up with a few shots to the face, his little fists like cue balls against my head. Even if I had fought back, I would have been no match for Bing, who was a professional and had slugged his way out of the Philippines, where fighting didn't mean putting someone in a headlock by the bike rack after school. He had suffered in life. He knew what he was doing. I hadn't, and I didn't. And he showed me the black lights.

I woke in a puddle of water by the pool, the two delinquents from the roof taking turns dumping a small plastic bucket on me and enjoying the hell out of it. Bing was gone. But the bag of money wasn't. It was sitting on the ground next to me, and I reached out and grabbed it with my good hand as a handful of people who lived in the apartment complex peered out through screen doors. In the distance, I heard the sound of sirens. I don't know if they were for me, and I wasn't about to stick around and find out. I reached into my pocket, pulled out a couple of hundreds, and handed them to the kids. My vision was blurry, and I was in more pain than I could ever remember being in before, but damn if they didn't look like the western version of those two little bastards who started all of it back in the motel parking lot with their bullshit fireworks.

I staggered down Flamingo Road, the lights of the Strip behind me. My lip was split, and I could feel my face swelling up. I started coughing, spat up some blood for a new wrinkle on things, and reached into my pocket for a bottle of painkillers, sitting down on the curb and working the top off with my teeth like an animal. I choked a couple of pills down dry, which I thought was going to make me vomit but merely resulted in more blood being spat out on the road, where cars rushed past and a billboard featuring the magician Pooh Jeter had run off with loomed. In the distance I could see the glowing neon guitar sign in front of the Hard Rock Hotel. I looked in the bag. Fished around with my good hand. I could tell it was light. Instead of twenty straps, it felt closer to fifteen or sixteen. And then it dawned on me. Bing had taken his money and left the rest.

I sat on the curb, covered in sweat. In dirt. In my own blood. My rescue of Howie Rose had ended like everything else had ended. It was a joke, like everything else was a joke. A complete and utter failure brought on by impulsive decision-making and terrible judgment. So what did I do but pull out my phone and make another stupid and impulsive decision.

"City and state, please."

"Essex Fells, New Jersey."

"How can I help you?"

"The number for Howard Rose, Senior, please."

"There's a Howard Rose on Vine and a Howard Rose on Rose-land," said the operator.

"Rose on Roseland."

"Hold for the number, please."

When I heard it, I was struck with another pang of sorrow. It was the same number from when I was a kid. I thought it might be the last thing in the world that hadn't changed.

"Hello?"

"Mr. Rose?"

"Who's this?"

"Ray Parisi."

"Who?"

"Ray Parisi," I said. "Howie's friend."

There was a long pause.

"Dominic Parisi's kid?"

"I guess."

"Whaddya want?" he demanded. "I'm going to work."

"What's that?"

"I said whaddya want?"

"I was calling about Howie," I said.

"You're calling about Howie?"

"Yeah."

"Is this your idea of a joke, Parisi?"

"No, sir."

"Then whaddya want?"

"I wanted to know if Howie lived in Las Vegas, by any chance."

"What?"

"Does Howie live in Las Vegas?"

The line went silent for about five seconds. I thought he might have hung up. Maybe he had done something. Maybe he was responsible somehow.

"No, Howie does not live in Las Vegas. What kinda question is that?"

"Are you sure?"

"He's been dead for eleven years," he snapped.

"What?"

"He's been dead for eleven years. You might have known that if you ever came to visit the kid."

"He's dead? How is that possible?"

"Are you on drugs, Parisi?"

"Some."

"Your father must be proud of you."

"He died," I said.

"Oh yeah?"

"This summer. He died. He left me six hundred grand. I don't know why. I don't know why he did that."

"I don't know why he did it, either. Now, if you don't mind, I gotta get to work."

"Six hundred twelve thousand, five hundred."

"Wonderful," he said. "Sounds like you're spending it wisely."

"I gambled it all away. Pretty much."

"Terrific."

"A lot has happened."

"What do you want, Parisi?"

"I wanted to know about Howie."

"Well, now you know."

"I'm sorry," I said. "He was a really good kid."

"I know he was a good kid. Think I need *you* telling me he was a good kid?"

A car sped by. Nearly ran me over. I didn't flinch.

"I guess you loved him."

"Of course I loved him. He was my goddamn son, you fucking fruitcake."

"That makes sense."

"Not for nothing, but you might want to consider getting yourself some kind of help."

"That's probably not a bad idea, sir. I'm a little fucked-up. I lost my wife."

"Your wife died?"

"No, she left."

"Well, that happens," he said.

"That happens?"

"Yeah, it happens. Shit happens. Where the fuck you been you don't know that?"

"I don't know."

"You want some advice, Parisi?"

"I could use some of that, yeah."

"Here's some advice, then: Call somebody who gives a shit. Or go fuck yourself. Either one."

HERE WE ARE NOW,
ENTERTAIN US

September 15

"The Pretender" came on Spotify today when Boyd and I were making break-
fast. It was the first time I've heard Jackson since I wore out "Late for the Sky"
after R and I collapsed. It's funny how you begin to feel once you've healed. I'd
thought "Late for the Sky" was the song that would always remind me of R,
of what happened to us, but I'm not in that place anymore. In reality, "The
Pretender" is the right song for R. I'm even beginning to find some compassion
for him in my heart, though admittedly not as much as I wish I could. Anger
is such a debilitating emotion. Poisonous and useless and small. I'm trying to
let it all go. He was a person who never had a childhood but also never grew
up. A person who never knew who he was, or at minimum couldn't admit who
he was. You have to feel a little bit for a person like that, don't you? To be a
person who has to pretend his entire life is beyond sad to me . . .

WITH THE BLOOD DRIED AND THE bag of cash in my hand, I wandered
about the Hard Rock Hotel in a daze, making my way past a long line
of display cases stuffed with music memorabilia. Familiar faces that had
beaten Kurt Cobain to the "27 Club" (Joplin, Morrison, Hendrix)
gazed out through glass, all of them young and invincible and mere
months away from their inglorious end. They were sad to look at, as
was a nearby photo of Paul and Linda McCartney, young and sun-

splashed and in love. I thought of listening to the Beatles on Saturday mornings in Myrtle Beach. Lucille would make biscuits and sausage gravy and dance around to "I Should Have Known Better" and "Eight Days a Week" and the rest of those jaunty '62–'66 tunes John and Paul seemed to zip off in their sleep. Thinking of how alive she was in those days before she got sick depressed me even more, and then it got worse when I chanced upon a picture of a boyish and barefoot Jackson Browne sitting in an open van somewhere on the California coast, his silky hair dangling in front of his eyes and the Pacific rolling in behind him. L played "Late for the Sky" nearly every day after she got home from South Carolina, and it was the last music I heard in my old house before the deal went down. The mournful slide guitar on the title track played over and over in my head during those early days at the Motor Lodge and nearly drove me mad with anguish. For my money, there isn't a song anywhere that's as heartbreaking as that one.

In the corridor outside the Pink Taco restaurant, a group of impossibly good-looking LA types was loitering around the hallway, talking to Mötley Crüe drummer Tommy Lee. He was holding court in front of a cigar shop with a giant mural of Che Guevara on the wall, and one of the hipsters pointed at it and said, "Check it out, it's that guy from the T-shirt." Zeppelin poured out of the overhead speakers, Robert Plant wailing about how it'd "been a long lonelylonelylonelylonelylonely time" (no kidding) as I made my way past more cases filled with KISS dolls and *Welcome Back, Kotter* lunch boxes and kitschy memorabilia of just about every pop icon you could imagine. I had never felt less nostalgic in my life.

The casino itself was like none I'd ever seen. A circular-shaped bar sat in the middle of the floor as a centerpiece, as if to suggest that gambling was secondary to socializing, and high-cheekboned twenty-somethings walked blithely past tables covered in purple felt. Giant blue globes hung from the ceiling in cast-iron casings, and inconvenienced cocktail waitresses strutted beneath them, looking for all the world like they had merely shown up to hang out and suddenly had drink trays thrust into their hands. It was late. Even the people who wanted to be there didn't want to be there anymore.

Dozens of guys who looked like they didn't care if they got a good night's sleep before their next soap-opera casting leaned on the circle bar, scoping out anything that was in possession of breasts and a pulse (the former more of a must than the latter). Behind the front desk, a sign read HERE WE ARE NOW, ENTERTAIN US, and just off the entrance, a cluster of guys who had taken advantage of a "Buy One Hip Black Suit, Get Two Free" sale at Men's Wearhouse hovered around a glass case containing one of Prince's outfits from the *Purple Rain* days.

"Dude was a fucking midget," one of them said.

"Yeah, but he got a crazy amount of ass," said another, and they high-fived and headed toward the circle bar.

I walked up to the cashier's cage and tossed my MGM bag on the counter. The second it landed, Erik, a floor manager with his hair slicked like Michael Douglas in *Wall Street*, popped up next to me and started a spiel. I let him gasbag for fifteen or twenty seconds before stopping him.

"OK. Honestly, what I want is all of that in dime chips, and that's it," I said. "I don't want any comps. I don't want anything but to be left alone. If that's not cool, I'll go somewhere else, 'cause I don't give a shit anymore, Erik with a K."

"Not a problem, amigo," he said. "But we've got to punch some forms for that kind of paper."

"Tell me where to sign, then leave me alone."

"Whatever you want, man," he said, signaling for a cashier to get the paperwork. "We're all about rock and roll and good times."

"Good times," I said.

"Ain't no other kind."

"Are you being serious?"

"Like a heart attack, bra."

"Get the fucking forms, Erik."

The music was good, the cards were bad, and by four A.M. the money was gone. The end of the inheritance. I sat in a side lounge off the main floor next to the Sports Book and got drunk for a change. It dawned on me fully and completely that it was all over. L and Boyd were getting married. I was broke. The cops would find me anytime. The best I could do was hop a bus to California, or Arizona, maybe, and live out the next fifty-six years of my life as Raoul McFarland. I drank Absolut on the rocks until I was so depressed that all I could think about was dying, and the different ways I might do it, and how all of them were nothing compared to what had already happened. I tried to think of something decent, anything, but nothing came to mind, and for a long time I just sat in the lounge and cried.

At one point a young maid came through with a vacuum cleaner. I had never seen anyone clean a casino before. They were places that just seemed to get spotless in the same way graffiti just seemed to appear on the sides of buildings. It was strange to see it taking place. I stumbled to my feet and tried to help her, but she didn't want me to.

"I can help. Let me help," I said, grabbing the vacuum.

"*No es necesario, señor,*" she said, and backed away from me.

"I can do it," I insisted. "I can help you. Let me help you."

"*Señor, por favor. Lo siento. No. No, señor.*"

The bartender looked over, and I could tell she was thinking about calling security. A grown man, drunk and in tears, grabbing at a vacuum cleaner at the crack of dawn was strange even by Vegas standards, so I did all I could, which was let go and sit back down. I pulled out my phone and looked at it. I wanted to call somebody, but whom? Who was there to call? Messages piled up even as I looked at the screen. Everyone I ever knew had heard about the Belmont Park incident. Friends. Neighbors. People I worked with. All the countless human beings I had met over the years but didn't really know.

I stared at the screen saver. It was a picture of L when she was three.

One Lucille had given me my first night in Myrtle, when we watched *The Man Who Never Was* and I started to get comfortable in my new life. Then, for some reason, I decided to call the Motor Lodge. I wanted to say something to Maurice. What, I do not know.

"Parkway Motor Lodge."

"Is Maurice there?" I said.

"Who this?"

"Let me talk to Maurice."

"Maurice is off, man. This is Angel."

"Angel. It's Ray."

"Holy shit, man! Bro. Bro. You are up *in it*."

"You do me a favor?" I said.

"Up in the shit."

"I know," I said. "I'm aware of that. You do me a favor or not?"

The maid ran the vacuum past me and did not make eye contact.

"Shit, you gave me that Mookie ball for my brother," Angel said. "That was straight up."

His brother, a fan of the '86 Mets, had been sick during the spring, and I had forged Mookie Wilson's signature on a ball for him.

"But I ain't doing nothing illegal," he continued. "This job is six kinds of bullshit, but it's all I got."

"I don't want you to do anything illegal. I just want you to go to the pound, pick out a dog, and give it to Maurice."

"What?"

"Maurice," I said. "I want him to have a dog. It doesn't have to be big. It can be a small dog."

"You want me to give the fat boy a dog?"

"Yeah."

"You kind of a crazy motherfucker, Ray."

"Can you do it?"

"What it run me?"

"It's free," I said. "They're free."

"Free I can swing."

"Get him a nice one. Small. But not mean. Make sure it's sweet."

"Sweet?"

"Yeah."

"You *crying*, Ray?"

I drained the last of my drink and wiped my face. I had no idea what I was talking about or where the dog thing had come from. Somewhere in my mind, I recalled Maurice saying, "I had a dog once, too." It must have been that.

"Will you do it right away?"

"I'm on it tomorrow. I'll take LaLa with," he said. "She can pick it. I don't know shit about dogs."

"Thanks, Angel. And one more thing."

"Digame."

"Don't let the Sarge take any more videos of Maurice."

"Yeah, that's fucked-up."

"It's so fucked-up," I said. My voice was shaking.

"Yo, you all right, Ray?"

I didn't say anything for a few seconds. I just stared at the bartender, who was wiping down bottles, and tried to pull myself together.

"And don't let him shoot any more deer."

"Yeah, that was fucked-up, too."

"Listen. You know a girl named Rosario Nuñez, Angel?"

"Don't know her."

"From Bridgeport," I said.

"Uh-uh."

"She's dead. She died."

"Never heard of her."

"It was in the paper."

"I don't read that shit," he said, and I heard a bell ringing in the distance. "Got enough bad news of my own. Yo, take it easy, Ray. Stay low. I gotta split. But I'm on that dog for you."

I hung up, wiped my face again, and dumped what was left in my pockets on the table in the lounge. I had a $100 bill, a $20, and a $500 chip that I'd meant to give to my cocktail waitress but hadn't. I gave the bartender the C-note and walked through the casino. It was late, and barely anyone was left on the floor. I could have cashed the chip in, used the money for a bus ticket, like I said, but I didn't care anymore. I walked up to my cocktail waitress and was about to give her the chip when she shuffled past me and said, "Cool your jets, Tiger. I'll get to you when I get to you. You don't need another drink, anyway."

I sat down in the empty Sports Book and stared at the final scores from the day's action. There was a time when I would have analyzed things, thought about who I might have taken and why, looked at the futures board, but not now. Now it was just a blackboard with lights. I pulled my phone back out and dialed one more number.

"Yellllo."

"Is Penny there, please?"

"You've got some balls, Ray. I'll give you that. I wouldn't mind cutting them off for you."

It was Dawn's sister, KC. She wasn't what you would call a fan.

"That seems extreme," I said.

"There's nothing I could do to you that would qualify as extreme, trust me. Been following you on TV, by the way. Nice work. You'll look great in orange."

"Where's Dawn?"

"A lot you care about Dawn."

"Where is she?"

"Dawn's not here, and if she were here, she wouldn't want to talk to you. Listen to me good, Ray. Get lost and stay lost. She finally met what seems to be a halfway decent guy the other day, and you don't need to be messing it up for her. It's not like you want her. Do the right thing for once in your life and leave her alone."

"Is it Ken from the aquarium?"

"Never fucking mind who it— *What? No, honey, you need to go to camp. And no swearing like Auntie KC. Swearing is bad. Even if you're talking to someone you detest.*"

"Let me talk to her," I said.

"There's no reason for—"

"Come on, KC. Just for a minute. I won't call again. I promise."

"She thinks . . . well. We told her some things."

"It's OK."

"Is it OK, Ray? I'm *so* glad you feel that way. It's *such* a relief."

The black-suit brigade walked through the Sports Book and stared at the board. They argued over Super Bowl future odds, the very bet I didn't place for Maurice, and took turns farting in each other's direction and cracking themselves up. I got up and walked back toward the lounge.

"Just let me talk to her for one minute," I said to KC.

"Then you promise you'll get lost?"

"Yeah."

"You have one minute," she said. "*Penny? One minute and then we're leaving, OK?*"

"*OK!* Hey, Uncle Ray!"

Her voice was enough to break your heart.

"Hey, baby."

"How's Brazil?"

"How's what?"

"*Brazil.*"

"Oh, Brazil's good," I said. "Very hot."

"What's it like there? I haven't Googled it yet."

"Well, it's hot, like I said. And there's a lot of South American people running around in white suits."

"How come?"

"'Cause they're fancy like that, I guess."

"Oh. OK. What time is it there?"

"I'm not sure. I lost my watch on the boat," I said.

"The boat carrying the palominos?"

"Sure. What did they tell you, exactly?"

"First I was mad when they said you couldn't take me to Central Park, but then Mom told me about the sick horses and how you were helping them, and then I wasn't mad anymore. I was being selfish. But now I'm not. Mom said you were going to a place in the mountains where there were no phones and that you'd be gone for a really long time."

Jesus. Even Dawn had given up on me. And why not? What the hell did I ever do to deserve anything from her?

"I am. I'm leaving right now. I wanted my last call to be to you."

"Really?"

"Of course. You're my girl."

"Why do you have to take the horses to the mountains? Why can't you take them where it's flat and you have a phone?"

Depression aside, it wasn't hard for me to continue the story. I always found it easy to talk to kids as long as they belonged to somebody else. And lying, we know, I've never had a problem with.

"Because there're healing springs there, and they don't have them anywhere else, and if we don't get them there, then they'll die," I said. "There's an epidemic all over the country. I've got twelve other people on my team, though, so I think we'll be able to save this batch and send the boats back for more."

"How did they get sick?"

"The people who were supposed to take care of them didn't do a good job," I said. "They didn't pay enough attention."

"But you're there now, so it'll be OK. *I know!* Aunt KC says I have to go."

"Don't go."

"Gotta."

"Tell me one more thing," I pleaded.

"Like what?"

"A fact. Something you haven't told me."

"I told you about the torpor."

"I know about that. Yeah."

"Lemme see. Oh. Sea horses are the only ones where the males carry the babies. Isn't that crazy? Boys carrying babies! Gotta go!"

"I love you, P."

"I love you, too, Uncle Ray. I'm proud of you for saving the palominos. 'Bye!"

I sat there for a long time and thought about how I'd probably never see Penny again. And how there was no one left for me to call. From the day I met L, there were always people around. When we lived in Atlanta, we were friends with everyone in Cabbagetown. We played on the softball team of L's firm. There were always parties to go to. Concerts to see. Even around town, you'd always run into people you knew from hanging out in different neighborhoods. People in Little Five Points you'd always see at shows. People at the farmers' market in the Highlands who were there every Saturday. People you'd run into at the Starlight drive-in. People tailgating in Athens. It was a full world. We played touch football in Myrtle Beach with the same group for years. When we moved back north, there were scores of people to see. L and I had to turn down invitations just so we could stay home together. There may have been a time, probably after my mother died and I went to prep school, when I knew something about loneliness, but if so, I don't remember it. I can't say whether my ability to make friends with just about anyone was something that came naturally to me or whether I developed it, but it didn't seem to matter. It all came so easy. If I got tossed out of one school, I'd just make friends at the next. It wasn't a big deal. I never spent a single nervous second in any room I ever walked into. But sitting there looking at my phone and realizing that there was no one left to call, I understood that all of the people I had met along the way were not really friends but just people with whom I shared something small and inconsequential at one point or another, and that L was right. I didn't have any true friendships at all. I had L, and I don't think I ever thought I would need more than her, and so everyone else just got whatever was left over. Loose joints and signed balls and good humor when there was time to kill.

After I started gambling, normal, stable people didn't have anything to do with me. I didn't know anyone like that anymore. The only people I did know were on the outside in some way, short on whatever the things were that made life something you were able to bend to your own will instead of being crushed by. I knew impressionable, fatherless little girls like Penny. Hopeful single mothers like Dawn. There were immigrant bookies like Bing Buli, who had no friends, and overweight motel clerks like Maurice, who also had no friends. These were the kinds of people I had come to attract. And the fact of the matter is that I took advantage of people like that. For companionship. For places to stay. For money. For convenience. The moment I got L back, they all would have been forgotten; I would have left them behind in a flash. Even then, even in Vegas, I found myself attracting those kinds of people. People who were hoping for something from me that they would never get. As I sat in that lounge, looking at that phone, there were not enough pills or bottles of Absolut in the world to keep me from facing the singular truth of my life: In one way or another, I had disappointed everyone who had ever cared about me.

As I walked across the casino floor, I saw Tommy Lee sitting at a roulette wheel. He was wearing a wifebeater and a straw cowboy hat with an exaggerated curved brim. Both his arms were covered in sleeves of ink. Sitting next to him was a girl with short pink hair whose implants looked like they might explode if she exhaled too heavily. I watched him play for a minute, and then something happened that I don't have any explanation for and am not going to speculate about, because you can go down the rabbit hole with that kind of thing and end up drawing some ridiculous conclusions. I had bronchitis, after all, and was treating it with copious amounts of pills and alcohol. I was concussed from Bing's beating. What happened could have been caused by dizziness and blind luck as easily as, say, divine intervention. I really can't explain it, but it happened nonetheless, and all I can do is tell you what happened and let you draw your own conclusions.

As I watched the ball settle into a slot on the wheel and the board get cleared of chips, I saw the number 11 swell to twice its size for a split second. No longer than one flicker of a caution light. I blinked and looked again, but nothing happened. I doubted I had seen it at all, but I was exhausted, and clean out of hope, so I placed my $500 chip on the 11. The Who's "Won't Get Fooled Again" was playing, and Tommy Lee slapped his hands in perfect time on the girl's knees. "Fucking Keith Moon, man," he said.

The dealer looked at the denomination of my chip, called out the play to a nearby pit boss, got a nod of approval, and whipped the ball around the wheel. It went around, around, around, around, around, around, around, around, around, around, around, lost steam, fell, clicked into one slot and another and another, hopped up, clinked and clacked, and made one last little *oomph* into place.

"Eleven winner eleven."

Tommy Lee slapped his cowboy hat on the table. "Dude! That's seriously fucked-up!"

The dealer called both Erik and the pit boss over, and Erik shrugged as I was paid out at 35-1. It came to $17,500. He didn't care. I had already lost $150,000 before that. And I'd probably give it right back in five seconds.

"Killer call, bro," Tommy Lee said. "You got the touch."

"This was Dostoevsky's game," I said.

"Here's to the motherfucker," Tommy responded, raising a shot glass and knocking back a Jägermeister.

I handed my original $500 chip to a passing waitress, then stared at the board, and once again a number swelled for a brief second. This time it was 23. I muttered, "The next number's twenty-three," to no one in particular, and Tommy Lee handed the girl with the pink hair a $100 chip and said, "Here baby, put this on twenty-three for Dostoevsky."

"Let it ride on twenty-three," I said.

The dealer was shocked and looked at Erik. He put his finger up, said, "Hold on a sec," and then disappeared over by the cage. As we waited, "Every Rose Has Its Thorn" came on. Tommy Lee shook his head in disgust. "What a buzzkill."

"Little 'Girls, Girls, Girls' would be nice," I said flatly.

"That's what I'm talking about, dude!" Tommy Lee sprang up and gave me a half hug and a soul handshake.

"You got some nice work there," I said, nodding at his tattoos.

He smiled. The girl looked at him and said, "When are you gonna get *my* name, Tommy?"

He held out his arms. Turned his hands over and said, "No room at the inn, baby."

Erik came back, gave the go-ahead, and the dealer zipped the ball. It went around for an eternity. I didn't even watch it. Everything had suddenly become clear to me. I knew what was coming.

"Twenty-three!"

The dealer's eyes bulged. Erik pinched the bridge of his nose. Tommy Lee slapped my back and said, "Holy shit, dude!" and the girl with the pink hair tried to give me a hug but could barely reach. Her boobs hit my chest like an air bag. Tommy Lee was ecstatic. He kept shouting, "What's next, kemosabe? What's next?"

I eyeballed the board. Nothing happened. And why would it? 11/23 was my anniversary. There was no number left for the year.

"I don't know," I said. "I don't know what's next. I'm all done."

"I like a man who knows how to go out on top. That's totally cool," said Tommy Lee.

Later, at the cashier's window, the only female over thirty-five in the entire building counted my chips. A couple of people stood behind her and watched.

"OK, Mr. Lucky. That comes to a total of—"

"Six hundred twelve thousand five hundred dollars," I said.

She looked at me. "That's right," she said. "Six one two five. How'd you know?"

"I don't know," I said. "I just had a feeling."

SOMETHING'S UP
IN MEMPHIS

May 1

It was a wonderful performance. One of those nights when Broadway feels like the center of the universe. I hadn't seen any Shakespeare in I don't know how long. Boyd had such interesting things to say as always. We ate hamburgers at Junior's like teenagers. I remember seeing Romeo and Juliet *with R once. He went on for an hour about how it was all the Friar's fault. Anybody who wore the cloth was suspect to him. He brought up Pastor Perry time and again. Father Phil, he calls him. He thought Romeo and Juliet would have lived happily ever after if it weren't for the Friar's meddling: He came up with the idea. He screwed up the letter. What business was it of his? What kind of crazy person suggested taking poison? Why didn't he get punished for it? God, that was a long train ride home. R wasn't goofing around like usual, either. He absolutely felt that the Friar was the only thing worth discussing as far as the tale of the Montagues and Capulets went. He kept on it the entire next day . . .*

I STOOD OUT IN FRONT OF the hotel and watched the sun rise over the Spring Mountains. Hipsters who had pulled all-nighters poured out of purple Hard Rock limos, stumbling toward the entrance of the hotel as I hailed a cab, climbed in, and told the driver to take me back to the MGM. There I was in Vegas, with $612,500 and a dream once again, heading toward the emerald gates to see if I could get things right the second time around.

See, something had occurred to me while I stood outside watching the first cathartic light of day break over a place that didn't deserve such softness and wonder. *She wasn't married yet.* L wasn't married. L was *getting* married. No one in their right mind got married during the week unless they were eloping, and she hadn't said anything about that. There was no present tense around the word *marriage.* It was future tense. And the luggage I saw on the day I borrowed the dog suggested some kind of destination, which also pointed to traditional weekend nuptials and not some town hall quickie. It was still dawn on Friday, after all. At worst, she'd be getting married on Saturday, and since that was the Fourth of July, it might even be Sunday. Granted, my obstacles were greater than ever, but if the roulette miracle had taught me anything, it was that you were never dead. I had heard countless athletes run out some version of "It ain't over till it's over," usually when they were on the brink of playoff elimination, and you know what? Sometimes they were right. Sometimes it wasn't over. Why couldn't I be the 2004 Red Sox? Had anyone ever come back from 3–0 down in a league championship series? No, they had not. Had the mighty Yankees ever suffered such an unlikely and inglorious collapse in all of their storied history? No, they had not. But what happened? Boston won four straight, then another four in a row in the World Series, and the next thing you knew, there were millions of New Englanders lining the streets of Beantown and the banks of the Charles to celebrate men who would never be forgotten. Men who changed the history of an entire region and eliminated an eighty-six-year jinx. Men who gave hope to countless souls who had long since stopped believing in miracles, or in the fairness of a cold and fickle universe forever ruled by clean-shaven men in pinstripes. Those men in Sox laundry had changed all that. Why couldn't I be such a man?

But there was much to do before the parades came for me. So much to do. First, I still needed to turn that $612,500 into $2 million. And then I needed to find out where the hell L was and get there. And then I needed to get her alone and convince her to come back to Georgia with me and leave that musty old shitbird behind. It was too much to think about getting done in twenty-four hours, too overwhelming, so I slowed my mind down and tried to be Zen, whatever the hell that really was. As we pulled into the drive of the Grand, I knew I needed to focus on one thing at a time, and the money would be first. I had to get the money. If I could get the money and find L, the Kinder House Plan might be enough to save me. After all, it was one thing to say goodbye to someone over the phone, but in person? After the kind of grand gesture I'd be unveiling? That's entirely different territory. I mean, we had spent nearly half of our lives together. I was the only man she had ever been with before the Ancient Mariner washed up on the fucking shore. We had history. And I had the secret to her heart. To her future, even. L talked about the Kinder House with a reverence it's hard to explain. I had clearly let her down, disappointed her deeply, but all that meant was that she still cared, and still carried with her the flickering hope that I would change. Do something selfless and dramatic. Wasn't that what all women wanted? Didn't they all want us to do what I was about to? Go all the way down the line for her? Of all people, shouldn't L have known how difficult things were? How tough life was? Not just for me but for all of us? Hell, life was so hard that you had to spend a third of it asleep just to have the energy to deal with the rest of it. Wasn't it time to cut this boy a little slack? I mean, let's remember one thing, and it didn't occur to me until I got that money back: *She called me.* If she wanted to get married in peace, why on earth would she call me and tell me it was happening? She could say it was about closure or whatever, but I was standing right in front of her not a few days earlier, and she chose not to say a word. They were getting ready to leave. The car was there. Bags packed. She could have told me and driven off, and there was nothing I could have done about it. But she didn't do that. She chose not to tell me, and then she called instead, and I don't think it's anywhere close to out of the question that she wanted to see what I'd do about it.

Now, why go back to the MGM when I could have simply walked into any house in town? Because fuck Bob Mota, that's why. I wanted to stick it to him, and to his hideous sidekick Manny C. But that would be gravy. There would be no time for shenanigans. No time for trying to replicate the epic run I had gone on when I first got there. Two spins of a roulette wheel had turned $500 into $612,500 (no wonder Dostoevsky was obsessed with that stupid game), and two hands of blackjack would turn the $612,500 into $2.4 million. That was the only way to play it now, and I wanted to see Bob Mota's rat face when it happened. And it *would* happen. Even the most cynical person in the world had to take what had gone down with Tommy Lee as a sign. Eleven and twenty-three? Those two numbers couldn't have been an accident. Maybe it was taking my beating from Bing Buli that had placated the gods. Maybe it was trying to save Howie Rose. Maybe it was saying goodbye to Penny. I don't know. But clearly things had shifted. There was no question about that. I didn't know how I was going to find L, but I definitely knew that I was going to win that money and figure it out. Just because I was on no sleep and numb from pills and alcohol didn't mean I wasn't seeing things clearly. I was seeing things more clearly than ever. My torpor had ended.

Mota wasn't in his office. He wouldn't be back until six P.M., and when I demanded that someone call him, wake his fat, bald ass up, there was no reply. I stumbled out into the nearly dead quiet of the casino with the bag of cash in my hands. I fished in my pocket, produced my room key, and took the elevator up to the suite. Sure enough, it worked. Mota had obviously gotten busy and hadn't bothered to inform anyone I had departed. The place was exactly as I'd left it, right down to the shopping bags Renée hadn't been able to carry with her when she'd left for work not ten hours earlier. Jesus Christ. Had it been only ten hours? Think about how much can happen in your life in ten hours. How everything can change entirely. Who knew that when you hit rock bottom, there might be a spring mattress waiting for you down there to break your fall?

I didn't make it to the bedroom. I face-planted on the couch and didn't wake up until late in the afternoon, when I felt a little over a hundred pounds on my back. It was Renée, amusing herself by sitting on me Indian-style, reading *Us Weekly*, until I stirred. I opened one eye. Barely pried the other, black one open. It took a while for me to focus, but I could make out my own image on the flat-screen in the room. CNN was covering my fugitive story. I looked around for a remote before Renée turned around and found out the truth about Raoul McFarland. Fortunately for me, she was fixated on my busted-up face.

"Holy moly! Like, what happened to you?"

"What do you mean? How was bingo?"

"What do I mean? Look at your face!"

"Oh. Yeah."

"*Cheese and rice*, Raoul. What the heck happened?"

"I ran into an old friend. It's nothing."

"Nothing shmuthing. I gotta get you some ice with the quickness."

She ran to the bar, which gave me the opportunity to find the remote, shut off the TV, and remove the batteries in the event that she got any ideas about turning the sucker back on. CNN was basically proof positive that the story not only had legs but was running around media outlets that had no sports component whatsoever. I knew from Maurice's texts that the story had swept across social media faster than anything since that teenage girl took a selfie at Auschwitz, but I didn't give a shit about that, either. I probably had less than twenty-four hours left at this point, and if I was kicking myself for anything, it was falling asleep and burning nearly a dozen hours I couldn't afford to waste.

"Here. Put this on your handsome face," Renée said, coming at me with an ice-filled towel. "Are you, like, gonna tell me what happened or not?"

"I was out in front of O'Sheas," I said. "This old woman was, you know, getting hassled by some drunks, and it escalated. I had to get involved. It was the right thing to do."

"Holy moly. The craziest stuff happens to you! You're amazing," she said, kissing my tender cheek. "You're like the coolest thing ever. Black eyes are crazy sexy, FYI. Any girl will tell you that."

"Hey, remember when you said you could find just about anybody on social media? Whether they're on it or not?"

"Yepper."

"I might need some help."

"Who you looking for?"

"Who'm I looking for?" I said, searching for a lie, which was never far away. "I'm looking for my sister. She's about to get hitched to a very bad guy, and the whole family is worried sick. No one knows where she is, and word is she's getting married tomorrow."

"The wrong guy can ruin your life big-time."

"Right? That's why I need your help."

"You're such a good brother," she said, hopping off the couch and starting to do lunges across the room. "Does she have a Spanishy-sounding name like you?"

"What?"

"Well, you're super-white-looking, and your name is Raoul . . ."

"Oh. Right. Yeah. Her name is Margarita."

"That's badass! I wish my name was Margarita. Renée is such a meh name. That's why I added the accent. To make it less meh. And also 'cause Renée Zellweger does that, and I liked that *Bridget Jones* movie. Did you know she was American? How crazy is that?"

"How can we find her?"

"Renée Zellweger? I don't know. She probably lives in Malibu or someplace fancy like that."

"Not Renée Zellweger. My sister."

"Ohhh. Margarita. Yeah. Right. Obviously. Blonde moment. If you give me a list of your sister's friends, I'll track her down, no sweat."

I choked down a couple of painkillers, poured a vodka pineapple, and started writing names on an MGM notepad as she finished up her impromptu workout. People we knew from Atlanta. From the firm. From Myrtle Beach. Man—what a list of traitors. They had abandoned me one and all.

"Is this enough?"

"Totally."

She whipped out her phone and iPad and went to work with the care of a DNA specialist. She also took her shirt off. I have no idea why.

"Do you—"

"*Silencio*," she said, holding up a hand. "I'm Sherlock Holmesing the fuck outta this situation."

"OK. Gotcha. I'm gonna run downstairs and talk to Bob Mota right quick. If we find Margarita, I may need to take their private jet. Time's of the essence."

"You're Joe VIP. They'll give you whatever you want," she said, not looking up.

I grabbed the bag of cash and headed toward the door.

"Raoul?"

"Yeah?"

"I'd hump a stranger for a Mocha Frappuccino right now."

"That's—"

"*Kidding.* That's gross. But maybe you can bring me one?"

"One Mocha Frappuccino, coming up," I said, heading for the door.

"You're a massive babe," she said.

Downstairs, Bob Mota looked up from his desk and shook his head when he saw me walk in, bag in hand. "Jesus Christ."

"Remember me?"

"Yeah. You look like the asshole who was here before, only worse. You're one of those cuckoo birds, aren't you, Parisi? Guy with a death wish or something like that. You look like you jumped in front of a car."

I tossed the bag on his desk. "My name's Raoul," I said. "Guess what this is?"

"It's too small to be a body."

I opened it and showed him the cash. "Six hundred twelve thousand, five hundred. On the nose. Sound familiar?"

"I'd ask what the fuck's going on if I gave enough of a shit," he said.

"Oh. If you don't give a shit, then I'll just go play it somewhere else. I'm putting it all on one hand. Then, after I win, I'm putting all of it on another hand. And then I'd like to borrow the private jet."

He and Lou Gehrig both looked at me. Mota smirked. Gehrig didn't.

"You mind if I ask you a question, whatever you're calling yourself?"

"Shoot."

"The fuck is happening here? Honestly."

"I can't tell you, Bob. All I can say is that you think there's one story going on, but in reality there's another, bigger story you know nothing about. I don't have time to explain it to you. You want my play or not?"

"Oh, I'll take your play."

"Let's go, then. Time is not on my side."

"That's the first thing you've said that makes any sense at all."

I told him I wanted privacy. And I didn't care who the dealer was. In my mind, it wasn't going to make a difference. Hell, they could have brought the Old Rooster Bollinger in to deal, and I still wouldn't have worried. I had this. I *knew* I had this. I have no idea why I'd gone so dark after talking to L. I have no idea why I'd taken that conversation as the nail in my coffin when it clearly wasn't. But maybe that was how it was supposed to play out. The roulette scenario certainly had brought the tale to another level and would make for great dinner conversation in Athens for sure.

Mota brought me to a small VIP salon. Two racks of chips were waiting, along with a dealer named Damon, a quiet Aussie with ADE-LAIDE on his name tag. Where had I heard Adelaide before? Had I read it somewhere?

"Raoul's going to play it all," Mota said to a couple of severe-looking men in suits who had followed us and were lurking like crows on a wire. Some kind of casino execs. Fuck them. They could watch all they wanted.

"Where's Manny?" I asked. "He should see this."

"Manny's at the lake with his wife," Mota said.

Jesus. Manny C. was married, and I was scrambling to save myself? How was that fair?

"That's too bad. He's going to miss the fun. And Bob, so you know, don't get any ideas about dropping a dime on me after I beat you out of this money. They'll take it when they take me, and you'll never see it again."

"Play the fucking game already, will you, Ray? You were on my last nerve two days ago."

I looked at the dealer. Rapped my hand on the table. "Gimme my twenty, Damon," I said. "That'll be enough."

I felt no fear. In fact, it was the calmest I'd felt since I had lost L to weakness and circumstance. As Damon moved to deal, I smiled. Was there any doubt that I had a couple of face cards coming? He snapped the first card in front of me. A 6. Wait, a *what*? OK. OK. No worries. No worries at all. A 5 would be next for 11. Then a face for 21. We'd do it that way. Take a little walk around the old block. Juice things up a little. Why not?

Damon put his hole card down, then snapped an 8 in front of me for 14. He turned an ace for himself. Oh *no*. No. A 14 on an ace? I couldn't believe my eyes. How was this happening? That was *my* ace in front of him. This was *his* 14.

"Jesus, Damon."

"Sorry, mate."

Mota stood to the side of the table and smirked at the suits. These motherfuckers, I thought. What kind of men conspired and rooted against love? The Aussie slid his hole card in front of the tiny plastic square that would tell him whether it was a natural blackjack or not. If he had a 10 or a face down, I was done for. The Hard Rock would have been nothing but a cosmic joke. The last laugh on old Ray Parisi. Damon looked down. Didn't move. Looked up. *No blackjack.* The suits frowned. They wanted the natural so they could show me the door for good. But they weren't worried. They knew I had no choice but to hit, and anything over a 7 would be *el busto* for Raoul. I closed my eyes. That lack of nervousness I had seconds earlier? Gone, baby, gone.

"All right. Gimme the seven, Damon. One time."

He looked at me. I'd like to think he was rooting for that 7. Aussies are generally solid people, and I felt like he was a good fellow. He was certainly no Ho. Damon snapped down what may have been the last card I'd ever see. A 3. I was stuck in no-man's-land. A 17 against an ace. There are a million ways to lose to an ace. It can be a 1 or an 11. The odds were bleak. In the movies, the player would do something outlandish here. He'd know that he was going to lose to that ace, and he'd do the unthinkable. Break every rule of basic strategy and hit the 17, though that's something only a severely handicapped person (or a booze- and drug-addled jackass who thought he'd lost his wife forever) would do. But there's no question the movie guy hits that 17, draws a 4, and inspires the suits to look at each other in utter shock and dismay. But this was no movie. This was my life. And I waved my hand over my cards like I was supposed to. I was finally learning.

Damon turned his hole card. There could be no face there, but a 7, 8, or 9, and I was done. He rolled it. It was another ace.

"Two or twelve," he said.

I ran numbers in my head. I had avoided a catastrophe and was left facing a disaster. There were still a million ways to lose. I started to wish I had just busted and gotten it over with. Where I once thought I may have been the recipient of some kind of divine intervention, it occurred to me that being saved and being killed slowly are not the same thing.

Damon snapped down the next card. A 4. "Six or sixteen."

Everyone stared at the table. Anything small and it was over. He turned over another 6. I thought for a moment it was 21. I think one of the suits did, too. But the math said otherwise.

"Twelve."

"Goddammit, give me that face," I said. "Please gimme the face."

The dealer took a deep breath. Turned a king. I slapped my good hand on the table: 22.

"Player wins."

Mota was emotionless. The suits were edgy. They had just seen a sure thing slip away: $1.2 million was put in front of me.

"One more time," I said. "Just one more. C'mon, Damon. I deserve this."

If it was tense before, now it was almost unbearable. Everyone knew I was playing only two hands. This was it. This was the end of my gambling life, one way or the other. I'd soon be just another cautionary tale, or a legend alongside Johnny Chan and the others.

"Paint me up."

Damon looked at the suits, then snapped down a queen.

"There you go," I said. "There's the paint."

He dealt his hole card and then gave me another queen. A beautiful pair of ladies. I stared at them for a moment as he dealt himself a 10, then turned his hole card. An ace and I was done. But it wasn't an ace. It was a 9. I jumped out of my seat and started running around like a mad dog. I circled the table no fewer than five times, extending both middle fingers and screaming, "Fuck you! Fuck you, motherfuckers! Fuck you!" over and over, until the suits walked away and Bob Mota sat down in a chair, a look on his face that someone might have mistaken for a smile.

When I walked into the suite, Renée was still shirtless and lying on her stomach, propped up on her elbows, with dozens of scraps of paper around her. She looked like a stripper pulling an all-nighter before finals. She looked up at me. "Memphis."

"What?"

"Something's up in Memphis."

Memphis. Of course. The son of a bitch was from Memphis. Why hadn't I thought of that before?

"The son of a bitch is from Memphis."

"Well, that's where— Hey, where's my Frap?"

"Shit. I got sidetracked."

"Augh. You're worse than Leslie," she said, then froze and looked at me with dead seriousness. "Oh my God. I'm so sorry I said that. It's so not true."

"It's OK. You want me to go back down?"

"It's cool. Just check this out." She started grabbing scraps of paper. "Look. Here's Kelly Hogan and her gross husband eating barbecue at a place called Pork with an Attitude. I think. That's in Memphis. And here's Pete and Elyssa Gaffney on Beale Street. Also in Memphis. What else? Here's Hope For-te-something—"

"Hope Fortescu. Jesus."

"—at the place the 'I have a dream' dude died. That's—"

"In Memphis."

"Right. And both the Hamiltons—they're so tacky—and Jordy Fowler posted pics from Graceland, where what's-his-face used to live before he got shot."

"Elvis? I don't think he got shot."

"Yeah, he did. In New York."

"OK."

"Of the twenty names you gave me, twelve have posted pics from Memphis, and everyone else has said something about going to Memphis for the holiday weekend. Every last one of them. But no one says anything about your sister's wedding. Which is pretty weird."

"That's because they don't want me to find out. I'm the only one who knows how bad this guy is."

"Do you think he's dangerous?"

"More than you know," I said soberly.

"Do you want me to come with you for backup?"

I thought about it for half a second. Showing up with Renée would be nothing short of a disaster.

"No, sweetheart. Things could get hairy. I need you to stay here. Keep your phone and your computer on you. I may need you to look up some things for me."

Her face fell. This was the second time I was leaving with no intention of coming back.

"If everything goes OK, I'll be back tomorrow."

"In time for the fireworks, you think?"

"Hopefully. Yeah."

"Your sister's really lucky, you know. And not just 'cause she has an ass-kicking name like Margarita. I wish I had a big brother like you. Or maybe one that wasn't so good-looking. It'd be weird to have a brother who was hot."

I gave her a hug and a kiss. I'd be lying if I said I wasn't going to miss her a little.

"Can I tell you something?" I said.

"Is it a good thing?"

"Yeah."

"Sure! Tell me!"

"You did a hell of a job, Renée. *Hell* of a job. You might have changed some lives here. I can't thank you enough."

I looked at her. Out of nowhere, tears were pouring down her face.

"What's wrong?"

She buried her head in my chest. She must know, I thought. She must sense the kind of person I am and that I'm not coming back.

"Hey," I said. "Renée. What's the matter?"

She wiped her face on my shirt. Looked up at me with big, moist eyes. She really was only a kid.

"Nothing. It's just that's probably the nicest thing anybody's ever said to me. Heck, nobody's ever been this nice to me before in my whole life. That shopping trip? I'm never going to forget it as long as I live. I used to think that I'd like to be a millionaire someday so I could go all the places I wanna go, but if all I ever have is that shopping trip, I think maybe that'd be OK. I mean, maybe I won't be a millionaire, and maybe I won't see everything there is to see, but after this week I'll still think I did pretty good and maybe better than some other people. At least I got out of Blowhio and did something different. And I met you. That's good, right?"

I held her tight. Whispered in her ear. "It's good," I said. "You did really good."

SWIMMING WITH
BRIDGEPORT GIRLS

August 8

. . . I told her about the last trip R and I took, when we met Jordy and Benny up at the Vineyard (Benny turned out to be another Great American Boy-Man, didn't he?). Our house was at the crest of a hill, and I watched R speed down on a beach cruiser one morning. He looked so unencumbered. So free. Golden hair wild in the wind. Sun on his face. Big smile. The next day I pulled a Schwinn out of the garage and walked it to the top of the hill. I looked down and started to go, my hand resting on the brake. My eyes immediately searching for potential trouble. My hand never left the brake. I couldn't remove it even if I wanted to. If there's any magic to youth, it's in not knowing all the things that can happen in life. That will happen in life. The bikes sit in a garage all year, rusting away, uncared for, and then they're yanked out in the summer and expected to perform. Tires can pop. Chains can seize. There are unseen stones in the road, and people parking, carelessly opening doors without looking. I remembered the Japanese girl struck by the cab door in Tribeca. Jennifer and Rodrigo's son going over the handlebars near the golf course. Those long nights in the ICU. The dim expression that settled on his face forever after. R blazed down that hill in thirty seconds. I tapped the brake and eased down in ninety. Maybe it's a small thing, but this is who we are now.

DURING THE BLEAK FIRST FEW MONTHS after I was asked to leave Archer Street and then hit with the world's swiftest divorce, I fell into the habit of both calling L at odd hours and appearing at our old house without invitation, usually after a meltdown at the casino. I wanted nothing more than to explain myself, she wanted nothing more than to have space, and these were frustrating and unsatisfying times, to say the least.

I tried a variety of tactics during this period. Aside from the incessant calls and visits (most of which led to neighbors turning on their porch lights or peeking out from behind bedroom curtains), I wrote lengthy letters heavy on nostalgia; I also tried the obvious (mix CDs), the obvious with a twist (flowers to her at work, which I delivered in a gorilla suit I rented from a Manhattan novelty shop), and the less obvious (walkie-talkies). For my troubles, I was either ignored or threatened with restraining orders. Having felt I was being punished for not telling the complete truth about what I was up to while she was taking care of her mother, I overcompensated by trying to tell the truth about everything else, especially my family. I overshared. This was also a poor decision, as it did not have the desired effect (making me appear more forthright in the present), but rather the opposite (making me appear more duplicitous in the past). I said and did all kinds of things I shouldn't have said or done, though the worst had to be the night I went over to her house with the newspaper article about the fifteenth anniversary of Rosario Nuñez's death. I don't know why I did it, though I guess on some level, I was looking for sympathy. How I thought I could achieve that, I can't rightly say. It wasn't a time of great clarity for me.

Momentarily out of credit options, I had spent a wintry Sunday in my room at the motel, taking the collar on an entire slate of NFL games and breaking one in a series of lamps I had to have LaLa in housekeeping replace without telling Maurice. Dawn was in one of her brief bimonthly periods when she wasn't talking to me, and most of my old friends weren't speaking to me because they had sided with L (or I wasn't speaking to them because I owed them money). After watching the Broncos blow a sure cover by giving up fourteen points in the final ninety seconds to the Chargers, I stormed out of my room and walked to the deli to get some fresh air and a newspaper. On the front page of the *Bridgeport Post* was the familiar face of a girl I had known years earlier, when I went to prep school in the area. As I think I said before, after my mother died, the old man sent me to a variety of prep schools in Jersey, where I excelled at sports, didn't study, and wasn't invited back for one indiscretion or another. It was decided that a change of state and scenery (along with some Jesuit priests) might do me some good, so I was sent to a place in Connecticut called St. Ignatius Academy that was roughly forty miles from where L and I ultimately wound up living. It was a boys' school, so there was nothing to do but play hoops and lacrosse during the week and hang out with girls on weekends. We divvied up our time between a group of local girls from Bridgeport we had met at the Wonderland of Ice skating rink, and some private school girls whose parents had a brownstone in Manhattan. The Bridgeport girls were mostly Italian or Puerto Rican, and they were always eager to hook up with a prepster, since most of the academy boys were from good families and drove nice cars and weren't anything like the guys they'd grown up with, most of whom wore wifebeaters and liked to race Bondo-caked Firebirds up and down State Street all night.

Friday nights in the winter were reserved for swimming with the Bridgeport girls. A couple of us would be sent down to the Wonderland of Ice, and we'd round up whoever wanted to come back to Hank Acker's parents' place in Greenwich and go swimming in their heated pool. It was covered by an enormous nylon bubble and sat behind a main house that had the dual luxury of twenty-two rooms and no parents, since Acker's father was a diplomat of some sort and always off in Brussels or Geneva or wherever it is mannered people practice diplomacy. Everyone would smoke dope, drink Four Roses, and skinny-dip before pairing up until it was time for the girls to get back to Bridgeport. Sometimes P. J. Cassill gave them a ride in his van, and sometimes they took the last train back from Greenwich station.

On Saturdays we'd all take Metro-North into the city and meet up with the private school girls at Trish Van Pelt's parents' place on the Upper West Side, which was always at our disposal. We'd play drinking games, and the girls would give us a hard time about what they jokingly referred to as our "Friday-night socials." James van Clive, who drove a red 911 and was the de facto leader of our group, would say things like "Well, if you prudes put out, we wouldn't have to go fishing in muddy waters," and I guess that was the crass truth behind the split weekends: The private school girls never gave it up, and the public school girls did. It was that simple.

Me, I liked the Bridgeport girls better, since they were more like the ones I'd grown up with in Jersey. They wore tight designer jeans and lots of eye shadow and listened to Prince (those girls could dance), while the private school girls wore turtlenecks and hair bands and Top 40'd you to death (those girls could *not* dance). Sometimes I'd go down to the Wonderland of Ice by myself and skate around with Rosario Nuñez, who had black hair and blue eyes and was by far the most beautiful girl we knew. James van Clive was desperate to hook up with her, and I remember riding around with him in his Porsche, listening to Pearl Jam, and him slapping my leg and saying, "Goddammit, Parisi, she's the only Puerto Rican chick I ever met who won't put out. You gotta help your boy out." Van Clive looked and acted like every character James Spader ever played in the eighties. His hair always looked like he had just gotten in from a day of sailing, he always wore black Ray-Bans, and his parents were filthy rich. Not getting what he wanted was entirely foreign to him. If he decided you were going to help him get a girl he wanted, then you were going to help him get a girl he wanted. He'd loan you his ride, give you cheat sheets he bought for biology tests, hook you up with the best weed, and invite you to Newport to go sailing in the summer when school got out. For that, he expected a favor when he asked for it.

I remember a couple of very distinct things about Rosario Nuñez.

One was that she had a deaf little brother. There were a couple of nights when she couldn't go skating on account of having to babysit for him, and I'd go over to her mother's place on Wood Avenue and sit with her. She sang him songs, which you could tell he liked, though I have no idea why, because he was deaf. It mystified me, but it was nice to see anyway, and it was the first time I discovered that you could spend hours watching a pretty girl do just about anything (L was living proof of this, as I probably spent a good four hundred hours of my life just watching her sleep, in sheer amazement). The other thing I remember about Rosario is that she was, without question, the most graceful ice-skater you ever saw in your life. Her long, silky hair would just kind of *whoosh* behind her when she'd jump in the air and do a spin. I think she could have been an Olympian if someone had pushed her in that direction, but that doesn't happen a lot in Bridgeport.

Van Clive was one of those guys whom girls knew better than to like but did anyway, and Rosario was no different, though she was different in that she wouldn't sleep with him. She told me one night that she wanted van Clive to respect her and asked my advice on how to best handle the situation. Being privy to what the guys from the academy really thought about the public school girls, I knew the chances of van Clive taking a Puerto Rican girl home to Newport to meet his parents were roughly the same as him getting a summer job working the fry bin at the Milford Burger King. I didn't have the heart to tell her that, so I didn't. Instead, I told her I could definitely see things working out.

In the spring, she asked him to her prom, and he said he'd go if she would go to our mixer with him. This was highly unusual, since everyone invited private-school girls to the mixers, and van Clive always went to functions with a girl named Emmy Banks who went to Miss Porter's. No one said anything about it until one afternoon when we were hanging out at Devil's Glen in Weston, a rock quarry we'd cliff-jump at during the day and sometimes take girls to at night, since it was secluded and you could sit and drink beers without the cops busting your chops. There was a dangerous leap off what was called Running Rock, where you had to get a running start and clear another rock face that jutted out into the water. Van Clive had badgered everyone into trying Running Rock that day, and we were tanning on a flat rock below it when a little hanger-on named Royce Petersen said, "Hey, Jimmy, what's up with you slumming with that Puerto Rican chick?"

The minute he said it, we all knew it was trouble, since it wasn't six months earlier that Petersen had made the mistake of continually calling him "van Clove" for his penchant for smoking perfumed cigarettes, and van Clive had broken his elbow with a tennis racket out in front of the quad. This time van Clive yawned, got up, flicked a cigarette in Petersen's face, and dragged him by his feet across the rock, whipping him into the shallow water and holding him under for a good five seconds before letting him go.

"Nobody's slumming, you fucking runt," he said as the kid flailed around and gasped for air. A couple of seconds later, van Clive helped Petersen out of the water and let him drive the Porsche home in apology, and the issue was forgotten until the next Monday back at school, when Acker asked him about it in the cafeteria in a more respectful manner.

"Shit, I'm not going to that bitch's prom," van Clive said, swigging from a carton of chocolate milk and putting his hand on my shoulder. "My boy Ray's gonna stand in for me when I tell her I have to go back to Newport for a family emergency. He doesn't mind that class of people, right, Parisi?"

I just shrugged, said, "Whatever," and then broke into an imitation of Anthony Hopkins in *The Silence of the Lambs* that everyone liked, because I was just learning then how to get along, and understanding that people were just how they were, and nobody changed anybody's mind about anything, so what was the point of getting too involved in things? So I ignored him, pretty much, and ended up taking Rosario to her prom. I picked her up on Wood Avenue, and after she got over the disappointment of van Clive canceling, we had a good time. After the dance, we went up to Devil's Glen and drank some High Lifes. I thought maybe I had a chance with her, to be honest, but she was too into van Clive. I remember she asked me if she could trust him, and I said, "Sure, everybody trusts Jimmy."

She told me how excited she was to come to a St. Ignatius mixer, how jealous all her friends were, and I was starting to feel sorry for her, knowing what I knew. So when she called the next week to thank me for going to the prom with her and seeing if I wanted to come babysit, I said I was too busy with school, which wasn't true, because we never studied. Cheating was so rampant that even the good kids did it. The fact that they let me graduate is a testament to the institution's lack of quality control. But I was feeling guilty, and when given a choice between being forthright or avoiding the situation entirely, I made the easy choice and either lied or didn't take her calls.

A week later, van Clive was a no-show at the academy mixer. He showed up later at Acker's afterparty with Emmy Banks, who was still fuming because van Clive was three hours late picking her up and never called to tell her he was having trouble with his Porsche. When I asked if he had called Rosario to cancel, he smiled and said, "C'mon, Parisi, what do you think I am?" and we all went swimming and hung out until the sun came up and the nylon dome started to glow in the early light. I remember sitting on the diving board and him telling me I was his best friend and the only person he could trust. He said he was tired of the States and might go overseas for a while.

That Monday, he was gone. Word was his parents had sent him to school in France, though no one knew for sure. A day later, a group of kids cutting class from Staples High School found a pair of red dress shoes on Running Rock, and when they climbed down, they found Rosario Nuñez lying facedown in the shallow water. I cried all day, and for some reason decided to call my father, who told me to stay out of things (a sentiment he followed up in a letter delivered the next day).

When the cops came to St. Ignatius to ask questions, I was to answer honestly but not elaborate. The son of immigrants, my father was always in awe of old money. He said rich people were good to know and bad to cross. A smart person, he said, knew to mind his own business in life. He did not consider me a smart person, which was why he felt the need to put pen to paper and remind me to shut my mouth. All he wanted was for me to finally graduate. I'd be legal soon. He could be rid of me.

James van Clive never came back to the United States. It was speculated that he changed his name and was living in Europe, though no one has ever confirmed that. The *Bridgeport Post* ran an article about Rosario Nuñez's murder on its fifteenth anniversary, and for some reason I took that paper with me to Archer Street and sat on the stoop of my old house and told L everything I just told you. I hadn't considered the implications of the story. Or the fact that L became obsessed with the school shooting in Sandy Hook and drove up to Newtown every weekend on one mission of mercy or another. Or that she grew up poor and was a public school girl at heart despite her scholarships and Ivy League education. I remember she sat there and looked at Rosario's picture for a long time, and also at van Clive's, which ran next to it, and said it was just about the worst story she had ever heard. It seemed to affect her in some profound way. If I was looking for sympathy because my prom date had been killed, I had gone to the wrong place, and afterward, when I'd call and ask if I could see her, she was fond of saying, "I don't know, Ray. Why don't you go swimming with Bridgeport girls instead. Maybe your grandparents can drive you." It became her favorite thing to say. Whenever I'd suggest getting together, her response was always the same: "Why don't you go swimming with Bridgeport girls."

She said it every time.

The logical question, of course, is why didn't I just tell the truth about my background from the get-go? From the very first night down the shore? It would have been so much easier, after all, and considering we were at the beginning of things, she would have understood. But I couldn't have known that then, so to be honest, it never crossed my mind. I mean, I hated my father enough to invent a story about him being dead, and the emotion that led to me concocting the tale was still pretty fresh (it had been only a little over a year since I had seen him), so the last thing I was going to do was tell a girl I was thunderstruck by that I was the worst kind of liar, a trafficker in invented tragedy. Her own father had died in a bizarre accident before her mom gave birth, and she thought that particular kind of loss was a thing that bound us. Though it was never anything we talked about, there was no denying it was there, and it was probably an accelerant to her trusting and believing in me so quickly, this idea that we were connected through such a specific kind of loss from the outset of our lives. I can see that now. But then? What the hell did I know about that or anything else? I was nineteen. My mother was a suicide. I hated and blamed my father. And so I tried on the pose of someone who was raised by his grandparents in the aftermath of tragedy, and while I can't really tell you why I started telling that tale, I will admit that I enjoyed the sympathy it engendered in people. It seemed like the perfect kind of lie, because it was the type of story people spoke of when you weren't around, and a thing they would never bring up when you were. You could bask in the warmth of sympathy without ever having to answer for it. And since you never had to answer for it, you kind of forgot about it.

On the night when I could have said something, I was in a place that can't be described as wholly of this earth. After nearly floating straight into the sky while dancing with L on the deck of the tiki bar, I went back and sat with her on the bank near the canal that ran behind the beach house she was sharing with her friends. I have no idea how we got on the subject, but I remember asking if she had ever been to DC and when she said no, I told her about some class trip I took to go see the cherry blossoms, though I had only read about them, to be honest, and had never been to DC at all. She hopped up, said, "Well, let's go check them out, then," and before you knew it, we were driving down the highway in the middle of the night in a borrowed Volvo wagon, holding hands and listening to Dire Straits' *Making Movies* on CD (the second track, "Romeo and Juliet," would become our wedding song after she wrote the lyric "You 'n me, babe—how 'bout it?" in lipstick on the dash). It was like we had decided to be a couple without even discussing it. As if we'd been a couple all along and were just waiting to meet so we could get things started. We fell into a familiarity I would never experience again in life with another human being, and one, to be honest, that I never looked for with anyone else. I would pile up acquaintances over the years, people who felt we were good friends, but the reality is that L was the only person who ever truly mattered to me. I had managed to fit in all my life, but there, with her, was the only time I ever felt like I belonged.

We rolled down through the tunnel in Baltimore, talking and talking and talking, her saying, "I like the white hair under an old dog's chin," and me saying, "I like watching Woody Allen movies in the middle of the afternoon," and her saying, "I like when little kids dress up as bumblebees on Halloween," and me saying, "I like those little leather helmets that falcons wear when they're in training," and her saying, "I like the fact that Scotland Yard isn't in Scotland," and me saying, "I like the way your freckles all seem hand-placed," and her saying, "Maybe you can be my Paul Newman, or at least write me a novel," and me saying, "I'll be whoever you need me to be till the end of fucking time, and *also* write you a novel."

As we rolled toward DC in the darkness, L put on Springsteen's *Live 1975–85*, and this is the moment when things could have been different. This is the time I might have liberated myself from a prison I wasn't even aware I was building. Before "The River," Bruce tells a story about his father. With just a melancholy acoustic guitar and a ghostly organ behind him, he speaks in a manner so earnest, so confidential, that it feels like he's talking directly to you, and not to what was probably close to a hundred thousand people at the LA Coliseum that night in 1985. I defy any living person to listen to the story and remain unmoved, and anyone with any father issues will be hard-pressed to keep from falling apart entirely. L and I held hands as he said this:

How you doing out there tonight? That's good. That's good. When I was growing up, me and my dad used to go at it all the time, over almost anything. I used to have really long hair, way down past my shoulders. When I was seventeen or eighteen, oh, man, he used to hate it. And we got to where we'd fight so much that I'd spend a lot of time out of the house. In the summertime it wasn't so bad, 'cause it was warm, and your friends were out, but in the winter, I remember standing downtown, it would get so cold, and when the wind would blow, I had this phone booth that I used to stand in, and I used to call my girl, like, for hours at a time, just talking to her all night long. And finally I'd get my nerve up to go home, and I'd stand there in the driveway, and he'd be waiting for me in the kitchen, and I'd tuck my hair down in my collar, and I'd walk in, and he'd call me back to sit down with him, and the first thing he'd always ask me was what did I think I was doing with myself? And the worst part about it was I could never explain it to him. I remember I got in a motorcycle accident once, and I was laid up in bed, and he had a barber come in and cut my hair. And man, I could remember telling him that I hated him, and that I would never, ever forget. And he used to tell me, "I can't wait until the army gets you. When the army gets you, they're gonna make a man out of you. They're gonna cut all that hair off, and they'll make a man out of you." And this was in, I guess, '68, when there was a lot of guys from the neighborhood going to Vietnam. I remember the drummer in my first band coming over my house with his marine uniform on, saying that he was going and that he didn't know where it was. And a lot of guys went, and a lot of guys didn't come back. And a lot that came back weren't the same anymore. I remember the day I got my draft notice, I hid it from my folks, and three days before my physical, me and my friends went out and we stayed up all night. When we got on the bus to go that morning, man, we were all so scared. And I went, and I failed. It's nothing to applaud about. And I remember coming home after being gone for three days and walking in the kitchen, and my mother and father were sitting there, and my dad said, "Where you been?" I said, "I went to take my physical." He said, "What happened?" I said, "They didn't take me." And he said, "That's good."

I tried to mask the tears in my eyes, but when I looked over to L, I could see she was crying, too. I could have told her everything right then and there. I think she would have understood. Certainly she would have. There was no depth to the lie then. Time and repetition are what make people feel betrayed, and we had neither of those things behind us yet. I could have told her, Look, what you heard about my parents isn't true. I don't know why I said that, but it's not true. What's true is something else. What's true is that when I was thirteen years old, my mother filled the pockets of a fur coat with my father's rare coin collection and walked off into the lake behind our house. I was at my friend Ben Langraf's house when my father showed up at the door. It was startling. I didn't think he knew who my friends were, much less where they lived.

I could have shared with L that my father told me what happened on the drive home, and how frogmen were in the lake when we got back to the house, and how otherworldly their searchlights looked beneath the dark water, and how I never forgot the image of a frogman who came out of the lake, put his slick hand on my shoulder, and walked off into the night. I didn't tell her that my father and I never spoke, and that the old man spent all of his time at his restaurant while I spent mine out of the house, just like Bruce, hanging out with friends until their curfews kicked in, and then talking on pay phones to girls late into the night. When I'd come home, he'd often be sitting at the kitchen table, just like Springsteen's dad, the glow of his cigarette the only thing visible in the darkness. He, too, would ask me what I thought I was doing with myself. He hated me, it seemed, and I hated him right back. Hated the way he played the patriarch with his staff. Hated his phony spiel with his regular customers. Hated the way he absorbed the attention and pity at my mother's funeral. Hated that he referred to what happened as "the accident."

I blamed him for what happened to my mother. For much of my childhood, she was gone on "research trips," and I assumed her absence was due to the fact that he was a philanderer, and she'd rather be absorbed in nature than bear witness to his crushing infidelities, even if it meant leaving your son behind. I had no proof, of course, but I felt like my suspicions were confirmed after I finally graduated and he told me that he'd fallen in love with a nineteen-year-old hostess and was selling the restaurant and moving to Michigan.

Again, I told L none of this that night. I didn't tell her that I accused my father of all manner of horrid conduct, and laid the blame for my mother's long absences and subsequent death directly at his feet. And I didn't tell her how he exploded, telling me that my mother's research trips weren't that at all, but rather stint after stint in the psych ward. She had struggled with schizophrenia since I was a boy, and they chose not to tell me, inventing tales of ecological adventures instead. I suppose this would have been the perfect opportunity to point out that I had been raised in the world of the big lie, and how that must have informed my own choice to make up the grandparents story, and that I was born anew, meeting L, and wanted to live with her forever in the clean light of truth. That connection was available to me, I see, but those words never came close to leaving my mouth. My desire was to live in a new place with L and never look back. Wasn't that a logical impulse? Wasn't reinventing yourself what being an American was all about? If Norma Jeane could become Marilyn and Zimmerman could become Dylan and Gatz could become Gatsby, then why couldn't Ray Parisi leave his own trash at the curb and roll right away? My love for L was the truest thing in my life. It never wavered. Shouldn't that have been all that mattered?

When we got down to Washington, it was drizzling, and there were no cherry blossoms to be found. I hadn't realized they were exclusive to the springtime, but L didn't care. As a dim light broke, we held hands and walked around in the quiet of morning. We climbed the steps of the Lincoln Memorial and shimmied up onto Abe's lap. Gave mock speeches on the great Mall. At one point, we made our way to the Vietnam Memorial. An uncle she never met, Lucille's older brother, had been killed over there, and L wanted to find him. The Springsteen story in the car had sparked her. I remember they had these books on brass stands so you could look up a name and know what panel of the wall to find it on. But L wasn't interested in that. She didn't want to look at the books. She had a reverence for things and was not a person who believed in shortcuts of any kind. Instead, she started at the very beginning and went name by name, running her finger down the slick black granite, taking in each stranger. Absorbing each person's memory somehow. Bearing witness. I was a shortcut person, of course, and immediately looked up her uncle's name in the book. I knew it would be hours before she came to it, but that didn't bother me at all. In fact, I don't ever recall being more at peace than I was at that moment. I sat on a stone bench and watched her with a look of wonder. As rain tumbled over the capital, I gazed at that perfect, luminous face reflecting off the black granite, and thought of the new, better half of the world that had just been cracked open for me. I sat alone, hatless and content, as my girl inched along the great wall, slowly tracing her index finger over the engraved names of the dead.

BEHOLD, HERE COMETH
THE DREAMER

September 15

When I mentioned going up to Newtown to help in some way, R blanched. He can't handle grief. He wouldn't even watch Sandy Hook coverage on the news, and whenever I got back, he'd act like I had been to the movies or something meaningless. He never wanted to talk about it. He wouldn't even take a stance on something as obvious as gun control. He couldn't understand how any of it had anything to do with him or me. R was truly mystified by how much it moved me. Why it mattered. He has no idea that it's all that matters. That it's all connected. Then again, this is a person who remembers 9/11 as an event that ruined his basketball league. Meanwhile, Boyd came up from Tennessee and set up a relief center for rescue workers with his own money. Made grilled-cheese sandwiches all night for weeks . . .

MGM's PRIVATE PLANE WAS PILOTED BY a guy who never told me his name and spoke precisely one sentence to me. Granted, I was passed out for the entire flight, but he did not greet me as a VIP or anything resembling a VIP (if anything, he looked at me like I was a potential hijacker). The only interaction we had was when he woke me up at the private airfield in Memphis, reminding me I had twenty-four hours before the jet would return to Vegas. It wasn't easy to get the plane in the first place. After shaking off what must have been an overwhelming urge to kill himself (or at least call the cops), Bob Mota had refused to let me leave town with the plane and the money. I could have one or the other, he said, but letting me out of his sight with the MGM jet *and* the money was out of the question. He reminded me that: 1) I'd have a lot of explaining to do if I tried to take the money on a commercial flight; and 2) the airport was probably not the optimal place for a fugitive to be showing his face, pocketful of Raoul McFarland identification or not. He was right, of course, and in the end we settled things the Vegas way: I paid him $75,000 in cash. In exchange, I got to take the duffel bag of money with me and had use of the plane for twenty-four hours.

I paid off Mota, then asked for a box and a FedEx label from his assistant. I put $325,000 in the box with a note written on Grand stationery that read "Penelope Dondero College Fund" and shipped it to Dawn's apartment, which left me with exactly $2 million in the bag, $10,000 in my pocket, and something resembling a clear conscience. It was as if losing everything and staring into the futureless pit of despair had loosed something in me. Suddenly I was able to instinctively know what the right thing to do was after a seemingly endless run of doing nothing but the wrong thing.

We landed in Memphis just before midnight on Friday, the third of July. The pilot gave me his cell number to contact him when I was ready to go back (that was never happening—I'd just give him a stack of cash and have him take us to Georgia once it was all said and done). I shook off the delirium of sleep, stashed the bag with the $2 million on the plane, choked down a couple of painkillers, and then whipped out my phone and started poring through a slew of messages from Detective Renée (I ignored all the other ones, which were the usual shitshow of threats and incredulity). She had been hard at work, updating me on the whereabouts of L's friends on the list I had given her and sending screen grabs and photos as well. You could tell she was enjoying the assignment.

"@hopefortescu is at cafe ole wt @clairehamilton, @bethmccarthy1, @fionasweeney."

"u land yt?"

"@philober sez gus chicken is da bomb. ew."

"manny c is a creeeeeeeep."

"cafe ole peeps goin 2 beale st."

"ur sisters friends suk."

"does margarita drink margaritas?"

"chk out ths cute hotel ducks!"

"miss u alredy!"

"u land yt?"

"raoooooooooooooool!!!!!!!!"

I looked at a picture of five ducks marching down a red carpet in an ornate hotel lobby (what the hell?) and kept scrolling through. There were multiple pics of Renée lounging around the hotel in her robe (and possibly a little less in one of them) and more updates on where people were eating dinner, but it was past midnight on the East Coast, a little after one in the morning, and information about where people were having dinner wouldn't help me. The pilot called me a cab, and while I was waiting, I kept sifting through Renée's texts and finally hit the jackpot.

"raoool! big crwd @wetwillies. 983 beale st"

"this is frm @hopefortescu . . . old skool party time @wetwillies w/ @p_gaffney, @suzannedeak, @bethmccarthy1, @clairehamilton, and benny fowler. benny's 2 cool 4 social mdia!"

I assessed some of the names and put them into two categories in my mind: Enemy and Ally. This was important, because I couldn't just roll into a bar and start asking questions. Some of them would call the cops, particularly the women, who considered me Public Enemy #1 and spread all kinds of bullshit rumors about Dawn Dondero and me over the past year. Hope Fortescu, for example, had ripped me so mercilessly that I have no idea how she found time to do anything else. She even sent out a Facebook picture that Dawn posted after graduating from hairdressing school, which I thought was a cheap shot. She was just the worst of the worst, Hope, and topped the Enemy list. Based on who seemed to be hanging out on Beale Street at the moment, things looked like this:

ENEMY: Hope Fortescu, Suzanne Deak, Beth McCarthy, Claire Hamilton, Fiona Sweeney.

These ladies were a five-headed beast of rumormongering and moral intractability.

ALLY: Benny Fowler. Pete Gaffney?

Benny was the last one who jumped ship on me, but only because his wife forced him to cut me loose. Gaffney I wasn't sure about. He was mildly trustworthy, but a self-preservationist at heart, and married to Elyssa, who hated me beyond reason.

I walked the tarmac out to a service road to await the taxi. Vegas was hotter, sure, but Memphis had a sticky factor that lent some credence to the whole "dry heat" thing that people who live in the desert try to pitch as justification for settling down in a place where triple-digit temps are the norm and any room without central air feels like a Cambodian prison cell. I must say that I enjoyed the humidity and felt instantly at home again in the South, where L and I had spent our first four years together and had some of the best times of our lives.

I figured my best play was to go to Wet Willie's, stay as incognito as possible, and try to avoid the women. If I could isolate Pete Gaffney, or better yet, get Benny Fowler alone, then I'd very likely get to the bottom of where this charade of a wedding was being held, and also where I could find L before she made the biggest mistake of her life. Gaffney was something of a wild card, like I said, but I knew Benny was unlikely to rat me out because: 1) though he went to Yale at the same time L did, I met him first; 2) Benny had gotten himself into a dicey situation not all that dissimilar to the Dawn misunderstanding and was simpatico on some level (his transgression was actually way worse, since he was guilty); and 3) I played in a basketball league with his brother, Jack, before he was killed in the Towers, and that fact deeply bonded us in his mind.

My cab arrived and we rolled toward Beale Street in the muggy Memphis night. It was a town I'd never been to, but I liked it immediately. It seemed to have a retro feel, an early-seventies vibe. A little down at the heels. I looked at the timeworn buildings and watched random fireworks popping in the distance as we drove into town, then got out on Beale, which reminded me a lot of Bourbon Street (save for the ubiquitous sound of blues instead of jazz). Throngs of people getting an early start on the holiday weekend jammed the streets, most of them either tourists or college kids, and all of them wasted. They were hanging off balconies, weaving en masse down Beale, swilling out of go cups, and basically howling at the moon from every possible direction, most of the guys in the standard frat-boy uniform of khaki shorts, oxfords, Top-Siders, and soiled baseball caps with exaggerated curved brims, and the girls just spilling out of clothes they all seemed to have rooked from a far younger sister's closet. Everyone was soaked in sweat and had cut loose any inhibitions they might have clung to a few hours earlier. *Sloppy* didn't begin to describe the scene.

I jostled my way down Beale, looking for Wet Willie's. Some yo-yo sporting a torn Grizzlies jersey decided that it might be hilarious to drop his pants, bend over, stick bottle rockets up his ass, and send them whistling into the crowd. It reminded me of the afternoon all of this started, with Bruce going wild and blowing my cover with L. I hadn't thought much about Connecticut since I'd left on my quest, and now that I had $2 million and was close to getting L back, I could barely remember having lived at the motel in the first place. It seemed to belong not only to another lifetime but to another *person* in that other lifetime, and that individual was definitely not me. I was a man with a plan. A guy on a roll. A legend on the floor of high-end casinos who stayed in swank suites and did his traveling on private jets. Why would I ever have lived at a fucking motel?

It took Johnny Ass Rocket about thirty seconds to wind up in handcuffs, and I lowered my head as I passed the cops, adjusting my shades as I went. I was safe amid the chaos, but I knew that I needed to be careful and was entering a delicate situation. I needed to avoid anyone on the Enemy list, somehow find L, tell her what I was doing as far as the Kinder house was concerned, and get her to come home with me before she made the blunder of the century and married a human pair of khakis. I couldn't afford any mishaps or get sidetracked in any way. I had seen enough war movies to know what could happen if you slipped up behind enemy lines.

The pills started kicking in hard just as I found Wet Willie's. The doors were open, and it was a free-for-all inside. It was sad to think that this was all human evolution had come to. I approached the bouncer, who put up a thick paw.

"Move along, tough guy. We're all done."

"But there's a million and a half people in there," I said as a couple of girls stumbled out onto Beale Street and vomited at exactly the same time. Their timing might have been impressive if it weren't so depressing.

"Already called last call."

I looked at the bouncer. He had "failed offensive lineman at a D-3 school" written all over him. The kind of beefy guy who went to the gym every day but refused to do cardio or anything involving the lower body. I handed him a hundred, which he held up to the light.

"Enjoy," he said before hollering "You bitches need to move it along" to the girls who were puking. No fewer than half a dozen people videotaped the retching. They must have been related to the Sarge.

I worked my way through the crowd. A house band massacred Marshall Tucker's "Heard It in a Love Song" with the help of a hundred mewling drunks. Strangers sucked face. Pools of stale beer and cocktails covered the floor. It was the first time I can remember being somewhere and feeling old. I looked for Benny Fowler. For the Hope Fortescu Quintet of Hate. It was nearly impossible to navigate the chaos, so I texted Renée to make sure I was at the right place: "Still Wet Willie's?"

She responded with a picture of Beth McCarthy, Hope Fortescu, Fiona Sweeney, Suzanne Deak, and Claire Hamilton arm in arm at the bar, slushy rum drinks in their hands and sloppy smiles on their aging, traitorous faces. They all looked just a few years away from entering their frosted-bob period.

I worked my way through the crowd, ordered a vodka pineapple, handed the exhausted bartender a hundred when she said she had already made last call, and then glanced down to the end of the bar. *Jackpot.* All five of them were there, hammered, posing for more pictures. There was no way they'd recognize me, but what was I supposed to do next? I needed an Ally. I slammed my drink and ordered another, giving the bartender another C-note, and then turned to a girl with a lip ring who was standing next to me, failing to get the bartender's attention. She was attractive, in her late twenties, had some bad ink, and was sweating like Ralph Fiennes at the end of *The English Patient*.

"Fucking bitch," she said, glaring at the bartender, who wouldn't serve her.

I slid my drink in front of her. "What's mine is yours," I said.

"Thank you, darlin'," she said, taking a swig without any concern that a strange guy had just handed her a drink. "I was fixin' to go off on that bitch."

I smiled. Took a sip for myself.

"We're inside, you know," she said, referring to my shades.

"I've got an eye condition."

"Oh, shoot. Pinkeye? I had it in college. It was no joke. 'Preesh on sharing the drink. Gentlemen are going outta style. I'm Jade, by the way."

"You want to make some easy money, Jade?"

"What?"

"How do you feel about making some easy money?"

She glared at me. "Girl takes a free drink and she's Polly Prostitute? She's the town whore?"

"I don't think you're the town whore at all. I'm just trying to get some information," I said, peeling off two hundreds and putting them on the bar. She dropped the attitude the second she got a look at the money. "See those five girls down there?"

"The ones havin' the photo shoot?"

"Yeah."

"What'chall want with them?"

"I need to find out what they're doing in Memphis. Actually, I know what they're doing here, but I can't ask them myself. I can't go into it. Basically, there's a wedding, and they're going to it, and I need to know when and where it is."

"They look like Yankees," she said, giving them a once-over.

"They are."

She pulled on her sleeveless flannel shirt. It was drenched. "Why you want to know about this wedding?"

"You don't need to know that. Just buddy up to them. You obviously have a great personality, so it should be easy," I said, laying it on a little thick and pulling out an extra hundred. "Here. Take this and buy them a round. She'll serve you."

"And the other two hundy is mine?"

"Yes, ma'am. Just find out about the wedding and report back."

"Okey-dokey, smoky," she said, scooping up the cash and heading toward the girls.

I tried to stare straight ahead, play it cool, but a quick glance down the bar revealed that Jade had made fast friends. She and Hope Fortescu had their arms around each other, and they were all toasting with shots of Jägermeister. Sure, I thought, treat a total stranger like Lady Di risen, but bury alive a guy you've known for fifteen years.

After about five minutes, Jade made her way back to me.

"Whattya got?" I said.

"OK, first of all? They're *amazing*. Especially Hope. She's so sweet."

It was all I could do not to tell her what a vindictive, duplicitous viper Hope Fortescu was, not to mention what a lousy judge of character Jade herself had turned out to be.

"They're here for a super-secret wedding, like you said. They wouldn't tell me where it is, but apparently the friend they're all here to see has some psycho ex-husband stalking her. He just got out of jail or something, and they're afraid he's gonna show up, so they all took a vow of silence. It's very *Ya-Ya Sisterhood*. They're Yankees, but they're all right with me."

"I'm sure the ex-husband is neither a psycho or a stalker," I said. "He's probably misunderstood and being demonized by people who never really knew him in the first place."

"That's not what Hope says. He's supposed to be cuckoo for Cocoa Puffs, this guy. I was like, y'all are awesome friends to keep a secret like this, so I didn't want to push it. Can I still keep the money?"

"Yeah," I said. "Keep it."

It was then that I spotted a familiar face in the crowd. It was the possibly trustworthy and possibly not Pete Gaffney, heading for the bathroom. I took my leave of Jade and followed Gaffney to the can, hoping I was right in putting him on my Ally list.

"Hey, man," I said, sidling up to the urinal next to where he was taking a leak. It was filled with vomit, naturally, so I stared straight ahead at an advertisement for a local strip club that was hanging over the urinal. There were no fewer than a dozen penises drawn on it. "Hey," I said again.

"Dude, I'm taking a fucking whiz over here," he said, and it wasn't until then that I remembered what a dick Gaffney was.

"Pete, it's Ray."

"Terrific."

"Ray Parisi," I whispered.

He looked over. Managed to see through the hair and glasses. "Oh, Jesus."

"How's it going?"

"Ray. Dude. You should *not* be here."

"What are *you* doing here?"

"I'm on vacation."

"In Tennessee? With everyone you know?"

"Ray, you're a fucking wanted man. You're all over the goddamn news. You ought to be worrying about that and not who I'm on vacation with. I mean—Jesus Christ. What the fuck are you thinking, coming down here?"

"I'm looking for L."

"You gotta let it go, man," he said, zipping up.

"I know about the wedding, Pete. I just need to know when and where."

"Ray, come on. I can't. You know I can't. The girls put up the wall. Any breach, and it's straight to the doghouse."

"Just tell me where I can find L, then. I just need to talk to her, and then I'm out of here. I promise."

He looked at me. Glanced around to see if anyone was listening. "You didn't get this from me."

"Copy that."

"I'm fucking serious, Ray."

"Don't sweat it. I never saw you," I said, and then I went on a coughing jag that he seemed to find more revolting than the bathroom, which was arguably the most disgusting room in the United States. Amerigo Vespucci wouldn't have stood for it.

"She's at Graceland."

"What?"

"She's at Graceland. Boyd's a big deal in these—"

"You know Boyd?"

"Of course I know Boyd."

"How?"

"Are you serious?" he said.

"Did he pay for you to be here?"

"What? Why would he— No. Listen. Boyd's a big deal in Memphis. Chief of police. The mayor. You name it. They're staying the night at Graceland. He got some kind of hookup. I don't know. Listen, Ray. I gotta go. I gotta split. You should get out of here. Turn yourself in. Something."

"I'm OK," I said.

"You're not OK. You look like a fucking train wreck."

With that, he started to walk out.

"Wait. Pete?"

"Jesus Christ," he said, turning around. "What now, Ray?"

"You know who the United States of America is named after?"

"Amerigo Vespucci. Why?"

"No reason," I said. Jesus, even a meathead like Gaffney knew that?

He shook his head and walked out. I followed suit a few seconds later. The bouncers were making a racket. They wanted everyone gone. As I made my way back to the bar, I pondered just what that Old Rooster was up to. What the fuck was my wife doing in Elvis Presley's bedroom?

There was no sign of Jade. At least not where I'd left her. You know where there *was* a sign of Jade? Down at the end of the bar, with Hope Fortescu and the anti-Ray alliance. I glanced down. She was showing them the money I'd given her, which struck me as a very negative sign, and sure enough, it was, since she pointed right at me. Fucking Jade. What the hell had I ever done to her?

Claire Hamilton took out her cell and started filming me. Beth McCarthy produced a can of Mace. Fiona Sweeney did a double take, reached into her purse, put on her glasses, and then whispered something to Jade. My cover was blown. Hope Fortescu marched straight to the door, naturally, and got in the bouncer's ear. He shrugged. She responded by grabbing a cop who was out front and getting in *his* ear. I watched her gesturing through the window, saw the cop turn, and

decided it was time to vamoose. I gave Jade the finger, then headed toward the back door, which led to an alley off of Beale. I made my way
back to the main drag, disappeared into the massive, sweaty crowd, and
was in the clear in no time.

I trudged through the Memphis night. My cover in town was
blown, and I had no information. It was not the start I was looking for.
I walked past FedEx Field and the Gibson guitar factory and away from
the lights of Beale. Two people were having sex against the ATM in the
SunTrust parking lot. A fistfight broke out directly in front of a one-
level brick law office. A loner repeatedly lit M-80s that sounded like
atom bombs in a Kroger parking lot. Memphis seemed to be treating
the approach of the Fourth of July like it might be the last day on earth.
I pulled out my cell and called Renée.

"*Hola!*"

"Renée, it's Ray."

"No duh. Wait, what?"

"It's Raoul."

"Oh. Obvi. I miss you!"

"Where are you?"

"In the suite. That's OK, right? Bob the dickhead is being all nice to
me now. He hooked me up with a massage. But that other guy? Manny?
He's the worst. He's like that douchey little horse that's always hanging
around with Winnie-the-Pooh and being in a crappy mood."

"Great. Listen, I need you to look up Graceland for me."

"Coolio. What do you want to know?"

"I don't know," I said. "Text me whatever info you can, like where
people sleep there. Anything like that."

"Hold on while I check," she said. "It'll take two secs. These
robes are the shit, by the way. I totally want to steal one. OK. No.
Graceland closes at five o'clock. It doesn't say anything about sleeping there. There's no whattycallits. Sleepovers. I don't think. What a
weird-looking house."

Mr. Insider with his bullshit connections, I thought. Whenever I thought it was impossible to hate Bollinger more than I did, he pulled another rabbit out of his puckered old ass.

"OK. Forget Graceland for a second. I tried Wet Willie's. Anywhere else?"

"Yepper. You need to check out a disco called Raiford's. I'll text you the addy. A lot of people are dancing there. I think it goes after hours. And Raoul? I think you're a pretty awesome brother to be doing this. Margarita's really lucky to have you looking out for her."

"Has there been any mention of the wedding?"

"Nope. But Fiona Sweeney wrote 'Big day tomorrow' on her Facebook. So it's like, you know, probably tomorrow."

"Thanks, Renée. Send me that disco address."

"Aye-aye, Cap'n! Hurry back, OK? Or I could come there. I mean, if you need me, just say so."

"I'll let you know," I said.

An hour later and I was at Raiford's disco, and if I thought Memphis looked and felt like 1972 before, then Raiford's drove the idea home with a forty-year-old hammer. White vinyl banquettes. Disco ball. Multiple fog machines. Dance floor with squares lighting up. Sly Stone blasting from the speakers. And an old black man wearing a crown and cape ("King" Raiford himself) spinning the funk. It was a wild scene, with a mixed crowd, more black than white. The place was all kinds of alive, only I wasn't looking for amusement, for a change, I was looking for information. And the only way I'd get it was to find my sole Ally. As I squinted through the fog, hoping to spot Benny Fowler, a black girl glided up to me and asked me to dance just when Raiford dropped "Wanna Be Startin' Somethin'" on the turntable.

"Ohhhhhh shit," the girl said. "Michael before the crazy. Let's do this."

We hit the dance floor, shook it up a little (so much for not being there to have fun), and then a group drifted through the wall of fog, led by a guy with a cleanly shaved head. He looked familiar. And terrible. An Ally who had taken a razor to his dome, for some reason.

"Benny?"

He looked up. Didn't recognize me.

"Benny. It's Ray," I hollered.

He was loaded. I took off my glasses. That did it. He hugged me harder than I've ever been hugged in my entire life.

"I can't believe it! Fucking Ray! What happened to your face?"

"Can we talk, Benny?"

Suddenly a tap on the shoulder.

It was Pete Gaffney, looking superior and disappointed. Why was he even there? Since when did any of these people party like this? Weren't they all parents?

"Ray, I told you—"

Someone bumped into him before he could admonish me. Gaffney overreacted, gave a blind shove, and then some more pushing followed, drinks got spilled, the girl I was dancing with started yelling, and in a matter of moments, the Raiford's dance floor went from the happiest place on earth to Black Friday at Walmart. Bouncers interceded and started herding everyone out to the sidewalk.

The most aggravated person out there was an older black guy in a mustard-colored suit. He looked almost exactly like Joe Frazier and was waving his clenched left fist around like Smokin' Joe, threatening all manner of southpaw violence on none other than Gaffney, who got a lot less tough beyond the anonymity of the dance floor. He played the innocent to the bouncers, but the old dude wasn't having it, and neither were his friends, all of whom were roughly seventy and dressed just as colorfully as he was (it looked like an old pack of Starbursts had decided to go for a night on the town). The posse tried to calm their guy, but he wasn't having it.

"I'll cut a steak off that motherfucker," he said, pointing at Gaffney, whose cries of "It wasn't me" were met with indignation by the crowd, most of whom wanted to know why white tourists like Gaffney couldn't just stay on Beale Street or go back to their hotel bars instead of spoiling everything at Raiford's.

"Come on, son," the old man said, waving his left fist some more. "Buy the ticket, take the ride."

As if the suit weren't enough, the guy's slang was unreal (threatening to "cut a steak" off a man struck me as inspired, and "buy the ticket, take the ride" wasn't far behind). I'd never heard anything like it. A bunch of people started recording him on their cell phones. They knew everything that came out of the old man's mouth was gold.

"The man shined me!" he hollered. "He shined me!"

"No, I didn't! I didn't shine you!" Gaffney squawked, though you could tell he had no idea what that meant. I didn't, either, but I loved the term, as did Benny Fowler, who had somehow lost all of his hair but not his sense of humor.

As Gaffney was led toward the curb and an arriving taxi, the Starburst Brigade headed back inside, but not before the old man stopped and tossed one more gem at Gaffney. "I'm a man," he declared. "I walk down the street. Remember that."

"Jesus," Benny said with a tinge of awe, "he just topped himself."

"No question," I said. "That one was next level."

The bouncer opened the cab door for the flustered Gaffney, and out poured Hope, Suzanne, Fiona, Claire, Beth, and Jade (*Jesus*). Before they could spot me, I grabbed Fowler, and we hustled off into the Memphis night.

"I'm a man," he said, following me.

"You walk down the street."

Benny smiled broadly. Gave me another sloppy hug. "That's right! Shit, I've missed you, Ray. Hey—what the fuck happened to your hair?"

"A better question is what the fuck happened to *your* hair," I said. "You looked like a second disco ball in there."

"Guy at work's going through chemo," he said. "We all shaved our heads in solidarity. Jordy went batshit. She won't even look at me."

"A guy at school?"

"No. Teaching's all over. I thought I told you that. I've moved up in the world. I'm installing chair lifts in the homes of elderly people who can't make it up the stairs. It's like being a mortician, except the clients talk back. Very inspiring stuff."

I gazed at his head. It looked awful, but it was a decent thing to do. I thought I should've done that for L's mom when she went through chemo instead of buying board games and trying to get her to act like everything was going to be OK. But I hadn't. Everything, it seemed, came to me too late.

The night was sweltering. Neither of us had any idea where we were going. We were just walking. There were run-down houses and abandoned estates everywhere.

"This town's a little grim," I said.

"Memphis is your colorful uncle who could never quite get his shit together, and now it's not funny anymore," he said. "He'll never turn it around, and everyone knows it. The best you can do is just keep him away from the children. Why the hell are you here, Ray?"

"No particular reason," I said. "You?"

"You know I can't tell you anything. My marriage is holding on by a thread, or whatever less than a thread is. I mean, we're not even staying in the same room. She finds out I'm even talking to you, and I'll get the door."

We walked on. Crossed some trolley tracks. Walked past a cluster of bail-bonds joints. Car-rental places. A bread factory. It was all industrial and hot and depressing. But I have to say, it gave me a good feeling to see an old friend. Outside of Dawn, Penny, Maurice, Bing, and the degenerates at the casino, I never saw anybody anymore.

"Jordy says you're living with some hairdresser?"

"I am *not* living with a hairdresser," I said. "Jesus."

"It's OK. You'll get no judgment from me. I fell for a nineteen-year-old who ate two bags of Skittles every class," he said, wiping his head with his T-shirt. "Jordy puts a bag of them in my lunch every morning just to turn the knife. If it wasn't for Chloe, we'd be all done, but I gotta be there when she wakes up. I mean, she's only four, Ray. What does she know about all our adult bullshit?"

"I don't know," I said. And I didn't. I didn't know what a four-year-old knew, but I guessed it could be a decent amount. Penny was five, and she knew all kinds of things.

"On the other hand, how long before she figures out her parents hate each other? It's not like Jordy hides it or anything."

I wondered for a second why it was somehow all right for Benny Fowler to have sex with a student but it wasn't OK for me to be friends with a hairdresser and sleep on her couch. How was he still part of the gang and I wasn't? Why did he have options and I had to go to extremes? I liked the guy a great deal, but the group reasoning was bullshit.

"I went hunting with my old man once," he said out of nowhere. "For geese. It seemed like the worst possible way a person could spend his time, so I never went back, but I remember him blasting one out of the sky and following the dog to it. I was mortified, seeing it just lying there. The old man looked at me. Said that geese mated for life, and they deserved to be shot for that reason alone. Jesus. I haven't thought about that in years. Why am I even telling you that?"

I thought about my old man. His letter was still unopened in my pocket. I wondered if anything was rarer than stories about good fathers. We walked on through the night. Passed a church. Then another. And another. And another. I stopped in front of one. Looked up at a cross spire.

"What do you think of Peter?" I said. "He strikes me as kind of a scumbag. I mean, for being an apostle. I think he's a lot closer to Judas than everyone thinks he is. He's just more of a smooth operator, don't you think?"

"I never really thought about it," Benny said.

"Somehow L got into the church thing. Father Phil from *The Sopranos* really did a number on her and Lucille."

"I know."

"Know what?"

"That L and Boyd are churchgoers," he said, stopping to get a breather. "I consider myself more of a lapsed atheist. Every once in a while I slip up and find myself believing in something."

"You know Boyd Bollinger, Benny?"

"Yeah," he said, sounding ashamed. "He's OK."

"Where's the wedding? I know it's tomorrow."

"Ray, come on."

"Where's L?"

"I have no idea. Jordy won't tell me anything. I think they've all identified me as the weak link," he said.

"Gaffney said she's at Graceland."

"Where?"

"Graceland. He said Bollinger knows everyone in Memphis, and he's getting to stay at Graceland."

"I was there yesterday," Benny said. "They won't let anyone go upstairs, where the bedrooms are. It's off-limits. Then again, he is Joe Tennessee, so maybe he has an in. I don't know. All I *do* know is that I need a fucking beer. Badly."

I agreed. Fowler pulled out his phone. Fiddled with one application or another.

"There's a 7-Eleven a few blocks away," he said, phone glowing.

We found it, grabbed two six-packs of Bud tallboys, and walked back out into the night.

"We should call a cab," I said, just before a major coughing jag hit me.

"You sound brutal," he said. "Heat should do you good. Come on, let's walk a little more. The Lorraine Motel is right around here."

We cracked a couple of Buds. Walked on. Every now and then random fireworks went up in the distance. It had to be five A.M.

"You hear about my neighbor, by any chance?"

"No one talks to me, Benny. How would I have heard about your neighbor?"

He killed his beer and popped a fresh one. "The neighbor's kid is a total wack job, right? Always has been. Acne. Body like Iggy Pop. Shooting squirrels. All of it. Anyway, he catches a bird and dismembers it. Like, clinically dismembers it. Then he goes to the playground and cuts his wrists up with the bones of the bird. Total scene. Blood all over the fucking seesaw. Just disgusting. What did his genius parents do? Put him on medication and bought him a Range Rover. That's it. I swear, these kids now—they're all fucked-up, Ray. You don't even know who might be packing in your own classroom. I was afraid to give an F to any of the guys. I'm not even kidding. It wasn't worth it. I swear, if I had my way, I'd homeschool Chloe. I'm terrified to send her out there. Hell, you know. You guys were involved in that Sandy Hook thing."

You could tell he was truly afraid. He had lost his brother in the most heinous way possible, and now it seemed that schools were getting shot up so often that people stopped paying attention unless there were really young kids involved, like up in Newtown, and even then people forget about it because another one was always right around the corner. It was a legitimate thing for him to worry about, and it seemed like an extension of my fears over swimming pools and deformities. And it wasn't true that I was afraid to go to Sandy Hook with L. I just didn't think we belonged there. I mean, she wasn't *always* right. She thought I couldn't deal with our blind neighbor, for example, but the reality was that he bored me by starting every sentence with "The way I see it" and then waiting for you to laugh. I wasn't spooked by him. He was just dull.

Benny swilled his beer. His good looks had vanished, and things seemed to be getting away from him. We were the same age, but he'd easily pass for fifteen years older.

"Never have kids, Ray," he said. "I'm serious. You'll never sleep again. When they're little, they won't let you get any rest, and once that stops, you end up keeping yourself up all night worrying about all the things that can happen to them in this fucked-up world. And at the end of it, they might not even like you. Hell, they might not even *talk* to you."

He lifted his can and drained the rest of it. His buzz had kicked back in. "The more you love something, the greater capacity it has to ruin you," he said, and boy, did that hit home.

We turned a corner. Found ourselves in front of the Lorraine Motel, where Martin Luther King Jr. had been shot. It was another place in Memphis that was frozen in time, though this one was kept that way on purpose. A pair of old Cadillacs were parked out front behind some ropes, tailfins gleaming in the lamplight. A giant white and red wreath adorned the second-floor balcony outside room 306, where it had happened. It seemed like such a great man should have died in better lodgings.

I looked at the plaque outside the motel:

They said to one another, Behold. Here cometh the dreamer. Let us slay him. We shall see what will become of his dreams. Genesis 37:19–20.

I shook my head. Man, that was heavy. We stared at the balcony for a while and then sat on the curb. Someone had spray-painted "Though Much Is Taken, Much Abides" on the sidewalk. I had no idea what *abide* actually meant, but it seemed like a very solid word.

"My brother really liked you, Ray."

"I liked him, too," I said.

"I'm sorry I haven't been a better friend to you. That email wasn't enough. It was chickenshit. You want to talk about all this trouble you're in? I'd be happy to listen."

"Not really."

"I get it. When everything happened with Skittles, I didn't want to talk about it, either."

"You actually call her Skittles?"

"Yeah. I don't know what I was thinking. Does anybody have any

238

idea what the hell they're doing? They don't tell you that about getting older, you know? That you won't really know anything. The thing that changes you isn't learning new things but learning old ones over and over until you lose all hope. Hell, anything having to do with the human heart is a fucking mystery to everybody. I mean, Einstein married his first cousin, for Chrissakes. And who the fuck can explain Yoko Ono?"

I cracked another Bud. They were getting warm already.

"You want to know why most marriages fall apart, Ray?"

"Not really."

"They fall apart because they're doomed by an inherent contradiction from the start. We want to maintain the fire of passion while also getting the daily comforts of hearth and home. But they can't coexist. Not for long. The person holding your hair when you're puking, the person whose dirty laundry you carry, the person whose face you see every day, that's not the person who's going to keep fucking you against the wall. The fire goes out. And it goes out because what does fire need to flourish? Air. Air and space. You get neither of those things in a marriage. Marriage takes place in a goddamn phone booth. There's nowhere to turn."

I didn't agree with him. I mean, I did agree with him as far as other couples went. No question. But that story? That story was not my and L's story. Our story was something else.

"Remember *Touch of Evil*?" he said.

It was another thing I had always liked about Benny Fowler: He was a first-rate movie buff.

"L and I saw it at Film Forum when we lived in the city that summer."

"Remember toward the end? Welles goes to see Marlene Dietrich and says, 'Come on, read my future for me'? And she says, 'You haven't got any,' in that great weary voice of hers. She was in her late fifties then, I think. It was over for both of them. Him worse than her. He was totally ruined. She just got old. Anyway, Welles says, 'What do you mean?' and Marlene says, 'Your future's all used up.' That's how I feel a lot of the time. That my future's all used up."

I nodded. No one understood that more than I did. Which was why I needed to stop sitting on the fucking curb, drinking warm beer, and get moving.

"Let's go to Graceland, Benny."

"Are you serious?"

I looked at him. He looked back at me. At the cast. The hair. All of it.

"Why not?" he said. "I owe you that much." He grinned, pulled out his phone, and called a cab. "OK," he said, hanging up. "Let's go see the King."

JESSE PRESLEY

August 8

Told the skywriting story today. Katherine just looked at me, and we both started laughing at the same time. "Do you need me to say it?" she said. I just laughed and said, "No, I think I can figure out the symbolism of that one!"

THE CABBIE DROPPED US ACROSS THE STREET FROM GRACELAND, IN A STRIP mall where the tours load up and you can buy everything from Elvis and Nixon paperweights to "Love Me Tender" hand cream. Across the boulevard was the house, a white-columned mansion that didn't seem like much from a distance. A wrought-iron gate with musical notes on it was adjacent to the guard shack, and a stone wall about six or seven feet high ran the length of the property. It looked easy enough to get over.

Benny and I trotted across desolate Elvis Presley Boulevard. Walked as far away from the guard booth as possible and assessed the situation.

"We can go right over here," I said.

"What about your cast?"

"Boost me, then lift yourself up."

"I don't know, Ray. I stopped working out when all the shit started. I don't think I can do it."

I looked at him. I think he saw his brother's disapproval staring back at him. The guy was a stud athlete.

"No worries," he said. "I'm good."

We looked around. No people. No cars. Still another hour or so before sunrise. He gave me a boost. Jagged rocks lined the top of the wall as a deterrent, but the hell with it. I placed my good hand on the sharp stones and tumbled over the wall. No lights came on. No alarm was tripped.

"We're good," I whispered. "Come on."

I waited for him, and then *whap*. I felt an incredibly sharp pain along my left shin. It was all I could do not to scream. "What the *fuck*?"

I looked down. He had tossed our four remaining tallboys over the wall. After a good deal of grunting and groaning, Benny fell over on my side.

"Thanks for the heads-up on the beers," I said, nursing my shin.

"Thanks for the heads-up on the fucking rocks," he answered, showing me his hands, which were bleeding. His khakis were torn up as well.

We stayed low to the ground and crept across the grass. I looked up at the house. It wasn't any more impressive up close. Somehow I'd thought it would be more *Gone with the Wind*.

"I thought it'd be bigger," I whispered.

"I thought the same thing yesterday," Benny said. "And the inside is the tackiest thing you've even seen in your life. Shit you wouldn't even buy at a flea market."

We sneaked up the right side of the grounds. Wound our way past an unimpressive swimming pool.

"What the hell's that? Over there."

"Gravestones."

"He's buried here?"

"Yeah. So is his stillborn twin brother. Jesse. He was born thirty-five minutes before Elvis, according to the guide."

"That's weird. I wonder what it was like to be Elvis's brother."

"You know what stillborn means, right?"

I thought about Elvis. It might have been nice for him to have a brother. It probably would have made a big difference in his life.

"You know where there are more fugitives than any place else on earth?" he asked. He was getting drunk. "Alaska."

"Why are you telling me that? I'm not going to fucking Alaska. I've got two million dollars in a bag on a private airplane. I've got a plan."

"What?"

"Nothing."

"What exactly is the plan here, Ray?"

"I don't know," I said. "The wall was as far as I thought it through. We're doing pretty good, though. I guess the next step is we sneak in the back somehow, and then we find out where the hell they are. Take it from there."

"Are you sure they're here? It doesn't make any sense."

"Gaffney said they were."

"Gaffney's a shithead."

"I'll tell you what he's not."

"A man who walks down the street?"

"Right," I said, grabbing a beer from him. Boy, had I missed Benny Fowler. "I really would have liked to have seen that guy cut a steak off him, to be honest."

"You and me both. Not for nothing, Ray, but you can't trust Gaffney. Elyssa hates you as much as Hope does."

"*Hate*'s a strong word."

"I know. That's why I used it," he said, killing another beer. "I don't know why he would help you. Hell, he sent out a mass email with that video of you and the jockey."

"That motherfucker."

"*Shhhh.*"

"What?"

"Get down," he whispered.

"Is someone coming?"

Someone was definitely coming. A flashlight swept across the gravestones. I looked around. There was nowhere to hide.

"Get in the pool," I said.

"I'm not—"

"Get in the fucking pool and keep your head down."

We both put our cell phones and wallets down. I lowered myself into the swimming pool and clung to the side. Benny did the same. It might have even worked if Renée hadn't texted me at that very moment. The flashlight landed right on my beeping phone. Then it shifted right onto us.

"Get out of the pool," came a voice from the darkness.

"Call me Raoul," I whispered to Benny.

"What?"

"Call me *Raoul*. I'm *Raoul*."

"Jesus Christ, Ray."

We crawled out of the pool. Stood there soaking wet. Shielded our eyes from multiple flashlights.

"Welcome to Graceland, gentlemen," said the voice. "Two-oh-one Poplar will be the next stop on your tour."

I grabbed my wallet and phone and quickly texted Renée as the cops approached: "Code Red! Fly to Memphis NOW!!!" In my mind, I was thinking—what was I thinking? That she could bail me out? I have no idea. It didn't matter anyway. I figured once I forked over the phone and the Raoul McFarland ID by the Graceland gate, it was all over. It would be only a matter of time before the Tennessee authorities figured out who I was and alerted the New York authorities, and then that would be that. Tackled on the one-fucking-yard line like Kevin Dyson on the last play of the Super Bowl back in 2000 (and naturally, he played for Tennessee).

I guess I had it coming to me. The reality was, I had never really suffered. I hadn't even experienced American suffering. I had never been to a Western Union. Never slept in my car. Never packed my life's belongings into a Hefty bag. Never eaten just ketchup. And I had never been incarcerated. It had all caught up to me, though. Once that door closed, there was no telling when it was going to open up. I was looking at a serious problem.

Only I wasn't, because once the Memphis PD got us to the Poplar Street jail, they never bothered to fingerprint us. They just tossed us in the drunk tank, either because that's what they do down there when people do stupid shit like try and break in to Graceland (and let's face it, that kind of nonsense probably happens all the time—I even heard a story about Springsteen doing it when he was younger), or because they didn't feel like doing the paperwork the morning of the Fourth of July, or because Benny insisted on dropping Boyd Bollinger's name every thirty seconds, which annoyed me immensely but may have been responsible for there being no fingerprints or mug shots taken, which would turn out to be a bitter irony for the old bastard once I took L back. Whatever the reason, I seemed to have lucked out, and was somehow in a better situation than Benny, who had to call his wife and tell her where he was (though not who he was with). When he got out, I'd have him call Renée and tell her where I was. I might still be alive yet.

We leaned against a wall as far away from the aluminum toilet as possible, though the cell wasn't any worse than the bathroom at Wet Willie's.

"Can I tell you something about Skittles?" Benny said, slumping against the wall, his buzz gone. "She made me feel alive. I'd fucking do it again if I had the chance. I'm not kidding. I'd install chairlifts for the rest of my life for one more bite of that apple." He looked at me. "Bukowski said that every man has a woman who put him under a bridge," he added.

"Or at least in a Motor Lodge," I said.

"You know—Jordy and I hadn't had sex in I don't know how long before I met Skittles. Porn ruined me, to be honest. It changed my expectations in a fucked-up way. You watch enough high-end porn with enough Russian tens, and the real thing starts to feel weird. Everything's imperfect. Too fat. Too hairy. Too loose. It looks like what it is instead of what it could be. But Skittles? That was what it could be."

It was another area we didn't have in common. I loved L's body, and our sex life had never come close to waning. I thought that maybe I'd introduce Benny to Renée. She was right up his alley.

I knew I should have been thinking about my next move, what I was going to do when we got out of there, but I was too tired. I was coughing up a storm (an effective tool when you're in a cell, since no one will mess with you); had no idea when we were getting out; and if Jordy had heard stories about the previous evening from any of the girls and took a guess who Benny was in jail with, then I might never get out at all. The best course of action seemed to be to sit there, let our clothes dry, and see what happened.

"At least we got to see the Lorraine Motel," Benny said.

For a guy who had never been to jail, he seemed very comfortable. Of course, that might have just been complete resignation revealing itself. He looked around the cell. A few white guys with terrible ink were passed out on the cement floor.

"You know, deep down, everyone thinks they're creative," he said. "It's a common human conceit. But all you have to do is look at your average tattoo to know that's a fucking lie."

I smiled, but I was tired, and eventually we ran out of steam, closed our eyes, and crashed out seated against the wall, until around noon, when we heard a guard yell, "Fowler! McFarland! Let's go!"

I was delirious and looked around the cell for McFarland until Benny elbowed me and said, *"You're* McFarland, genius."

We walked out into the harsh light of a sweltering Memphis afternoon. Jordy was standing in front of a rented Chevy Malibu, arms crossed, but she was too far away to recognize me.

"You better go, man," Benny whispered to me. "Head any direction but this one."

Before I could make a decision, she started walking toward us.

Either curiosity or instinct had gotten the better of her. She wanted to get a look at Benny's Graceland buddy.

"Shit," Benny muttered. "The jig's up."

Jordy marched up the stairs. Took off her sunglasses. Stared at me.

"You wait in the car," she said, handing Benny the keys to the Malibu. "You can turn around, Ray. You're going right back inside."

I didn't move. She shrugged. Marched toward the entrance of the police station. Benny handed me the car keys. "Go," he said. "Take the car."

"You sure?"

"Go. I honestly don't give a shit anymore."

I was hesitant. Running from the police station didn't seem like a great idea, but neither did making off with Jordy Fowler's car.

"Don't worry about me," he said. "It's over anyway. She's never going to forgive me. And let's face it: I'll be fine. She'll make my life miserable over Chloe, but what can you fucking do?"

He hugged me, and then I ran down the stairs and hopped into the Malibu. It had a nice new-car smell.

"Ray!"

I lowered the driver's-side window.

"L's getting married tonight!" Benny hollered. "Nine o'clock. Peabody Hotel."

I nodded. Punched the gas. Drove away from the jail and adjoining courthouse as calmly as possible. I must have passed no fewer than a dozen patrol cars before clearing the complex and rolling into the parking lot of a First Tennessee Bank and checking my messages. I had received either texts or calls from pretty much every single person in the United States except Renée. She was either in the air or had found the batteries to the remote.

I knew I wouldn't be able to just stroll into the Peabody and talk to L. Word was out that I was in town, and the cops would be none too happy when Jordy told them that they'd just let Ray Parisi walk.

I figured it was time to change my hair color again, so I zipped into a Walgreens, bought some Just For Men Real Black 55, and went to the bathroom at a nearby RaceWay station to do another dye job. It didn't turn out to be much of a change from what I currently had, so I went back to the Walgreens, grabbed a Norelco home-grooming kit, returned to the RaceWay bathroom, and gave myself a buzz cut.

Satisfied with my decision, I strolled back out to the Malibu, which I had parked behind the station, and then looked up when I heard a buzzing in the sky. Above me was an old biplane pulling a banner advertising Fourth of July drink specials at none other than Wet Willie's.

I had to laugh. Things come full circle somehow. I had hired exactly that kind of plane to propose to L out in Montauk years earlier. My friend Matty Besser had just started his own skywriting business, and he'd offered me a great rate to give him a try and be his first client. I didn't think it was the world's most original idea, but he sold me on it pretty aggressively, so I took L out to Montauk on the Jitney, ostensibly to celebrate her finishing undergrad. We had agreed that we'd wait until she'd finished at Emory and possibly even gotten through law school before we got married, but I couldn't wait, so I borrowed some money from a friend in Atlanta (Marty Tepper, now that I think about it), bought a ring, and arranged everything with Matty Besser the weekend before L was to start up at Yale. I called Lucille and told her about it, since L didn't have a father to ask for permission, and she started blubbering over the phone. She was a real romantic, Lucille, and loved the Montauk plane idea, though again, I didn't think it was very original and thought about abandoning the plan the entire bus ride out there before deciding to go through with it, mostly because I really wanted to ask her but couldn't think of a better way to do it.

We walked along the shoreline at sundown. My heart was pounding, and I was trying to engage in normal conversation without giving away what was coming up. I knew she'd say yes, I knew she loved me, but I was still terrified. I kept glancing up, waiting for the biplane to appear on the horizon, and finally it did, gliding through the late-afternoon sky with such elegance that it was all I could do not to stare at it and give things away before the writing started. It looped and twirled, and suddenly smoke began to trail behind it.

W I L
W I L L Y
W I L L Y O
W I L L Y O U M

L looked up, a smile beginning to crease her perfect face. After the M, more smoked poured out, but it just spat into the sky without form, and then came a sputtering, the sound of the engine dying, and soon all was silent. The biplane glided along for a few moments, and then it spiraled toward the water. Matty leaped out, opening a bright red parachute, and drifted down as the plane plummeted, crashed into the water, and broke into pieces. There was nothing left of it. Matty continued his leisurely descent, easily maneuvered the parachute, and landed in the shallow water not twenty yards from where L and I stood, mouths agape.

After the authorities came and the cleanup began, we went back to our hotel for dinner. Since Matty was fine and no one was around to get hurt, we both realized that we had one of the great proposal stories of all time on our hands. An unoriginal idea had turned into a wholly original story. We were so excited to start telling the tale to our friends and Lucille, first and foremost, that I forgot to actually propose. We were done with our entrées and perusing the dessert menu when L sighed and said, "So I'm assuming you have a ring?"

We delighted in telling the story for years. It symbolized everything that we felt was unique about us. Countless people said it should be in a movie (which it was supposed to be until I started surfing with Cyrus instead of writing with his brother). And then years later, when L returned from Myrtle Beach, she started framing the story in an entirely different manner. She began to view the Montauk incident as a tale of foreboding, a glimmer of impending doom, not something to be celebrated as an anecdote but rather an ominous and portentous sign that never should have been so blithely ignored. This was the kind of revisionist history I was up against.

After I gave myself the crew cut and climbed back into the Malibu that Jordy Fowler no doubt had already reported as stolen, a wave of texts poured in from Renée. She had just arrived in Memphis, and all her messages must have been backlogged. There were a slew of "where r u?" "whatz goin on?" "R U OK?" missives, and then a picture of ducks swimming in the fountain of a fancy hotel. "at the peebody. wait n 4 u in lobby! where r u?" read the last one.

Well, what do you know? She had gone to the Peabody because the ducks were cute, no doubt, and had accidentally stumbled into where the wedding was. This was ideal for me, as I couldn't really show my face there, shades and black buzz cut or not. Renée had come through, and while I should have been pleased that I'd had the foresight to have her fly to Memphis when I was about to be arrested, the more I thought about the entire situation, the more enraged I got. L thought she was going to sneak off and get married without me finding out about it? No way. Not in this life, and not in any subsequent lives, either. I kicked myself for wasting time partying in Vegas, but I tried not to dwell on that and instead remembered that I was the guy who'd gone from having about a hundred bucks on Wednesday to having $2 million on Saturday. How many people have ever been able to say that? And how many people would have had the instinct to get a fake ID that ultimately saves their bacon? And how many people would have not only figured out that something was fishy on the Boyd front, but also discovered where the fishiness was taking place? I had done the impossible and still had eight hours left to find L. All in all, I was doing pretty damn well, wasn't I?

I texted Renée, told her to stay where she was, got directions to the Peabody from a trolley driver, and parked the stolen car deep in the hotel garage. I put on my shades and walked upstairs into the lobby as carefully and quietly as possible. My clothes had dried, the cough had subsided, and my buzz cut made me feel anonymous, if only because it was so new to me. I'd never shaved my head before, and it made me feel a little like an outlaw, which I guess is what I was.

It was an old hotel, luxurious by Memphis standards, and again, it must have been something to see in 1972. In the center of the room was the fountain Renée had sent me pictures of, but there were no ducks swimming in it. I saw a uniformed cop milling about by the concierge stand, and over near the elevators stood another uniformed cop. In the lobby bar, a cluster of people in hideous patriotic garb drank Bloody Marys and mimosas. I recognized some of them, but there wasn't an Ally to be found. On the bar TV, highlights from that morning's Coney Island hot-dog-eating contest played. (I participated in the event on my show years earlier, managing to choke down seven Nathan's Famous hot dogs before I vomited, delighting and disgusting the enormous Stillwell Avenue crowd in equal measure.)

I finally spotted Renée sitting by an old woman playing the piano. She was wearing red-framed Wayfarers, an American Flag slip dress, and red, white, and blue Chuck Taylor high-tops. While there were a lot of aggressively patriotic outfits on display throughout the Peabody, none of them came close to touching Renée's. She looked like the Founding Fathers' wet dream.

I walked around the corner to the gift shop, which was basically to ducks what the Graceland shops were to Elvis, and texted Renée: "Come to the gift shop." Two minutes later, she strolled in. And walked right past me.

"Pssst. Renée."

She turned. Looked right through me.

"It's Raoul."

After a professional double take, she got it. "Holy disguise! I mean, *whoa*. You look soooo different. But still totally hot. Like, Channing Tatum hot."

"Thank you."

"You like *my* outfit?"

"It's outstanding," I said. "You're the American Dream."

"Hey—I found out about the ducks. It's this whole thing. You wanna hear about it? It's, like, totally tradition here. Wait—why do you look like that?"

"My sister has turned everyone against me. I have to be very careful," I whispered. "They don't know what I know about this guy."

"Has he killed somebody?"

"I'd, you know, rather not say," I said.

"*Cheese and rice*, Raoul. Your sister can't go marrying a psycho," she said, taking off her glasses and wiping them on her dress. "This is getting so *Law and Order*. I love it. What's the plan?"

I looked at her. Obviously the plan was to find L, but I wasn't sure how to do that. One thing I was sure of was that I needed to have the money with me when I did find her. I couldn't just tell her about the Kinder House Plan. I had to show her. Once she got a look at what I'd done for her, I'd be home free, but I needed to get that bag of cash. Two million dollars would say a lot more than I could, especially since I looked like my own ugly twin who had been dragged behind a car for six miles.

"I think I'm gonna get one of these duck tote bags," she said. "Which one you like best?"

I looked at the rack of bags. They all featured ducks. "I'm leaning toward the one with the ducks."

"Hardy-har."

I bought Renée a tote, texted the pilot, and we cabbed it out to Wilson Airfield. There's a distinct possibility that Renée was even more excited than she had been at the Forum Shops. She had somehow become part of a grand adventure with a rich and colorful character, and most important, he needed her. He had sent for her, and if he needed her this much after just a couple of days, how much might he need her in the days ahead? There were two people in that taxi carrying grand visions of the future. Futures full of adventure. Of romance. Of the world as it was meant to be. But the fact of the matter was that there was room for only one happy ending there in Memphis, and let's face it: This was *my* dream. This was *my* story. Renée deserved a lot more than a duck tote bag for her troubles (hell, she deserved her own miracle, just like I did), but that wasn't something I was thinking about. I'd like to say I was, but it's not true. The clock was ticking. I had to get to L. Nothing else mattered.

Nothing else had ever mattered.

YOURS AND TERRIFIED

September 15

. . . he was one of the most beautiful writers who ever lived. Maybe the most beautiful of them all. I think Gatsby *is the only perfect book ever written. Not a word wasted. But that oft-quoted line of his about there being no second acts in American lives? That was just wrong. It seems to me that there's nothing but second acts in American lives. It's our whole narrative . . .*

RENÉE AND I MET THE PILOT at the plane, got the duffel bag of cash, and headed back toward the hotel in the blistering heat. The jet would be leaving at ten P.M. with or without us. On the way back, we decided on a plan. I'd wait in the rental car and stay out of sight while Renée hung around the lobby bar and tried to find out where in the hotel the wedding was taking place and where Boyd Bollinger and L were staying. Once I got that info, I could figure out a way to get L alone (this part of the plan had to remain flexible), make my case, and get back to the plane by the deadline. Would there be a lot of crap to sort out after? Sure. But according to some texts from Maurice, the jockey was going to make a full recovery, I didn't have any priors, and my wife knew all the best lawyers in New York. It'd be a hassle, but with L back, what did a couple of court appearances and some community service matter? I was planning on doing a lot more volunteer stuff anyway. It obviously mattered to L, and now that I understood that, I could make the necessary adjustments and be a better citizen and partner. This was how people grew, right?

It was stifling hot in the garage, so while Renée went off on her assignment, I ducked across the street for some barbecue. I was too wound up to eat, though, so all I ended up doing was taking out my phone and Googling "Ray Parisi Wanted." Let me tell you something: You don't want to get into trouble during a slow news cycle. It was too early to care about presidential politics, there were no climate-related catastrophes burying poor people in mountain regions, and no one had gotten beheaded in a few days, so my story was getting way more play than it might have under different circumstances. I clicked on a *Huffington Post* article. There was a video with an interview. The place looked familiar. So did the guy being interviewed. It was none other than the Sarge.

"You want it straight? There's something wrong with Parisi," he barked. "Knew it the second I laid eyes on the guy. He's weak. No character. No toughness. Just like that one over there."

As the Sarge pointed, the camera swung and captured a sheepish-looking Maurice, peeking out of the motel lobby door. I was a little disappointed that there wasn't a dog with him, but maybe it was back in the office.

Unable to eat and having no further interest in exploring the Internet shitshow, I went back to the garage and sat in the car. I had nodded off at the jail, but I hadn't slept soundly in ages. The last good night's sleep I'd had was probably with L. I had basically been a walking zombie ever since I started going to bed under the watchful eye of a doomed sea captain, and while I'm not going to blame fatigue for the bad decisions I made before my banishment, I think it contributed to some of the things I did after. They've done a lot of studies on this. You're just not yourself without the proper rest.

After taking a couple of painkillers, I was out. Completely zonked. I think there's a good chance I could have slept for three days straight if I hadn't been woken by a punch in the face.

"Wake up, *Ray Parisi!*"

My aviators cracked and fell off my face. I looked up. Saw a swirl of bright yellow and flashes of red, white, and blue. It was like staring into the sun while being attacked by the American flag. Then I got hit again.

"You son of a bitch!"

I managed to get my good hand on the door handle and tumbled out onto the pavement of the parking garage, getting back to my feet while the onslaught continued. What the hell was happening? Was this another bad dream? Did Bing Buli come back for seconds? As with the banging on my door back at the motel, there were a lot of potential candidates for this onslaught.

"You stinking liar!"

My attacker finally stepped back. Threw a pair of red Wayfarers at me.

"Your sister *Margarita's* getting married, huh?"

"Renée—"

"You don't even have a sister! Your ex-wife is getting married and you're on the television and I know who you are, you son-of-a-bitching liar!"

"Renée. Calm down, for Chrissakes."

"I will *not* calm down!"

I looked at Renée. She was on tilt. She was either going to fall to the ground and have a breakdown or take the tire iron out of the trunk and bludgeon me to death in a Memphis parking garage.

"You're a crazy person and a liar and a stalker, and you're going to jail!"

"Hey. I am *not* a stalker."

"Like fun you're not. I heard them all talking about you and then I saw you on the TV and then they all gathered around the bar and watched it and I listened to everything and your name is not Raoul McNothin'. You used to be a TV guy and you don't even have a sister and that guy Boyd didn't kill anybody. *You* almost killed somebody.

You're the one they want to keep from the wedding. *You're* the one who's going to jail."

"Will you just calm down and let me explain?"

"Oh, hey, Renée, come to Memphis, Tennessee. Come help me save the day. I'm Johnny Nice Guy. I'm Tommy Trust." She gave me a blistering look. Then she went and picked up her Wayfarers. It seemed to settle her down some. But not a lot. "G'head and talk, Mr. Plastics. Mr. BS."

"I—"

"Why is everyone in the world a liar? Huh? Why does everyone have to treat me like shit? Is it so hard for anyone to tell the fricking truth and be nice?" This was when the tears started to come. "I saw a video of you with kids playing baseball. It had a skillion views. What happened to you? You used to be awesome. Now you're a bad person."

"I'm not—I'm telling you, I can explain."

"Oh, can you? Well, I'm a rabbit, then."

I looked at her. *What?*

"Like, I'm *all ears*."

The rage was subsiding, and mascara was leaking down her cheeks. I didn't really know what to say to her. Truth be told, time was short, and I was wondering if she had gotten any info on the wedding or L's whereabouts before she'd made her discovery. I wasn't in a position to ask her about that, though. It's the problem with most conversations. You spend all your time avoiding the stuff you truly want to know about.

"I didn't mean to lie to—"

"I told you, I Googled you," she said. "I know everything."

"Fine," I said. "I'm sorry I lied to you. I didn't mean to. I mean, I did mean to, I guess, since I did it, but I didn't want to hurt you. I didn't mean to do that. I just need to stop this wedding, and I guess I figured—"

"You figured I wouldn't help you if I knew you were trying to get your GD wife back. I shoulda known. I shoulda known you weren't interested in me. No one's interested in me except for one thing, which is always a big nothing. And you weren't even interested in that."

She started bawling. I put my arm around her. Almost brained her with my cast. She buried her head in my chest and sobbed, but then she seemed to think better of allowing me to comfort her and pushed me away. A car drove down to our level and then turned around and went back up the ramp.

"You made me think about the future," she sobbed. "You made me think about pretty things."

"Jesus," I said. "I'm sorry. You're a great girl, Renée."

" 'You're a great girl, Renée.' Augh. Why don't I barf now?"

She leaned against the car. The fire went out of her. And then the hurt. All that was left was the resignation. It was the worst of the three. It was impossible not to think of Dawn.

"You know what?" she said, wiping her face. "Life's like that retarded guy said in that movie my mom likes. It's like a box of chocolates, except every time you bite into one, you find out it's just a ball of crap. And then when you get the taste out of your mouth, you think, Heck, maybe it was just that one, I'll try another, and then that one is a ball of crap, too. You eat one ball of crap after another until there's none left. That's what life is."

She looked at me with red eyes. "You're a ball of crap, Ray."

With that, Renée marched away. I have no idea where she thought she was going. She was in a strange city. She couldn't have had much money or booked a return ticket. But I didn't stop her. I should have. She wanted me to. But I didn't, and the reason I didn't was because I was running out of time, and in the end it was a matter of priorities, like everything was. Is that selfish? I don't know. When people say someone's selfish, it just means that they're not on that person's priority list, and it upsets them. That's all. Because the truth of the matter is every-one's selfish. Everyone's trying to survive. To get situated and straight before they can help somebody else. You can't call that selfishness. It's just life. That said, I should have stopped her. I shouldn't have let her walk off alone like that. But there was no time to lose. L had called me for a reason. She had to know I'd find her. Sacrifices had to be made.

As Renée disappeared, I pulled out my phone and looked at the clock. It was almost seven P.M. I panicked. How was it seven already? How long had I been out? I left the duffel bag of cash in the trunk, put on my bent shades, and took the stairwell up to the lobby, stopping to wipe the blood dripping out of my nose. Again, the place was packed, and this time I saw Hope Fortescu and her beleaguered husband, Roger, walking toward the elevators, dressed to the nines. I stayed out of sight. Explored the ballrooms on the second floor. All were empty. I ducked back into the stairwell. Started climbing. On the fourth-floor landing, I passed a black kid in a catering outfit. He couldn't have been over nine-teen and looked exactly like the actor who played D'Angelo Barksdale on *The Wire*.

"'Scuse me. Does this place have a bridal suite?" I asked.

"Fuck happened to you, man?"

"Long day," I said. "Bridal suite. Yeah or nay?"

"Yeah. Up on six."

"Anyone in there?"

"Have to imagine," he said. "There's a wedding tonight. On the roof."

"You know who?"

"Rich white people. Who else? They even got the ducks. Nobody ever got the ducks before."

I pulled out my phone. Pulled up a picture of the ducks walking the red carpet toward the lobby fountain. "These guys?"

"Uh-huh."

"What's this all about?"

"Tradition. They do it twice a day. Down at eleven. Up at five. Tourists eat it up."

"What's so interesting about ducks swimming? What else are they supposed to do?"

He smiled. Shrugged. "People like stupid shit, man. What can I say?"

I nodded. Lord knows there wasn't any quibbling with that statement. "Listen. You got any interest in making some easy money?"

"Always."

My first thought, straight from the movies, was to get my hands on a catering uniform.

"Whatcha want a catering uniform for?" he asked.

"Because I want to see who's in the bridal suite without getting recognized."

"A uniform don't cover your head," he said logically. "And your head's pretty fucked-up."

"That's a good point."

Let me admit right now that I wasn't thinking clearly. I think I had some kind of PTSD situation going on. I had been in three fights in under forty-eight hours, and while Everett from Wisconsin and Renée were not exactly terrifying opponents, Bing Buli had done a number on me. And then there were the drugs. And the bronchitis. And the fact that I was two hours away from losing the love of my life. I was clearly on the ropes, but it was late in the fight, and I just needed to hang on, gather my strength, and throw one last haymaker.

"Here's what we do," D'Angelo said. "First, how much money we talking?"

I pulled out some bills. "How's a grand?"

He shot his hand out. "I'm Warren, and I'm most definitely at your service."

"I was hoping your name was D'Angelo."

"For a G, you can call me whatever you want. Now, you just wanna know who's in there? That all?"

"Right."

They wouldn't be together before the wedding. Question was, who was in there, Bollinger or L? And if it was Boyd, where was she?

"OK. Here's how it is. I'm gonna knock on the door. Say I got a question about the setup in the ballroom."

"I thought the wedding was on the roof."

"It is. But the cocktail party's in the ballroom. Rooftop level, but inside."

"Gotcha."

"I'll put a phone in my pocket, peeking out like this, and record everything at the door, and then I'll show it to you so you can see who's in there. No one will know what's up."

"Great idea, Warren," I said, coughing up a storm.

"No worries, brother. But you gotta cover your mouth."

I covered up. It went on for a while. God, was I falling apart.

"You got a phone? The video on mine's jacked."

I handed him my phone. "Don't you want to know what's going on?"

"Not really," he said, gesturing to the money. "Far as I'm concerned, I already know who's in there. Ten members of the Franklin family."

He dashed off. I sat on the stairs and waited. I took out the first love letter L had ever written to me. I'd had it folded in my wallet for more than fifteen years. She had written it after the first time we slept together. No one ever belonged to a person more than she belonged to me. She told me she wanted to spend every second of the rest of her life with me. She told me it made her sick to write because I wasn't by her side. She told me she had never felt anything like this in her entire life and never would again. She signed it "Yours & Terrified."

Warren returned. "Your shit is blowing up," he said, showing me my phone. Messages were flooding in for a change. Then he played the video. It was Pete Gaffney at the door for some reason, his shrew wife,

Elyssa, behind him. Warren was smooth. He congratulated them before saying there was a question about the ice sculpture in the ballroom. They said they weren't the couple.

"Sorry," Warren said on-camera. "Isn't this the bridal suite?"

"The couple's not staying here," Gaffney said. "They were going to, but the bride has a nut-job ex-husband on the loose. We can call them for you."

"It's OK," Warren said. "It's a minor issue. I'll just speak to the wedding planner. No need to disturb them."

He clicked off the video. Handed me my phone back.

"You should have gotten them on the phone," I said.

"And said what?"

"I don't know. Asked where they were."

"That would be pretty suspicious," he said, handing me the money back.

"Don't be crazy," I said. "A deal's a deal. Plus, I can really use an ally here."

Warren gave me a long look. "You're the guy he's talking about, right?"

I shrugged. He smiled.

"Ah, shit. *Shit.* I know who you are. They're all talking about you. You're the guy on TV, right? That sports dude? Cut off all your hair, didn't you?"

"Possibly."

"It's cool. Your secret's safe with me, man. If all these stiffs are against you, you gotta be all right. Come on. I'll show you where it's going down."

We walked up to the roof level, where signs reading PRIVATE EVENT hung everywhere. Inside the ballroom, preparations were taking place. No expense was being spared. I kept my head down. It was pointless being up there. All I could do was fuck things up. My best bet was to wait until L arrived and then somehow get her isolated. How, I didn't know, but Warren had replaced Benny as an Ally, so at least I wasn't alone in my quest.

A sign on the door leading to the roof read REMEMBER TONIGHT, FOR IT IS THE BEGINNING OF ALWAYS in calligraphy. I was fuming. Could you believe this motherfucker? What the hell did Boyd Bollinger know about *always*?

We went outside. White chairs and a white-canopied altar were set up. Flowers were everywhere. From the roof, you could see the Mississippi River. The bridge leading into Arkansas. Something seemed to be going on along the banks of the river. Warren nodded toward the activity. "Dude's spending. Special wedding fireworks combined with the city fireworks. Rented out Mud Island for the after-party, too. You don't wanna know what that must've run."

I looked over at a marble room encased in glass. A black guy in a burgundy uniform was fitting five ducks with bow ties. We walked over.

"These them?" I asked.

"Don't normally let the ducks do nothing but swim in the fountain," the man said, "but they got 'em walking down the aisle tonight. Groom's got juice."

God, was I sick of hearing about Boyd Bollinger's local influence. It was fucking Memphis, for Chrissakes. It wasn't like the guy shut down Times Square. I turned and looked at Warren. "What time does this bullshit start?"

"Cocktails and hor d'oeuvres in the ballroom at eight. Out here at nine for the ceremony. Then the fireworks. Then they all go to Mud Island. Maybe it'd be easier to catch her then?"

"She'll be married by then."

"Right. Sorry, man."

I considered things. Even though time was very short, I knew my instinct was right. The best thing was to lie low. Use Warren as my eyes and ears. I pulled out another $1,000. Handed it to him. "I'm going to need more help."

"Brother, we were tight five minutes ago. You're about the best friend I got now. You just paid for fall semester."

The plan we devised was simple. I'd hide in the garage, and Warren would find the bride. When he did, he'd text me. Then he'd do his best to concoct a way to get her alone, at which point I'd make my move.

"I can't tell you how much I appreciate this, Warren."

"Shoot. You're a little crazy, but we don't mind a little crazy in Memphis."

I made my way back down the stairs and into the parking garage. Sat in the car. The stolen car. With $2 million in the trunk. And cops upstairs. Every time a text came in, I had to look at it to make sure it wasn't Warren, and that wasn't a lot of laughs, especially since Dawn was killing me. She must have not gotten the money yet.

Time ticked away. I was helpless. It was looking like I might not pull this off after all. Finally, at close to eight-thirty, word arrived: "Bride in 605."

I texted him back. "Great work. Where are you?"

"Roof. Cops in lobby. Cops in ballroom. B careful."

"Who else is in 605?"

"Buncha bitches," he wrote.

"Tell me about it."

"Meet me on 4th floor landing."

I grabbed the duffel bag and ran up the stairs. Met Warren.

"I guess I don't want to know what's in there," he said, looking at the bag.

"You don't."

"Please tell me this ain't a Columbine situation."

"It's not. Tell me—how can we clear 605? Fire alarm?"

"Fire alarm won't get her alone," he said.

"Why not?"

"'Cause she'd run out with the rest of them. Think, man."

"Well, I can't knock on the door. Those chicks will have me arrested on the spot."

"No doubt. Manager just did lineup and told everyone to be on the lookout for you. Showed your picture around. Didn't look like you, but still. You got all kinds of heat. I actually kinda respect it now that I know you ain't lookin' to kill anybody."

"Maybe those girls will go up for the cocktail party?"

"It's already going on. No one in the bridal party is there. Groom's making the rounds, though."

"That son of a bitch."

"Dude take your girl from you, Ray? That what this is about?"

I nodded.

"Shit. She got some daddy issues. Don't know what to tell you, man."

"We need a helicopter," I said seriously.

Warren put his hand on my shoulder. "I like you, Ray. I wanna help you. But you gotta help yourself, too. Talking about shit like helicopters is not gonna help you. You feel me?"

I nodded again.

"You gotta play this straight. Trust me."

I followed him up to the roof. The party in the ballroom was in full swing. I couldn't help but peek in. Everyone I ever knew was there. Traitors in evening wear, every last one of them. Warren led me outside. It was 8:40 P.M. The rooftop was empty. We went over toward the ducks' penthouse. They all had their ties on. They were like the other traitors, only with webbed feet. I hated all of them.

"Listen up, Ray. This shit's settin' off in twenty minutes. Now gimme your phone. I'm gonna film you," Warren said.

"Why?"

"'Cause you can't be runnin' out here like it's some damn movie. They'll have you in bracelets in five seconds. The chief of police is in the ballroom right now. So's the mayor."

"Tell me what to do," I said, handing him my phone.

"You're gonna ask to talk to her. Then I'll take the video downstairs. They'll probably fire me for this, but it's a bullshit job. I got my license. I can always deal blackjack in Tunica for the rest of the summer."

"Blackjack," I muttered.

"You ready? We don't got much time. This needs to be convincing."

"OK, so what? I pick up a duck and threaten to throw it off the roof?"

"What the fuck you talking about?"

"Bad idea. It'd just fly away with its stupid bow tie on."

"It'd drop like a stone, man. These ducks don't fly."

"Really? Then maybe it's a good idea."

"It's a bad idea," he said. "You'll look crazier than you already look."

"True. What if I went to the edge and threatened to jump unless she talks to me? She knows I'm afraid of heights. It could be effective."

"You on something, brother?"

I didn't answer. Did I really have to?

"OK. You don't threaten the ducks, and you don't say you're gonna kill yourself, either. That's helicopters all over again. It's the opposite of where I need your head at. Just be as normal as possible. Just say you wanna talk to her for five minutes and then you'll leave. Be sincere. Do *not* do anything crazy. We're runnin' outta time. I can't do multiple takes."

He held up the phone. Hit record. Pointed at me.

"Hi. I know I shouldn't be here. I'd—"

"Hold on. Take your sunglasses off."

I did. He got a look at my black eye.

"My bad. Put 'em back on," he said, pointing the camera again. "G'head."

"Hi. It's me." I looked at Warren, who gave me a thumbs-up. "I just want to talk to you for five minutes. I have something important to tell you. I'm not going to do anything to the ducks. That good, Warren?"

"I'm still filming."

"Sorry. Warren will be delivering this message. He's a good kid. Please don't have him fired. He shouldn't be dealing blackjack. Dealing blackjack is depressing. Anyway, please talk to me, OK? It's important. Thanks. Oh—don't you think he looks like D'Angelo Barksdale?"

Warren rolled his eyes. Raced off. I walked over and looked at the duck setup. It was bigger than some apartments I'd lived in. I gazed out over the river, then turned and looked at the altar. Walked under the canopy. Set the duffel bag down. I thought about what a simple affair L's and my wedding had been. How happy Lucille was, her red hair free-styling, her gown cut low, as always (if I had a buck for every Lucille cleavage joke I ever made, I could have bought the Kinder House ages before). I remembered how she'd pulled me aside afterward and told me that while I might have lost one mother, I had gained another. She held my face when she said it and made me look her in the eyes. Of all the adults I've known since I was a boy, she loved me the most. I missed her terribly. I felt like if she were still alive, none of this would be happening. She could have counseled L. Talked sense to her. Hell, maybe if Boyd Bollinger had ever gotten a look at Lucille, he would have lost interest in L. They were the same age, after all. What was so hard about staying in your fucking lane?

I heard the door to the rooftop ease open. Warren stepped out, and for a moment, my heart sank. He had failed to convince her to talk to me. But then who came lumbering out the door but my dog? Bruce was wearing a black vest with a pouch on his back and came running, or what passed for running for him. He wasn't moving that well, if you want to know the truth. I dropped to my knees to love on him, and then I looked up to see none other than L walking through the door and out onto the roof. She nodded at Warren (man, was he good), and he closed the door.

She walked toward me wearing an off-the-shoulder gown. Her new short hair was silky and perfect. It would have been the most breathtaking sight imaginable if the dress she was wearing weren't intended for another man. But still, there she was, an inscrutable look on her face. She seemed peaceful and not at all angry, though that didn't seem logical. I stopped petting the dog and looked up at her. It was all I could do not to cry at how beautiful she was, and where we were, though I knew that I had a job to do, and not much time to do it, and any negative or morose thinking was not going to help me. It was time to pull it together. It was time to bring it all home.

THE MAN
WHO NEVER WAS

July 17

. . . Boyd and I watched an interesting documentary on a famous Australian known as the Somerton Man. He was found on Somerton Beach, just south of Adelaide, in December 1948. They call it the Tamam Shud case. There was a scrap of paper found in a pocket of his suit with that Persian phrase on it. Tamam Shud means ended or finished. The page was torn from The Rubaiyat *of Omar Khayyam. A local man found the book in his car with the page missing and what looked like code written in the margins. Investigators have tried to piece together the clues to who this man was for decades, but they've never been able to. It reminded me of Mom and that lousy movie she loved to watch with R. I cried for an hour after. I miss her so much I can't breathe sometimes . . .*

LOOKING BACK, I SEE THERE WERE a lot of times I might have realized that things were slipping away. That's obvious to me now. Of course, when you're in the shits, and you've dug yourself a serious hole, it's difficult to get a good vantage point on things, since you're, you know, *in a fucking hole.* And it's hard to find a way out of the hole, because you're the one holding the shovel that got you into it in the first place. Maybe another kind of person would have just told the truth, asked for help, but I was never that kind of person. I was the person who kept digging and hoping there was something useful at the bottom of things.

By the time L called and said I should come down to Myrtle Beach to see her and Lucille, I had been gambling hard-core for months and was at least $70,000 in debt, not counting the back-and-forth with Bing Buli. She told me to fly, but I figured it would do me good to drive, get some road between me and the hole, and I must admit that it felt nice to roll the windows down and hit the highway in the middle of the night. I had made that drive down 95 so many times with L over the years, and it was nice to remember those trips, with Bruce shoving his head out the window and me and her blasting tunes or listening to books on tape and holding hands. I thought about it the whole way down, how she'd put her bare feet up on the dash, the way she'd hold her skirt up to the breeze, how the sun would shine on her face when she napped. For a long while, I stopped worrying about my predicament and just thought about how much I missed her and how good it would be to hold her again.

I figured I owed Bruce for the Prince and Pawper sentence, so he was along, the old traveling pro at my side. He slept through the Mason-Dixon but perked up when we hit North Carolina. That was where L loved to stop and load up on fireworks, which I did myself, filling a shopping bag with all manner of Roman candles and shower cones that I envisioned all of us shooting off on the beach once I got down there. It's a long, long stretch through North Carolina, but Bruce shoved his face out the window the entire way. I think he knew he was going home somehow. He was probably hoping for a return to Atlanta, or maybe even the Athens barn where he was born, but he would take Myrtle Beach, though he was afraid of the ocean and had made a career of mad dashes for the shore, thinking about taking the plunge and then retreating, barking at the waves in a long-running personal beef, as if making a racket would change the fact that he was a sweet but cowardly dog.

By the time I got to Myrtle, Bike Week had taken over. Route 17 was choked with hogs, grizzled riders revving their engines and raising all manner of hell. They had completely taken over the Lakewood campground and places like the Iron Gate Saloon, where leather-clad rednecks congregated in the parking lot, sprayed beer in the air, and listened to local bands covering the bulk of the Lynryd Skynyrd catalog. It was complete mayhem, and Bruce wanted no part of it. He got down on the floorboard and buried his head under the passenger seat.

I stopped at the Inlet Square Mall to buy some presents, though I didn't really know what to get and wound up buying a bunch of board games. It took me forever to get to Lucille's place on account of the bikers, who were spread out three wide across the road and inching along like they didn't have a care in the world, their old ladies on the back of their motorcycles in tank tops and bandannas. I must say, they looked like they were having a good time.

Lucille lived in a one-level prefab home near the beach that she liked to call "my trailer," even though it wasn't really a trailer and it had a nice little deck on the front. Heck, it even had some office space in the back, though she stored so much junk out there that you couldn't do any writing in it (not that I ever did any writing in Myrtle Beach, or anywhere else, for that matter—I had given up that pretense once I got a little celebrity). L was annoyed that I had driven down and not flown, like she suggested, but her face lit up when she saw the hound, and watching her reunited with Bruce on the porch was something to see. I had to wait until they were done wrestling around to get a proper greeting of my own, which ticked me off a little, although she was always an animal fanatic and you could find yourself getting in the neighborhood of ignored if there were dogs around. And horses—forget it. You didn't exist if a horse was anywhere nearby.

Finally it was my turn, and she hugged me and kissed me like we hadn't seen each other in a million years, which we hadn't. Everything felt perfect, like it always did with her, and I was overwhelmed by the feeling that what we needed to do was stay in Myrtle Beach with Lucille and never go back to Connecticut. Just leave everything behind and live down south again. I could toss my cell phone in the ocean, and that would be the end of it. Nobody would ever find us that we didn't want to find us. I know that sounds naive in this day and age, but I really believed it in the moment.

Out on the porch in the twilight, life seemed to make sense again, with Lucille's neighbors all waving hello to me and the dog running circles around L and her standing barefoot in front of the screen door, her long legs easing dreamily out of cutoff denim shorts. Her beauty was astounding. If it weren't for the encroaching mosquitoes and the distant and ominous rumbling of motorcycles, we could have stood out there forever.

Lucille was sleeping when I went inside, and I threw my bag in the guest room where L and I always stayed, though she was living in that room now, and it seemed strange to see her things organized all over the place. I didn't like it. But then I thought about my things mixed in, and all of us there together, cozy as cubs, and the feeling that we should stay overtook me again.

As I looked around at what I decided would be my new room, L opened the bag of board games. "What are these for?" she asked.

"I figured we could all play some games, since the girl's cooped up. Brought some fireworks, too."

"She's not *cooped up*, Ray. She doesn't have the measles. She's dying, fifteen feet that way."

"Nobody's dying," I said. "That's ridiculous."

"What's ridiculous is you bringing board games and fireworks to a funeral. Did you bring a suit?"

"What do I need a suit for?"

She looked at me in a way that I had never seen her look at me. Anger flashed across her face, then it went away. She ran her hand across my cheek. "Beautiful boy," she said. "You can get one from the mall. Come on, let's take Chicken Little to the beach."

I didn't want to take the dog to the beach. I wanted to lie around with L. But the minute Bruce heard the word *beach*, he went into psychotic mode, and that was that. I was starting to think that I should have left him at the Prince and Pawper, or maybe Dawn's, since he was jamming me up all over the place. I thought that he had a lot of nerve going ballistic when he heard her say *beach*, since all he ever did was embarrass himself down there. He had no shame whatsoever, that dog, and he was acting like it was *their* reunion, not ours. I said "Maybe you'll get in the water like a real dog" to him, to cut him down a little, let him know that he was rubbing me the wrong way and needed to step back and let me have some alone time with my girl, but he wasn't fazed and kept up his nonsense like I hadn't said anything at all. I guess when it comes down to it, he was as in love with her as I was.

The next morning I was sent into Lucille's room. L told me not to get her riled up. She said it was the first time her mom had asked for a hat, and L didn't like that. I asked her why Lucille wanted a hat, and L told me she didn't have hair, and when I said, "Really?" she said, "Just what exactly does the word *chemotherapy* mean to you, Raymond?" in that voice I wasn't at all getting used to.

I was a little cranky as it was, since the stupid motorcycles never shut up all night, and L let Bruce sleep in the bed, and I got exactly no sex whatsoever, and was never in the ballpark of getting any. I polished off a cup of coffee and went in to see Lucille. She looked smaller and older than I had ever seen her, even though she was wearing a lot of makeup and had a knit hat on her head that looked like those things people put on teakettles. She always had this huge mess of red hair, and now all she had was this ridiculous hat. I didn't like it and was very uneasy. I was already out of sorts from the night before, like I said, and those fucking bikes had started up again in the distance.

I went over to her and kissed her, did what I thought was a pretty decent job of acting like she looked fine, and frowned when the exhaust pipes got louder than usual.

"The Grim Reaper's revving his engine," she said.

"That's not funny," I said. "It's just rednecks making noise."

I walked to the window and saw Ed Cole, Lucille's neighbor, washing down his golf cart. It was gorgeous out. Normally it would have been a perfect time to take a drive over to the batting cages. Get in some cuts.

"Whatcha thinking about, handsome?" she said, and her voice sounded smaller. It was all I could do not to cry.

"The batting cages," I said, even though before I went in the room, L had said, "And don't start talking about the batting cages or nonsense like that, you hear me?"

"Can I tell you something?" she asked. "Come, sit next to me."

I went over to the bed and sat on it. Over in the corner, poking out of a box, was a picture of Lucille and her dipshit of a third husband, Randy Sparks, a golf pro who had run off to play some low-rent tour in Japan and taken along a girl from the Inlet Square Applebee's who most certainly was not there to caddie. You only had to meet the guy once to know it was going to be a disaster. It was the kind of luck Lucille had in men, and she joked about it all the time, since that's the kind of person she was. You've never in your life met anyone who could laugh things off like she could. There are a lot of kinds of people in the world, but for my money, I'd say Lucille's kind is the best to have around, and I think that's what people would have said about me before everything happened and they collectively decided that my jocularity was masking more troubling character traits.

"Of all the things I'm going to miss, can you believe that's one of the big ones?"

"What is?" I said.

"Going to the batting cages with you and playing 100."

We played this game called 100 where you were awarded a certain number of points for a hit that the others determined to be a single, double, triple, or home run based on its trajectory and velocity. The thing that made the game entertaining was trying to argue whether you were being treated fairly by the judges in between pitches flying in at you. The easiest way to get L off her game was to give her a single on a clear double and watch her nearly get beaned trying to argue the call like a lawyer. There is no telling the number of laughs we had at those batting cages.

"We'll go when you get better," I said.

"OK," she said, and grabbed my hand. It was all bones. I looked back out the window.

"What's going on out there?"

"Ed's washing his golf cart."

"Him and that cart."

"You know I would have come earlier, except she said not to," I said. I was feeling guilty. It was hard to remember what I had been doing all those months. Gambling and the casino and Dawn and Penny's apartment seemed a million miles away.

"I know, honey. This was an important time for us. It's meant a lot. It's funny. You have a child, and you take care of it, and then one day it's taking care of you. You wonder where all the time in between went."

"I guess," I said, though I didn't want to think about that. I looked at the wallpaper instead. I never noticed how ugly it was. It looked like someone had shot a pelican at close range. Everything in the room was depressing. Especially the bones in her hand. And the hat. And her voice. It all reminded me of Howie Rose and the time I went to visit him after he had fallen out of the tree and gotten paralyzed. I remember his mother gave me this *Encyclopedia Brown* book to read to him. It was the longest afternoon of my life. All I wanted to do was get out of there and ride off on my bike. And there I sat in Lucille's room, just wanting to get out of there and ride off on that golf cart. I felt bad for a second. It seemed like a person should grow out of that kind of thing.

"You gonna tell me what's on your mind?" she said.

I wanted to tell her about Howie. About how there's not much good I remember from when I was a kid, except for building model rockets with Howie Rose, and how he always carried a Swiss Army knife and would cut any candy he had in half and give it to you without you even asking. I wanted to say that. And tell her that I had never gone back to see him after that first time, even though he was my best friend, and how I'd avoided eye contact whenever I would see his father around the neighborhood. I couldn't tell her those things, though, because I had already lied about my childhood, and I couldn't share anything like that even if I'd wanted to. I had imprisoned myself.

"Nothing," I said. "I'm not thinking about anything."

"You don't like this, do you, Raymond?"

"What's that?"

"This. Being here."

"I wouldn't say that," I said. "I would have come earlier, like I said, but the boss said not to. Plus, I've been working on this new show idea."

"L said you might get a new show. I miss watching you in the afternoons. You were the most entertaining one. What's it about, or is it top secret?"

"What?"

"The new show."

"Oh, I don't know," I said, which couldn't have been truer. "It's, you know, investigative in nature. Issues and what have you. For example, casino gambling could be a possible segment."

"Have you gone to the casinos?"

"I've done some research, yeah."

"Do you watch or play?"

"Mostly I just watch. You know. Pretty much."

"You and I would have had some fun in the casino," she said. "We would have broken them. I can't believe we never thought to go to Biloxi."

"We'll go soon," I said. "We can still go. I can teach you."

"What will we play?"

"Blackjack."

"Oooh, blackjack. I like the sound of that."

She closed her eyes. For a second, I thought she had fallen asleep, and I thought about getting up and checking on Ed's status with the golf cart, but I stayed put and held on to what was left of her hand. I looked at her. It was hard to believe she was the person I once knew. How could it be? Where had all that beautiful red hair gone? What the fuck was this?

I thought of the first time L and I had gone to Myrtle to visit her. L was tired from the drive, but Lucille and I hit it off and stayed up late, drinking margaritas and going through old photo albums. While I was clearly alert to the fact that I had stumbled into being loved by the greatest girl alive, I couldn't look at the old photos without being overcome by a vague sense of loss. A sense that I belonged in this new life and always had, and I had been robbed of every moment up until the time I met her. I felt like it should have been *me* with her in all those pictures. It should have been *me* picking her up for her first date. *Me* in the prom photo. *Me* in front of the Christmas tree. It was as if my life suddenly made sense, because, to be honest, I did feel like an orphan then. I mean, wasn't anyone looking for a home a kind of orphan? Did the details truly matter that much? Is it really anyone's fault what they're born into? Aren't we *supposed* to find our home in the world?

Lucille and I stayed up until sunrise that first night, and she played her favorite movie for me, an old one from the fifties called *The Man Who Never Was*. It was a World War II story about how the Allies took this corpse, dressed him up as an officer, loaded his pockets with top secret military plans, and dumped him into the sea off the coast of Spain. The plans were fakes, of course, and designed to make the Nazis think the Allies were invading one place (Greece, I think) when they were really planning to invade somewhere else. It was a great plot but pretty boring overall. Lucille liked it less for the espionage and more for the idea of a man who never was. She found it inspiring that a nobody in life could somehow become a somebody in death. She saw hope in his story. That there could be meaning to your life even after your death, and you could accomplish something as one person even if you were born another (this much I could relate to). Like a lot of people who grew up poor, she saw everything in aspirational terms. People at the bottom need to believe in the possibility of rising to the top. They need to believe that anything can change at any moment. That everyone was just one good break away, one chance meeting with a benevolent stranger, from the opportunity for a new and better life. She carried that attitude with her until the very end. She was hope incarnate, that woman.

I felt her hand lightly squeeze mine. She wasn't asleep. I was fighting back tears at that point. I couldn't take the bones.

"I'm glad you came," she whispered, "but I kind of wish you hadn't."

"Why?"

"Because you're not yourself. You don't like being here, and I guess I don't like it much, either. With other people, this seems OK. I can talk about it. I'm fine with it. I usually just sit here with my bald little head. You're the first person I put this silly hat on for."

"You don't have to wear that thing for me," I said.

"I know. But I just knew you wouldn't like it."

"It's an OK hat."

"Not the *hat*, honey. *This*. I knew you wouldn't like *this*. And now that's got me thinking about what there is not to like about it. Which is a lot. I'm embarrassed for you to see me like this."

"You look fine."

"No, I can tell by looking at you how I look. I know you, honey. You don't hide things well."

"Everybody has tells."

"Tells?"

"Little habits that give poker players away."

"I like that," she said. "A gambling term. Give me another."

"On tilt," I said.

"On tilt?"

"On tilt is what they call it when you're losing, and you're mad about it, and you make terrible decisions because you're mad and can't control your impulses."

"Have you seen it at the casino?"

"I've seen it," I said.

She closed her eyes again. I looked out the window for a change.

"Ray? I need to talk to you."

"OK."

"About L."

"OK."

"Are you listening?"

"Listening to what?"

"Ray."

"I'm listening," I said. "I'm all ears over here." I leaned back and put my head on her shoulder. That was all bone, too.

"Sweetheart, I have never meddled in your life. I wouldn't. I love you. You're the son I never had, and I love every last hair on that handsome head of yours. You've been such a joy to me. But you have to know how difficult this is for L. And how difficult the miscarriage was, too. She feels very guilty. She thinks she's being punished for that decision you made back when she was in school."

"I didn't make that decision," I said quickly.

"Not *you*, honey. You as a couple."

I thought about that rainy day in Atlanta. The slick roads on the way to the clinic on Peachtree Dunwoody. It wasn't something we ever talked about. Never once. I had forgotten about it entirely.

"That was a long time ago," I said.

"I know, but she feels like she's being punished for it."

"That's retarded."

"She feels it."

"It's probably that stupid priest messing with her," I said. "Religious people like to work on you like that."

I told you that during the time L had been away, some priest had been hanging around the house with her and Lucille, riling them up in the way they do. I imagined he looked like Father Phil from *The Sopranos*, who was always chumming it up with the Mob wives, eating their food and flirting with them until Carmela called him on his shit.

"Pastor has been a great comfort to both of us," Lucille said. "I don't think I could make it through if I didn't feel there was more than just this. That Jesus had taken my sins for a reason."

"You haven't done anything wrong. If there's a Jesus, then he's got to like you more than just about anybody."

I had no idea where all the religious stuff had come from. Neither Lucille nor L liked church people. They rolled their eyes at them. They used to love to say, "I wanna do right, but not right now." I think they got it from a country song. That was the only religious philosophy I ever heard out of them. Now it was all about Father Phil, or whatever the fuck his name was.

"I wanna do right, but not right now," I said. "What happened to that?"

"Right now is here," she said softly, and here came the tears again, and I had to squint hard to hold them back.

"I think we should all move down here," I said. "I got a bunch of board games. We can start having some fun again."

"I think you should settle down," she said, ignoring the idea about all of us living in Myrtle Beach, which was too bad, because it sounded so good to me.

"We have a house and jobs. How much more settled can we be?"

"You know what I mean. You're getting older now. She wants a more stable life. A family life. Do you understand what I'm saying?"

I turned my head away from Lucille and stared at the pillowcase, which was covered with all these little purple birds I had never seen before. I thought it was an odd choice for a pillowcase, and that Penny would have liked it, and maybe even knew what kind of birds they were.

"Ray?"

"I understand," I mumbled. "I wanted the kid, too."

"I don't think she believes that."

"No, she does."

"No, angel. She doesn't. You're not listening. Do you know that poem she loves, 'Not Waving but Drowning'?"

"No, but I've been meaning to do some more reading. I went to Barnes and Noble. Got a bunch of the classics."

"Do you understand what that title means? 'Not Waving but Drowning.'"

"I don't know," I said.

"It means sometimes people don't notice important things."

"I hear ya."

"It means they think one thing is happening, but another thing is really happening."

"I understand."

"Are you scared, baby? Is that it? You can tell me. I won't say anything. I'll take it to my grave."

"That's not funny," I said.

She smiled. "Gallows humor."

"Nobody's dying. You said so yourself. You just said we were going to go to the batting cages and play blackjack. I mean, you just got through saying it." I was seconds away from losing it.

"I know, honey. We will. But first tell me what you're scared of."

"I'm not scared. I just don't like changing things."

"Change is good," she said.

"Why?"

"Because it's necessary to grow."

"I guess. I don't know. You have to worry a lot about a kid. It could drown in the pool."

"You don't have a pool," she said.

"No, but other people do."

She shook her head. "I know you hear me."

"I do," I said. "I hear you. I'm on it."

"You sure?"

"I'm sure. I promise I hear you."

"Good. Now I'm going to close my eyes. You talk for a little while. Tell me a story about my daughter."

"What kind of story?"

"Something from everyday life."

I had told our origin story a million times, how I knew it would be forever when we'd driven to DC that night, so I went with something else.

"Before we moved, it snowed in Atlanta, and everyone freaked out, like they do, and made a run on the Kroger," I said. "They cleaned the place out like a nuclear apocalypse was coming. We only got maybe three or four inches, but the roads were empty, and L and I took the truck out. We were skidding around. Acting up. She was driving and doing her crazy-Southern-girl thing. We went over to Oakland Cemetery. You know that old cemetery near Memorial Drive? It was all covered in snow and really beautiful, and there was no one there. L and I walked around and stood in front of graves and made up stories about the dead people. What they did. What they were like. Who they loved. Stuff like that."

"That sounds like you two."

"Totally," I said. "Anyway, we were standing there, and L bent down to wipe off one of the stones, and when she looked up at me, some snowflakes were caught in her eyelashes. She had that white hat on that you gave her, and her eyes looked really clear, and the snowflakes were just hanging on her eyelashes. I couldn't believe how beautiful she was, you know? I couldn't believe I had stumbled into this life. I'm sorry. That's not really a story. Nothing happened. But it was a great day."

Lucille lightly gripped my hand. "I love you, sweetheart," she said.

I sat up and looked at her. "I love you, too," I said. "I love you so much."

She smiled, but her face was sinking in on itself. You could see her cheekbones and eye sockets. And then there was the hat.

I started to cry. She was all hat and bones. I couldn't take it.

"This is bullshit," I sobbed, and she reached out as I put my head down into her hands.

"It is," she whispered. "It's complete bullshit."

And that was the last time I ever saw her.

BECAUSE YOU WERE MINE

September 9

I worry about what will happen to him sometimes. Even though I know that's not my domain anymore, it's hard to stop feeling responsible. But he'll be fine. He's Ray. I can actually see him living in California, enjoying being the single man at cocktail parties. He's perfect for that place. But that's sad to think about. Is there any version of this that isn't sad to think about?

L STOOD ON THE ROOF OF the Peabody and looked me over. The signature-covered cast. The black buzz cut. The busted sunglasses. The bloodied clothes. The hacking cough as I tried to smile at her. None of it seemed to bother her. She looked at me as impassively as a seasoned mortician takes in a fresh cadaver. I felt like my instincts were right. That this was what she'd been waiting for all along. She had wanted me to step up, and now I was. So what if I looked like I'd been through hell. I mean, hadn't I?

"He seems a little gimpy," I said, nodding at Bruce. He was so happy to see me. I hoped it was rubbing off on her.

"He's fifteen years old, Ray," she said, handing me my phone back.

"No, he's not."

"Have it your way."

"How long do they live for?"

"Fifteen is already a long time."

I scratched his head. He was a handsome old boy. He wasn't dying.

Though I did wonder if maybe I shouldn't have given him Pringles and French-bread pizza so often.

"He's a spring chicken," I said, letting him lick my sweat-covered face. "You're just getting started, aren't you, boy?" I scratched his ears. Looked at what he was wearing. "What's this contraption he's got on?"

"He's the ring bearer."

I stood up. Stared at him. *Et tu, Bruce?* He glanced away in shame. There was so much white on his face. He was old, once you looked for it.

"It's OK, pal," I said, patting his head. "It's not your fault. This has been a difficult situation for everybody."

L sighed. Walked past the makeshift altar to the four-foot wall lining the rooftop's edge. In the distance, cars crept across the bridge into Arkansas, and families began to line the banks of the Mississippi, waiting for the fireworks as the final light of a long summer day bled away.

"You surprised to see me?" I said, walking toward her with Bruce, who plopped down at her feet.

"Not particularly. It's not like no one saw this coming."

She seemed resigned, which I took as a relatively positive sign. She had been nothing but angry for so long. Not to mention she had basically admitted that she knew I'd show up if she called me. Which she had.

"Warren kind of looks like D'Angelo from *The Wire*, right?" I said, trying to start things on an even keel, since that was a show we once spent an entire winter devouring. "Remember how bummed we were when he got killed? I mean, it wasn't as bad as when Wallace got shot in season one, but still."

The door to the rooftop opened again. Out stepped the Old Bastard himself, Boyd Bollinger, wearing a tux, his silver hair coiffed. He stared at me incredulously as L walked toward him. I watched as she spoke to him in a low voice. He nodded as she touched his face. I wanted to go brain him with my cast but decided that wasn't the right thing to do. He kissed her cheek, then turned to go back inside, taking a last look at me as he did. I stared daggers at him. He thought he was going to use my dog as a ring bearer? To marry my wife? Think again, motherfucker.

"You're lucky," L said, walking back toward me at the roof's edge.

"How's that?"

"Boyd is very well connected here, Ray. The chief of police is in the ballroom right now."

"I know," I said. "It's all I'm hearing about. I think they're going to change the state flag to a pair of Dockers in his honor."

"If he were a different kind of man, he'd have you arrested."

"If he were a different kind of man, he'd date someone his own fucking age," I said, then immediately regretted it. "Plus, I didn't do anything. I'm standing on a roof. It's a free country."

"You're a wanted man, Ray."

"I don't see where that's any of Boyd's business."

"You've spent the past eighteen hours trying to ruin his wedding. How is it not any of his business?"

"This is bullshit," I said. "I haven't done anything."

"Really? Then why are you on every channel on TV?"

"I don't want to talk about that. That's not important. That doesn't have anything to do with this."

She gave me a long look. You could tell she couldn't believe what I looked like.

"Fine," she said. "Since I'm indulging you, you can indulge me and tell me how you found out about this."

"You called me and told me."

"How did you find out I was *here*?"

"Renée figured it out. She works at the Girls of Glitter Gulch. She's not a dancer, though. She just works in the front of the house. She's trying to get a job at Wet Republic."

She closed her eyes for a moment. "Is she friends with Coco? I'd appreciate if you told whoever that is to please stop leaving me messages. And sending photos. I got a picture of a Chihuahua at a nightclub. What on earth could that mean?"

"I have no idea what you're talking about," I said.

She gave me the look I didn't like. "Raymond, from what I hear, you marched into a bar, flipped off Hope and the girls—"

"I was flipping off Jade."

"—ran out of said bar one step ahead of the police—"

"That was Hope's fault."

"—started a brawl at a disco—"

"That was Gaffney."

"—broke into Graceland—"

"I thought you were there."

"—and—why on earth would you think I'd be at Graceland at five-thirty in the morning?"

"I don't know. Gaffney said Mr. I Know the Chief of Police had a connection. He said I'd find you there. Ask him."

It seemed ridiculous after I said it. Why had I put Gaffney in the Ally category, even with a question mark? He was always an Enemy.

"He lied to me, didn't he?" I said. "I wish that old dude in the great suit had kicked his ass."

"No one's kicking anyone's ass. And if Pete told you that, it was just to protect me. That's all anyone's tried to do."

"They're all a bunch of traitors," I said. "Even the ducks."

"Keep talking like that, and I'm going inside and letting the police take care of this."

I figured she didn't mean that, but I shut up anyway.

"Shall I continue listing your escapades since you got here?"

"You don't—"

"You got arrested at Graceland—"

"Not charged."

"Somehow got Benny involved— He and Jordy are getting divorced, by the way. Well done."

"It's for the best. He was happier with Skittles."

She gave me the look again. "You got arrested. Somehow got out—"

"Fake ID."

"—stole Jordy's rental car, from the police station, no less—"

"Benny told me to take it."

"—and now here you are."

"Here I am."

"What the hell do you want, Ray?"

I looked at her. Got distracted for a second by the blue speck on her lip. "You've got something on your lip."

She glared at me. That oldie wasn't playing.

"Look," I said. "Mistakes were made. Let me admit that up front. But I have something important to tell you. Here, let me show you first." I reached for the duffel bag. "You remember the guy who called you about that inheritance? Ira Schnauph?"

"Mention anything to do with your parents again. See what happens."

"Fine. Here."

I unzipped the bag. She looked at the cash with less surprise than I'd expected. This was a once-in-a-lifetime opportunity to see that much money up close, and she acted like I was showing her half a poppyseed bagel.

"That's two million dollars."

"Great."

"It's mine," I said. "It's ours. I mean, it's for the surprise I came to tell you about."

"I've had enough of your surprises for one lifetime, sweetheart."

Sweetheart. Nice. Good sign.

"This is a good surprise," I said. "It's got a happy ending. It's like *Gatsby*."

"Gatsby ended up facedown in a swimming pool, Raymond. Three people went to his funeral."

"Well, before that," I said, kicking myself for not finishing either the movie *or* the book. Jesus. What the hell happened to the Old Sport? I thought he had everything under control. "It's for the Kinder house."

She looked at me blankly.

"I'm buying us the Kinder house. I talked to Marty Tepper. He's setting it up. We can start over. Raise dogs. Have a family. Anything you want."

She gave no reaction. None whatsoever. Instead, she walked toward the first row of white chairs and sat down. She didn't say anything for a few seconds. I have to admit, I was hoping for a more enthusiastic response.

"Oh, Ray," she finally said.

I sat down next to her.

"I don't even know what to say right now," she said.

"Don't say anything," I said, leaning close to her. "Let's just take off. Or we can have Warren drag the priest out here, and he can marry us again. Then we head down the stairwell. Move back to Georgia. I've got a private jet waiting."

She leaned away from me. Looked at me like I had just suggested we assassinate the chief of police in the ballroom.

"I'm not living in the *Kinder house*. I wanted to live there when I was a *child*. And I'm marrying *Boyd*. I'm not— My God, Ray, what's wrong with you? What happened to you?"

I didn't like the way she said that. Or how she was looking at me.

"Nothing's wrong with me," I said. "I was in a torpor, is all. A torpor. I'm out of it now. I'm awake now."

"I can't believe I even came out here," she said, more to herself than to me. "The girls think I'm crazy. But I thought I owed you this. Do I owe you this?"

"You don't owe me anything," I said. "Other than a second chance."

She seemed numb. "I guess I thought maybe we could say goodbye to each other with a little decency."

"Decency?"

"Yes, decency. I thought we deserved that much. Don't we deserve that much?"

I started to panic.

"You can't love him," I said.

She sighed. "I'm sorry, but I do. I do love him."

"You can't. Not like you love me."

"It's a different kind of love," she said. "I don't know what else to tell you. It's time for you to move on. You should find someone else, too."

"I can't believe you just said that to me."

"I can't believe any of it. But here we are."

"You blame me for everything," I said, trying to keep it together. "But I was on tilt."

"I don't blame you for everything," she said quietly, looking out at the darkening sky. A silver tracer whistled beyond the bridge, popped, and shed its embers into the Mississippi. "I can't believe we're here," she said. "I can't believe this is who we are now."

It was the saddest thing I'd ever heard her say. All I wanted to do was fix it, but I didn't know how. Everything I'd tried had failed. I heard a sound near the duck penthouse. Looked over. They were all lined up in their bow ties. They seemed to know their schedule had been delayed and didn't like it. They all looked out the glass, judging me, the little fuckers.

"You were supposed to have Paul Newman qualities," she said, still more to herself than to me.

"I do."

"Not Paul Newman in *Slap Shot*. Paul Newman in real life."

"What's the difference?"

She smiled sadly.

"Please," I said. "I have so much I want to tell you."

"We're past all that. It's— We're past all that. I should have known from the beginning, but I didn't. I loved you so much."

She stood up. Straightened her dress. My God, the beauty.

"It's not fair," I said, tears welling in my eyes. "I'm still me."

"I know."

"I'm still the guy waiting for you on the bench."

"I know you are, sweetheart. I'm just not the girl at the Wall anymore. You're trying to get someone back who doesn't exist. Can't you understand that? Can't you see that?"

"You exist," I said. "I'm looking right at you."

She started to move away. She was done.

"I want to talk to Boyd," I said, coughing for a few seconds after I said it.

"You're not talking to Boyd. He's done enough for you. He allowed this to happen on his wedding day. It doesn't have anything to do with him, anyway."

"It— Are you insane?"

Her eyes flashed. The melancholy disappeared, and the anger came back.

"This is the end of all this craziness, do you understand me? *The end of it.* You're going to let this go once and for all. You're going to let me live my life. You're going to let Warren take you out through the service entrance, and you're never going to bother us again. That's what a man who loved me would do. Are you that man or not?"

I started crying. There was no stopping it.

"I came out here to say goodbye to you with a good feeling in my heart," she said. "You were my whole life for so long. I'll *never* forget you. I'll carry you *everywhere*. But this part of my life is over."

I looked at the sleeping dog. The ducks. The people along the river. What was the point of any of it?

"But I've got all this money."

"Do something good with it," she said, starting to edge away.

"Wait," I said. "I'll write you a novel. I can write you a novel."

"I don't want you to write me a novel." She gave me a look of exhaustion and finality. "Just say goodbye, baby."

She started crying. You could tell she didn't want to. Then she held her hand up to my face. I pressed my forehead into it as hard as I could. It was a thing we used to do.

"My beautiful boy."

That was it for me. Her touch. Those words.

"I'm a good boy, aren't I?" I sobbed. "Aren't I a good boy?" I don't think I was even talking to her anymore. "Please tell me I'm a good boy."

"You're a good boy, OK? You're a good boy," she said, grabbing both sides of my head. "Now say goodbye."

She let me go. Whistled for Bruce. He took forever to get to his feet. Looked at me with cloudy eyes. They were fading into a milky otherworld. My God, he was going to die, wasn't he? They started to walk away.

"I loved your mom," I yelled, though I don't know why.

"I know you did," she said, stopping. "She loved you, too. She adored you. You were her son."

"She didn't have to wear a hat for me."

She smiled sadly again. "But people always wear hats for you, Ray. Don't you see?"

She and Bruce continued on past the rows of chairs toward the door. Toward the ballroom. Toward the rest of her life. I knew I'd never see either of them again.

"Wait. *Wait*," I cried. "Swimming with Bridgeport girls."

"What?"

"Swimming with Bridgeport girls. Why did you say that? Why did you talk about that?"

"I was just angry," she said, turning back toward me. "Looking for reasons. I'm past that now."

"I want to know."

"Baby, please."

"That was just a story I told you," I said. "I didn't do anything wrong. It didn't have anything to do with me."

"I know it didn't. I've got to go, sweetheart." She turned away again.

"But I didn't do anything wrong. *Hey.* Did you hear me?"

"I heard you."

"Why are you punishing me?"

"Please let me go."

"Answer me."

"It doesn't matter, angel."

"But I didn't *do* anything."

"I know," she said. "I know you didn't."

"What could I have done?"

"Nothing."

"Tell me."

"I don't know."

"Tell me."

"Ray—"

"Tell me."

She exploded. "*I don't know*, all right? I don't know. But *something*, OK? *Something.* My God! Do you know what kind of gifts God has given you? Did you ever think about that? Did you ever *one time* think about that? You could have been *anything*. Anything at all. People love you. They *love* you. They tell you things they'd never tell anyone else. They trust you. They hang on your every word. You're smart. You're handsome. You're funny. You have *everything*. You've been given *everything* in a world where people have *nothing*. And you just don't care. You don't do anything."

"What was I supposed to do?" I said, bewildered. "Why did I have to be the one?"

"Because you were special!" she said. And then, quieter, "Because you were *mine*."

"I don't—"

"Goodbye, Ray."

LAIKA

. . . maybe in the end you simply had to accept that you had no control. Maybe that was the thing to learn and give yourself over to. That there would always be so much you didn't know. That you couldn't stop. Currents never rest, do they? Invisible forces are always gathering. They are gathering right now. Compromised blood is coursing through our veins. Seemingly motionless clouds are forming in storm patterns over our heads. Buildings are listing imperceptibly beneath our feet. All around us, things are falling away. Silently eroding. You cannot stop any of it. All you can do is live in this world, and live in it with courage.

WELL, I DIDN'T GET ARRESTED. I took the service stairwell to the street, hailed a cab, and went out to the airfield. The cabdriver must have been confused. I looked like a guy who had a Greyhound bus in my future, not a private jet. Of course, I also looked like a guy with all of his earthly belongings stuffed into a duffel bag, and that wasn't quite true, either. Later, when the press came, he would identify himself as the man who drove me. Have his brief moment in the spotlight. How could he have known I was carrying $1 million? he would say. And why hadn't I given it to him? He damn sure could have used it. It was one of the many, many things they got wrong in all the stories that followed. For one thing, it was $2 million in the bag, and for another thing— Ah, forget it. It doesn't really matter. This isn't a world that cares about the truth. Maybe it was once, but if so, it isn't anymore. And a liar can't exactly spend a lot of time lamenting that, can he?

We drove out to the airfield, where the MGM jet sat on the tarmac in the clear night, its stairs down and door open. I gave the taxi driver a hundred bucks, got out on the service road, and walked to the plane. The pilot looked at his watch as I boarded. He was getting ready to leave. Then he jerked his thumb. "You got company," he said.

There, curled up asleep, mascara dried on her cheeks, was Renée. She had her thumb in her mouth like a child, and was sound asleep, her Peabody-duck tote bag on the seat beside her. I looked at her for a long time. Watched her breathing in and out. Her hands were so small. Her eyelashes so long. She looked closer to Penny than anybody who should be working the cashier's cage at a strip club. I opened the duffel bag. Reached in and started stacking until there was exactly $1 million in the tote.

I kissed her forehead and walked to the door. Looked at the pilot. "Take her back to Vegas," I said. "She's VIP."

I headed for the stairs to the tarmac. Turned one last time. "You know who this country is named after?" I said.

In the distance, cherry bombs exploded. Bottle rockets whistled. Lone tracers streaked through the sky. Night had fallen.

"Amerigo Vespucci," he said, not turning around.

I sighed. Reached into my pocket for my last two painkillers. Stuffed in there, folded up, was the "RAY" letter from my father. I put it back in my pocket, swallowed the pills dry, walked down the stairs, across the steamy tarmac, and out to a dark road leading to exile. I trudged through the heat of the night, carrying the bag of money like a child in my arms. On and on I went, a man with no plan and no future to execute it in even if he had a plan. Between the heat, the distant explosions, and the random flashes in the sky, it felt like

I was in a Vietnam War movie in the moments before an air strike. I thought of the Wall in DC, L's face reflected off the black granite, then I shut it out of my mind. Whatever that was had happened to somebody else.

The bag was heavy, and I stopped to catch my breath. Felt my phone buzzing in my pocket. I took it out as a call was coming through. It was Marty Tepper. News on the Kinder house, no doubt. I looked at the phone, tossed it into the weeds alongside the road, and kept walking, soaked in sweat, until I eventually ended up in a neighborhood I was probably not welcome in. A long line of shotgun shacks. Dark faces behind rickety screens. Dark faces on weathered lawn furniture. Dark faces clustered on patches of baked dirt that passed as yards. All eyes were on me. Adults. Children. Stray dogs. Firecrackers rat-a-tat-tatted. Smoke bombs hissed. And then a series of high whistles began. Silver tracers zipped like meteors across the night sky. All eyes turned up. Electric bouquets of flamingo pink and gas blue bloomed in the darkness. Platinum concussion bombs flickered and boomed. On and on it went, a shower of light and possibility, breathtaking and strange as life itself. The faces of the adults carried no less wonder than those of the children, and when the grand finale wound down, there came a final flurry of silver streaks spreading out like spiders, falling like tiny diamonds. The onlookers gasped and grinned as the embers connected and formed a perfect image of a bride and groom in the night sky. And so it was done.

Tamam Shud.

Tears filled my eyes as the applause ended and the smoke cleared. I sat on the dirty ground. Absently reached into my pocket and opened my father's letter. It was unsigned and contained just two words: "We're Even." I stared at it. Dropped it to the ground. Reached into my wallet and took out the "Yours & Terrified" letter. I couldn't read it, and I dropped that, too. Stuck to it was a laminated card I had gotten in one of the gambling books I had bought when this all started: "10 Keys to Being a Winner." I had followed precisely none of them.

I guess if there was one thing I wish I had told someone, one memory I might have shared with L or Lucille or anyone who had a sympathetic heart, it would have been this: On the June night my father came to get me, I watched a frogman in the lake from my bedroom window. Ambulance lights were flashing. My father was speaking to the paramedics and the police. They had already taken my mother from the water. Yet there was still a lone lamp sweeping beneath the surface of the lake. One last frogman. What was he looking for? I wondered. Why hadn't he left with the others? I thought for a moment that it must have been the rare coins. Was he collecting my father's treasure from the lake bed? Had my father actually asked them to do that? I walked downstairs and out the door in my bare feet, moving across the dewy grass in a kind of daze. A torpor, I guess. There was no moon. The sky was a deep charcoal smear, and the only light came from the lake. The ambulance had gone. I approached the water's edge just as the frogman was emerging. He looked enormous in his black wet suit, alien in every way, and I stared at him as he gathered his equipment and prepared to leave. I remember he placed his slick hand on my shoulder as he walked past. The water seeped through my T-shirt. Outside of all my countless moments with L, it's the only time I can ever recall the touch of another human being. It's my only memory of it. Of course, this, like everything else, is true and not true. It's true that I don't remember any other touch, but it can't be true that I never experienced any. That couldn't possibly be right. Yet the memories are not accessible to me, and so a false thing can become a true one, and become even truer somehow with the passage of time. That I've learned.

When my father waved me back to the house, I stepped on an

antique silver coin. Felt it beneath my bare foot. In the days that followed, I found that if you looked down from my window, there would often be glimmers of silvery light, sudden flashes that ricocheted through the yard on sunny days. The coins that had fallen out of my mother's pockets on the way to the lake had become embedded in the grass, and on those bright days I could stare at the flashes and remember her a little, remember her in a way that is entirely lost to me now. When I told my father about them, he had a bulldozer brought in and tore up the yard, filling it with sand. I would never see those coins again, never grab the tail end of one of those silver streaks and follow it to a place in my mind where maybe I could see her again. When I told L I didn't have a mother or a father, it was another false thing that was truer than a true thing. But she didn't see it that way, and maybe she was right not to. Maybe everything in life was part true and part false, but your job was to stand on the true side and deal with the rest, not try and make believe anything was all one way or all another. Even my father, for all his bullshit, was a man who, when he proposed to my mother, filled a yard with hundreds of monarch butterflies he had gotten from the Meadowlands. She adored monarchs, so he kayaked out into the swamp, painstakingly caught each one, carried them to a van, and transported them a hundred miles, the butterflies wildly fluttering around him as he drove the turnpike, the future wide-open and golden in front of him. The man with the bulldozer was also the man with the butterflies, and there's no sense in acting like one of those things is truer than the other. It all just comes down to what stories serve your story. Because we must forever play the hero, everyone else gets the part we assign them. Dominic Parisi played his part, and now he's gone, with all the others.

When I stood up, I could see that everyone had returned to their tiny homes save for a family who stood in the dirt and looked up at a bright, lone light. I thought maybe it was a star, but then I could see it inching almost imperceptibly west. It could have been Renée in the plane. It could have been anything at all. And maybe the not knowing was what captivated them. I watched them stare into the sky. There was a shirtless boy, no older than five or six, and a wary man my age, and an old woman, hair like a gray flame. I approached them. They looked at me curiously as I handed the man the duffel bag. I glanced at the old woman and the boy, lightly touched his shoulder with my own slick hand, and walked away. I heard the zipper open moments after I turned. Felt their eyes on me as I departed. They were no doubt wondering what was happening. Was this some kind of prank? Was it real? And if it was real, why was it happening? What kind of a man would do such a thing? What circumstances led him here?

"Who are you?" I heard the man ask as I vanished into the night. "Hey, man. Who are you?"

I walked through the neighborhood and off toward the great unknown, his question trailing me like a ghost. Who was I? Who *am* I? Am I the Pretender? Don Quixote? The Somerton Man? Am I Elvis's dead twin? Raoul McFarland? Or am I simply, in the end, the Man Who Never Was?

I looked up at the westbound light, stopped in my tracks, and for some reason thought of Laika the Space Dog. Born a stray on the frigid streets of Moscow, brought in to the warmth of the science center, surrounded by attention she could only have taken as love. I thought of her hopeful new chapter in a home with children, with toys on the floor, and the smell of bread, and the touch of small hands. All the warmth of belonging. How it must have seemed that the promise of this life had been fulfilled. How it must have seemed that all the hardships were the price you paid for the better things. But it was not to be. Laika was taken from the home in the morning. Led outside under snowy skies. She was driven back to the science center, strapped down, and shot out into the universe in a steel capsule, spinning slowly away from the home she thought she'd found. Untethered entirely from the known world, she must have looked into the deep and endless darkness and wondered what was happening to her. Why am I weightless and alone? she must have thought. Why have I been forsaken?

ACKNOWLEDGMENTS

THE FIRST DRAFT OF THIS BOOK was written in a series of spiral note-books nearly fourteen years ago in the Cabbagetown neighborhood of Atlanta, fueled entirely by heartbreak, two-liter bottles of Georgia water (Coca-Cola), and two-for-one 79-cent hot dogs from a gas station long since razed. It was a terrible, lonely, desperate time. Naturally, I miss it sometimes.

Years before, when I was a kid, I used to ride the Metro North from Connecticut to New York just to read beneath the great dome at Grand Central Terminal. I'd sit there for hours and disappear into weathered paperbacks, fifty-six miles and entire worlds away from home. It was there that I discovered that someone you had never met—a beautiful stranger, perhaps no longer even of this earth—could make you feel understood somehow. That is the great relief of art, and to me, one of the great wonders of life. I had to be a writer.

This, of course, is easier desired than attained, hence spending nearly fourteen years on a novel that most of my heroes probably could have written in six months with half the soda and none of the hot dogs. But that's all right. You start out wanting to be the best, sure, but in the end you come to find that merely belonging is not an insignificant reward. It's a club I doubted I'd ever belong to, to be honest, but I worked the fields, kept the property up, and toiled by night, and when no one was looking, I snuck in and put this baby on the shelf with all the others.

It's been a long time, and some of the people who provided guest rooms and stocked fridges and all manner of support are lost to me now, but it's lovely to remember them and their decency and generosity. Virginia and Mike King. Betty and Jim Sullivan. Marci Lackey. Courtney and Gail Watkins. Thank you. I'm reminded suddenly of my old Decatur roommate Matt Perry, hopping trains in the Emory switchyard, trying to be Jack and Neal in the Kerouac phase all we wannabe writers go through, and of my girlfriend in those lean but enthusiastic years, Tracy Ruffin, and her wonderful mother, Beryl, lost to an aneurysm so young.

I'm also forever grateful to Jeff and Linda Campbell and their glorious daughter Tracy. I'd also like to thank the old Point Pleasant crew, Jose Romano, George Neal, and their better halves, the Wilczynski sisters, Amy and Jill, who encouraged me while writing the novel before this one that did not end up on a shelf in the club but died a merciful and just death in the low hum of a high-end shredder.

Naturally there has to be a girl involved, so I must thank my old beloved, Rachael Keller, who inspired that original frenzy of work in the fall of 2003, and also a gentleman's bow to her father, Jack, and also to brother Rick, who read early chapters a lifetime ago and was a true supporter. I'd also like to thank Bret Bader, Jim Donnelly, David King, Colleen McDonnell, Jennifer Zinner, and all the wonderful friends I grew up with in Fairfield, Connecticut. And much love to some of the fine friends who have made life in Los Angeles and beyond something far greater than it would have been without them: Bryan Callen. Dov Davidoff. Laura Chinn. Carin Besser and Matt Berninger. Fernando Chien. Merritt Lear. Margarita Levieva. Timmy Riley. Brantley Gutierrez. Gio Cianci. Boyd Holbrook. DJ Joo. Sam Sheridan and Patty Jenkins. Jimmy Burke. Catherine Hardwicke. Lizzie Olsen. Rachel Nichols. Joel Edgerton. Saori Wall. Samantha Ellison. Carolina Bartczak. Jade Bartlett. Elyssa Samsel. The great Renee Zellweger. And my Cali family, mighty Gavin O'Connor and Brooke Burns.

And to the SWBG team, who believed in me more than I believed in myself: the Gotham Group's indomitable Ellen Goldsmith-Vein and

Lindsay Williams were champions from the start, and I never would have slipped into this club without them. Thank you, guys. They led me to Sterling Lord's Doug Stewart, all class, loyalty, and faith, and ultimately to Simon & Schuster, where I was fortunate enough to have Jofie Ferrari-Adler be my editor, someone who shared my dear mentor Pam Durban's belief that no work was finished until "you exhausted the story's potential for meaning" (she talks like that because she can). This novel would have been inferior without Jofie's guidance and without the faith of the team above. Thanks also to Jofie's many colleagues at Simon & Schuster, especially Jonathan Karp, Marysue Rucci, Richard Rhorer, Julianna Haubner, Sarah Reidy, Stephen Bedford, Alison Forner, Kristen Lemire, Amanda Mulholland, Beth Maglione, Benjamin Holmes, and Carly Loman, as well as copyeditor Beth Thomas and cover designer Lynn Buckley.

Finally, I want to thank my family, who graciously allowed me to drift thousands of miles away to follow the dreams of a boy on a commuter train. This book is for my intrepid mother, Marina, who shares my lifelong love of movies; my fiercely loyal brother, Nick; my incredible gentleman-nephews Dylan and Zac (who is already a better writer than I am); Ed and Barbara Coe; my lit-loving sister-in-law, Mary; the greatest brother-in-law a guy could ever hope for, David Coe, whose own talent is matched only by his decency; and the rock of our little tribe, my dear, dear sister, Staci, who has my eternal love, gratitude, and respect.

Oh. And to Bruce Springsteen and Paul Newman. Just because.

Anthony Tambakis
Venice, 2017

In loving memory of Anastasiya Povolotska.

ABOUT THE AUTHOR

Anthony Tambakis is the recipient of the Paul Bowles Fellowship for fiction writing and a renowned screenwriter. He is currently adapting the 1961 novel and film *The Hustler* for Broadway and penning the screenplay for *Swimming with Bridgeport Girls*, his first novel. A native of Fairfield, Connecticut, Tambakis lives in Venice, California.